STRANGE DAYS

BILL OF THE DEAD SAGA

THE TOME OF BILL - 9

RICK GUALTIERI

DEDICATION

For Alissa, Joey, Connor, and Rai. You guys make every day both wonderful and a little bit strange.

ACKNOWLEDGEMENTS

Special thanks to my badass beta crew: Don, Walter, Faith, Kristi, Chris, Ebony, Simon, Reeban, Chris again, and Jana. Your feedback helped put the bite back into this book.

1

JUST WHEN I THINK I'M OUT

"Look at what I can do, Uncle Bill!"

An unexpected shiver ran down my spine at my goddaughter's words, as if someone had driven a dump truck over my proverbial grave.

There'd been no alarm in her voice, nothing to give me cause to shit a brick. For all I knew she was doing nothing more than playing with her dolls, yet that sudden feeling of barely contained panic only grew worse.

The hell?

I was watching Tina for the weekend while her mother was away on business, and though I couldn't exactly claim to be an expert when it came to babysitting, this wasn't the first time I'd done so.

It's not like anything weird had happened to cause such an intense feeling of dread, and trust me, I know weird. Hell, I'd once had a front row seat to the apocalypse and lived to tell the tale.

At first glance, I wouldn't blame anyone for not believing that. Fuck it. *I* barely did. I'm a near-sighted, thirty-one year old programmer of average height and ... *slightly* below average build. One might not think from

1

looking at me that I'm anything special like, say, a former vampire who'd once saved the world – and no, I'm not being metaphorical. I may not be that old, but I've seen some shit.

Since those days, my threshold for what I considered to be disastrous had been upped ever so slightly.

But that was the past – dead and buried, so to speak.

It had been five years – right before Tina's birth, as a matter of fact – since anything seriously out of the ordinary had happened to me. Yeah, there had been one *minor* incident about two years ago, something I really didn't like to think about, but I'd long since chalked that up to the universe throwing out one last *fuck you* before letting me get back to my regularly scheduled life.

Maybe that was it. The anniversary of the barely averted end of the world had recently passed. I had company flying in for a reunion of sorts, but otherwise there'd been no fanfare to mark the date. It was possible that survivor guilt was worming its way through my subconscious, causing the knot of unease in my gut.

"Come see, Uncle Bill. I can make fire!"

Or maybe not.

Please be playing with matches, I said to myself, racing toward the guest room.

I looked in at the familiar contents: bookshelves lined with toys and action figures – a sort of shrine, if you will, to its former occupant, Tina's father and my best friend, Tom. He hadn't been quite as lucky as me when it came to surviving Armageddon, something I still occasionally struggled to let go of.

Dwelling on the past could wait, though, as my eyes locked onto his daughter, the small girl with brunette pigtails sitting in the center of the room.

I *really* should have been a lot more startled to see a ball of green flame floating above her outstretched hand.

Shit like that wasn't normal, at least not anymore. But again, there was that strange feeling in my gut. I could almost taste the weirdness in the air, making the sight before me unexpected but not entirely surprising.

Mind you, that didn't mean I wasn't terrified out of my fucking skull.

Tina giggled and flicked her hand, causing the ball of unnatural fire to bob up into the air before landing again an inch or so above her palm.

So much for a nice boring day.

"Um, hey, Cat," I said carefully, using my nickname for her. "What'cha got there?"

She turned to me and smiled, her eyes momentarily lighting up the same color as the fireball dancing above her fingertips. It was all I could do to keep from pissing myself.

Memories from an earlier time raced through my mind – clashes with the Magi, the collective name for the warlocks and witches who'd once dwelled in the shadows of this world. If memory served me right, their spells had a tendency to be color-coded according to purpose. Green, if I recalled correctly, wasn't from the friendly side of the Crayola box. Not by a long shot.

We closed the door, destroyed The Source. This shit doesn't exist anymore.

Except that, despite my brain's insistence to the contrary, it apparently did.

Tina, for her part, continued to smile the innocent grin of a child too young to understand she was playing with the magical equivalent of a cruise missile. "Isn't it cool, Uncle Bill?"

"Yeah, cool is ... one word for it." Did I mention that talking to kids wasn't one of my specialties?

"I was thinking about the man in that movie we watched. The wizard ... Ganny."

My left eye twitched for a moment. "I think you mean *Gandalf*, sweetie. Trust me, there's a difference."

She shrugged, unconcerned. "Yeah, that's his name. I thought about him and then it just appeared."

I was tempted to ask how, but then remembered she was a preschooler, still at an age where shows about talking hamsters were considered high entertainment. Besides, I already knew at least part of the *how*. Tina's mother was a former witch, after all.

But she wasn't anymore. *No one* was ... or at least that had been my assumption up until this moment.

How is this even fucking possible?

Sadly, any answers would have to wait as Tina got to her feet and faced me.

"Wanna play catch?"

A better person would have done ... *something*: called 9-1-1, grabbed the fire extinguisher, or maybe even tried to wrestle the magical death ball away from Tina. I, however, froze as every instinct in my body refused to process whatever the hell was happening.

So this is how it ends. A five year old was going to do what a legion of monsters had failed at: kill me with extreme prejudice.

But then, just as she was about to lob the orb of fiery doom toward me, it winked out of existence. It didn't fade, or pop, or any dramatic shit like that. It was as if a light switch somewhere had simply been turned off.

"Oh poop!" she cried before covering her mouth, as if she'd said something dirty. "Sorry."

Considering the litany of colorful words dancing on the tip of my tongue, I wasn't about to call her kettle black. Besides, I was too busy counting how many years had been scared off my life.

Oddly enough, though, freaked out as I was, I realized that strange feeling in the back of my head, the one that had struck when Tina first called out to me, seemed to fade away in the same instant her spell had. Of course, no longer being in the line of fire probably didn't hurt matters either.

I pushed all that aside, however, because of one simple fact: whatever the hell was going on, I was in *way* over my head.

Fortunately, one upside to surviving the end days was knowing others who had, too – people who I could talk to about this stuff without sounding batshit crazy.

My first instinct was to call Sally, my old partner in crime. Though she might not have been as spry as she'd been in those days, she had a sharp mind and an ability to cut through bullshit like a hot knife through butter.

But this wasn't just about me. A little girl, barely old enough for kindergarten, had just conjured a ball of energy containing enough eldritch power to seriously fuck up my insurance premiums. Keeping this from her mother made me a piss-poor godparent. If she found out after the fact, I'd deserve whatever verbal ass-kicking came my way.

She'd been called away at the last minute, filling in for a sick colleague at some trade convention. Busy as she was, though, I had a feeling this was worth the interruption.

I pulled out my phone and dialed her.

"Hey, Christy. It's Bill. I think we have a bit of a problem."

"...um, so call me back when you get a chance."

Goddamned voicemail! There'd been a time when the

whole point of cell phones was to actually reach someone. I probably should have sent her a Facebook message or maybe a Snapchat instead. Chances were she'd see that sooner.

Either way, it left me back at square one – dealing with the little girl from Firestarter, still happily playing in her father's old room as if nothing out of the ordinary had happened.

I glanced toward my own bedroom for a moment. Not too long ago there'd been someone else living here I could have turned to for guidance, but those days were likewise over. Pity, because she'd have had a much better shot of surviving Tina's...

The downstairs bell rang, pulling me from those unhappy thoughts. Someone wanted to be let in, although, I noted, it was way too early for any of my guests to arrive. *"Oof!"*

In my haste to reach the door buzzer, I tripped over one of the dozen or so boxes cluttering my living room, each labeled with an illustration of a Morticia Addams lookalike and the words *Immortalis – Age-Defying Cream.*

I managed to catch myself before I face-planted on the floor, but just barely. "Goddamnit!" Fucking Dave and his stupid get-rich-quick schemes.

Almost like clockwork, Tina's voice came floating out of the bedroom. "You said a bad word!"

"I know." That was another quarter in the swear jar ... definitely not my idea. "Sorry," I called back, hitting the intercom. "Can I help you?"

"Bill Ryder?" a male voice replied.

"Yep, hold on." I pushed the button to unlock the downstairs door. Then, almost as an afterthought, I pressed the intercom again. "What's this for?"

There came no reply save the hiss of static. Oh, well, it

was probably UPS or maybe an Amazon driver dropping off a package ... not that I was expecting anything. But that didn't mean much. I also hadn't been expecting all these boxes from Dave, my former dungeon master. Yet here they were anyway.

I swear to God, dude, if you sent me more of this shit...

Alas, my friend's dipshit proclivities were of minor importance compared to the issue at hand – magic, real magic, the kind that should have been impossible.

And yet, Tina had summoned a ball of energy with seemingly as much effort as it took to lift her hand.

Maybe it was possible this was nothing more than a freak occurrence. I'd once, about four years back, seen her mother conjure a few sparks when the pilot light on her stove blew out. A bit of residual energy, she'd called it. Even so, that had barely counted as a cheap parlor trick. What Tina had done was full-blown sorcery, the kind that suggested...

There came a knock on the door, derailing that train of thought. *Huh.* That was strange. Usually the delivery guys just dropped their stuff in the downstairs hall and took off. It had taken me three freaking trips to carry all of Dave's shit up last time.

Guess I shouldn't complain at being spared the effort.

The knocking became heavier, more insistent.

"Okay, hold on. I'm coming." I reached out to grab the doorknob when, all at once, it felt like a great weight fell upon my shoulders – a heaviness in my bones that stopped me in my tracks.

"I did it again, Uncle Bill!"

I turned my head toward the sound of Tina's voice just as something hit the door from the other side, hard enough to partially dislodge the frame from the wall.

What the fu...

Sadly, before I could finish that thought, the entire door exploded off its hinges, sending me flying across the room.

2

FANGS FOR THE MEMORIES

Once upon a time, during deader days, such a hit would have barely fazed me. Pity that was long past.

I landed hard, the wind knocked out of me, and skidded across the wooden floor before stopping next to my love seat.

In between the stars currently dancing before my eyes, I spied two men step through the now splintered remains of my apartment door. Had they been big no-neck gorillas, I maybe wouldn't have been too surprised, but they were both of average size. Unless one of them was secretly the world's greatest kung-fu master, something was definitely not right here.

The first of the intruders stepped over to me. He was about my height, with an athletic build and a blond crewcut. Before my vocal chords could stop shaking enough to form coherent words, he bent down, grabbed hold of my shirt, and dragged me to my feet as if I weighed nothing.

"It's been a long time, Freewill."

Freewill? That was most certainly not good. I didn't

9

recognize the guy holding me up, but that didn't mean much. In times past, the entirety of the vampire race had known me by that title, stupid as it might be, acknowledging me as a rare breed of their kind. But most of them were gone, dusted. And any who were left were like me – normal, human – unable to kick down doors like they were made of balsa wood.

Finally, the haze in my brain cleared enough for me to speak. "Sorry ... I don't ... answer to that anymore."

I'm not really sure what I hoped to accomplish. Even in D&D you'd be hard pressed to get a monster to back off with such a lame response, no matter how good your dice roll. Oh well, I'd always been a glass half full kinda guy.

"That matters little," he replied. "The Last Coven *requests* your presence."

Last Coven? Was that supposed to be a joke? The ruling body of the vampire nation had once been known as the First Coven – the thirteen most powerful vamps on the planet. But again, they were gone, extinct, nothing more than dust in the wind.

"Last Coven? Does that make you guys the ass-end of the gimp suit?"

Rather than knock my head off, as I probably deserved, the man grinned at me, displaying grossly elongated canines.

Fuck!

It was impossible. Yet, at the same time, some small part of me still wasn't surprised. Though it was hard to tell with my head still ringing, that strange feeling from before, like someone tap-dancing on my grave, seemed to not only be back, but worse than last time. What the hell was going on?

Sadly, any introspection was cut short as my two uninvited guests weren't finished screwing with my expectations of reality. The one holding me up like an economy-sized piñata blinked and his eyes turned gold – irises, pupils, the whole thing.

Double fuck!

But that was even more impossible. The only vamps who'd been able to do that...

"Come on, Uncle Bill. Come see the..."

Tina's voice trailed off as she stepped into the living room, no doubt noticing the two freaky-eyed strangers manhandling me.

The surprise appeared to be mutual, however, as she was carrying another ball of magical energy ... this time red, yet another color from the lethal end of the rainbow.

For a moment, it was as if time stopped. The two vampires, for lack of a better word, turned and stared at the pint-sized sorceress, all while keeping me suspended six inches off the ground like human laundry hung out to dry.

Then a strange thing happened – or stranger anyway. Talk about a weird day.

The orb of red death hovering above Tina's hands winked out of existence. As it did, the arm holding me up began to shake, as if from exertion. A moment later, I was dropped to my feet.

By the time I steadied myself, the vampire's eyes had changed back to normal. There was a look of surprise on his face that told me it hadn't been on purpose.

What the?

He turned to his friend, a fucker with medium-length brown hair and hipster goatee, then nodded. The other guy reached a hand into his jacket for something. Call me cynical, but I doubted it was an apology card.

Though I wasn't even remotely what one might call a

competent fighter, I'd gotten into a ton of scraps during my time as the vampire Freewill. Sure, back then I'd had super strength and accelerated healing to back me up, but the important thing was I knew how to take a punch as well as when to throw one of my own.

While the first vamp, guy, whatever was distracted, I socked him in the side of the head. Unsporting of me, but fuck that noise. History was written by the victors, and being outmanned, I needed every advantage I could get.

Truth be told, I expected to do nothing more than break my hand. Vampires, assuming that's what these guys were, weren't unbeatable, but they were tough as fuck.

Not these assholes, though. My fist impacted with a meaty thud and the blond guy stumbled into his hipster buddy, stopping him from retrieving whatever he'd been about to pull out – probably not Bible tracts.

For a moment, I stood there as stunned as they were. Hell, it was almost like they were ... human.

Then it hit me, albeit fortunately not as hard as the door had. Tina's power winking out had coincided with the one vamp suddenly getting a lot weaker. Could the two be connected? More importantly, did it mean these fuckheads were now as vulnerable as anyone else?

My punch seemed to confirm that. Problem was, I didn't know when or even *if* their wonky powers would turn on again. However, I was more than aware that shit would rapidly go south for me if it did.

I needed to turn the tables and quickly. Fortunately, I had something in my possession that was just what the doctor ordered.

I rushed forward and plowed into the duo, keeping them off balance. Even if they were no stronger than me, they still had me outnumbered ... meaning I was in for an ass kicking. But maybe I could stall them long enough.

"Tina!" I cried, glancing her way.

Her eyes were wide with surprise and fear. Good. She realized this wasn't a game. That was going to be key to our survival. She stepped forward, as if to help me, but I waved her off. "No! I need you ... *oof* ... to go into the other room."

That broke the impasse on her face. She nodded and turned around.

"No, the *other* room."

I was busy hammering my two assailants with overhand blows, more designed to keep them on the defensive than do any real damage. It wasn't particularly impressive looking, but you use what you have. "I need you ... to ... get the thing ... I told you never to touch."

"But you said not to touch it."

Ah, gotta love kid logic. It's only when you want them to break the rules that they become interested in following them. "I give you permission ... *ouch* ... to touch it. Get it for me."

"But..."

"*Now!*"

That got her moving. Just in time, too, as a wild swing to my shoulder sent me staggering back several paces. It hurt, but it definitely wasn't vampire powerful, as evidenced by the fact my arm wasn't left a bloody stump.

That gave the first guy room to properly face me, a knot on the side of his head from where I tagged him. Not bad. Pity I'd probably have a matching bruise on my fist. Punching was easy when you're a movie star or an undead monster. When you're a regular dude ... not so much.

But that was the least of my problems. The second guy – Hipster McFucknugget, let's call him – produced a stun gun from his jacket. Not good.

Even with vamp powers, getting electrocuted had sucked. I really didn't care to relive that experience as a regular guy.

"Surrender, Freewill," Blond Crewcut said. "We won't hurt you if you come peacefully."

"Peacefully?" I asked, trying to keep him between me and the one with the miniature cattle prod. "Next time, ask instead of kicking my door off the fucking hinges."

He actually laughed at that. "We are the true shepherds of this world, finally reawakened. Despite my words, please don't assume your prior status holds any sway here."

Yep, he definitely sounded like a vampire – arrogant, sanctimonious, and with his head so far up his ass that I was surprised he could draw breath.

"Uh huh," I replied, stepping in. "Shepherd this, asshole."

As I'd learned in the past, the best time to strike was when someone was busy giving you their conceited "I'm better than you" speech. The words were barely out of my mouth when I let fly with my fist, intent on wiping the grin off his face.

Did you ever have one of those dreams where you're fighting for your life, but you can only throw punches in slow motion, no matter how hard you try? Sadly, it was kinda like that, only I was wide awake.

Two things happened almost simultaneously. The vamp's eyes turned golden yellow again, telling me I was as fucked as a prostitute on two for one night. But even as I realized my punch would be ineffective, that weird feeling in the back of my head returned. With it came a strange lethargy, as if all the energy in my body had been instantly sucked away.

Was this some weird-ass new vamp power I'd never heard of? No idea, but if so, that would make these guys far more terrifying than they already were, and they were already a good ways down that path.

Blond Crewcut caught my fist as if it were a Wiffle ball lobbed at him by a clumsy two year old.

Incredible pressure clamped down on my hand, causing me to cry out in a less than manly way. Yet, from the look on his face, he'd barely exerted himself.

He shoved me away, thankfully before he could turn my hand into a sack of powdered bones, then turned to Hipster McFucknugget. "Finish this. Neutralize the Freewill and bring him with us."

"The girl?" Hipster asked.

Crewcut shook his head. "Leave the Magi. But, if she tries to follow ... do what you have to."

Red flashed before my eyes at hearing his words, instantly pushing away the strange tiredness I felt. Of all the things I hadn't missed about the vampire nation, the casual disregard for human life – as if people were nothing more than walking Cheetos – was at the top of the list. Sadly, it wasn't the same type of rage that would have once propelled me to new heights of ass-kickery. No, this was just regular anger, impotent in the face of their superior...

"I have it, Uncle Bill!"

I spun, moving toward Tina's voice as I did. Sure enough, my godchild had proven to be a godsend.

She was standing in the doorway to the third bedroom of my apartment, the one I now mostly used for storage. In her hands was a sheathed broadsword nearly as long as her body and almost too heavy for her to lift.

But this was no crappy replica designed to hang on some LARPer's wall.

It had once belonged to Joan of Arc.

And though the textbooks say she was a warrior and martyr, her true history was a bit more interesting.

She'd been an Icon, a legendary warrior imbued with the power of faith magic, who'd once used this sword for the same thing I was hoping to do now – slay the shit out of some vampire assholes.

3

THE PEN IS MIGHTIER

Don't get me wrong, Joan of Arc's sword wasn't some magical artifact I just so happened to have lying around. I'm a programmer by trade. That's not exactly a profession that leads to Indiana Jones type treasures such as what I grabbed out of Tina's hands.

See, Joan hadn't been the only Icon. History was actually full of them: legendary heroes – the Shining Ones – powered by their own belief in themselves. Achilles, for example, had been one, leading to his legend as the ass-kicker of Troy. And there were many more, all culminating in the last of their proud line – my ex-girlfriend Sheila.

I still wasn't sure why she hadn't taken the sword when she'd left, but right then, I wasn't about to look a gift horse in the mouth. And to think I'd almost donated it to a museum. Well, if this was about to become my life again, fuck that shit. I'd take staying alive over a tax write-off any day of the week.

"Stay back," I told Tina. "It isn't safe."

That might have been the understatement of the century. It was the middle of the fucking afternoon on a sunny day and two vampires were in my apartment, bent on kicking my ass. If that didn't scream emergency, then I didn't know what did. Sadly, it wasn't the type one called 9-1-1 for.

The vampires grinned as I drew the blade, no doubt thinking it was little more than an oversized letter opener.

Come on, work!

Thankfully, those smiles were wiped off their faces once it was free of its sheath. Just the day before, it had been a grey hunk of metal – sharp as fuck, but otherwise fairly unremarkable to look at. Without knowing its true history, one might have easily dismissed it as a cheap replica from the Medieval Times gift shop. Fortunately, whatever was allowing these vampires to ... err ... vamp up, wasn't playing favorites.

The blade lit up with a soft white glow – the power of faith magic. I winced, waiting for the pain, but then remembered that sort of thing didn't affect me anymore. The sword – minus the pointy parts, of course – was now harmless to me. The glow wasn't as brilliant as when Sheila had wielded it at the height of her power, but it was enough to give me some comfort as the two vamps charged forward.

The problem with sword fighting is it looks easy. I mean, hell, you watch Conan the Barbarian once or twice and you'll walk away thinking all you gotta do is twirl a blade around in your hands and voila – instant badass.

Real life didn't quite work that way.

My sword fighting skills were possibly even worse than my proficiency as a brawler. I'd hoped to end this, but instead stood there like a doofus, waving the sword in front of me like a baseball bat as I tried to ward off the vamps.

The only upside was that, against the undead, this blade was more like a lightsaber, guaranteed to flash fry vampires, zombies, and other paranormal assholes.

We were at an impasse, or at least I thought we were.

Hipster McFucknugget stepped in, trying to use his superior speed to his advantage, but I was ready for that. I countered and took a swipe at him ... bingo! Clumsy as my swing was, I managed to slice his arm and he fell back with a cry.

My victory screech was prematurely silenced, however, as I realized that all I'd done was shred the sleeve of his shirt and leave a painful-looking, but relatively minor burn mark on his arm.

The fuck?! This sword contained the residual power of the Icons who'd wielded it. The mere act of picking it up had once been enough to cause my hand to break out in blisters. Slicing a vamp with the blade was a surefire way to coat yourself in a fine layer of dust. That guy should have been nursing a stump instead of...

And then I remembered these weren't normal vamps, as if the word normal ever applied. Most vamps had pitch black eyes and tended to avoid being out in the middle of the day lest they get flash-fried. Not these guys, though.

Near the end of things, right before we sealed the world off from magic and creatures dependent on it, a new race of vampires had emerged – one that was immune to sunlight and far less susceptible to the fires of faith.

The thing was, so far as I remembered, there'd been only two of those neo-vamps – neither of which were these chuckle-fucks – and, afterwards, they'd both reverted to being human again like me.

Hadn't they?

Yeah, one of them was a bit of an anomaly – a three hundred year old vamp who'd survived where all others had been rendered dust, their bodies aging to match their true years. All except her. But she'd been rendered powerless by the event. And even if not, she'd been a mule – okay, more of a full-on jackass – incapable of siring new vampires.

In short, none of this made any fucking sense!

If I was hoping for answers, though, I was in for disappointment. Hipster's arm was already healing. I'd been hoping to burn him with the righteous fires of faith but instead all I'd done was the equivalent of holding up a lighter and asking him to play some Skynyrd.

Blond Crewcut took advantage of my shock to slap the sword from my hands, sending it tumbling away into the corner. "I was told you might have that. There was a time when I would have trembled before it. But no more."

"Wait, *you were told?*" I asked, trying to buy time to think of ... something. At the very least I was hoping some heroic last words sprang to mind.

No such luck. Both vamps rushed forward and were on me like a new suit. Hipster slapped me, rattling my teeth, and then Crewcut followed up with a backhand. I staggered, feeling that lethargy come over me again. That, or it could have simply been the result of being pimpslapped. Whatever the case, a wakeup call came in the form of a fist to my stomach, doubling me over and leaving me retching.

It was obvious they were toying with me – hitting me hard enough to make me regret being born, but not so hard to put me down for the count.

I was starting to guess the reason why. Someone had probably ordered them to bring me in alive for whatever reason. However, vampires were assholes by nature, so these guys naturally figured they'd tenderize me a bit first.

And they were doing a hell of a job at it. I was all but done but, as much as that sucked for me, I remembered there was someone else in the apartment – a little girl they'd already threatened to neutralize.

Poor Tina had already been through enough in her short life. She'd almost been fried in utero by a crazy powerful witch and then lost her father before she'd even been born. Sure, she didn't remember any of that, but I did.

It was enough to make me realize I needed to end this in the only way I could.

"Enough," I wheezed, spitting out a mouthful of blood and holding up my hands. "I'll go with you." It was all I could do to keep from calling these guys out as the shit-birds they were, but I was out of tricks. I didn't want to provoke them any more than I already had. "Just promise me you won't hurt the girl and I won't fight you."

"Is that what you call this?" Hipster scoffed. "Let's be very clear. I could snap both your necks like matchsticks and there's nothing you could do to..."

"You leave my Uncle Bill alone!"

The room lit up an angry green, casting me in shadow. I dared a glance behind me, knowing what I'd see. Tina was aglow with power. Energy crackled around her, and it looked a hell of a lot angrier than what she'd been playing with earlier.

It was something to remember. Yes, she might have been cute as a button, but she was also a witch and, judging by the look of things, every bit as potent as her mom had once been.

Instinct kicked in and, rather than tell her to calm down like a responsible adult probably would, I instead dove out of the way and hit the deck.

Good timing, too, because a beam of energy shot out of Tina's hands, hot enough to singe my eyebrows.

The vamps were fast, but we were in an enclosed space with limited maneuverability. Before either of them could do anything to stop her, the blast hit the floor in front of them and exploded in a torrent of bright hot power.

4

BLAST FROM THE PAST

I won't lie. I figuratively kissed my ass goodbye, certain that the building was about to collapse beneath us. What a way to go – taken out by a pint-sized Zatanna.

Imagine my surprise, then, to look up several seconds later and realize I was still alive.

Better yet, there were no vamps in sight.

For a moment, I thought they'd been dusted, as the living room looked, quite literally, like a bomb had gone off in it, but then I realized most of the damage was superficial. A scorched floor, cracked windows, and a lot of broken stuff, but the blast hadn't been as powerful as I'd feared – albeit whether that was a result of Tina being so young or holding back, I wasn't sure.

A part of me was afraid to ask.

That would have to wait anyway. As the dust settled, I heard the sound of footsteps racing down the stairs. Even if Tina hadn't completely ass-fucked those vamps, they'd gotten enough of a taste to retreat ... for now.

I ran to the window, almost slipping in a puddle of

Dave's fucking skin cream along the way. Grr. Why did I let the asshole send me so much of this shit?

Sure enough, the two vamps raced out of the building and tore ass down the street, but at a human pace. Whatever was happening, it seemed to be on the wane again. Maybe Tina's blast had coincided with the power shutting off, so to speak, muting the explosion but rendering the two assholes powerless enough to have felt it.

I stepped back, realizing that fuzziness in my head was likewise gone. Good. The last thing I needed was a siesta. Muted power or not, it was unlikely the ruckus in my apartment had gone unnoticed.

Though I wasn't about to call the cops, that didn't mean they wouldn't be called. And then what?

I stepped back and considered this, leaning against my kitchen counter.

The world had seen some pretty messed up shit five years ago, during the final days of the war that had raged between the vampire nation and their ancient enemies – Bigfoot, of all things. Hell, nearly half the population of Boston had been erased from existence, turned into a primeval forest thanks to Sasquatch magic.

The press had even come up with a nickname for those dark times. They called it the Strange Days.

Yeah, I know, but I never said it was a *good* nickname.

For some time afterward, a lot of scrutiny was given to what had happened. There'd even been talk of Congress authorizing a new federal agency to investigate and regulate the paranormal. Yep, for a short moment in history, *The X-Files* was almost a real thing.

Problem was, following the conclusion of it all, there was no paranormal left to regulate. In one fell swoop, partially thanks to yours truly, the doors between worlds were closed, driving out the things that went bump in the night.

As time passed, with no weirdness in sight — save the typical craziness of the world — interest waned. Soon, people started turning to other more "rational" explanations for what had occurred — mass hallucinations caused by chemical warfare and other ludicrous shit like that. In short, anything that made more sense than magic, vampires, and murderous monsters.

For half a decade we'd lived in a world that was more mundane than ever before in history. Sure, not everyone wanted to forget what happened, but most did. There was enough denial out there to make it a fair bet that telling the authorities the truth would do little except get me locked up as a weirdo.

Forget magic. My living room currently looked like a meth lab gone wrong. Add in the contents of the boxes that Dave had sent me and it was as if someone had thrown a mad bukakke party for good measure.

Needless to say, there was little doubt that calling the cops would result in Tina being taken away by protective services. True, that might not be a bad thing if those vamps came after me again, but there was also her mother to think about. If Tina was removed from Christy's care because of me, I would feel awful about it.

Also, not to be a petty dick, but if these strange magical outbreaks affected her, too, then I really didn't want to be on the receiving end of her bad mood. We were in a good place, she and I, and being vaporized would kind of mess that up.

Speaking of Christy, I pulled my phone out of my pocket. *Fucking A!* The screen was cracked. Guess it was back to ruggedized cases. Luckily it still seemed to be working, at least well enough to tell me my call hadn't been returned yet.

Where the hell was she?

That was something I'd have to figure out later. For

now, I realized I needed to make Tina and myself scarce. If we could get out of the building before anyone noticed, we might be able to make this look like a case of breaking and entering. Then, later on, I could play dumb to the cops and hopefully this would blow over without an official investigation.

I let out a mirthless laugh. What a joke. Back in the day this shit would have been easy. The police, or at least the higher ups, used to have agreements with the vampire nation to sweep stuff like this under the rug. Now I had to do it the hard way.

"Did something funny happen, Uncle Bill?" Tina asked, looking at me wide-eyed.

"Life, Cat," I replied. "Life is funny sometimes. Some days it keeps us on our toes. On others, it gives up all pretense and drops a bowling ball on them."

"This is yucky. I don't like it."

Oh, I was so fucking dead if Christy found out about this.

After surviving the near end of the world, I'd found myself in possession of more liquid assets than I knew what to do with – a gift from Sally. Much like the rest of the vampire nation, Village Coven – formerly of SoHo – had been flush with cash. But with no vamps anymore, those funds were left sitting around waiting for someone to claim. Considering Sally had been in charge of the coven's finances, it wasn't hard to guess who that someone had ended up being.

It wasn't exactly hitting the Powerball, but it was more than enough to purchase the apartment building in the Bay Ridge section of Brooklyn that I'd called home throughout all the nonsense that had occurred. Some might have been pragmatic and moved far the fuck away, opting for a big house in the suburbs, but that had felt wrong.

This building, and the apartment on the top floor in particular, had been like a port in the storm, our fortress of solitude. It had been as much a part of things as I had. It didn't seem right to casually abandon it just because I could afford to.

Mind you, it still kind of sucked to be a landlord. I mean, I didn't know shit about fixing things. I mostly just called someone when something broke. But, there was one perk to the whole deal, a little something I'd had installed shortly after acquiring the building, paid in cash with a little extra thrown in to make sure there was no paperwork trail: a hidden subbasement exit which led to the sewers beneath.

It had been little more than a throwback to scarier times, one that I figured I'd never need to use. But I was now thankful for that little bit of paranoia, or I would be once we got out of the disease ridden hell we were trekking through. Thankfully, it was only a few short blocks to the nearest exit, a side tunnel that led to a subway maintenance stairwell.

Even so, with a young girl riding along piggyback, a few blocks in a filthy sewer tunnel was still pushing my luck. "What do you say we keep this a secret between us?"

"Why?"

"Because I don't want your mother to worry."

"But it's gross."

"Did I mention there might be a trip to Build-A-Bear in it for you?"

"Ooh! Can we go today?"

Say what you will about love, but bribery was the universal language as far as I was concerned.

Fortunately, our journey wasn't a long one. Double

fortunate that it had been dry the last several days, meaning the filth we tromped through was at least mostly dry filth. Underground adventures like these hadn't been any more fun as a vampire, but at least back then I had the advantage of knowing I'd emerge without contracting the bubonic plague.

Speaking of vampires, how was I to know whether these weird magical ... pulses, for lack of a better term, were localized to my apartment? I'd taken Tina down below so as to escape scrutiny, just in case unfriendly eyes were watching the front door.

Problem was, the underground wasn't exactly a safe place back during the Strange Days. Visions of monsters with bright orange eyes and mouths full of stalagmite teeth danced in my head as we traversed the last few hundred yards to the exit. I kept those thoughts to myself, not wanting to scare my godchild, but I'd have to be mindful of such things the next time we needed to beat a hasty exit.

In truth, I needed to face facts. The rules had suddenly changed and with no warning. I had no clue what was happening or why I was involved. But, most of all, I didn't know how far it reached. And until Tina was safely back in her mother's arms and far from harm's way, I needed to at least try being less stupid.

And part of that probably meant not traipsing around with her in the fucking sewers of New York City.

Thank goodness fate smiles upon small children because we managed to make it to the subway unmolested, if a bit dirtier than we'd started out. Oh well, it was a warm day, so it wasn't like we'd be the most fragrant people sitting on the subway to Manhattan.

And, thankfully, weekend traffic was heavy enough so that I felt relatively secure in the crowd, just in case those two assholes had somehow followed us.

Before boarding the train, I'd checked my phone. Still nothing from Christy. That was starting to get worrisome, but it was nothing I could fix at that moment. Instead, I texted Sally and let her know we were heading over, that it was super important, and to please meet us at the Office.

Looking down at the message, I smiled at my subconscious use of capital letters. Sure, it was *an* office. But it hadn't been *the* Office in roughly five years. Nowadays it was the North American headquarters for the Pandora's Light Foundation, a nonprofit humanitarian aid organization that Sally had founded – providing counseling, shelter, and all sorts of other services to the Tri-State area's downtrodden.

Its purpose was a far cry from the bloody atrocities committed there when it had served as the prime hangout of Village Coven. Yet, now, with strange shit afoot, it somehow felt fitting to call the place by its old name ... at least until we could be certain these magical surges were nothing more than an aberrant quirk.

It wasn't until we boarded the train and were underway that I realized I hadn't given her any details as to why this meeting was important. I just naturally assumed she knew, having fallen into the old habit of thinking Sally had more of a clue than me, when it was more than possible the opposite was true in this case.

I wasn't about to pretend this shit was like riding a bike. It wasn't and, even if it was, I was no longer sporting the same equipment. I'd downgraded to a smaller, lighter, and far more squishy model. But perhaps it wasn't all bad. When I'd first been turned into one of the undead roughly seven years ago, it had been easy to laugh at things, knowing I could take a punch if need be. Don't get me wrong, I could still laugh at the ridiculousness of it all. But I was a bit older, maybe a smidgeon wiser, and a hell of a lot more killable now.

Go figure, but somehow that last one offered me a bit more clarity than I'd once had.

Hopefully it would even be enough to keep us alive.

5

OLD FACES, NEW PROBLEMS

My desire to meet Sally at the Office was only partially inspired by dumbass nostalgia. It was also because her foundation operated on the weekends, meaning there were bound to be a decent number of people around.

True, safety in numbers only mattered if the boogeymen had an aversion to tearing through those numbers. There was also the fact that anyone who knew where I lived would likely also know about the Office, but I still liked our chances better in a crowd than in another apartment where the only people we could rely on for help were ourselves.

Besides, as awesome as Tina had been back at my place, I didn't want to hedge my bets on a five year old pulling my ass out of the fire again.

We signed in downstairs – improved building security was yet another change since the bad old days – and rode the elevator up. Tina had only known this as a good place, and I didn't care to dissuade her of that notion, so I kept my memories to myself on the ride up.

So many things had happened here, probably even

more so than at my apartment. I wondered if Sally had kept Pandora's Light in this place for the same reason I'd bought my apartment building. Of course, it was also possible she had a really good lease stemming from the time when our *negotiations* were done by creatures who could rip a man's spine out if they didn't like the way talks were going. Sally was nothing if not pragmatic.

Fortunately, the ride up was quick, meaning my trip down memory lane didn't last long. Good thing, too. There were some stops along the way I really didn't want to relive ... like most of it.

Less fortunate was stepping out of the elevator and seeing that the place appeared to be dead, which was perhaps a particularly poor choice of words this day.

Pandora's Light was naturally less busy on the weekend, running with a smaller staff and shorter hours, but it was usually still pretty hopping. I'd been a volunteer long enough to know how it all worked and this was ... not typical.

My hopes fell even further as we reached the doors to the foundation. In years past these had been big, solid, and completely opaque ... mostly to hide the crimes against humanity being committed inside. Now they were your typical glass corporate doors, leaving me with a very good view of the reception area inside and the fact that it, too, was completely empty.

"Tina, stay behind me."

She didn't question — just fell back a step. Probably a good thing since I really didn't have an answer as to what I would actually do to protect her in case things went south. I didn't own a gun and I'd left the sword back at the apartment, not wanting to be arrested riding the NYC subway system with it.

I opened the door far more hesitantly than I wanted to and we stepped in. The office floor, usually alive with people, conversation, and muffled phone calls, was now quiet as the proverbial grave.

Disturbingly fitting in a way because, as I stepped closer to the receptionist desk, I caught sight of the body lying on the floor behind it, drenched in blood and viscera.

It was Sally. They'd gotten to her first.

We were too late.

Just fucking with you! Gallows humor and all that shit. Guess the old memories really were coming back strong.

Anyway, my bullshit aside, Tina and I stood in the empty receptionist area looking around for maybe all of thirty seconds before the sound of approaching footsteps caught my ear, the accompanying click-clack noise telling me their owner was likely wearing heels.

Sure enough, a few moments later my former coven partner – once Sally Sunset, now known by the somewhat less ridiculous moniker of Sally Carlsbad – stepped around the corner.

She bent down and held out her arms, a big smile on her face, as she laid eyes on Tina.

My godchild, for her part, ran to her without hesitation and gave her a big hug.

What a difference half a decade could make. When I'd first met Sally she'd had the appearance of a femme fatale in her early twenties ... multi-hued blonde hair, hot as a fucking neutron star, and with an equally volatile attitude.

Back then, she was far more likely to gut someone like a fish than hug them.

Now, though, she appeared her true age – mid-fifties with short, dirty blonde hair greying slightly at the edges, and a few more age lines on her face. She was still in fair shape – definitely a cougar if she had the inclination to be – but now she looked like she'd be more at home sitting in a board room than shaking her ass on a stripper pole.

I still wasn't sure which look I preferred more ... okay, that wasn't entirely true. Let's be realistic here. I'm not quite as shallow as I was back then, but she'd been the proverbial piece of ass, even if she was just as likely to kick mine for saying it.

What hadn't changed, though, was her sharp mind, always seemingly two steps ahead of me. It was that part I was really counting on.

Memories aside, she appeared at ease upon seeing us, which made me feel a bit better about the empty office, but only slightly. "Um, not to sound paranoid, but where the hell is everyone?"

Tina pulled back from Sally and gave her a serious look. "Uncle Bill's been saying a lot of bad words today."

Sally stood up straight and put one hand on her hip, somehow looking taller than her five foot nothing height. "Has he now?" She looked at me with a smirk that quickly fell away. "What happened to your face? Did you fall into a door?"

"More like one fell into me. Again, where is..."

"I gave everyone the rest of the afternoon off after I got your text. Was kind of a slow day, not much going on. Figured it would give us a chance to talk."

Not good. That told me she either wasn't aware what was going on or wasn't concerned. "Shit! That's not what I wanted you to..."

"Ooh, you said..."

"I know, Cat. Money in the swear jar when we get back. I promise. In fact, I might toss in an extra hundred the way this day's going."

Sally crossed her arms in front of her and narrowed her eyes. She wasn't stupid by any means. No doubt she was beginning to come to the conclusion that something wasn't kosher in my life. "What's got you all frazzled? They cancel Comic Con this year?"

"Lock the door and let's head back to your office."

"Why?"

"Because my apartment looks like a freaking war zone right now thanks to two vampires who didn't get the memo that they were supposed to be dead."

Needless to say, that got her attention. She locked the doors, armed the security system, and led us back to her corner office – still in the same spot it had been when she was overseeing functions of a far more bloody nature.

One major change, however, was the small play area set up right outside of it.

Some of her volunteers occasionally brought their kids to the office, but I had a feeling it was mostly for Tina since it only became a thing once she was old enough to visit.

Sally gave her a juice box and snack then sent her to play so we could talk – the glass windows of her office allowing us to shut the door while also keeping an eye on her.

I was still debating where to start when I saw her step around a small pile of boxes stacked next to her desk, all of them stamped with the Immortalis insignia.

"He sent you some, too, eh?"

A look of confusion crossed her face for a moment,

then she looked down and laughed. "I was meaning to ask you about that. Kindly tell your idiot friend we accept donations, but cash is a lot more preferable than boxes of shit."

"Dave ... means well."

She locked eyes with me for a moment.

"Okay, fine, he doesn't. He's supposed to be taping a live infomercial next week while he's in town. He shipped me a bunch, too. Asked me to hand out samples to everyone I know like I was his personal sales monkey."

"Huh. I hope he doesn't expect me to play Avon lady because fuck that," she replied. "What the hell is this crap anyway?"

"Hand cream."

"Seriously? Any reason why?

"He lost his medical license ... again, and I guess he's just trying to make a living."

"He's not still experimenting with...?"

"No idea. Don't know. Didn't ask. Besides, it's just moisturizer."

She shrugged dismissively. "Not like I care. Never liked him to begin with."

I wasn't about to argue. Dave was an ... acquired taste, in that he was kind of an asshole. But asshole or not, he was still my friend, and yet another of the small group who'd survived the events of five years ago.

"So I assume that means you haven't tried it yet," I said.

"Why would I?"

I was tempted to point out the anti-aging cream part of the label, but figured that might get me decked. "I don't know. Everyone needs to ... moisturize every now and then."

She narrowed her eyes. "Please tell me you haven't been using it to jack off."

Rather than answer that somewhat personal question – it was only a few times – I quickly changed the subject. I'd allowed myself to be lulled into a false sense of security by her presence. It was time to get back on track.

I brought her up to speed as quickly as I could – free to use whatever adjectives I wanted now that I was out of earshot of the little girl trying to bankrupt me with a swear jar.

"How the fuck is that even possible?" Sally replied once I was finished, the kind auntie veneer cast to the side. That was fine, though. This was the side of her I was most comfortable with. "Vamps don't exist anymore. They were wiped out when we destroyed The Source."

"Thanks for the history lesson. I was there. I'm also aware that every witch and wizard on the planet has been firing blanks ever since, yet that didn't stop the little girl out there from nearly incinerating my living room with a goddamned fireball."

"She did, eh?" Sally asked, a half grin on her face. "Can't say I'd be sorry to see that shithole burn down. No idea why you still live there, especially after Sheila dumped your..." She trailed off, no doubt noticing the glare o' death I was giving her. "Anyway, guess she takes after her mother. Speaking of which, what's up with you two? I've heard ... a few things."

I knew where this was going, but we needed to prioritize here. Save the rumor mill shit for later. "She's on a business trip and I can't get in touch with her. I'm getting kind of worried."

Sally waved a hand. "She's a big girl. She can take care of herself."

"I hope you're right."

She threw me a wry grin at my note of concern, then asked, "Do you think she noticed?"

"What?"

"That magic is a thing again?"

"No idea. But I can't see how she could have missed it. Even I felt it, and it's not like I have any residual hankering for blood in my system."

"You did?"

"Yeah. Didn't you? Hell, I was surprised you didn't try calling me first."

She shook her head. "Obviously not. Didn't notice a thing. I was going over marketing proposals before you texted."

"No ... um, headaches, anything like that?"

"Nope. Nothing out of the ordinary."

"That's strange." I explained to her first that weird sense of dread, then that feeling of tiredness.

"Are you sure you're not just coming down with something?"

"You mean aside from pant-shitting fear?"

"As usual, thanks for the visual."

"Anytime." I paused and turned serious. "You do believe me, right?"

She rolled her eyes, a familiar gesture. "I wish I didn't. I really do. I'd love nothing more than to ask what you've been smoking so I know to stay far away from it. But I can't. After all this time, I think I know how to read you. So, no. I don't think you're full of shit."

"Glad to know I have some integri..."

"That still doesn't mean it makes any sense." She stood up, stretched her back, and started to pace. "I don't know. I guess it's possible for there to maybe be some sort of ... stutter, I guess, in the fabric of reality. And I suppose I can buy a Magi tapping into it. I mean, who knows how that magic crap works anyway? But vampires? That simply shouldn't be possible. The things, extra-dimensional spirits or whatever you want to call them, that made us vamps got sucked out of us like a freaking Hoover."

I couldn't help but grin, so she pointed a finger at me. "Don't even think of making a blowjob joke, Bill. I might be old enough to be your mother, but I'd still put money on me kicking your ass."

I chuckled. "Me too, grandma."

Normally she'd snipe back, but she merely shook her head and sat down. "I won't lie. Some days I really do feel my age. I mean, I was okay when *this*," she gestured down at herself, "happened. Figured I owed karma for all the stuff I'd done as a vamp. But that was then. Now ... it just sucks to feel old."

I considered that. When The Source was destroyed, all of the vamps in the world – a not inconsiderable number – had reverted back to human. That wasn't all, though. Their bodies had quickly deteriorated to match their true ages. It had been a death sentence for most. Within minutes they withered, died, and turned into piles of old bones. For those who hadn't lived past their normal lifespan, the results were a mixed bag. Vamps like me, Dave, and my ex-roommate Ed – who'd only been undead for a short time – saw almost no change. Sally, however, had been a vamp for about thirty years. As a result, in the space of seconds she went from being an eternal bikini babe to middle-aged. At the time, she'd claimed to be okay with it. My ribbing aside, though, her confession was the first I'd heard that might not actually be the case.

"I do what I can – eat right, work out when I'm able to, but it's not the same." She looked me in the eye, sounding weary as she spoke. "Is it wrong to occasionally wish I could have the old me back ... not the bloodthirsty monster, mind you, but the rest?"

I opened my mouth, but she waved me off. "You don't have to say anything, I know it's stupid. Even so, if what you told me is true... God, I hate to steal lines from movies. That's your schtick. But, I can't help but feel I'm too old for this shit."

"Believe me, I get it. I had to fight off two vamps on my own."

"But how? And no, I don't mean the fighting part. How could they even exist? The door's closed. Hell, even if ... and that's a big if ... it were opened again, something would have to act as a catalyst. You remember Calibra's story about how the vampire race was created, right?"

Hard to forget. Calibra, known as the White Mother to some and Ib the First to others, had been both a master mage as well as the first vampire, a being over five-thousand years old. In a monologue worthy of a James Bond villain, she'd told us how the undead first came to be – basically a major magical fuck-up on her part that resulted in human souls being merged with the spirits of ... things, I guess, from outside this reality.

Her screw-up soon became a self-sustaining process. These new entities, vampires, required blood to survive. However, by feeding, a vamp could then *infect* a person – their venom, for lack of a better term, essentially acting as a lure for another spirit to enter our world and merge with the victim.

It was only by closing The Source that we broke the cycle, ripping all of those spirits out of their human hosts and banishing them back to whatever Hell they'd come from.

Sally was right. There were a lot of things that would need to happen, most of them seemingly impossible, for vampires to reappear in this world. That wasn't even counting the fact that the ones I'd seen hadn't been normal garden-variety vamps.

"There's something else, too."

"You mean that's not all?" she asked, massaging her temples.

"The ones who showed up at my apartment were neo-vamps. Golden eyes, cool with sunlight, all that shit."

She actually laughed, but there was little humor behind it. "Then it's even less possible. There were only two of those: Ed and your creepy wannabe girlfriend."

"Thanks for the reminder."

"Anytime. So, about Ed..."

"So far as I know, he's on a plane right now. Should be landing at JFK in..." I looked at my watch, ready to dismiss it as having plenty of time left, but then remembered I'd left my car back in Brooklyn. "Shit. I gotta leave to pick him up in a few." I made a mental note to keep track of the time. "But anyway, last time I talked to him, he was just Ed. Not to mention I don't recall giving him any reason to kill me."

"He did live with you for several years. Maybe it's all catching up to him."

I flipped her the finger, keeping it low so Tina didn't see me through the window. "Be that as it may, I highly doubt it. Problem is, he was the only person who could make new ones. Gan was sterile, or so she claimed."

Sally nodded. "More importantly, she's dust in the wind. Good riddance, too. Wish I'd known which pile of ashes down there was hers. Might have grabbed some as a keepsake."

"Yeah ... dust." You'd think, as an adult in his early thirties, I would have developed a bit of a poker face by now. Unfortunately, there were still some subjects that made me squirm.

"Bill?" Sally asked.

"Yes?"

"Why are you fidgeting?"

"I'm not fidgeting."

"Yes you are. Is there something you're not telling me?"

Shit! So far as I was aware, Sheila and I were the only members of our circle who knew that Gan was alive. She'd approached us two years ago, just as our relationship was getting off the ground. I wasn't sure if it was a miracle or curse, but Gan had inexplicably survived where all other ancient vamps had perished.

Not only that, but she'd started aging normally. For three hundred years she'd lived as an eternal twelve year old, but when we saw her, she'd looked to be in her teens. Mind you, our meeting hadn't been all wine and roses. Her purpose for seeing us was to give fair warning that she'd be coming for me one day and, sadly, not in a revenge sort of way.

Weirded out as Sheila and I had been, we'd both agreed that it was probably for the best to keep it to ourselves.

Why? I don't know. Maybe because there was nothing any of us could do about it now. We were all human again, not murderous monsters.

My hesitation in answering Sally as I considered this did not go unnoticed.

"Bill, I'm going to ask you a simple question. I hope the answer is yes, but if you're lying, I'll know. My hip is a little sore today from Zumba class, so please don't give me an excuse to put my foot up your ass." She leaned over her desk and put a sweet smile on her face. For a moment, she looked like the old Sally, meaning the young Sally. Her expression bespoke of innocence and hope, which was complete and utter bullshit. It was the look she usually gave me right before she flipped the fuck out. *Oh boy.* "Was Ed the only neo-vamp who survived?"

"Um, not entirely."

"Good. Now we're getting somewhere. Let's go for the bonus round. Is that little fucking bitch still alive?"

I glanced out the window. Tina was still happily

engaged in the play area. *Please want a drink of water or to use the bathroom.* Sadly, she appeared quite content for the moment.

Oh well. Time to rip off this bandage and see how much it hurt. "I ... didn't exactly ask to see her ID or anything."

There came a scraping sound – Sally digging her nails into the desk. "How long have you known?"

"Two years."

"Does anyone else know?"

I told her what had happened, all the while watching her nails begin to bend as she put more pressure on them. Safe to say, she wasn't all too pleased.

"And you didn't think to inform the rest of us?"

I let out a long sigh, one I'd been subconsciously holding ever since that day outside the cemetery when Gan had revealed herself. "She was ... human."

"That's not the point. How the fuck did she survive?"

"I don't know. She didn't either."

Sally gave up trying to gouge a furrow in her desk in favor of pounding her hand onto the surface. "God-damnit, Bill!"

"I'm sorry."

"You should have told us. You should have told *me.* "

I held up my hands in placation. "You're probably right, but tell me this. What good would that have done? Seriously? What would you have done about it?"

She rubbed her hand, glaring at me in silence for several seconds before nodding as if to acknowledge I had a point. "Not too long ago, I would have..."

"Yeah, *before*. But that's not you anymore."

"I might have made an exception for her."

"And gone to jail for life?"

"Would have been worth it."

I smiled. "Maybe. But like I said, she was as human as

you and I. And even if she wasn't, it's not like she could infect anyone else."

Sally took a deep breath and looked me in the eye again, dead serious. "I understand that. But what you don't understand is what this potentially means."

"Fine. Spell it out for me then."

"If even one, *just one*, person survived that hell who shouldn't have, then that means it's possible others could have as well."

6

WITCH WAY IS UP?

I tried to convince Sally to come with me to pick up Ed. Unlike with Dave, she actually liked my former roommate. Hell, they'd even sort of pseudo-dated back in the day, at least when I hadn't been busy cockblocking them.

Ah, good times.

Regardless, with the weirdness afoot, I wasn't comfortable leaving her alone. True, there was no indication that anything that was happening involved her, and there hadn't been any more of those magical surges since we'd arrived in Manhattan. At least I assumed that was the case judging by how Tina hadn't blown any holes in the floor yet.

Sally's response was to direct my attention to the safe beneath her desk, within which sat a nine millimeter semi-automatic. It was a far cry from the hand cannon she used to carry during her fanged days, but less likely to knock her on her ass. For my part, I didn't bother to ask if she had a permit. I had a feeling it was better if I didn't know the answer.

Nevertheless, she was adamant that she'd be okay. By

then I was running too late to argue. So, with a parting shot about hoping those weren't famous last words, Tina and I headed out, promising to keep in touch should the day continue to be ... surreal.

Mind you, I might have preferred surreal to the horror that is driving to JFK on a weekend. We rode the train back to Brooklyn, seeing nothing out of the ordinary on the way, then hopped in my car and proceeded to rot in traffic. I swear, we could have walked there faster – not that I wanted to.

Thankfully there was one bright spot in a horizon filled with dipshit drivers.

About halfway there, my cell rang. I quickly glanced at the caller ID on the center display – ah, we'd come so far from the days of driving around in Ed's old junker – then answered even quicker. "Thank goodness you're okay."

Okay, perhaps that was an overly melodramatic way to say hi, but fuck it.

There came a slight pause from the other end, which led me to believe either Christy was giving her phone a weird look or a sinister voice was about to reply, "We have the witch, Freewill."

Fortunately, it was her. "I'm sorry I didn't call back sooner. My phone was charging and I was stuck in a planning meeting that went on forever."

"Hi, Mommy!" Tina called from the back seat.

"Hey, baby girl. Are you in the car?"

"Yeah, we're going to get Uncle Eddie."

It wasn't just an honorific title like mine. In a few months, Ed would officially be her uncle, being that he was engaged to Tom's sister Kara. I still had trouble wrapping my brain around that. He'd never been what I would consider a family man. Hell, during our time living together, he barely qualified as having human emotions ... and this was before the bizarre circumstances that led to him becoming a neo-vamp. But that was neither here nor there at the moment.

"That's great. Tell him I look forward to seeing him. Let me talk to Bill now, okay?"

"Okay, Mommy."

"I'll see you soon." And just as quickly, her tone changed, indicating she was addressing me. "I'm pretty sure I know why you called."

"I'm going to venture a guess that you felt it, too," I replied.

"Hard to miss. It was like someone flipped a switch in my body. One minute, all was normal. The next, the power was back on again. It was..."

"Weird?"

"Wonderful." Her voice grew wistful. "Like being blind and then given a single glimpse of daylight."

Wonderful wasn't quite the word I'd use to describe my day, but I guess I could understand where she was coming from.

Not everyone had adjusted to normal life as well as she had. In the months following the destruction of The Source – basically the portal for all extra-dimensional power, magic, or whatever the fuck in our world – several support groups for ex-Magi had popped up.

From what Christy told me, the suicide rate for former mages was through the roof, made worse by the fact that it wasn't exactly something they could talk to just anyone about. Witches and wizards had only other former Magi to talk to, and most of them weren't exactly an upbeat crowd. Despite being labeled a traitor in the waning days of the war, due to siding with us instead of falling in line with her people's returned *messiah*, it wasn't long before Christy started volunteering her time at a local Magi support group.

It was ironic, in a way, because it had inadvertently led to Sheila walking out on me.

A year of blissful relations. It was probably more than I should have hoped for, especially with my dating record. But I'd truly believed Sheila and I were meant to be together. Hell, we'd survived the end of the world – two legendary beings, the Freewill and the Icon. You get past shit like that and you've gotta think you're in it for the long haul.

Turns out the long haul was a bit shorter than I expected.

And the road to that personal hell was entirely paved with good intentions.

I knew that Sheila felt some guilt at the part she'd played in things. Not in stopping the end of the world, mind you. She was perfectly cool with that. But it had come at a price. First there was Tom. He'd sacrificed himself in the end, but Sheila was the one who had to do the sacrificing – running him through to unleash the power contained within his body, combining it with her own energy to close The Source. She'd survived the ensuing explosion – he hadn't.

But that wasn't all. Destroying The Source had fulfilled a prophecy hanging over her head, one which proclaimed she'd destroy the Magi. It hadn't been quite the genocide she'd feared, but it had still effectively neutered them as a people.

It sucked for them, but the vast majority of Magi had been assholes to me during my vamp days, so I couldn't say it bothered me much. Problem was, Sheila didn't share my attitude. Unbeknownst to me at the time, the guilt of what she'd done had slowly festered inside her.

It was Christy who'd first suggested she come to one of her support meetings. It was meant to be a way to heal old wounds. Sheila was no longer the Icon and the Magi no longer had their magic. They were all just people now. Christy thought that by talking to one another, it could give both sides some closure.

Maybe that had been the case for some, but it changed something inside Sheila. After that, things weren't the same between us ... *she* wasn't the same.

I didn't notice at first, mostly because I'm a clueless idiot. It wasn't until it was too late that I realized she'd internalized the pain she saw in those broken souls. She blamed herself for causing their misery, and it was eating her up inside.

And then she was gone ... leaving behind only a short note, her sword, and my broken heart.

I forced myself back to the present. I'd dwelled enough on all of that this past year. Yeah, it had hurt, *a lot*, but I'd gotten over it ... with a bit of help. Diving back into that cesspool of depression wasn't something I cared to do again, especially not with vampires kicking down my door.

"So ... did anything strange happen on your end?"

Christy let out a wistful sigh. "Well, the rest of the meeting was definitely not fun. I was trying to pay attention, but all I wanted was to feel the power flowing through me again."

"What happened?"

"Nothing. By the time we wrapped up, that feeling had passed."

I had to suppress the urge to laugh. Here I was, worried sick about her, and it turned out she was simply stuck in a stupid meeting with some asshole executives.

Not exactly a kind fate, mind you, but it definitely beat my afternoon. "That's it? Nothing else?"

"Isn't that enough? I mean, how the hell ... I mean heck," she corrected, obviously mindful of the sensitive ears listening in, "is that even possible?"

"I was kinda hoping you'd know."

"No idea."

"I was afraid you'd say that."

There came a brief pause in the line. "At first I thought it had to be a localized phenomenon, maybe residual power in the surrounding earth, something I accidentally tapped into. But then I saw your message. If you were able to feel it, too..."

I was about to say something to that, but she cut me off. "Hold on a second. How did you sense it? I'm attuned to these things, or was anyway. But you're..."

"Just a garden variety human?" I replied. "Trust me, I'm aware. But two things clued me in. First, was finding Cat playing with a fireball..."

"What?!"

Tina leaned forward in her car seat. "You should have seen it, Mommy. It was cool!"

Oh yeah, I was never gonna be asked to babysit again. "Calm down."

"Don't tell me to calm down! She's only five!" The tone in Christy's voice was a mix of disbelief and sounding a bit peeved. I could understand that latter. As for the former, she'd once mentioned that witches typically came into their power during their teens, kind of like the magical equivalent of the X-Men.

However, Christy's pregnancy had been marred by some *stressful* events, including being captured by Calibra, the White Mother, and having her unborn baby force-fed a shit-ton of magical feedback as way of torture. Tina had survived, apparently no worse for the wear, but even back then Christy had wondered whether the experience had changed her in utero.

With the Strange Days over, it hadn't seemed a big deal. Now, though ... I guess we finally had an inkling as to the answer.

"It's a good thing, too," I quickly replied. "Because she saved my bacon after two vamps kicked in the door and used my face as a punching bag." Hmm, perhaps I could have worded that a wee bit more delicately.

"Oh my God! Is..."

"Before you freak out, they didn't lay a finger on her. She's fine."

"But ... that's..."

"Impossible? Way ahead of you on that one." Oh, yeah. My babysitting card was definitely getting revoked.

I had a feeling Christy wanted to do nothing more than scream at me through the phone, but instead she paused and I heard several deep breaths from her end. "You're both okay?"

"Five by five." Fine, maybe that was a stretch, but I figured it might be best to save the details for when she could yell at me in person. "Isn't that right, Cat?"

"Uncle Bill hit them with a sword. It was great."

Okay, that probably wasn't helping much. Before Christy could freak out further, I headed her off at the pass and gave her the rundown on what happened, trying to downplay things as much as I could without the little girl behind me calling me out as a fibber. Christy didn't sound even remotely pleased by the time I was finished, but at least she was a bit less frantic.

"I ... still don't understand how that's *possible*."

"Me neither. I'm open for suggestions."

"And you're sure you're both..."

"We're fine. Seriously. We wouldn't be heading to JFK for a pickup if we weren't."

"Thank goodness." She let out a sigh. "I'm going to tell my boss I'm not feeling well. I'll be home in a couple of hours."

I opened my mouth to argue with her, then abruptly shut it again. She was right to be heading back. Nobody had been seriously injured yet, but this didn't strike me as something that should be so easily blown off. Strange shit was going on and I, for one, would feel a fuckload better with a badass witch close by.

Mind you, that didn't mean I couldn't have a little fun to hopefully lighten the mood.

"You could always..." I grinned at the road ahead, "apparate there."

"It's not called that and you know it," she replied sternly.

"Relax, I'm kidding."

She let out an annoyed huff, but when she spoke again, she sounded calmer. "I guess if you can crack jokes then it can't be that bad."

Well...

"Head over to my place after you pick Ed up. I'll meet you all there."

"Will do."

"And please keep my little girl safe."

"With my life if need be."

I meant it, too ... although, for the record, I really hoped it didn't come to that.

7

A VAMP BY ANY OTHER NAME

Christy told me she'd make a few calls on the drive home, see if anyone in her circle had any clue what was going on. It wasn't much to go on, but it was all we had, and it probably gave her something to keep herself occupied with for the time being.

On my end of things, the remainder of the drive to the airport was blissfully uneventful ... if slow as fuck.

Go figure – the world might once again be descending back into chaos, but Ed's flight still arrived on time. Combined with our late start and the traffic, he was already waiting for us in the terminal when we arrived, looking about as pleased as I expected.

"It's about fucking time." Despite his gruff greeting, his next act was to bend down and give Tina a big hug before doing the same to me. He looked pretty much the same as the last time I'd seen him: an inch or two shorter than me, thin, with close-cropped brown hair and a perpetual look of apathy tattooed on his face. He'd maybe put on a few pounds in the last year, but otherwise he was still the Ed I remembered.

With the pleasantries out of the way, he stepped back

and let out a huff of breath. "You wouldn't believe the weird-ass flight I just had."

"Try me."

Ed and I compared notes on the drive back to Brooklyn while Tina played in the back seat with a doll he'd brought for her – suck up.

Turns out his weirdness rivaled mine. He'd been sitting next to some yappy old lady on the flight when suddenly he developed an intense craving for her blood. He got up to use the restroom, thinking maybe the stewardess had given him some bad peanuts, only to see a pair of golden yellow eyes staring back at him from the mirror.

Something like that would have seriously fucked up a regular person. Ed, however, simply locked himself in the bathroom until it passed, then went back to his seat.

"Three hours of nonstop chatter about her fucking cats later and I was kind of wishing I'd given in to that craving."

"That definitely would have made your trip through airport security a lot more interesting," I replied, keeping my tone neutral despite being seriously freaked out by the fact that somehow his vampiric powers had returned. It didn't make sense.

Before we got to that, though, it was my turn to regale him with tales of the supernatural.

Ed listened and, when I was finished, replied, "So what you're saying is, I should have booked a hotel room."

"Fuck you."

"Ooh, Uncle Bill, you..."

"Yes, I know, I said a bad word. You know, Uncle Ed said one, too. How come he doesn't get the third degree?"

Tina was quiet on that one. Little snitch was apparently only interested in bankrupting me.

Ed swiveled in his seat to face her. "A fireball, eh? Cool. High five!" They slapped hands, then he said, "Your Uncle Bill and I need to talk for a few. Here, play with his phone for a bit."

"Okay."

"What's wrong with your phone?" I asked as he unplugged mine and handed it to her.

"Nothing, but I already gave her yours."

Dickhead. "Stay out of my browser history."

Tina occupied for the moment, Ed turned toward me. "You sure they were neo-vamps?"

"Willing to bet on it."

"But how?"

I glanced at him out of the corner of my eye. "That's what I was going to ask you."

He nodded. "Fair enough. But, just in case you were wondering, It's not like I've been able to do any of that stuff since we stopped..." He snapped his fingers. "What was that chick's name again?"

"Calibra?"

"Yeah, her. And I know for damned sure that – despite the temptation on the flight over – I haven't bitten anyone, at least not in recent years."

"Yet the fact remains they were there and far more real than I would have liked."

For a short while, Ed had been hot shit in the vampire world. Sheila had attempted to save him after he'd gotten bitten – infusing him with her faith magic just as he was in the process of turning.

The end result had been *unexpected*, turning Ed into

something never before seen in the entire five-millennia plus history of the vampire-race. Calibra and her minions had referred to him as the pure one, obviously knowing nothing about my ex-roommate's dating history. He'd become a vampire with all our strengths, yet seemingly few of our weaknesses. Sunlight didn't burn him, and things like faith magic and silver went from being lethal to merely annoying. Even better, he was capable of biting regular vamps and passing on his infection, revamping them, so to speak.

There were only two downsides as far as her high and mightiness was concerned: Ed was immune to compulsion, and the neo-vamps he created all appeared to be mules, incapable of turning others.

Calibra had been in the process of trying to *correct* these flaws within him when we finally brought her bullshit to an end.

"Are you sure none of Calibra's guinea pigs survived?"

"Certain of it," he said. "It was the same thing over and over again. She'd force me to bite one of her followers, try to compel them, then dust their ass when it failed. End of story. I didn't see any who got away." He looked out the window, no doubt remembering those dark days. "Except for that psycho girlfriend of yours. But it's not like she wound up in any better shape than the rest of them when all was said and done."

I turned and glanced his way for a moment too long, unsure how to break the news about Gan, then had to swerve to avoid rear-ending an asshole who was double-parked. "Fuck! And yes, I know that's a bad word."

"You still drive like shit," Ed remarked.

"Bite me."

"Poor choice of words, all things considered."

"You may have a point..."

"Hold on," he said, interrupting me. "Remember when you finally rescued me from that crazy bitch?"

"Didn't you say the same thing you said at the airport, about it being fucking time?"

"Not that. I meant later, when shit started to go down and all those prisoners escaped."

"You'll have to be specific. I was a bit occupied at the time."

"There was a group of vampires down there Calibra had been keeping prisoner. Anyway, they saw how I was immune to her compulsions, so they asked me to bite them all so they could fight back."

I tapped a finger on the steering wheel. "Oh, yeah. I remember now. We found you standing over their bodies, trying and failing to look like you were a badass. Did anything ever come of that?"

"Nothing as far as I know. I bit them. They died ... again, I guess. But we stopped everything before they could rise up and be of any use."

"How old were they?"

"No idea. Didn't come up in our conversation. But they seemed to have their shit together, so they couldn't have been all that young."

I shook my head. "That means they got dusted when everyone else did."

"That would be my assumption," he said. "So where's that leave us?"

"Same place we started: with two neo-vamp assholes who shouldn't exist."

"Sure you didn't hallucinate them?"

"Doubt it."

"I don't know. Maybe you accidentally smoked something laced with Borax."

"I kinda wish I had, but my living room says otherwise."

"Hah! Still glad you bought that place?"

"I'll admit, I'm beginning to reconsider the wisdom of that purchase."

I finally found a parking spot within walking distance of Christy's apartment. I then texted Dave to let him know where we were. He was likewise due to arrive soon, but in his case there was a car already lined up for him at the airport, courtesy of the Buy Mor Network.

Our plans had been so simple. We were all supposed to hang out tonight, then sit down for a pick-up game of D&D tomorrow. After that, Dave was due in Manhattan to film his infomercial before a live studio audience, leaving me and Ed to putz around on our own.

Of course, that was before the world decided to kick my ass for old time's sake. Figuring this shit out and surviving it was now top priority.

That aside, I was still happy as hell to have Ed around, and not just for the scintillating conversation. As strange as it was that he was vamping out again, it would be a good heads up if another magical pulse hit, not to mention a shit-load more subtle than Tina conjuring high explosives. Also, as messed up as it was that his powers were back, it could be handy if those other vamps tracked us down again – even if, at the end of the day, Ed was an even worse fighter than me.

Therein lay another potential problem, though. What if he and those two assholes weren't the only ones this was happening to? That one vamp had mentioned a Last Coven. While covens could technically be witches, too, I couldn't help but think that wasn't the case.

Then there was Gan. I hadn't seen her in two years, but it seemed too much to hope that she'd gotten hit by a bus in that time. Were these pulses affecting her, too? God, I hoped not.

Unlike my former roommate, her sense of *restraint* wasn't exactly renowned. Sure, she was older now – around seventeen if my math was right. But that was only physical. Mentally, she was over three hundred. The rules of maturation didn't necessarily apply in this case. Even if they did, teenaged girls weren't exactly the most stable bunch.

Either way, she was an X-factor. I didn't know where she was, had no way of contacting her, and wouldn't have even if I did. With any luck, the lovesick little psycho wasn't even aware of any of this.

I pulled out my spare key and let us into Christy's place. It was smaller than my apartment, but a lot better decorated. It felt like an actual home whereas, even after all these years, mine still kinda screamed crash pad.

Still, homey or not, there were some items there that stood out in contrast to the normalcy. One in particular caught my eye, as it always did – a glass curio off to one side of the living room. Inside, front and center, was a singed and broken Max Adventure doll, an old action figure from the seventies. I doubted it was worth much, especially in its current condition, but it held a special place in our hearts because it had once housed my friend's soul.

Technically speaking, Tom died about a week *before* he sacrificed himself to save the world, his neck snapped by a vampire warlord. That would have been the end for most, but his spirit somehow ended up merging with the doll, allowing him to stick around long enough to help us stop Armageddon. The explosion that ended it all finally freed him, allowing his spirit to soar to whatever reward awaited us in the great beyond.

Even with Christy's vast knowledge of the supernatural, none of us were certain what that might be, but I held out hope for the best. Tom had been a hero in the end. He deserved nothing less.

"Make yourself at home," I told Ed, pulling myself back to the present. "I'd say to put something on, but Christy's TV is all frigged up."

"Oh?" he asked absentmindedly as Tina ran past us to go play in her room. I couldn't help but notice he'd turned toward Max Adventure as well.

"Yeah, the remote's all screwy. Keeps changing channels on its own." I stepped over and clapped him on the shoulder. "How are you holding up?"

He turned away from the doll and laughed. "So far so good. No more cravings for blood clots."

"Well, if you need me to, I can run to the corner deli and get some rare chop meat. Probably best I can do on short notice. Wouldn't want you looking at me and getting all hangry."

"I'm pretty sure you count as junk food. Besides, Kara's been super strict about that. Think she wants me to go vegan. Ugh."

"Vegan? But she was a vamp, too."

"The irony is not lost upon me."

I made a whipping motion with my hand. "How are you going to break this to her?"

"That I like hamburgers?"

"That you might like them still screaming."

He shook his head and sat on the couch. "I'm not even sure there's any news to break. I mean, I feel fine, as in human fine. Maybe it was just ... a onetime fluke?"

"I might agree if a pair of assholes hadn't kicked down my door. When someone does the whole..." I lowered my voice an octave. "*You will come with us or you will die* spiel, I tend to take it out of the coincidence column."

"I picked a hell of a time to visit New York again, didn't I?"

"Your timing is quite impeccable, I'd say."

"I knew I should have gone to Vegas instead."

"Hells no," I replied with a grin. "You remember what happened there, right?"

"Oh, yeah. How about Palm Beach?"

"That should be fine, although there's a first time for everything..."

I trailed off at the sound of a key in the lock, tensing up before I remembered supernatural monsters usually didn't bother with things like picking locks.

The door opened and in stepped Christy. Her dark hair was a bit windswept and she seemed somewhat harried, not too surprising all things considered, but otherwise she looked as good as she normally did, which was to say pretty darn fine.

She locked eyes with me. "Tina?"

"In her room playing."

In the space of an instant the worry vanished and her face brightened into a smile. She turned toward Ed. "Hey, stranger. Long time."

"Ditto." He walked over and gave her a big hug.

Once they disengaged, she sauntered up to me and put her arms around my neck. "As for you. Thanks for keeping my little girl safe."

"Anytime."

"And here you thought you were done playing the hero."

"Well, I never quite said I was the..."

My words were cut off as she pressed her lips to mine.

Oh, did I fail to mention this part?

It was still kind of new for both of us. Just sort of

happened a few months back. But it felt pretty good nevertheless. I still wasn't sure where it was going, but...

"Whoa," Ed proclaimed. "When the hell did this happen?"

I pulled away and turned to him, both of us smiling sheepishly.

Before we could answer, though, a voice from behind us spoke first.

"More importantly, when the fuck is it going to end?"

I spun toward its source, but that strange weariness from earlier hit me again mid-turn and it was suddenly all I could do to keep from falling to my knees.

However, the sight before me was more than enough to overcome any desire for a nap.

"Tom?"

8

THE SPIRIT IS WILLING

"No fucking way." The words came out as a whisper. It was equal parts shock as well as not being capable of more. It really was an effort to stay upright.

Mind you, that seemed a minor inconvenience compared to who, or *what*, was standing there in front of us.

It was Tom, but not in the flesh. He was colorless and semi-transparent, looking kind of like a Star Wars hologram before Hollywood figured out CGI. But there was no mistaking his look or voice.

"Wait just a second," he said, his eyes opening wide. "You guys can actually see me?"

I nodded numbly.

"Fuck yeah! It's about goddamned time!" Then, just as quickly, the smile dropped off his face and he glared at me while raising his middle finger. "Can you see *this*?"

I nodded again.

"Good. What the fuck, dude? It's bad enough you can't keep a woman of your own. You gotta try stealing mine? Emphasis on try."

"Tom?" Christy asked, her voice cracking.

"Holy shit," Ed muttered. "I ... oh, fuck."

My brain just barely registered the panic in Ed's voice, still dumbfounded by what I was seeing. I glanced back at him only to find golden eyes staring at me over a pair of plus-sized canines. *Oh, fuck* was right.

So much for this being a coinciden... "Ow!"

Something burned my arm and I stepped back, the lethargy momentarily dispelled. When I turned to look, there was a yellowish glow emanating from Christy's body. I'd like to say I was surprised, but by then I was pretty sure those circuits had all been blown.

"Watch it with that," I said, rubbing my arm.

She turned her head toward me, tears in her eyes, as if seeing me for the first time. "S-sorry. I-I didn't mean..."

"Hit him again, babe," Tom said, a grin on his spectral face. "Teach him to keep his micro-dick where it belongs."

In the space of an instant, the situation had ratcheted up from weird to batshit, but the crazy wasn't done yet. Tina came skipping out of her bedroom. Prismatic energy crackled all around her, making her look like the world's cutest nuclear warhead. "Mommy, you have to see..." She stopped when she saw her father, or whatever he was. "Oh, hi, Daddy."

"Hey, Cheetara," Tom replied conversationally, as if this were a normal thing.

She looked between us for a second or two, then said, "I heard you yelling. Are you mad at Uncle Bill?"

"Don't worry," he said. "I'm just giving him shit."

"Hey!" I protested. "How come he doesn't get the swear jar?" It was, perhaps, the least-important question I could have asked in that moment.

Tina, for her part, shrugged. Magical power continued to crackle around her, but her face was the picture of childlike innocence. "I don't think Daddy has any money."

I half expected her to add "duh," but instead she turned toward Christy. "Mommy! Look at what I can ... oh pooh!"

And just like that, it was over. That dizziness evaporated as quickly as it had hit me, like injecting caffeine straight into my veins. In that same instant, Tina ceased being a pint-sized power capacitor and became just a little girl again.

Tom had just enough time to let out half a sigh and then he winked out of existence, as if he'd never been there at all.

I stood there for several long seconds, my mind on complete overload. When I finally got enough sense of myself to face the others, I saw that Ed and Christy were both back to normal as well.

I'd been starting to get an idea of what to expect from these magical surges, but what had just happened now was completely off the map. Tom was dead. Hell, we'd had a funeral for him. There was a big headstone down in New Jersey with his name on it.

But this...

Christy's face was a jumble of emotions. Tears streamed freely down her cheeks, but I couldn't tell if they were tears of joy, misery, or fright. Maybe all the above. I sure as shit was having trouble processing what I'd just seen.

I mean, how many people throughout history have wished they'd been given one more chance to tell a loved one how they felt?

We'd just been handed a miracle beyond all miracles, and what had we done with it? I'd bitched about a fucking swear jar.

Goddamn, I was a moron.

"Why?" Christy asked. "How..."

"On that note," Ed interrupted, getting his shit together before the rest of us, "how about I fix everyone a nice stiff drink? I don't know about you guys, but I have a feeling this is going to make a lot more sense with some vodka."

Christy only had gin and a few hard ciders on hand. But it was enough to get us started.

For several minutes we sat and drank in silence. I think we were all waiting to see if another surge was going to happen and whether Tom would reappear. Problem was, seeing wasn't necessarily believing when it came to things of a supernatural nature.

"Please stop that, honey," Christy said idly. "Conjuration isn't a game."

Tina stopped staring at her outstretched hands, as if willing the magic to come back. "Uncle Bill thought it was neat."

I laughed. "Yeah, well, Uncle Bill is going to have to pay about three thousand dollars to get his apartment fixed now."

"Sorry."

"Don't be," I replied to her. "Without you there, I'm not sure what would have happened. You're a natural with this stuff."

"But she shouldn't be." Christy sat back and took a long sip of cider. "You do realize how big of a problem this is, right?"

"No, not really." I guess this tangent was easier to talk about than the six hundred pound gorilla in the room.

"She's way too young to manifest powers, much less at

that level." Christy lowered her voice. "Seriously, did either of you feel the energy she was radiating?"

I fixed her with a blank stare. "Sorry, guess my PK meter is on the fritz. Next time I run into Egon I'll have to..." I trailed off as a thought hit me, something we all should have noticed had we not been busy freaking the fuck out. "Hey, Cat. Why did you say hi to your dad like it was no big deal?"

The wide-eyed expression on Tina's face reminded me she was five and probably being asked something that was above her mental pay grade.

I was just about to rephrase it, when she said, "Oh, that? I see Daddy a lot."

"A lot?"

"Yeah. Sometimes he plays with my toys at night. Or he sits on the couch watching TV." She giggled. "He likes to watch shows with butts and stuff."

Butts and stuff. Yeah, that sounded like Tom.

Christy leaned forward, looking visibly disturbed. "Can you see him now, sweetheart?"

She shook her head. "No. Maybe he's in the bathroom. I can go check..."

"That's okay." I saw the bottom of Christy's lip begin to tremble. Truth be told, mine was probably going to start, too.

"How come you never said anything, Cat?" I asked, my own voice on the verge of cracking.

"She did," Christy replied, fresh tears running down her face. "Oh my God, she did."

"What do you mean?"

"Little things," she said, barely holding it together now. "Things like Tom came to tuck her in, or said her new dress was pretty. But I..."

I put a hand on her shoulder. She didn't need to say more. Such a thing would've been easy to dismiss as a child's imagination, even for those of us in the know about the supernatural. Hell, even now, it was hard to believe this could possibly be real.

Christy looked like she had more questions, a lot more. Couldn't blame her on that one, but I doubted there was much point in grilling Tina. There was only so much detail we were going to wring out of a five year old.

Fortunately, we didn't have to.

Just as I was mentally debating the merits of interrogating a child about her dead father, something from across the room caught my eye. At first, I thought it was a trick of the light, but I quickly saw that wasn't the case. Max Adventure, still locked in the curio, was glowing. Light was spilling out from within it through the chipped and broken plastic of its body.

I stood up to point this out and just as quickly fell back down again, my breath caught in my throat and my heart skipping a beat.

But nobody seemed to notice.

Tom was back, which meant the magic was as well.

Not only was he back, but he was standing right in front of me, thrusting his crotch toward my face.

"Daddy's being funny!" Tina cried.

"Yeah, gobble my foot-long, bitch," Tom said, before backing up a step. He looked down at us, apparently realizing we could see him again. "Um, no homo."

"You do realize nobody says that anymore, right?" Ed replied dryly.

"Mommy, what's a..."

"That's enough, Christina," Christy snapped. "We don't use that kind of language here."

"But..."

"*Do we?*" She narrowed her eyes at Tom. They were still damp, but fresh determination now shown in them, the same kind I'd seen during much darker days.

"Um, nope," Tom said after a beat, smiling sheepishly. "Bill, put a quarter in the swear jar for me, will ya?"

"What?!"

"I said that's enough," Christy repeated, ending our banter. "Everyone, please be quiet for a moment. I need to concentrate ... and see if I remember this right."

Before I could ask what she was trying to remember, she grabbed a bottle cap from the coffee table in front of us and used it to slice a shallow gash in each of her palms.

Okay ... not quite the reaction I was expecting.

She stood, raised her arms above her head, and began to chant, the words coming out in some unintelligible language. Ed and I shared a quick glance as a swirl of blue and purple energy surrounded her.

I didn't know magic from dick, but it sure as hell seemed like her memory was just fine.

The only question was, for what?

Before I could focus enough to remember if I'd seen this particular color combo in the past, a bubble of sorts coalesced around us. The wall of shimmering magical energy expanded until it stretched almost to the edges of the living room.

More importantly, all at once I could breathe again, which was definitely convenient. That bizarre tiredness was still weighing me down, but it wasn't nearly so bad. More like minor fatigue than anything else. I could deal with it.

Unfortunately, whatever weight was lifted off my shoulders seemingly fell onto Christy's as she collapsed onto the couch next to me.

"Are you okay?" Tom's ghost and I asked simultaneously.

Christy held up a hand and nodded. "Just like riding

... a bike." She smiled. "I'll be fine. Haven't ... exercised those muscles in years. My stamina isn't what it used to be."

"Fascinating, I'm sure," Ed replied, his eyes once again that freaky golden hue. "Care to clue us in?"

"Time bubble," Christy explained with a tired grin. "Advanced blood magic. Kind of forbidden actually."

"You don't say," I commented, pretty much dumbfounded.

"Yeah, but who's left to judge me?" She took a deep breath and I could see that purplish energy still swirling in her eyes. "Anyway, I've temporarily slowed down time for us. We are living in the space between heartbeats, if you will. Every second is like an hour."

"Cool!" Tom replied. "It's like the..."

"Hyperbolic time chamber on Dragonball Z?" I finished for him.

"Exactly! Fucking awesome." Then he frowned at me. "Wait. I'm supposed to be mad at you. It isn't cool to plow another man's field, you know."

Whatever this thing was, it sure as shit sounded like Tom.

"You're funny," Tina proclaimed.

"Honey, I need you to go to your room," Christy said, interrupting our banter.

"But I want to see more magic."

"*Now*. The adults have to talk. Mind me, young lady."

Tina gave her mother her best sulking glare, then turned and stomped off. Personally, I had to question the wisdom of ticking off someone with the power of Dr. Strange and the restraint of a young child, but I kept that opinion to myself.

Just as Tina reached her bedroom, she stepped through the spell's wall and there came a brief flash of light as she became frozen in place. Hold on. I saw her leg move ever so slightly. She wasn't entirely frozen, just moving at a pace even a snail would consider tedious.

"She's in normal time now," Christy said as way of confirmation. "It'll give us some room to talk."

I raised an eyebrow at her. "You just happened to have an advanced spell like this sitting around waiting to use?"

"Light reading."

"Excuse me?"

"I still have all of my old tomes," she explained, sounding stronger than she had a few moments earlier. "Every so often I pull them out and go through them again."

"Interesting nostalgia you have there," Ed said.

"Some people collect trading cards. I have my own hobbies."

"Gotcha," Tom's ghost said. "So why don't we get rid of these two fuckheads so we can spend a few moments of quality time together..."

"That will be quite enough." Though she still looked upset, her voice was steel itself. Being that she once again possessed the power to ass-fuck the laws of nature, arguing with her didn't sound like a smart move.

"Good," she said after a few seconds of silence. Then she turned to Tom and pointed a hand at him, one that was now glowing an angry red. Guess her stamina was better than she let on. "As for you, you're going to tell me what you are and what the hell is going on. And you'd better pray to whatever god you serve that I like the answer."

9

A GHOST OF A CHANCE

"**W**hat do you mean, you've been here all along?"

"Exactly what I said," Tom's specter replied. "After we blew up that orange jizz pool, I was all like high five to Sheila, but she left me hanging. Then you guys came over and started crying and shit. At first I thought you were all fucking with me, but then I realized you weren't. Talk about messed up."

"That's unreal," Ed muttered.

"Tell me about it," Tom continued. "I couldn't even go all invisible man and have some fun with this shit. Turns out I can't get more than twenty or thirty feet away from that thing." He pointed toward the glass curio containing Max Adventure. "Let me just say, though, I am super glad you guys didn't toss it in the trash. Can't say I wouldn't have. Stupid thing isn't worth shit."

"It's worth everything to me," Christy said in a small voice.

Tom shrugged. "Yeah, I guess there's sentimental value and all that crap. And hey, maybe I should be happy it's not worth anything. Imagine how that would have sucked if you'd pawned it and the new owner had turned out to be a chronic masturbator."

Goddamn, this was hard to swallow. A part of me felt this had to be someone trying to trick us. It's not like mimicry was unknown among mages or supernatural monsters. But he was so ... Tom.

He turned and gestured at me, seemingly oblivious to the internal struggle we were all waging. "Oh, and by the way, dumbass, I was rooting for you and Sheila. Don't get me wrong, I didn't want to watch you guys bone or anything, but I was really hoping you'd go the distance. Of course, then you had to fuck it up."

"I didn't fuck anything..."

"And now I finally realize why. This was your plan from the start – trying to seduce the fine piece by my side. Not that I can blame you. She's..."

"Sitting right here," Christy stated. "That's a discussion for another time."

He opened his mouth to say something.

"I mean it." She glowed red again and Tom quickly held up his hands in supplication. "Good. Because I can't hold this spell forever." She took a deep breath. When she spoke next, I could see she was losing out to her emotions again. "I just want to know ... how?"

"Not following."

"You say you've been here all this time. Five years of not being at peace, of not being able to talk to or touch anyone else? How ... how are you..."

"I think what Christy is trying to say, man," Ed offered, "is how on Earth are you still sane? Assuming it is you."

Tom flipped him a ghostly finger. "Fair question, dude, with a very simple answer. I watched a lot of TV." He saw my questioning look and said, "Yeah, that was me changing the channels. Took forever to figure that shit out.

I swear, fuck that stupid *Ghost* movie for making it look simple."

Christy shook her head. "But with no human contact..."

"Oh, that was no big deal," Tom replied, turning to me again. "Sixth grade."

"What about it?"

"You and Johnny Collins?"

I shrugged, having no idea what he was talking about.

"Jesus Christ, am I the only one here not going senile? Remember that time you guys decided to fuck with me by pretending I was invisible, acting like I wasn't there?"

It took me a second to dig up the memory. "Oh yeah. We did, didn't we?"

"Well, I just kept telling myself that's what you were all doing."

I stood up. "We played that prank for maybe two days before we got bored with it. We're talking five fucking years here."

"I know," he replied. "I just figured you guys were being assholes about it."

It was unbelievable, almost inconceivable. At the same time, it was an answer that sounded exactly like something Tom would say. "So how is it that Cat can see you?"

"Her name is Cheetara, dude."

"Her middle name is Cheetara and I'm not calling her that in public."

"Why not?" he asked. "What happened to you, man? You used to be cool. What? Lack of pussy turned you into a hipster douche or something?"

I stepped up and pointed a finger at his wispy chest. "I am not suffering from a lack of..."

Christy threw me a glare and I immediately clammed up. Ed might be a vampire again, but she still had my vote for the biggest badass in the room, one who I really didn't want to tick off.

Ed stepped between us like a referee. "Based on the fact that Tina can perform magic when she's not supposed to, maybe it's her. Maybe she can see you because she's special." He then grinned at our former roommate. "And I mean special as in good, not like you."

"Suck it, old man," Tom said with a laugh.

"Old man? I'm only..."

"Fucking thirty. You're like my grandpa, for Christ's sake. Whereas I, being dead and all, haven't aged a day."

He did have a point, albeit it was kind of a poor one to use to win this argument.

"Need I remind you," Christy said, likewise rising. "I'm that *old,* too."

Tom immediately backpedaled. "Yeah, babe, but you're like a fine wine ... whereas these two cock-suckers are more like moldy cheese with limp dicks."

Goddamn. Despite his insults, this felt *right*, like the conversations we used to have before he died. There was still a chance this was some kind of deception, but if so, it was a damned convincing one.

Christy stepped past us, headed toward the curio. "I'm willing to accept that our daughter can do things that are beyond her age. What she went through while I was pregnant could have affected her. Much as I've tried not to think about it, you don't absorb that kind of power and remain unchanged." Though her tone remained strong, I could tell this was a truth she didn't want to admit. "The thing that confuses me more is how you're..." Her voice broke for a second, but then she took a deep breath and continued. "Still here. I sensed the others leaving this world. I think we all did."

I nodded. When Dr. Death – the murderous spirit inhabiting my body, and the very thing that made me a vampire – was finally dragged back to wherever he'd come from, I'd definitely felt it. It had been like someone tearing my soul in two and then hoovering half of it up. I'd heard the screams of the others in my head, spirits from another plane of existence, all being dragged out of their host bodies as they were sucked back to wherever they belonged.

"And it wasn't just vampires," she continued. "It was everything. All of it. Every soul, spirit, or extra planar being that didn't belong here. Even the Jahabich, the spirits trapped inside their bodies anyway, were able to move on."

"But not Tom," Ed surmised.

Tom, for his part, shrugged. "I like living in New York. All my shit's here."

"It shouldn't have mattered," Christy said. "Unless..." She pulled out a key and unlocked the cabinet. Once it was opened, she reached in toward the still glowing action figure but then hesitated. Rather than grab it, she closed her eyes and a soft yellowish glow suffused her.

A moment later, Max Adventure floated out of the case and hovered in front of her.

"You could have just worn gloves, babe," Tom said. "There's a pair in..."

"Hush," she commanded. "If what I suspect is true, then it could be *unwise* to touch this right now."

She made a gesture and the figure began to slowly rotate in the air in front of her. I glanced over at Tom to see if he did the same, like some freaky voodoo doll, but he stood there looking as confused as the rest of us.

"How do you not drop through the floor?" I asked, breaking the uncomfortable silence as Christy examined the doll.

"Beats the fuck out of me, man."

Christy studied the action figure for several minutes,

all while Ed and I continued to grill Tom on the weirdness of his ghostly state.

He was explaining to us how nice it was to not have to get up in the middle of a movie to take a piss, being that he had no bladder, when Christy finally glanced back at us.

Sweat stood out on her forehead, strain plainly visible on her face. Hell, she looked to be on the verge of passing out. Past her, I noticed that Tina had taken maybe another step or two toward her bedroom in all this time. It kind of gave me the shivers. Imagine being trapped in sped-up time, like in that old Star Trek episode. Pity I couldn't remember how they eventually resolved it.

Christy made another gesture and the action figure floated back into the display case, which she proceeded to lock.

With that done, she took a step toward the couch before stopping again. "I'm sorry, but that's all I have."

As abruptly as she said it, the weird shimmering around us disappeared. Just like that, Tina resumed marching into her room at normal pace.

Christy staggered and both Tom and I stepped forward to catch her. However, only one of us was solid enough to do anything about it, and it wasn't him. Petty of me, perhaps, but he'd been giving me shit ever since reappearing.

Too bad that weariness hit me again like a baseball bat to the nuts. It was all I could do to not drop her and send both of us crashing to the floor. If this lasted much longer...

Before our eyes, Tom winked out of existence with nothing more than a quick, "Oh shit."

In that same instant, my body pepped up again, saving me from looking like a total wuss.

The fuck? I understood what was happening to

Christy and even Ed, to a degree anyway. When the power came back on, so, too, did theirs, even if his shouldn't have. But me ... why the fuck did I feel like death warmed over whenever those pulses hit? It didn't make sense.

Mind you, none of this really did.

For now, though, I helped Christy to the couch before she fell over.

After a few more minutes, she waved me off. "I'm okay, thanks."

"Just making sure."

"Well, maybe not that *okay*."

"I really don't think any of us are," Ed replied. "Not after that. And, just between us, I'm getting seriously tired of that on/off bullshit. It's like one minute I feel fine, then the next I want to sink my teeth into someone."

"I appreciate your restraint," I said, "but how are you even sporting fangs again? You should be just as normal as me. Not that you ever were, but you know what I mean. Any ideas, Christy?" I was tempted to call her babe, just to be a dick, knowing Tom could likely see us, but that seemed a bit over-the-top douchey.

For now anyway.

The color had returned to her cheeks, which was good, and she looked almost back to normal. Pretty amazing, considering she was telling the laws of nature to take a flying fuck just minutes earlier. "I have no idea what's going on there. But I think I know why Tom is still with us."

"He wasn't ready to move on?" Ed offered.

Christy shook her head. "Nothing so banal. I think it's the doll."

"Action figure," I corrected. Then, a moment later, I said to the thin air, "You're welcome."

"It's not the action figure itself that matters. It's what it's holding."

Christy got up and approached the display case again. Inside, the cracked visage of Max Adventure had stopped glowing. Once again, it looked like nothing more than a broken toy.

"It's the Apollo's Prism," she said at last. "Not only did it survive, but it somehow fused with him."

10

SHOWTIME AT THE APOLLO

Five years ago, when the world had been busy trying not to end, the city's electrical grid had become a bit unreliable.

In response, Christy's coven had worked their voodoo and created a ball of energy in our basement that covered our power needs, while the rest of the neighborhood was plunged into the proverbial Stone Age. It was awesome.

Less awesome was learning later that this wasn't simply some magical Duracell. No, we're talking some serious shit. Our resident witches had essentially created a self-sustaining tear in reality through which endless power flowed. That was terrifying enough by itself, but then a little birdie by the name of Gan had casually mentioned that this thingamabob – called an Apollo's Prism – was ever so slightly volatile, to the tune of leveling an entire neighborhood if it exploded.

So, of course, rather than run for the fucking hills, Christy repurposed it after Tom's soul got stuck in Max Adventure, to power a sort of solid glamour that temporarily restored his body.

All was well and good ... right up to the point when Sheila blew him up to shut down all magic in our world.

Ah yes, the rabbit hole for that little adventure ran deep indeed.

"The explosion," Christy explained, "I thought it destroyed the prism along with The Source, but I was wrong. I think it only rendered it inert."

She was trying to keep her tone businesslike, but I could tell it was an effort. I knew her too well to be fooled. Not that I could blame her. Her dead fiancé, the father of her child, had suddenly returned in Casper form. Oh, and go figure, just a few months after she'd started a relationship with his best friend.

I swear, what a tangled web of fuckery the universe sometimes wove.

"Why didn't I see it back then?"

"Because you were knocked out at the time," I offered, drawing a glare from her.

"That was a rhetorical question."

I glanced at Ed and he shook his head to let me know I was on my own. Ah, where would I be without his moral support?

"The Source," Christy continued, apparently undeterred by my dumbass comment. "They were standing in it at the time."

"I know. We were there."

I got the impression, however, she was less explaining it to us so much as talking to herself, trying to figure this out. Ed and I were merely the peanut gallery. "The Source wasn't just a portal, though. It was a physical catalyst, one that could fuse the spirits of the dead to a corporeal source."

She was talking about the Jahabich, the army of rock monsters Calibra had created via infusing trapped souls into the very earth of the underground cavern where The

Source had resided. Tom had, coincidentally, been drenched in Jahabich *blood* when he'd died.

"His spirit," she continued, following that same train of thought. "It became attached to this doll in the same manner, by their blood. But, what if the combination of the prism, the doll, and The Source affected him again ... right as the portal was collapsing?"

"You mean, it kinda glued them all together?"

Ed laughed. "I bet your parents are so glad you went to college."

I threw him a dirty look before focusing on Christy again.

"In a sense," she replied. "But that would explain why he couldn't move on. His attachment to the doll would have been weak. It was just a flimsy physical construct. But if his spirit became fused to the prism, too, then its power might have been strong enough to hold onto him while everything else was sucked away. Then, when it went inert due to The Source's destruction, he lacked the raw energy to manifest."

"Maybe." Ed's tone said he didn't entirely buy it. "But that glamour spell looked and felt solid. Now he's just a..."

"A ghost?" she finished for him. "No. I don't think he actually is. What we usually think of as ghosts are mostly psychic imprints, an echo left behind. True intelligent hauntings are rare and usually indicative of non-human entities trying to break through to our world."

Okay, I suppose that made sense. Can't say I'd watched too many reruns of *Ghost Adventures* since saving the world.

"If I'm right," Christy continued, "his soul is still intact. It's the prism itself that isn't. It wasn't destroyed in the explosion, like we all thought, but it's weak, damaged." She smiled sheepishly. "Please don't misunderstand what I'm saying. It's still dangerous. I didn't have enough time to properly examine it just now, but I have little doubt it could kill everyone in this building were it to become unstable."

Ed stepped up and looked at the doll in the case. "A word of advice, if I may. That might be something you don't want to share with your landlord."

"No shit," I replied. "So what do we do? I mean, we can't leave him like that ... stuck in limbo."

"Except he's not stuck in limbo." Ed stepped back and turned on the TV.

"So your way of dealing with this crisis is to see if *Doctor Who's* on?"

He narrowed his eyes at me. "You do realize you're an idiot, right?" Before I could say anything to that, he continued. "Hey, Tom, if you can hear me, change the channel."

For several long seconds nothing happened, but then the channel changed. Holy crap. Tom hadn't been shitting us.

"Like I said," Ed explained. "Not in limbo. He's here. He can see us, we just can't see him. But now that we know he's around, maybe we can communicate."

"Via the TV?"

"Ed's right," Christy said, perking up a bit. "We can set up a system. One channel for yes, change two for no. Something like that, at least until I can figure out a way to free his spirit."

I started to nod, but it quickly turned into a head shake. "Wait. You mean find a way to bring him back, right?"

"Excuse me?"

"That was the plan back then ... to bring him back. Well, not the entire plan. I mean, we still wanted to fuck over the bad guys, but we were going to try to restore him, too."

Ed smiled. "He's right. This could be a second chance to fix that."

I wasn't sure what that would do to my and Christy's burgeoning relationship, but I wasn't such a selfish ass that I couldn't look past the end of my own dick when it came to my best friend. I'd sooner have him back and be shunted off to Dumpsville – population me – than know we'd passed up a chance to save him.

Mind you, I had no fucking idea how to do that. It wasn't like he was an operating system we could simply reinstall into a new machine.

Christy shook her head. "That's not the natural order of things."

"I think we left the natural order on the side of the road a long time ago."

"His spirit needs to move on."

"Tina needs her father."

She glared at me, such intensity in her eyes that I actually backed up a step. "Do you think I don't want that?"

I held up my hands. "Not at all."

"Because I do. But his soul is being tortured right now, stuck here as it is. It should be free to go to whatever awaits us *after*."

It was hard to argue against that, but maybe *I* didn't have to. "Yo, Tom. Are you currently suffering in eternal torment?"

A few seconds passed then the channel on the TV changed once, and again.

"That's two, no. I rest my case." I turned to Ed. "All in favor of trying?"

We both raised our hands.

Christy put a hand to her face and rubbed her eyes. "What you're asking is impossible, yet you're making it sound like it's as easy as crossing the road."

"Who's to say it's impossible? Hell, I'm pretty sure I've

seen the impossible at least three times today alone. Something is changing. I don't know what, and I sincerely doubt it's for the better. But maybe we can use it to our advantage, make some good come out of this."

Her eyes became glassy. "I ... just ... don't know." Christy's words were lost in a sob.

I stepped in and put my arms around her. "Neither do I. But we're in this together, all of us. You're not alone here."

Almost as if in response, the TV started changing channels rapidly.

I quickly let go and stepped back. "Jesus fucking Christ, okay. I get the hint."

Just as quickly, Tina's voice floated to us from her bedroom. "You said a bad word, Uncle Bill."

Oh, for fuck's sake!

11

INFODUMPMERCIAL

Despite my big words, not a lot came of it ... at least not immediately.

That was the last of those strange pulses for the day. So far as I could tell, the world once again reverted to the way it had been – and preferably would remain – magic free.

Even knowing Christy's apartment was haunted by my best friend and that something needed to be done about it, I was glad for the reprieve. Powerless as I was, I can't say I looked forward to getting jumped again by supernatural assholes.

Ed and I eventually returned to my place. Turned out I'd gotten lucky. The cops had stopped by, but had written up the whole thing as a break-in while I was out. I had to give a statement, professing extreme ignorance when it came to the burn marks in my living room, but in the end they walked away looking for a burglar who neither existed nor had, oddly enough, actually stolen anything – including the antique sword left lying in the corner.

Fortunately, we'd gotten another break. Dave had left a message that the producers of his infomercial had splurged for a hotel room close to the studio where they were broadcasting. He'd be crashing with us afterwards, but it gave us some breathing room to work.

That left us to clean up the mess. Thank goodness Ed was around to help. Fortunately, his stepdad was a salt of the Earth type, so he'd picked up a couple of useful life skills along the way ... meaning we were able to install a new door semi-competently.

By the next day, my place was back to being livable again. The work almost finished, I gave Dave a call back. However, it was less to catch up and more to ask if he'd experienced anything strange during the last few days. As one of our small circle of former vamps, I was curious whether the pulses had affected him. That said, I let him lead the conversation. Dave had been on the fringe of our group back then, so if all was right in his world, I wasn't sure I wanted to burden him with the fact that things were turning weird again.

Considering that all he talked about was his stupid moisturizing cream – bragging about sales and bugging me to pester all my friends about it – I felt safe in the assumption that everything was hunky dory in his self-absorbed corner of the universe.

At least someone was having a normal weekend.

I stepped out of the bathroom, having taken a piss break, and found Ed holding Sheila's sword.

"You know that's not a toy, right?"

The look he gave me suggested his opinion of my intelligence had just dropped a notch. "No shit, d'Artagnan." He swung it lightly, then leaned it against the wall. "Didn't you say this lit up, too, while you were fighting off those vamps?"

"Yep. Just like the old days. Except it didn't burn me like a tater tot, and kinda works like shit against your progeny."

"How many times do I have to tell you they're not mine?"

I shrugged and flopped onto my still singed couch. "Are you sure? Maybe you went on a weekend blood bender and got so shitfaced you don't remember knocking up a bunch of vampire baby mamas."

He laughed. "Think I already read that novel. But getting back to the sword..."

"What about it?"

"Considering it went all lightsaber, did you perhaps think to call its former owner and ask if maybe she did, too?"

I stared blankly at him for several seconds, the synapses of my brain firing off multiple signals that I was indeed a fucktard.

Holy shit, how could I be so fucking stupid?

I'd been so preoccupied with vampires, witches, and Tom's ghost, I hadn't even considered it. Well, okay, there was also a slight chance that subconsciously it was still something I didn't want to deal with.

Nevertheless, Ed had a point, a potentially important one.

Just because he and the Magi could tap into these strange pulses didn't mean they were the only ones. Sheila was another X-factor, one I should have considered from the very start. Hell, I'd even used her fucking sword.

If everyone else's powers had reawakened – albeit temporarily – then shouldn't it stand to reason hers might have as well?

I was pretty useless in a fight against just about every nasty thing that might be lurking in the shadows waiting for the next pulse. And, if we're being truthful, I was mostly okay with that. My time as the Freewill was done. I was out, finished, and quite happy to be *retired*.

But I still had friends in the game.

If things were going to get dangerous and, let's face facts, they already had, they could use a powerful ally by their side. Who better than the legendary Icon, the last defender of humanity?

Sure, it might be a bit awkward to have my ex-girlfriend, who'd dumped me like ten pounds of shit in a five pound bag, team up with my prospective girlfriend – the one working on a way to resurrect her dead fiancé – but...

Oh yeah, this was a clusterfuck. No two ways about it.

Before I could let how bad of an idea this might be overpower my resolve, I pulled out my phone and pulled up Sheila's number in my contacts.

As my finger hovered over the dial button, I let out a chuckle.

"Something funny?" Ed asked.

"Sheila. Remember how when we first started working together I could barely say two words to her?"

"First started? It took you three fucking years to talk to her."

"You know what I mean. It's just that, we haven't spoken since she left. No replies to my messages or anything. And now, after everything we've been through, I realize I'm back to where we started. I have no idea what to say to her."

He clapped me on the shoulder. "The more things change, the more they stay the same. God, I sound like my mother."

"Welcome to adulthood," I replied, hitting the button. "Now, if we want to live to see old age, we'd better hope I come up with something quickly."

12

PRIVATE SCREENING

"Here's a thought," Dave said. "If you two lovebirds want to whisper sweet nothings into each other's ears, then go get a room. Otherwise, shut the fuck up. My show's about to start."

Ed and I glanced at each other, exasperated looks on both our faces, then we turned back to the TV, trying to be quiet so as to not set Dave off again.

Two days had passed and Sheila still hadn't returned my calls. I was starting to get worried. It was one thing to not want to talk about us, but the shit going on kind of trumped relationship woes.

Still, it was probably stupid to think she'd call back in the middle of the night, so I put my phone away and pretended to concentrate on what was playing on the screen.

I'd made the mistake of forgetting to DVR Dave's live showing, something he'd been harping on ever since arriving. *Fortunately* for us, the Buy Mor Channel decided to show an encore performance ... at one in the morning.

Dave himself wasn't too put out by this. Sales had apparently been healthy following the first play through.

Besides, according to him, losers who made impulse buys from their TVs were up at all hours anyway. So the time didn't matter much.

I tried not to laugh. That was Dave in a nutshell – about as far from being a people person as one could get and not be a serial killer. The person on the TV, however, was pure fantasy – Dr. David Cheng, a *caring* physician emphatically proclaiming his desire to help the elderly regain their youthful shine.

"Fuck yeah," Dave said from next to me, cheering his own performance. "I should get a fucking Oscar for this shit."

"That's the movies," Ed replied. "Emmys are for television."

"Like I really give a flying fuck."

I'd invited a bunch of people – Christy, Sally, some of my consulting buddies, a few of the neighbors. So far, however, it was just the three of us here to *enjoy* the show.

I couldn't say I was surprised. Sally couldn't stand Dave. Truth of the matter was Christy couldn't either, but at least she had the twin excuses of having a small child and being busy researching resurrection spells.

The rest, well, I couldn't blame them for not giving a damn about some snake oil salesmen hawking skin cream ... even if it wasn't actually bad stuff.

What? My hands get chapped easily when I type on my laptop.

That's my story and I'm sticking to it.

Either way, I still had several cases sitting near my door – something Dave kept pointing out as if it were a personal failure on my part that I wasn't being a good sales slave.

God, what a fucked up world I lived in, and that wasn't even counting the supernatural.

To think that once, years ago, he'd been a promising

medical resident, not to mention a pretty good dungeon master – even if he was an asshole about it most of the time.

Then things had turned weird. Dave was one of the first people I told after being turned. He'd agreed to help me out, but there was a price: blood and tissue samples for his research. Ostensibly, it had been to help me, but the reality was more along the lines of making himself rich.

Neither had worked out. Since then, he'd lost his license, had his ethics questioned by just about everyone, and bounced around from project to project, all while his parents probably lamented the mountain of student loans he'd racked up.

And now here he was, using his credentials to pawn skin cream.

Yep, it was a tossup which of us fate disliked more.

TV Dave was busy spouting bullshit while his scantily clad assistants aided some elderly patrons in applying his crap to their wrinkled faces. "What sets Immortalis apart from other so-called age defying creams are special patent-pending proteins I've developed in my never-ending quest to help you stave off the ravages of time."

"Patent-pending proteins?" Ed asked.

Dave barely shrugged. "Technically speaking, a patent is pending ... even if it hasn't been submitted yet."

"And you're sure it's safe?"

"Didn't kill any of our lab animals, so far as I know," Dave replied with a laugh. "Relax. It's all harmless, except when it comes to sales. People eat that secret formula shit up and ask for seconds."

"Better hope the FDA doesn't say otherwise."

Dave smiled at me. "It's all in the wording, man. That's why you gotta keep this shit vague. You only offer suggestions, no promises, and maybe the occasional bullshit like seven out of ten users claimed to feel younger afterwards. There's no way to substantiate that."

On the screen, TV Dave reflected that grin, but in a far less predatory manner. "If you act now, we'll throw in an extra jar for free. Just pay shipping and handling."

I reached up to rub my eyes. A yawn escaped my lips, turning into a choked squeak as the breath caught in my throat.

One moment I felt fine. The next it was as if all of my organs seized up. I couldn't speak, couldn't breathe, and couldn't move except to drop limply back onto the couch.

"Oh suck it up," Dave griped from next to me. "It's almost over. Then you can go to bed, you lazy fuck."

He was right about me being tired, but it had nothing to do with staying up late. That strange weariness was back and worse than ever. It was as if every part of me weighed a thousand pounds, my lungs included.

With supreme effort, I managed to turn my head ever so slightly toward Ed. He was already aware, his hands in his mouth feeling the fangs which had sprouted.

"Um, I'm not feeling too well," he said, making sure to keep his yellow eyes averted from Dave. "Bill, could you show me where you keep your ... aspirin?"

I tried to move, but sorta just flopped in place, still fighting to fill my lungs. Thankfully Ed was neither stupid nor glued to the TV like the actual doctor in my apartment was.

He stood up and dragged me to my feet, almost yanking my arm out of its socket in the process.

"Ow," I squeaked.

Ed gave me an apologetic look, probably having forgotten that, aside from fangs and weird-ass eyes, his strength was now several times greater than it had been mere moments earlier.

He threw me a wink then hooked one of my arms over

his shoulder. "I know you're tired, but I really need to take something for my ... stomach."

Fortunately, the act of being upright eased some of the pressure and I was able to take a few shallow breaths. They weren't much, but at that moment, it was like ambrosia.

Supporting my weight, Ed helped me lurch to the bathroom.

Just as we got to the door, though, he hesitated and turned back. "Um, are you feeling all right?"

Dave threw him an annoyed glance. "Aside from you bothering me, right as rain. Why?"

"Just checking. Thought maybe that takeout from earlier was bad."

"Nope. The only shit I'm worried about is the shitload of cash I'm going to be making from this." With that, he went back to staring admiringly at himself.

As Ed closed the door behind us, I heard Dave say, "Try not to suck each other off too long. The show's not over yet."

Judging by how I felt, I had a feeling he was right. This was far from over.

13

IN MY TIME OF DYING

"What's wrong with you?" Ed whispered.

"No ... clue," I replied, focusing all of my attention on drawing breath.

"Do you think it has to do with *this*?" he asked, flashing his fangs.

I'd kept the tiredness I'd been feeling to myself as everything else seemed more important, but now, with it bowling me totally over, it didn't make sense to lie. "Maybe ... yeah, probably."

"Okay, so why isn't it happening to him?" Ed hooked a thumb toward the door. "He was a vamp, too."

"Beats ... the ... shit out of me."

It made no fucking sense. From what Sally had told me, it was the same for her – nothing – and she'd been a vamp a lot longer than the rest of us. Yet, whatever was happening, it seemed confined to me and was getting worse.

What a joke. Everyone else affected got more powerful, while I was slowly turning into a pile of human jelly. I didn't know what was happening, but I had a feeling it wasn't good.

"Is this, I dunno, a Freewill thing?"

I shrugged as best I could while propped up against the toilet. I guess that was possible. Freewills had been a rare breed of vampire, with abilities above and beyond the normal bloodsuckers. But why would that affect me now? I was human.

Dr. Death was gone. There was no trace of him left in me, not even residual nightmares. And if there had been, it should have made me stronger, not turned me into the equivalent of a thirty year old newborn.

My phone buzzed in my pocket, distracting me from my paranormal pity party. I flopped like a fish trying to get to it, until Ed finally noticed and helped me out.

"Try not to get too excited by this."

"Fuck ... you."

He pulled my phone out and looked at the screen.

Sheila?

Perhaps sensing my unspoken question, Ed shook his head, then held the phone up to his ear. "Hey, Christy. Everything okay? Yeah, we noticed it. Trust me on that."

He glanced down at me. "Bill? He's..."

I shook my head, not wanting her to worry about me with everything else on her plate.

"...Entertaining Dave until this passes. I'm in the bathroom waiting for my eyes to change back to normal. No, we didn't tell him. Yeah, I think that's for the best, too."

It probably wasn't fair to keep Dave out of the loop, but I knew my former DM. Chances were his primary concern would be annoying the shit out of us for DNA samples.

"They are?" Ed asked into the receiver. "Huh? What was that? Tell him to stop talking about his dick for a second. I can't hear what you're saying."

"Tom?" I wheezed.

Ed looked at me and mouthed, "Who else?" before giving his attention back to the phone.

I was tempted to tell him to put the fucking thing on speaker, but knowing Dave, he'd yell at us for interrupting his moment of triumph. It might also lead to some uncomfortable questions.

There was something to be said about keeping our circle small for now. Though the world as a whole had mostly gotten back to normal, people hadn't forgotten the Strange Days. I had little doubt the news would eventually spread to the general populace but I, for one, didn't want to be responsible for any doomsday cults springing up. Society had dealt with enough of that shit in the days following the cancellation of the apocalypse.

Mind you, word was already starting to spread in certain circles. The Magi community in particular had definitely taken notice.

When last we'd spoke, Christy told me her Sunday evening support group had been abuzz with chatter. Some were ecstatic to be given a taste of their former power again. Others were fearful, partly by what it meant, but mostly because they were afraid it wouldn't happen again.

Much as I had my own problems to deal with, I still found that a bit worrying.

A lot of ex-Magi were unstable. Many had been living broken lives for the last five years, unable to come to grips with the fact that they were no longer special snowflakes.

While some were no doubt able to handle the magical pulses in stride, there were probably far more acting like addicts who'd been handed the keys to the crack house. It didn't strike me as a good combo.

Sadly, Christy had been too preoccupied to discuss it for long. She was still uncertain about bringing Tom back, but had dove into her research with both feet nevertheless.

Even if she hadn't been busy, though, it's not like any of us were the designated babysitters of the Magi community.

"You are? Seriously?" Ed replied into the phone, dragging me from my thoughts. "Are you sure that's a good idea? Okay, relax. I'm well aware you know what you're doing. Just be careful. All right, we will. Do you want us to come over just in case?"

"What's going on?" I asked, vaguely aware that the current pulse appeared to be a long one. Fortunately, my condition seemed to have stabilized a bit. At the very least I could breathe again, even if I still felt like hammered shit.

Ed waved me off, then got back to the conversation. Fucker was eating up my battery. The least he could do was give me a play by play.

"I still don't like it," he continued, holding up what was apparently the uninteresting half of the conversation.

I was contemplating smacking the shit outta him with my toilet brush when he started to wrap things up. "Okay fine. Yes. I promise. Yes, I know there isn't much we can do. All right. See you then. Oh, and Christy ... be careful."

Ed stared at the phone for several seconds, at least until I managed to swing my arm hard enough to whack him in the side.

"Huh?"

"Sorry to inconvenience you, oh lord of the undead, but care to clue me the fuck in?"

"Oh, sorry, it's just..." His stomach made an audible gurgle. "Oh crap. Listen, I don't want to worry you, but I think we *really* need to go buy that raw chop meat." He licked his lips as he spoke, staring at me as if I were the last slice of pizza.

"Don't get any bright ideas. This all you can eat buffet is currently closed."

He shook his head. When he turned to me again, his yellow eyes still twinkled in the fluorescent light, but that look of longing on his face was gone. "Trust me, biting you in the bathroom isn't exactly my idea of fine dining."

"Food snob."

"How are you feeling?"

"Like a pile of stepped in dog shit. I don't know what's going on, but I could barely breathe when that pulse first hit."

"Are you okay now?"

"Not really, but I'm holding it together."

"Any idea what's causing it?"

"If I did, I'd have told you. Now, care to fill me in on what Christy said, or should I just lie here polishing the floor with my...?"

All at once, it was as if a fifty pound weight were lifted from my chest. Not only could I breathe freely again, but the rest of my body took the hint that it was still alive.

I looked up at Ed. In the space of him blinking his eyes a few times, they were back to normal. Almost in the same instant, his stomach stopped growling. "Oh God, that's so much better. For a minute there I thought I was going to start rooting through your garbage for used Band-Aids."

"If you do, hand me my phone first because I want a picture of that shit."

He flipped me off. "Seriously, though, we should probably find an all-night deli before that happens again."

I stood up, happy to find the last of the wooziness gone. "In a minute. First tell me what she said."

"For starters, she said to be ready for another pulse. If this weekend is any indication, they seem to hit in batches."

"Just great. Maybe you should go food shopping while I lie down in the bathtub and get comfortable."

He shrugged. "Might not be a bad idea..."

"Hey," Dave called to us from outside. "Stop blowing each other in there. You're missing the show."

I narrowed my eyes at the door, then turned back to Ed. "Perhaps we should both head out for a while."

"Are you sure you don't want me to eat him instead?"

"Don't tempt me."

Despite his complaints, Dave was far too engrossed watching himself to give us any shit about going out, especially after we told him we were gonna grab a couple of six packs to celebrate his awesome triumph.

"Cool," he called after us. "Just don't get any of that cheap shit you like. I have standards."

I was still commenting how his standards didn't seem to preclude fleecing old people out of their Social Security checks when Ed and I stepped out onto the sidewalk.

"Stay close," he warned.

"Relax. The only people out this late are probably too drunk to bother us."

"Who cares about that shit? I just don't want you embarrassing me by taking a face plant on the concrete if another of those surges hits."

"My hero."

"Or I could just leave your ass."

I stepped closer to him. "Okay, Romeo. Care to finally clue me in on the rest of what Christy said?"

He looked away. "You aren't going to like it."

"Name me one thing there is to like about any of this."

"Tom's back."

"Fair enough."

"Oh, and I really dig being super strong again."

"That's two. I said one."

He chuckled but it didn't hold much mirth. "That's okay, because this next one could count as a negative twelve if it goes badly. She's trying to stabilize that Apollo's thingy."

"What?"

"She told me she's conducting a ritual that might let Tom stick around longer."

Ed was about as well-versed in magic as me, but he tried his best to explain that the prism was a complex working of magic as far as miniature dimensional portals went. One didn't fix it by slapping on some duct tape and calling it a day.

"I get that part," I replied. "But how's she planning on getting Tom back without blowing us all up?"

"By feeding it even more power," he said, somehow keeping a straight face. "She called in some help and together they're going to try widening the ... breach, I guess."

"She wants to widen the breach? You did see Pacific Rim, right?"

"Only about half a dozen times. But anyway, she said the idea is to force the prism to pull in extra energy during those pulses."

I stared at him. "So she wants to turn it into a hydrogen bomb because atom bombs aren't scary enough."

"Will you shut up and let me finish? She thinks she can get it to act like a magical capacitor, holding a charge so that Tom can manifest even when the power's off."

"A ghost battery? Not a bad idea."

"My thoughts exactly."

"Minus the part about it being all explodey."

He shrugged. "I didn't say it was a perfect plan."

"We should get our asses over there."

"You think that didn't occur to me?" he replied. "Hence why I asked, dim-bulb."

"What did she say?"

"That we'd just get in the way."

I stopped and turned to face him. "I probably can't argue with that. Still, I was kind of hoping she'd find a way to bring him back that didn't involve overloading the warp core he's attached to..."

"Spare some change, buddy?"

We both spun toward the voice, coming from a small alleyway near where we stood. Just inside, a skinny bearded man sat amidst a pile of rags and cardboard. The *delectable* aroma that drifted out spoke of garbage mixed with urine.

"Help a fella out?" he asked in a raspy voice. "I ain't been able to hold a job since the Strange Days."

Ed sighed and reached for his wallet. Then he paused, standing there with his hand in his pocket.

Finally, I took the hint and reached for mine. "Hold on, cheapskate. I think I have a fiiiivvvv..."

The word caught in my throat, dissolving into a thin gasp as my lungs abruptly decided to go on strike. Then, before I could grab Ed's attention, the world upended itself as I collapsed face-first onto the sidewalk.

I had just enough time to look up and see my former roommate still facing the alley.

So much for catching me, I thought, as darkness closed in and I saw no more.

14

MY BLOODY VALENTINE

I wasn't sure how long I was out. Couldn't have been long because, when I woke up, my nose was still bleeding onto the sidewalk.

Ouch.

I still felt weak as a baby, but whatever had happened appeared to have cleared up enough for me to regain consciousness. Yep, those pulses were definitely getting worse. Pretty soon, I was going to need a jacket made of bubble wrap.

For now, though, I managed to push myself up to my elbows. It wasn't much, but it was enough to glance around and notice the street and sidewalk around me were both empty. Ed was nowhere in sight.

"Where ... the fuck ... did..."

That's when I heard it – a noise halfway between a slurp and a suck, as if someone was polishing off a particularly good milkshake.

I turned toward the sound, not entirely surprised to see that it was coming from the very alleyway we'd stopped in front of just ... however long ago.

Likewise unsurprising, I spied a figure hunched down

in the shadows. His back was to me, but I recognized the shirt – bearing the proud logo of San Diego ComicCon.

"Ed?"

The figure in the alleyway tensed as I spoke.

"Please tell me ... you're munching on some fried chicken you found in the garbage."

Mind you, that wasn't much better than what I suspected was going on. Sue me. My brain was still in the process of booting up from my impromptu collision with the sidewalk.

"Oh, fuck."

Yep, that was Ed's voice, all right, and his tone suggested he was doing something far worse than dumpster diving.

"What did I do?"

"That's what I'm trying to find out, dickhead," I called out, doing my best to crawl in his direction.

Ed turned around and, for a moment, I thought everything was okay. But then I realized it was only because he was still draped in shadows. He took a step forward into the light cast from the closest street lamp.

"Holy shit!"

He was drenched in gore, as if he'd found a swimming pool full of blood and had decided to dive right in. Nasty as that was, he knelt down before me, panic in his eyes, and grabbed hold of my shoulders with hands still dripping with blood.

"Oh man. I liked this shirt," I weakly protested as he hauled me to my feet like I weighed nothing. I looked him over and realized the only part of him that wasn't covered in red were his eyes – still that strange golden hue.

"I ... couldn't help myself."

"Say it, don't spray it," I replied, closing my mouth so as to not get any dead hobo in it.

He walked us back over to the alleyway, getting

enough blood on me so I looked like an accomplice, and pointed toward something on the ground. "What the fuck do we do?"

"Hold on," I said. Being upright had once again cleared my head a bit, but I was still unable to do much more than rely on him to hold me up. "Let my eyes adjust for a second and ... Jesus fuck burgers! Did you throw him in a fucking blender or something?"

I wished I was exaggerating. Back in the day, I'd seen my share of vampire kills. Most weren't pretty. Vamps had a tendency to ignore proper table etiquette. But the hungrier a vampire got, the more their self-control slipped. And, well, Ed must've been pretty damned hungry.

The former homeless man was now a shredded pile of homeless meat. It looked like he'd been run over with a riding mower ... at least half a dozen times. "Goddamn, dude."

"I didn't..." He lowered his voice. Now sated, I had a feeling common sense was returning, enough for him to remember we were out in public. "I didn't mean it."

"I'd hate to see what would happen if you did."

"What are we going to do?"

In years past, stuff like this could've been handled with a single phone call. Problem was, it had been a long time since Village Coven had paid its dues to the Patrolmen's Benevolent Society.

What Ed had done here was murder in ... pretty much every degree known to man, and probably a few new ones.

There was only one option, so far as I could see. "We need to get the fuck out of here."

Ed's vampiric strength was more than enough to pry open a manhole cover for us to slip down.

Thank goodness I'd had reason to tour the sewers with Tina a few days back. It had given my memory a nasty, but much needed, refresher course on the local tunnels and exits.

Sadly, I still wasn't much help for doing anything except pointing and then slumping onto the ground while Ed worked.

After some trial and error, in which I ended up being dropped into a pile of something unpleasant, we made it down below, where I was treated to an underground piggyback ride back to my place, echoing the one I'd given Tina a few days prior. Quite the way to end the evening.

If there was one upside, though, it was that, by the time we emerged in the subbasement beneath my building, the muck from the sewers had somewhat camouflaged the blood coating us.

Now we simply looked like dirty scumbags instead of dirty scumbag murderers.

Ed, for his part, was unusually quiet during all of this. Neither of us was innocent from our time living through the first apocalypse. But it had been years since we'd been forced to kill something. And, in all fairness, that homeless guy hadn't exactly been a matter of life and death so much as a midnight snack.

"Let's head to the second floor. Apartment 2A," I said.

"Why? That's not..."

"I know where I live, numbnuts," I replied. "That's the Martinez's apartment, but they're down at Disneyworld for the week. We can use their shower to clean up before going back upstairs."

"It's good to be the owner," he remarked, dragging me up the stairs with him.

"Not really."

"So then sell this place already."

"I..."

"I'm serious," Ed replied, sounding eager to talk about anything other than what he'd done. "Yes, there's lots of memories here, but a good many of them are shitty ... literally. Hell, you remember when that Night Razor guy broke in and took a dump in our living room?"

"Hard to forget... Whoa!"

Ed's grip on me slipped, but in that same instant my muscles got a wake-up call. Thankfully, I was able to grab the bannister and steady myself before I went tumbling back the way we'd come.

"You okay?" he asked after a moment, his eyes and teeth back to normal.

"I'll be a lot better when we finally figure out what the hell is going on. That was a long one."

He looked down at himself. "Too long. And now, to top it all off, I have a really bad taste in my mouth."

"Can't imagine why."

"Go fuck yourself."

I let Ed hop in the shower first. He needed it more than I did. While he was cleaning up, I ransacked the Martinez's linen closet for towels. Those were easy enough to replace. I was tempted to see if they had any clothes that would fit us, but that seemed a more serious crime. Besides, out of shape I might be, but Arturo Martinez still had at least fifty pounds on me.

He also had one of those apartment-sized washing machines. It more than made up for being a shitty host to the two blood-drenched guys making themselves at home in his place.

When Ed finally emerged, clad in a towel, he no longer looked like the sole survivor of a horror movie. "Our clothes done yet?"

"Have a seat," I replied. "It's going to take a while."

He flopped down onto the couch, giving me more of an eyeful than I needed. "How about crossing your legs when you do that?"

"Nobody told you to look."

Fucking cock. "Fine. While you air out your taint on the Martinez's sofa, I'll go clean up."

The shower was not only cleansing, but it gave me time to think. Unfortunately, what came to mind wasn't entirely pleasant.

By the time I was finished, Ed had transferred our clothes – now thoroughly ruined by about a gallon of bleach – to the dryer, leaving us to wait a bit longer.

"That was a bad one," he said as we settled down.

"I'll say."

"What I did to that guy..."

"Trust me, I noticed."

"I don't understand how I could lose control like that."

I nodded. "Been giving that some thought."

"Any useful insight from the Freewill?"

"Nothing more than a theory."

He laughed mirthlessly. "I don't even have that much. So hit me with it."

I hesitated for a moment, knowing he wouldn't like what I was about to say. "What if you weren't cured like the rest of us?"

"Excuse me?"

"I mean when we all became human again. What if we only thought you were, but you actually weren't?"

"That doesn't make any sense."

"I know. Just hear me out. I'm applying Occam's Razor here ... as opposed to the Occam's woodchipper you threw that homeless guy into."

Ed narrowed his eyes. "You're fucking hilarious. You know that?"

"So I tell myself. But enough of my comedic genius. When The Source closed, collapsed, imploded ... whatever the fuck, the spirits, for lack of a better term, sharing our bodies got sucked away, leaving all vampires human again."

"Thanks for the history lesson. I was there."

"Yeah, but you're also different — a new breed of vamp that nobody had ever heard of before. Not even Calibra, and that chick was older than dirt itself, literally."

"Okay, and?"

"So, we kind of know what you can and can't do, but we've always applied regular vampire logic to it. What if the changes inside of you went deeper than that? What if Sheila's magic affected you even more than we thought?"

He reached a hand up to the scar on his neck, faded but still there. It was in the shape of her hand, where she'd touched him with her healing magic in a bid to save him from the vampire bite that was killing him. Fun times, I tell ya. "How so?"

"Beats the fuck out of me," I replied. "I'm making this shit up as I go. But here's a thought. What if the connection inside of you between that spirit, if you will, was also different than a regular vamp ... stronger, as in strong enough to resist being pulled out when everyone else was evicted?"

"Okay," he replied, getting up and walking into the kitchen. "The problem with that theory is that I've been as normal as you these last five years. Correction — probably *more* normal."

"What are you doing?"

Ed opened the refrigerator and peered in it. "Looking to see if they have anything to drink. We already stole their towels. I doubt they'll mind if we swipe a few beers, too."

"I see your vampire side is affecting your already questionable morals."

"Eat a bag of dicks. You want one or not?"

"Fuck yeah."

After we'd settled back onto the couch to enjoy our ill-gotten gains, I turned to him and continued. "I was thinking about that ... not the beer, but that you've been human. However, what if you only appear to be human?"

I got up, almost lost my towel, then began pacing once I'd fixed it enough to not give Ed more of a thrill than he deserved. "Think about that doll Tom is connected to. The magic in it wasn't destroyed like we thought, just rendered inert. Well, what if the same thing happened to you? What if your powers were simply, I don't know, turned off instead of removed altogether? And now, with these weird pulses, they're activating again."

"I suppose that doesn't sound any crazier than anything I can think of."

"But it gets better," I continued. "That also explains why you went apeshit on that guy back in the alley. If whatever is inside of you didn't get sucked out when the rest of our things got sucked out..."

He raised an eyebrow. "Phrasing."

"Deal with it. Anyway, the thing ... spirit, inside you. What if it was dormant but still there? And now, with these pulses, it's slowly waking up again. Problem is, that part of you hasn't eaten in years, which would make it a lot hungrier than normal. Hence why you completely pulped that guy as opposed to taking a quick drink."

Ed appeared to consider this.

"Or you could just be a sick fuck and have been hiding it well all these years," I offered as a counterpoint to my argument.

⟵⟶

We continued to debate the ins and outs of my, admittedly hastily thrown together, theory. The more we talked, though, the more it made sense and the more dismayed Ed became.

"Kara's *really* not going to like this."

"Which part?"

"The part about me not being human, idiot. If you're right, then that means I haven't been human all this time. Hell, I might never be fully human again."

I nodded. "Yeah, there is that. But, if we can figure out what's causing these pulses and stop it, then the thing inside of you can go back to sleep again and you can go back to pretending to be a reasonable facsimile. I don't see the problem."

"Kara's the problem," he snapped. "She wants kids."

"I thought you didn't..."

"I got overruled," he replied bitterly.

I waved my hand and made a whipping sound.

"This isn't funny. She's going to flip out when she learns."

"Why? She was a vamp for a while, too. Looked like she fit in pretty well with the crowd."

"At the time," he explained. "But she's not a teenager anymore. The further we've moved away from that time, the more she's had to think about it. Those aren't exactly happy memories for her."

I opened my mouth, but no snark came out. It wasn't much different than what had happened with Sheila. I'd assumed that because I'd made my peace with things, she had, too, but that wasn't the case. "Sorry, man. I didn't know."

He shrugged. "It is what it is. I mean, on the upside, this might change her mind about kids. I guess that's a plus..."

The dryer buzzed, sparing us from an unpleasant conversation that really was none of my business.

I stood up and walked over to it. "Let's get dressed and head back upstairs."

"What are we going to tell Dave?"

"Who cares? This is Dave we're talking about. If it doesn't concern him, he won't be listening anyway."

"Fair enough."

We got dressed then I retrieved our phones from where I'd tossed them next to the washer. I was about to stuff mine back into my pocket when I realized there was a notification on the screen. "Hold on. I got a text."

"From who?"

A part of me was hoping it was from Sheila, while another part hoped it wasn't. "Probably Dave wondering where we are with his beer. He..." I glanced down at the phone for a better look and the words dried up in my throat.

"What is it?"

I held the screen up for him to see. A text had come in right in the middle of that last pulse. From the time stamp, it was probably right around the time we were busy hoofing it through the sewer system.

The text was from Sally, and it contained only two words.

They're here.

15

THE DEVIL YOU KNOW

I tried Sally's number for perhaps the twentieth time. Ed was behind the wheel of my car, which was fine. I was far too worried to concentrate on driving.

We'd spared just enough time to run upstairs to grab my car keys. Dave was mercifully asleep in Tom's old room by then, thank goodness. We didn't need any stupid questions from him slowing us down.

I found my keys while Ed stepped into his old room, emerging a few seconds later with Sheila's sword. "We might need this."

I didn't argue – just turned and headed out the door again.

The streets of Manhattan were never truly empty, but traffic was mercifully sparse during the wee hours of the morning. Even so, the trip seemed to take forever as I continued trying Sally's number.

She'd have had no reason to be at the Office this late – her days as a night owl long behind her – so I directed Ed toward her apartment.

Ironically enough, it had also once served Village

Coven, a former safe house that she'd purchased during a particularly dark time.

After the world didn't end, Sally had it renovated and then moved in. Morbid as that might have been to some, it was already paid for: prime real estate in one of the most expensive cities on Earth.

Of course, it was also located in the middle of fucking SoHo, because that seemed to be where my bad luck was centralized in this universe.

We parked in one of her reserved spots and ran to the door, heedless of the fact that we were carrying a broadsword in the middle of the city.

Ed hit the buzzer to be let in, but there came no answer. He tried again, giving the button an obnoxiously long press, guaranteed to wake even the dead — poor choice of words as that was.

"Come on, open up," I muttered.

No response came, so I stepped to the outside door and began to bang on it. It swung open on my first hit, revealing the jamb had been snapped.

Definitely not a good sign.

Sadly, despite this once being a vampire safe house, it had since been remodeled more for function than fear. If we all got through this mess unscathed, I had a feeling it wasn't a mistake we'd ever make again.

"Come on!" I cried, leading the way with Ed hot on my tail.

Please be okay!

Sally was the building's sole tenant, her apartment occupying the entirety of the fifth floor. The walls and floors were made of soundproofed concrete. Good for vampires back then but, sadly, equally good for them now if any decided to pay a visit in the middle of the night, as I now feared was the case.

Those fears solidified in my gut as we reached her floor, only to find the door kicked off its hinges.

"Shit!" I stepped inside and drew the sword, heedless of the fact I was a normal guy, likely wading in way over my head. "SALLY!"

Ed hit the light switch, illuminating the living room enough for us to see that the place was trashed. Sally had impeccable taste when it came to her furnishings, sparing no expense when it came to hiring the best decorators. She may have run an organization tasked with helping the needy, but she'd never quite bought into suffering for the cause.

It was the space of seconds to take in the broken glass and overturned furniture which had replaced the carefully laid out Feng Shui or whatever the fuck it was called – a leather sectional upended, a chandelier lying shattered on the floor, bullet holes riddling the big screen TV that once hung on the wall. Whatever had happened here, there'd been a hell of a fight.

"Where is she?" Ed asked.

"I don't know. You check that end." I pointed him toward the kitchen. "I'll check over here."

Though the apartment was massive by New York standards, it didn't take long to search. Sally had favored an open floor plan, no doubt from her years sharing communal living space with other vampires.

The bathroom was intact, if empty. Except for ruffled sheets on the bed and an open drawer in the night table, the bedroom was likewise untouched. I was no private eye, but my instincts told me she'd been woken by the sound of intruders breaking in and had stopped long enough to grab her gun before confronting them.

I stepped out and rejoined Ed, who'd likewise finished his sweep. "Anything?"

He shook his head. "No sign of her, but I found a kitchen knife in the living room with blood on it."

"Whose?"

"That's the sixty-four thousand dollar question. I also found this." He held out the remains of a cell phone, crushed beyond use. "I'm guessing she didn't get a chance to dial 9-1-1."

"I'm not sure she would have," I replied, just barely holding it together. "Not if she knew who ... what they were."

"Even if she didn't at first, I think she figured it out quickly. Check it out."

He directed my attention back toward the entrance. I'd been too focused on Sally to notice earlier, but the security panel next to the door was nothing more than a scorched mess of metal and fused plastic. That wasn't all. Now that I took a moment to slow down, I could see strange burns marring the walls in a few places.

"The fuck?"

"Call me crazy, but I don't think vampires did all of this."

A wave of guilt immediately washed over me. "This is all my fault. I shouldn't have told her. If she'd thought for one second this was a normal burglary she would have called the cops instead of me..."

"Don't do that shit to yourself, man. Do you really think the police would've made a difference? That pulse was more than long enough for these assholes to do whatever they needed to do."

He was right. That last pulse was the longest we'd seen so far, but I doubted it was long enough to organize a hit like this on the fly.

Had they been staking Sally's place out, waiting for their moment to strike? Between the attack on my apartment and now this, the timing not only suggested it, but pointed to things escalating beyond just a couple of vamps.

But if so, how did they know when to act? Sitting around, waiting for the magic to randomly turn itself back on, didn't seem like a sound strategy to me.

"I have a bad feeling about this." Talk about the fucking understatement of the decade.

"Do you think she's..."

"I don't know what to think," I snapped, it coming out harsher than intended. Taking some deep breaths, I tried to steady myself. I couldn't help Sally while I was in a blind panic. Neither of us could. Mind you, I wasn't sure what I could do otherwise, but thinking rationally was at least a start.

"She's alive," I said after several long seconds.

"How...?"

"It would've been easy for them to figure out she'd texted me. They could have simply left her body for us to find if they wanted to. They took her, which means she's alive."

"But why?"

"Beats the fuck out of me."

"Do you think it's *because* of you?" Ed asked. "Oh, don't look at me like that. You said they called you Freewill. If they knew that much, then it's not hard to assume they could've known about your history with her. If they were trying to get to you, then kidnapping Sally would be the next best thing because..."

"I'd come racing to the rescue?"

"More like you'd offer yourself up in exchange. No offense, man, but I'm not sure you're in any shape to rescue anyone."

Much as I wanted to shout him down, he was right. I was powerless. They could dangle Sally right in front of me and there wouldn't be dick I could do about it. This wasn't my world anymore.

So then why were they trying to drag me back into it?

"Do you think it's a revenge thing?"

Ed appeared to mull this over. "Let's face facts. You did piss off a lot of people back in the day. But they're all dead now."

"Not all."

"Sheila?" he offered.

I looked at him sidelong. "Maybe I wasn't the best boyfriend in the world, but I wasn't *that* bad."

"You did keep her sword."

"She left it behind. No forwarding address."

"Okay, okay. I was just grasping at straws."

"I meant the Magi," I said. "They're not the only group that hated me, but they're pretty much the only ones left. Not to mention, look at this place."

"You do make a compelling argument."

I shook my head. "This still doesn't make any sense, though. I mean, forget magic for a moment. If they wanted me dead, they could have run me over with a car. Why do all of this?"

Ed hesitated for a moment before saying, "Maybe they wanted to hurt you first."

He may have had a point. People like Christy were the lucky ones – strong enough to survive in a world without magic. From the sound of things, though, the majority of the Magi community had been leading sad, broken lives, for which I was at least partially responsible.

Still, this all seemed too convoluted for petty revenge. And besides, none of it explained those vampires. I said as much.

"So where does that leave us?" Ed asked after a long pause.

"Fucked," I said. "Utterly fucked. The ball's in their court, whoever they are."

"So what now? We wait for them to call with their demands?"

"Beats the fuck out of me," I replied, leaning against the dining room table, one of the few pieces left relatively unscathed. This was all so unreal, more so because it was Sally.

She'd always been more the type to leave a trail of bodies behind, superior foes or not. Even now, it was hard for me to think of her as vulnerable. Of course, with bullet casings and knives scattered about, maybe vulnerable wasn't quite the right word. "Who knows? Maybe we'll get lucky and they'll turn her again. Then she can kill their asses for us."

"That is a highly unlikely outcome," a female voice replied from back near the entrance, causing us to whip toward it so quickly I'm surprised we didn't snap our own necks.

Standing in the doorway was a lithe form topped by glittering green eyes and long black hair. "The Progenitor here is the only one with that capability. All the rest of the new breed are sterile. Mules if you will, myself included."

I could only stare in horror as Gansetseg, adopted granddaughter of Genghis Khan, stepped forward into the light. Shit had been steadily going downhill for us ever since this had all started. But where I'd thought they were mere bumps in the road, I now saw we were actually on a roller coaster and had just crested the big hill ... one that went all the way down to my own personal Hell.

16

THE GANG'S ALL HERE

E d backed up a step, his voice way too calm for my personal edification. "Bill, please tell me that isn't who I think it is."

As our *guest* continued forward, I offered silent prayers to every D&D god I knew of in the hopes that one might be real and in the mood to listen. Sadly, my eyes weren't playing tricks on me. And people wonder why I'm not a churchgoer. "Hi, Gan."

She wore a sly smile on her face as she put one well-manicured hand on her hip, adopting a very mature looking pose. She'd definitely grown from when last I'd seen her.

For most of our ... acquaintance, Gan had appeared as a twelve year old child, but that was nothing more than a facade. She was actually well over three hundred. Five years of normal aging had been kind to her, however. Gone was the cute little munchkin, and in her place stood someone who could've marched straight into any high school in America and taken over the top clique with a snap of her fingers. In short, she'd finally become the one thing she'd wanted more than anything: a woman. And hey, go figure. She'd ended up taller than Sally.

Mind you, despite her appearance, I was still creeped out, and it had nothing to do with whether or not she was still jailbait.

The Gan I'd known was batshit crazy, a remorseless murderer, and inexplicably head over heels in love with me. I had little doubt those labels still applied, but a small part of me had hoped she'd found a boyfriend in the last few years ... maybe some nice Goth kid who shared her disdain for humanity.

"Beloved," she purred, a predatory glint in her eyes.

So much for that theory.

She looked like she'd stepped straight out of a catalogue, wearing a casually cut summer dress – black with red and gold highlights. The illusion was only marred by a brief glimpse of yellow earrings beneath her hair. I didn't need to ask to guess they were likely a certain square-pantsed cartoon character, one of her few obsessions aside from me and enslaving the world.

I guess we all had to have hobbies.

She glanced around, idly surveying the scene as I waited for the tirade that was certain to come. It was only a matter of time before Ed got over the shock and lost his shit over the fact he was staring at someone who should've been little more than a pile of dust deep beneath the Earth's surface.

Oh, yeah, I was gonna get an earful about this one.

"From the condition of this apartment," Gan said, her tone one of boredom. "I shall assume they've appropriated your whore."

And just like that it was five years earlier ... I was still the Freewill, she was the vampire prefect of China, and Ed was the poor sap she'd once tried to wash down a bowl of Apple Jacks with.

Except it wasn't. We'd changed, *all* of us. I needed to remember that.

"I see you've lost some of the physical definition you once had," she continued, undressing me with her eyes. "Excellent. I always preferred your more mundane appearance."

"I've been busy," I replied with an uncomfortable shrug. "Haven't gotten a chance to hit the gym lately."

"Are we really having this fucking conversation?" Ed snapped, finally joining the fray. "I mean, did I just cross over into the fucking bizarro universe?"

Gan, for her part, smiled as she continued to address me. "I have always found it interesting that fate chose one of your cattle as Progenitor of our new race. For all the seers of the world, it would seem destiny occasionally likes to throw ... what is the phrase ... a curve ball."

Her English had improved, too. I barely detected an accent. But perhaps that was a discussion point for another time. "Why are you here, Gan, and what do you know?"

Ed narrowed his gaze my way. "Is it me, or are you not nearly as surprised as you should be?"

"Oh, I'm pretty damned surprised."

"Is that a fact? So then why aren't you shitting your pants right now?"

"Because I have the right amount of fiber in my diet ... and I might've sorta known she was ... alive."

"Do tell. And I'm just finding this out, *why?*"

"You were busy being engaged."

"And what about everyone else, or were they busy, too?"

"The Shining One is aware of my survival, as well as my intention to reclaim my beloved," Gan explained, stepping past him and eyeing the sword in my hand.

Ed turned to me. "Is that why she left?"

Gan let out a small laugh. "Doubtful. I believe her shift in affections had more to do with regret over the part she played in decimating the Magi."

"Wait," I said. "How do you know that?"

"Is it not obvious? I've kept close watch upon your life." She paused for a moment, a brief shadow of annoyance crossing her face. "At least until recently."

"Of course you did. Because why would a person's privacy mean anything..."

"Hold on," Ed interrupted. "Let's not skip past this. What changed?"

"Um, yeah," I added, glad to steer the discussion elsewhere. "What he said."

Gan held my gaze, all mirth gone from her eyes, making her truly look like the adult she'd always wanted to be. "It is because I became aware of an increasingly focused effort to reignite The Source."

I had about a million questions, and I'm pretty sure Ed had an equal number of accusations. Before we could pummel each other with them, though, Gan, in that maddeningly disinterested voice of hers, suggested we relocate to a place that wasn't currently an active crime scene.

As much as I didn't want to admit it, that made sense. There didn't appear to be any clues left behind as to where Sally had been taken. But with Gan's overly convenient reappearance, combined with her utter lack of surprise at what she'd seen, I had a feeling she could provide us with some of the insight we were lacking.

Waiting outside, double parked at the curb, was an enormous black limo with diplomatic plates. Couldn't say I was surprised. Gan was not only heir to her father's fortune, but she'd also been the only survivor of the apocalypse with the means to capitalize on the vast wealth left behind by the vampire leadership.

In short, she was fucking loaded. No wonder she'd been able to keep tabs on me. One didn't need super powers when they were up to their eyeballs in cash.

Gan offered us a ride in her ridiculously overblown vehicle, complete with a burly, no-necked driver, but I respectfully declined, fearing she might toss Ed out at the first red light, leaving me trapped with her for some *quality time*. No, sir, I did not want that.

I was still worried to all hell about Sally but fortunately calm enough to drive. That was good, because I didn't think Ed was.

"Spill," he said once we'd shut the doors. "And don't give me any bullshit because I am not in the mood."

"I'm gonna go out on a limb and assume you didn't enjoy that little reunion back there."

"Let me put it this way. I'd be less upset had a Bigfoot walked in and shit on me."

Ah. Well, that definitely put some perspective to his current temperament.

I brought him up to speed, telling him how Gan had approached Sheila and me two years ago after he'd already moved to California. The truth was we'd spent quite a few nights of our burgeoning relationship debating whether to let anyone else know. But, in the end, it had seemed a dangerous bit of knowledge to share. Gan might have been powerless, but the little nutbag had made it more than clear at the time that her homicidal tendencies were very much intact.

That and I think we were both hoping our meetup with Gan had been a one-time thing, despite her assurances otherwise. Hell, I'd almost managed to convince myself it was little more than a shared hallucination ... fate's way of giving Sheila and I the push we finally needed to become a couple, at least until she walked out on me.

"You should have told us," Ed said when I was finally finished.

"I know."

"Especially once all of this weird shit started happening."

"Sorry, but I was hoping she wouldn't show up."

"It's not even that, moron," he replied, looking at me from the passenger seat as if I were a base idiot. "Think about it. For the past couple of days we've been wracking our brains wondering where the hell these other vamps came from, when all along you had a clue."

"She didn't make them."

"I know that, genius. But she survived, which should have been impossible. I guess your crazy theory about inert spirits is starting to make more sense. I mean, hell, she's three hundred goddamned years old yet looks eighteen."

"Seventeen," I corrected.

"Whatever the fuck. It's not like I'm asking her out." He shuddered as if considering how badly that would end for him. "The thing is, we've been wondering who created those vamps who showed up at your door, but maybe that's not what we need to focus on."

"It isn't?"

"No. Maybe what we should be asking is whether this means others may have survived, too."

He was echoing what Sally had said when last I'd talked to her, something I'd tried very hard not to dwell on, perhaps stupidly so.

Talk about an unpleasant thought. I'd met a lot of ancient vampires during my short tenure among the undead, most of whom hadn't liked me – Calibra, Alexander the Great, the rest of the First Coven. I'd seen them all turn to dust, alongside my friend James, the one elder vamp whose death I regretted.

But I saw now they had a point. What if Gan hadn't been the one-off miracle – or curse – I'd assumed?

We drove in silence for several more minutes, both of us no doubt contemplating the ramifications of this, until he finally asked, "So where are we heading?"

"Huh?" That was a good question. Had Gan not shown up, I'd have said Christy's. But not now. Those two had sort of hated each other back in the day. "My place."

"You do remember Dave's there, right?"

"Can't be helped. None of the old safe houses exist anymore, I don't have keys to the Office, and I sure as shit don't want to take Gan anywhere Tina is."

"Probably a good idea."

"Tell me about it. Speaking of which, remember how she mentioned being too busy to spy on me lately?"

"Hard to forget."

"Since she didn't bring it up – and believe me, she would have – I'm going to assume she doesn't know about me and Christy. I think it might be best if it stayed that way."

Gan had tolerated Sheila, offering her a modicum of respect as the Icon. But Christy was another matter entirely. Those two had started off trying to kill each other and had never quite gotten over it. Now, though, I had a feeling Gan would see our relationship as little more than an excuse to take up old habits. Keeping them apart probably wasn't an option, but making sure certain things stayed on the down-low was probably wise.

Ed, being no stranger to any of this, quickly nodded his agreement. "So what do we do?"

"We can't keep Christy out of the loop. She's one of the few people with a clue as to what's going on. I'll text her and tell her to come by my place." I glanced at the time. "Or maybe wait until she's awake. Anyway, I'll say that things have taken a turn for the worse and we'll explain when we see her. Oh, and that she should find a sitter for Tina."

"You're not going to tell her about Gan?"

"Over the phone? Are you fucking crazy? She's liable to show up with every hex she knows, and I don't want that to happen until we've all had a chance to compare notes."

I was setting up a potentially explosive reunion between two enemies, with me smack dab in the middle. Not only that, but we still had to figure out a way to save Sally, wherever she might be.

My God, it had been a long day and the sun wasn't even up yet.

Sadly, I had a feeling the next few hours weren't going to be a walk in the park.

17

BITTER REUNION

We got back to my place just as the sky was starting to lighten, beating rush hour. It was a minor victory but I'd take it. The last thing I wanted was for the world to get ass fucked because we were stuck sitting on I-278.

I walked over to Gan's land yacht and asked if she'd be so good as to find another place to park it. I don't know why, but it didn't seem like a good idea to call extra attention to ourselves right then.

If Gan had any misgivings, she didn't show it. She simply commanded her driver as if he was little more than the cattle she used to refer to humans as. As a vampire, she'd tolerated nothing less than complete obedience from her servants. Human or not, I got the impression nothing had changed in that regards.

As we walked up to my floor, she said, "I do so miss visiting you here, my darling. I find it ... quaint that you've remained in this wretched domicile."

"There's a lot of memories here," I commented dryly.

"They must be truly special to abide such a place. I

have dozens of properties across the globe and none of them manage to produce an odor as unique as this one."

Ed snickered from somewhere below.

"Yuck it up, asshole. You used to live here."

"Perhaps better living arrangements can be arranged for you, Dr. Death."

Desperately trying to ignore what she was implying, I replied, "Don't call me that. It's not who I am anymore."

"I disagree," she said with smug surety.

"That was the name of the monster inside of me. He's gone now."

"No, my dearest. It is a name you and you alone earned. It is who you are and who you shall forever be."

I could practically feel her breathing down the back of my neck as we got to my apartment door. Sadly, I didn't have nearly enough alcohol on hand to erase the memory of her existence. On the flipside, blacking out piss-drunk in her presence probably wasn't a great idea to begin with.

I reached for my key and considered Dave. I hadn't wanted to drag him back into this. He wasn't a part of things this time around. There was also the fact that I really didn't want him pestering people for blood samples again. I had enough shit on my plate already.

Sadly, I was low on options. If only Sally had hung onto more of our old safe houses. It would have provided a neutral location for us to deal with this crap.

But why would she have? Who would have guessed this would be happening? More importantly, who would have guessed it would be happening to us – *me* – again? It was like I was living out a shitty movie sequel. Kinda made me wish they'd killed off my character in the first one.

Anyway, hindsight is twenty-twenty, I suppose.

This was the hand I'd been dealt and I couldn't afford to ask for new cards. Sally's life was likely on the line. Who knew what would happen to her if we failed to act ... or who might be next?

At least in my own apartment I had some modicum of control. I could hopefully ease everyone into the situation, whether it was the fact that Sally had been kidnapped or Gan was alive.

Yeah, I considered as I pushed open the door, I could control the narrative here. There would be no surprises to...

"Dude, where the fuck have you been?" the semi-transparent form of Tom asked from right in front of me as I stepped in.

"Jesus! What the fuck?!"

He laughed at my surprise. "Pussy out much?"

"What are you doing here?" I cried.

However, even as I asked the question, I could see he wasn't alone. Christy was sitting on the couch. Oh yeah, she had a key. I probably should have remembered that.

Next to her sat ... oh crap, what was his name? Vincent something-or-other. He was a former Knight Templar, a group of holy rollers who'd done nothing but give me grief back in the day. Now he was retired from that life, happily married to a witch of all people – Kelly, one of Christy's coven sisters.

Guess that's who she'd called in to help out, which was cool by me. I liked Kelly. The only reason I didn't hang out with her more was because she'd been tight with Sheila which, of course, made things a bit awkward since the breakup. I glanced around, not seeing her immediately, but maybe she was in the...

Hold on.

My addled brain had somehow glossed over the fact that Tom was both here and visible. Since I wasn't busy keeling over at the moment, that had to mean Christy had been successful in whatever mojo she'd worked.

Um, it also apparently meant Dave was aware of this, too, because he was sitting in the love seat, looking like he'd gotten way too little sleep to be cheered up by this revelation. But he could wait for now.

I looked at Tom, then back toward Christy. "How did you..."

Sadly, all of this had caught me completely by surprise, enough to make me momentarily forget that I hadn't returned to my apartment alone.

"Dude!" Tom admonished, stepping past me. "It's bad enough you gotta dip your wick where it don't belong, but now you've got a side piece, too?" He covered one side of his face with a spectral hand, shielding it from Christy's view and mouthed, "High five".

Fucking idiot.

If his reaction to seeing a now grown Gan was ... disturbing at best, Christy's was somewhat less welcoming. She stood up, her eyes narrowing. "It's not possible."

Gan, for her part, sauntered past me like she owned the place. She gave Tom the barest of glimpses, hardly raising an eyebrow, before facing Christy. "Few things are impossible, witch. I would think one such as yourself would be well versed in such matters."

So much for controlling the narrative.

Those two – oil and water on good days – approached each other. But then Dave stood up and slipped between them, extending a hand toward Gan.

"I don't believe we've met. I'm Dr. Cheng, and you look like someone who'd benefit from..."

"Don't," I warned, too late.

Faster than my former DM could finish his sales pitch, Gan grabbed his hand, twisted, and flipped him onto the hard floor. "We have previously met, and I remain unimpressed," she said. "Try to touch me again and my response will be considerably less generous."

Less generous?

With Dave out of the way, Christy and Gan stood facing each other.

Christy eyed her up. "You've gotten ... taller."

"And you have gotten older," Gan shot back. *Ooh, burn!*

"Wiser, too."

"You would need several more lifetimes to match the breadth of my knowledge."

Okay, this had potential to get ugly. I stepped forward, but Tom put a hand on my arm, or tried to. All I got was a weird staticky feeling as his hand passed through me. "Dude, chick fight."

I turned and glared at him. "Really?"

"What? I might be dead, but that doesn't mean my priorities aren't straight."

Goddamned idiot! "All right, you two, calm down. We have more important issues at hand than sniping at each other."

"Such as why she's alive?" Christy asked me.

"Yeah, Bill. Why don't you bring everyone up to speed?" Ed said from behind me, stepping in and shutting the door.

Instead of taking the bait, I took a deep breath, long enough for Dave to pick himself up off the floor and give Gan a wide berth. Then I turned to Vincent. "Hey, man. Long time. How are you?"

"Confused," he replied.

"Join the party. Where's your better half?"

"She's back at my place watching Tina," Christy said.

"Yeah, you should have seen her," Tom added. "She may be small, but she kicks all the asses. Takes after her old man."

I glanced from him to Christy, my eyebrows raised.

However, she replied, "I'm not sure I want to go into the details in front of present company."

Gan shrugged as if she couldn't have cared less. "Then perhaps I, too, shall refrain from sharing what I know. Pity, as I believe it could benefit the whore."

"What?"

"It's Sally. They got to her during that last surge," I said, giving Gan some side eye at her less than generous nickname.

Whatever disgust had been on Christy's face at Gan's reappearance immediately gave way to worry. "Is that where you've been?"

"Yeah. She managed to send a text to me."

"So you just ran over there without letting us know?"

"I'm sorry." I stepped toward her then hesitated, realizing almost too late that I'd been about to put my hands on her shoulders – a somewhat more intimate move than I probably wanted to make in front of a jealous three-hundred year old psycho.

"Personal space, fucker," Tom said in response.

Dumbass.

"Not now," Christy hissed at him. "Is she okay? Where did they take her?"

I held up my hands and explained what Ed and I knew, as well as what we didn't know which, sadly, greatly outweighed the former.

When I was finished, Vincent asked, "Did you call the police?"

"No. I talked to her a few days ago and she insisted this wasn't something we wanted to bring the authorities in on."

"Perhaps her warning was for during those ... pulses, as you called them. But otherwise, those ungodly devils are as mortal as the rest of us. The police might be able to track them down and..."

"They will not," Gan interrupted before turning to me. "Your friend is not anywhere the authorities of this city can get to. Of this, I am certain."

"And you know this how?" I asked.

She looked up at me and smiled. I made a silent vow that if her next words threw any more shade Sally's way, I'd deck her then and there – damn the rules of decency and sportsmanship.

However, she simply replied, "It is because they came for me first."

18

BEATING OFF THE ENEMY

"They *what?*"

Gan made to sit, then took a look at my couch and apparently decided against it. "Twice, as a matter of fact. They came for me first. Then, soon after, an attack was staged against one of my facilities. Regretfully, they were more successful in their second campaign."

"How'd you get away?" I asked.

She let out a laugh. "Escape was never part of the equation, dearest. Though they managed to overpower my bodyguards, they found me a much harder target to subdue."

"Let me guess," Ed replied, eyes narrowed. "You've been getting your powers back during those pulses, haven't you?"

"Indeed. It is most glorious to feel the pull of eternity again, even if only for a short time."

"You did? Err, do?" I glanced at Christy to gauge her reaction, but she was apparently still too annoyed at Gan's survival to pay me much heed. Yeah, that was going to be a fun conversation later.

135

Regardless, the fact that Gan was alive and her powers were working again seemed to reinforce the theory I'd laid out to Ed earlier. It was one more piece to this puzzle, albeit not a particularly promising piece.

"It is of little consequence, though," Gan continued, "for this happened some months ago, long before these anomalies began."

What the? "But why?"

"I will admit, at first I was confused. Even more so because I recognized the fighting style of my attackers."

"How so?"

"It was not dissimilar to techniques employed by the elite guard assigned to our former prefectures."

"Former prefectures? Like the one in Boston?" Ed asked. "So you think these fuckers were vamps?"

"Perhaps," Gan replied. "As I said, it moderately surprised me, considering I thought myself the sole survivor amongst our elders."

Oddly enough, that didn't make me feel better at all. "I'm going to assume that means you think these guys weren't newbs."

"It was unheard of for the elite to recruit any under a century in age."

"That would be a yes."

"I have so missed your sense of sarcasm, beloved."

"Focus, Gan. What happened?"

"A group of would-be invaders infiltrated my home and confronted me. I, of course, beat them off."

Tom started to snicker. If this hadn't been such an unfunny matter, I probably would have joined him. "Fought them off."

"Excuse me?"

"You fought them off. There's a difference."

"As you wish. The fact remains, my capture was seemingly only one of their objectives."

"How so?" Vincent replied.

"After they escaped, I learned they'd made off with a laptop containing sensitive data.."

"A laptop?" I asked. "That's very modern of you."

"A necessary evil in this day and age, I'm afraid. It was foolishly left unattended by a servant in my employ. I, of course, had him blinded for this oversight."

"What?" Vincent cried, standing up. "How could you?"

Ed stepped in and put a hand on the former Templar's shoulder. "Let's maybe focus on one war crime at a time. We can deal with her afterward."

Gan chuckled as if she thought their comments quaint. Yeah, this was heading downhill fast. I needed to keep us focused. "What was on the laptop?" I asked.

"Information regarding a facility of mine in Damascus."

"Damn-ass-cus," Tom said before being shushed by Christy again.

"Yes," Gan said with a nod. "It was breached roughly a week later. The data stolen was sufficient to circumvent the security measures in place."

Damascus? A memory flashed through my mind of Sally and I being held prisoner by Calibra. She'd told us a story of how, long ago, she discovered a tunnel leading deep into the Earth. That had been the start of everything: the creation of vampires, our war with the Sasquatches, and all the horrors which came after. More importantly, this tunnel still existed, somewhere beneath the modern city of...

"I can see by the look on your face that you are piecing things together," Gan said. "It does my heart good to watch your mind at work."

"This facility in Damascus..."

"Yes, my love. It houses the very same tunnel I walked

out of five years ago in my quest to reach the surface – the lone passage that leads to The Source."

"You know where it is?" Christy asked.

"I not only know where, witch, but I own the mosque that sits above it, as well as most of the surrounding neighborhood."

"Wait," I said. "You can't just buy a mosque."

Gan smiled as if she thought me a cute but dull-witted puppy. "The local government is in constant need of funds. I can assure you, everything there can be had for a price."

"Way to respect their religious beliefs," Ed remarked.

Gan let out a mirthless chuckle. "The Source is the one truth of this world. All other ideologies stem from its existence."

"Nonsense," Vincent barked. "Those are lies the darkness wants us..."

"Let's save the theological discussions for later." I turned back toward Gan. "Are there any other atrocities you want to confess before getting to the point?"

"None come to mind," she replied in a matter of fact tone before resuming her story. "A small strike team breached this facility, securing it long enough for a sizable group to enter the tunnel and collapse a section of it behind them. That itself spoke of their dedication, as without The Source the caverns below are little more than sterile rock."

"A sizeable group?" Christy asked. "All vampires?"

Gan raised an eyebrow. "I think you know better."

"Magi."

"Indeed. Working together in collusion with these elite guardsmen, as well as some others."

"Others?" I asked. "What kind of whackjobs would be crazy enough to sign up for a one-way trip to a dead cavern?"

"The non-human kind."

"Like ... dogs?"

She shook her head. "Not all extra-planar creatures were sent home when The Source was destroyed. Only those of a spiritual nature or tethered to their home planes via a greater power returned. Many purely physical beings remained behind."

I glanced at Christy and she nodded. "I've heard rumors, but nothing substantiated. Theoretically it's possible, but such entities would be rendered as powerless as the rest of us."

"Indeed," Gan replied. "Minor beings – imps or goblins as your culture might label them – left behind to rot in the shadows, unable to integrate into human society."

"Desperate," Christy said in a small voice. "Perhaps even more so than the Magi."

"So what was the point in all of this?" Ed asked. "Besides burying themselves alive."

"The Source, obviously," Gan replied. Before any of us could point out the impossibility of such a thing, she continued. "Doors, even heavily sealed, can be reopened, provided one is clever enough."

"Or has something on the other side which wants in badly enough," Christy replied, her face turning a shade paler.

I turned to her. "Excuse me?"

"The witch is not as ignorant as I assumed," Gan said.

I considered this. "Something that wants back in ... like vampires?"

Gan shook her head. "An interesting theory, but unlikely. Many who were driven out of our world are inconsequential. Even the entities who once empowered the undead are but disembodied spirits, little more than jackals prowling the forest. Fearsome perhaps, but nothing compared to the great beasts which rule those lands."

"Why does that sound ominous?" I asked.

"Because it is," Christy replied with a tired sigh. "The old gods. They were locked out, too. Most had long since retreated from our world, forgotten religions that..."

"Not all," I replied, remembering back to the time when I managed to piss off an actual death god.

"No, not all," she confirmed. "But a lot. And those that retained a toehold on our reality had mostly agreed to the provisions of the old Humbaba Accord."

Ah yes, the treaty that had kept the vampires and their ancient enemies – Sasquatch – from going to war for thousands of years ... at least until I'd gotten involved. Not one of my finer moments.

"Alas, the Accord is now null and void due to the eradication of both races," Gan replied. "But perhaps therein lies opportunity for the old powers."

Christy nodded, her rivalry with Gan apparently forgotten for the moment. "The history of the Magi tells us that in ancient times the old gods strove to forge followings among the human race. Once established, these pockets of worship were jealously guarded. However, petty as they were, the gods realized that all-out war would do nothing but destroy their hard-won spoils. As a result, many were content to allow their high priests to forge treaties with neighboring religions."

"Kind of like what cable companies do," Tom's ghost surmised.

Christy turned to him and smiled, eliciting a minor stab of jealousy from me despite the poor timing. "You're not entirely off base. But the old gods were fickle. Stuck in a state of stagnation with their fellow immortals, many eventually grew bored and withdrew from this world."

"So why give a shit now?" Dave asked, making it a point to keep the couch between him and Gan. Probably a smart move.

"With the destruction of The Source," Christy continued, "those old boundaries were erased, old treaties nullified. A being strong enough to punch back into our reality could, in theory, establish a wide swath of influence before others were able to respond."

"Okay, fine, but how the hell would someone even contact them with The Source gone?" I asked. "Pretty sure email isn't an option."

Gan grinned at me, mirroring Christy's smile to Tom but in a much more predatory way. "The ears of the old gods are sharp and ever listening for those who know how to call out to them."

"She's right," Christy said. "If one knows the proper rituals and is prepared to pay the price in blood, one could conceivably be heard."

Well, if that wasn't disturbing as fuck, I didn't know what was.

"It all sounds like bullshit to me," Tom scoffed.

"Agreed," Vincent replied with a resolute nod. "The one true Lord holds sway here. He cannot be so easily..."

"Not that, dumbass! I mean, it isn't the fifteen hundreds anymore. People have seen Ghostbusters. They aren't going to drop to their knees just because some asshole plops down in the middle of Manhattan and proclaims themselves Gozer. Fuck no. They'll get on the phone and tell the Army to send in the stealth bombers."

"Air Force," I corrected, "although you have a point. I mean, yeah, some assholes will be happy as clams to start sacrificing goats. But I like to think plenty more will be skeptical. We're not exactly living in the Bronze Age here."

"No, we are not." Gan held my gaze, her eyes sparkling in a way that was definitely not platonic. "But do not think the old powers are so naïve. Many who exist beyond the veil possess vast intelligence. They will surely pick more contemporary means to spread their influence than, for instance, burning bushes. Despite your belief to the contrary, my love, your species has always shown a proclivity toward subservience."

"My species?"

Gan smiled. "It remains to be seen what I and the Progenitor are. I'd thought myself human, but these last few days have left that in question."

"Kara is so not going to like this."

Ghost Tom turned toward Ed. "Dude, nobody wants to hear about you porking my sister."

"Seriously?" I asked. "That's what you're most worried about right now? If I'm hearing this shit correctly, we've got maybe Cthulhu and Odin standing outside the door waiting to hand out pamphlets, while a bunch of crazies are down below helping them pick the lock. Worst of all, these fuckers kidnapped Sally for some reason." I turned to the rest. "Does that about cover it?"

Gan clapped her hands together. "I have so missed your fire."

"Um, thank you, I guess."

"But you are likely also incorrect."

"I am?"

Gan tented her fingers as if preparing to lecture us. "I have merely put forth one possible scenario. What is actually happening might be far different. The sporadic nature of these fluxes of spiritual energy is strange, not at all in line with what I might expect from what we've discussed."

"Then what the fuck have we been talking about?!"

Christy put a hand on my arm. "You need to calm down, Bill."

"It's kind of hard to calm down."

"Believe me, I know." She glanced at Tom out of the corner of her eye. "Nobody knows that more than me. But shouting won't save Sally."

"Then what will?"

"I'm not sure, but we're making progress. We know more now than we did a few hours ago, as well as have more..." She glared at Gan for a moment. "...allies helping us."

I turned away from her and took a deep breath. "I know, and I've been trying to do my part, too."

"Nobody is saying you haven't."

"I know that, but..." This next part was going to be a bit awkward, considering how the relationships within our small circle had evolved. "I've been trying to reach Sheila. If these pulses have been affecting you guys, maybe they've been doing the same to her. If so, I have a feeling we're going to want the Icon by our side when we face off against whatever is waiting for us."

Gan stepped in, interjecting herself between me and Christy as if she wasn't there. *Ugh!* "I would expect no less from you, my love, but I think you'll be disappointed nevertheless."

"Don't start," I snapped. "Things have changed between us. Sheila and I ... well, she's not on your hit list anymore."

"As I am well aware," Gan replied. "What I meant is that you'll be disappointed to learn the reason why you've been unable to reach her."

"And that would be?"

"Because she was with those who attacked my facility in Damascus."

19

DOWN THE RABBIT HOLE

Gan pulled out a cell phone, proving she'd definitely modernized since last I'd seen her. She scrolled to the video app then held the screen up for the rest of us to see. "This footage may upset you, my love, but I thought you should see it with your own eyes." Despite the words of concern, her tone was chipper. Whatever was going on, she wasn't exactly broken up over it.

Black and white CCTV footage played on the screen. This had to be the aftermath of the attack she'd told us about. Downed security guards, broken doors, and smashed electrical equipment could all be seen, albeit it didn't look like any mosque I'd ever heard of.

"This is the underground complex beneath the public façade," Gan explained as if reading my mind, proving she was every bit as creepy as I remembered. "It is, *was*, considerably more modern than the rest of the structure."

A large group — I was hesitant to call them all people — entered the frame from the top of the screen and began making their way through the ruined facility. All were heavily laden with supplies, carrying crates, backpacks and...

Oh no! Please don't let it be true.

Sadly, the footage was of high enough definition that there was no mistaking Sheila as she walked onto frame in the midst of the throng of invaders. She was clearly unarmed and, for a moment, I held out both the hope and fear that she was their prisoner, but even without sound I didn't quite believe that. She appeared aghast at the destruction around her, but so did many of the others. At the same time, the relaxed gait with which she carried herself, and the fact that she appeared at ease with those holding weapons, suggested she wasn't being coerced.

Nobody poked, prodded, or in any way did anything remotely threatening to her as she passed through the scene from top to bottom.

"Goddamn it, Bill," Tom said from over my shoulder. "Your dick is so limp you sent her over to the dark side."

"You're really not helping..." I turned and the words died in my throat. Tom was flickering in and out, kinda like an old TV with a crappy signal.

"Hey," he replied, seemingly unaware that his batteries were running low, "all I'm saying is that if you had my skills, your woman would still be around with a smile on her..."

"Enough!" Christy snapped, shutting him up.

I could handle being dumped ... mostly, but this went beyond that. The Icon ... Sheila ... was a force for good, humanity's shining beacon in the darkness. She didn't do things like *this*.

But that had been *before*. Apparently we were in unknown waters now, a future never seen or mentioned by the prophets of antiquity. The old rulebook had been tossed out the window at some point, and only now was I beginning to see that.

"It was not my intention to cause you pain, beloved," Gan said, that same chipper attitude coloring her voice. "Merely to enlighten you."

I rounded on her. "You knew about this, *all this time*, yet you kept it to yourself until now?"

Her good cheer seemed to slip at my outburst, but I had a feeling it wasn't because I was yelling. "I am embarrassed to admit I didn't anticipate their success. Up until recently, I assumed they'd go mad with hunger, trapped as they are, until they eventually turned on each other. That would have solved the issue without any need for direct intervention."

I couldn't believe what I was hearing ... well, okay, I could. The thing was, I wasn't sure which was worse: that Sheila was apparently helping to reopen the very doors we'd almost died closing, or that Gan would have happily sat back and let her starve to death if it hadn't worked.

"Face it, dude..."

"I said that's enough," Christy repeated before turning to me. "Come on. Let's go for a walk. You need to remove yourself from the situation, and I need a few minutes to think."

Tom and Dave both began to protest. However, before we could reply to either, Tom winked out of existence. Guess whatever voodoo they'd done to the prism had run its course for now.

"Stay here with the others, please," Christy said to the thin air. Then she handed her purse to Vincent. "Would you mind keeping an eye on this for me?"

"I will guard it with my life."

"Hopefully it doesn't come down to that for a *wallet*

and some *credit cards*," Ed replied, throwing us a quick wink. "I'll help hold down the fort."

Christy thanked him while I turned to Gan.

I expected her to insist on tagging along. Problem was, I doubted we could stop her. It was five against one, but I'd seen her fight. Vampire powers or not, she put the lethal into lethal combat skills. It was probably too much to hope she'd discovered the joys of chilling in front of the TV with a bowl of ice cream.

However, rather than argue, she bowed and said, "My apologies, beloved. At times I forget that such matters can be overwhelming to a mind as young as yours. I will wait for your return."

"Um, thank you."

"For one hour. Then I will come looking for you." She turned to Christy. "If my love is in anything less than pristine condition when next I see him, I shall be ... displeased."

Dave approached me as I backed away toward the door, but I held up a hand. "Go wait in your room or something."

"But..."

"And try not to pawn off your hand cream on the teen titan again."

Christy waited until we were out on the street to speak, far outside the thirty foot radius Tom had told us about.

"This week keeps getting better and better," she said with a sigh.

"I'm assuming Max Adventure is in your purse."

She nodded. "I'm glad I thought to put it in there before heading over. I'm really not too keen on certain members of our company finding out about it."

"Yeah," I replied, figuring I should rip off the apology bandage as quickly as possible, "about Gan being alive..."

"It's okay." She took my hand in hers, catching me by surprise. "I can't say I'm happy, but I understand. Knowing wouldn't have done anything but cause undue panic. And it's not like we could have done much about it."

"Well..."

"I don't like her, but I get it. As far as you were concerned she was human, until recently anyway. Tempting as it might have been to do something *distasteful* to her, the war's over. The ancient powers are cut off from this world. Holding onto old grudges is toxic."

"That's very understanding of you."

"I'm still annoyed."

"As is your right."

"But I can't imagine any of this is easy on you either, especially considering what we just saw."

I couldn't help but shake my head. "What a fuckery. My ex colluding with the enemy, whoever they are, while yours is back from the grave. Although, just for the record, I'm pretty sure my issues don't hold a candle to yours."

"Maybe. But yours might be responsible for mine."

"There is that. Speaking of exes..." I held up our intertwined hands. "Where does that leave us?"

Christy shook her head. "Honestly, I don't know."

"A fair answer."

"But not a simple one." We turned the block and kept walking, the commuting crowd starting to fill up the sidewalk around us. "The fact that Tom could actually be a part of Tina's life overjoys me. Nothing is certain, I know that, but..."

"You have hope?"

"I've always had hope, but this is different."

"Because you still love him?" Yeah, I was leading the

witness. Sue me. If I was going to get dumped, I wanted it to be sooner rather than later.

She chuckled, but it held very little humor. "That's the part that's not so simple."

"How so?"

"I thought it would break me when Tom died. Between that and losing my powers, it was almost too much. But I had all of you by my side and then I had Tina, and at some point I knew I'd make it. Giving up wasn't an option. Still, for the longest time, the only thing I wished for was a few more moments with him, a chance to say goodbye. Some nights I'd wake up in a cold sweat certain he was there in the room next to me."

"All things considered, he might've been."

"I realize that now. But regardless, I grieved for him. It took me a long time, but I finally made my peace with it. I moved on." She glanced at me. "We both did."

"We didn't have a choice."

"Of course we did. Don't be silly. At first, I thought whatever we have was just because we were both lonely, but now I'm not so sure. We've always been close ... outside of maybe that short stretch when I was trying to kill you."

"I seem to vaguely recall something along those lines."

She let go of my hand long enough to elbow me in the side. "It was a different time, a different me. And that's kind of my point. I'm older now. I've lived my life, endured my pain, and it's made me stronger. But then, seeing Tom again and listening to him talk..."

"It all came rushing back?"

"No." She stopped and shook her head. "Yes, *some* of it. But not all. As I said, I'm older, maybe even a bit wiser. But Tom, he's still..."

"Tom?"

"Yes! It's like he's been in stasis these past five years.

He's a ghost in our world. There's been no chance for him to live and grow, and also no reason to. Don't get me wrong, I'm amazed he hasn't been driven insane by his isolation. It speaks to an amazing amount of willpower."

"I was going to say base dumbassery."

She smiled. "Maybe a bit of that, too. I won't lie. He still has that same ... innocence, let's say, that drew me to him to begin with. And now that he's back..."

"It's kind of weird?"

"Weird doesn't begin to explain it. The only thing I know for certain right now is I can't leave him like that. I have to do everything in my power to..."

"You don't have to explain. I agree one hundred and twenty percent. And, just for the record, it seems like you're making progress."

Christy turned away for a moment.

"What is it?"

"That's another problem."

"What is?"

"What we did. It shouldn't have been possible, not in the time we had. I'm not complaining, don't get me wrong, but it shouldn't have worked."

"Oh?"

"Creating the prism was the work of a full coven combining our powers over the course of several days. Even then, I'm fairly certain the only reason we succeeded was because the walls between realities were in the process of being knocked down thanks to the war. But I only had Kelly to help me this past week, and she's only a catalyst witch."

"A catalyst what?"

"It doesn't matter. It's a Magi thing. Regardless, with only a few days to create a ritual to modify the prism, then barely an hour to perform it, it should have failed outright, or at least taken several tries. But it worked."

"That's good."

"But only because we cheated."

"How do you cheat with magic?

"Tina."

Oh. "Really?"

"I didn't want to involve her, but Kelly convinced me that we could act as the foci while she merely provided some extra power for the incantation."

"And that worked?"

"Far better than I ever expected." From the tone of Christy's voice, I got the impression she was less than pleased.

"So why isn't that a good thing?"

"It is good, for Tom anyway. When a pulse hits, the prism not only taps into the extradimensional power it normally channels, but it now stores some, too. In theory, the more it charges, the longer he'll stay with us. The problem is Tina. Or, more precisely, the sheer amount of energy she's able to instinctively summon."

"Let me guess, she's a bit of a firecracker?"

"More like an atom bomb." She saw the look I gave her and pursed her lips. "I mean it, Bill. I've met some powerful mages in my time, grand mentors with decades more experience than me. But none of them even remotely approached the raw power I saw my daughter channeling. It was as if we had a whole coven assisting us."

"Okay, but didn't you say you could bind her until she was older?"

"The truth is, I'm not sure I can."

"Oh please. I've seen the things you can do."

"This isn't false humility," she replied. "I was once considered a prodigy among my people. But this goes beyond anything I've ever heard of. The only other witch I've seen who could blow away the bell curve like this was..."

"Let me guess. The White Mother?"

Christy nodded, a shadow of bitterness crossing her face. "Exactly. And there's no way of knowing how much of her power was artificially augmented by The Source. I won't lie. It frightens me."

"Tina?"

"No, I'm not scared *of* her. She's my daughter and I love her with all my heart. I'm scared *for* her. What if..." She trailed off.

"*What if* what?"

She shook her head. "Never mind for now. I'm just wool gathering because I'm worried."

"Tina's a peach. The people we *should* be worried about are all at the center of the Earth, fucking with things they shouldn't be. God, I can't believe Sheila is actually helping them. I mean, she's the one who blew it all up to begin with."

Rather than tell me I should give her the benefit of the doubt, Christy instead said, "About that..."

"What?"

"I have ... a confession to make."

"Let me guess," I said with a mirthless laugh, "a part of you hopes she succeeds?"

"Not quite. The truth is ... I sort of knew this was coming. Not *this* exactly, but I knew what had been bothering her."

"In retrospect, I guess I did, too."

"No. I mean I *really* knew ... including that she was planning to leave you."

"What?! How?"

"Because she told me."

I stopped on the sidewalk as her words registered in my addled brain. "She *told* you? When?"

"A few weeks before she left. I tried to talk her out of it."

"Why didn't you tell me?"

She looked me in the eye. "Because I knew it wouldn't fix anything. Her mind was made up. And then, after she was gone, I thought it would only make you feel worse."

"Holy crap."

"I swear, I didn't have any idea how far she'd take it. I thought she just needed to find herself. Maybe volunteer or do some missionary work – things to help ease her conscience. I never guessed she'd ever do something so reckless or dangerous."

We stood there for several long minutes, silence passing between us on the rapidly filling sidewalk.

I was tempted to scream at her, but the truth was, her sins weren't all that different from me keeping Gan's survival a secret for so long. And deep down, I hated to admit it, but I knew she was right. Who could have ever suspected that Sheila's guilt would manifest itself in this way? Hell, even if I had known, what could I have done? Gone with her?

I wasn't sure I saw myself traveling the world, like some half-assed Kwai Chang Cain, counseling depressed mages. Even if that had happened, there's still no fucking way I would've agreed to some crazed plan to open our world up again to the things beyond.

And Sheila probably understood that, which is why she'd slipped out without even saying goodbye.

Holy shit, what a fuckery.

But Christy wasn't at fault for any of it.

Instead of yelling, I put my hands on her shoulders and smiled. "Is it me, or do we both suck at this communication thing?"

She actually laughed, her eyes bright with moisture. "When it comes to the fate of the world? Maybe."

"Ain't we a pair?"

She leaned in for a hug. "I guess we are, Freewill."

20

WORLD BUKAKKE CHAMPIONSHIP

As much as I had tried to convince myself that a clean break was best, I was happy to find myself still in the running. The truth was, I had no idea where my relationship with Christy was headed, especially now, but I was glad we weren't simply hitting the off switch and pretending it never happened.

At the same time, we had to acknowledge there were trying times ahead for us all. And with Gan in the picture again, it was likely to be coupled with bouts of unnecessary bloodshed. Because of that, we talked a bit more and decided it might be safest to forgo any public displays of affection – for now anyway. Assuming we didn't get lucky and return to find Gan dead from an overdose of smugness, there'd come a time when she'd inevitably find out about us, but hopefully we could attend to the matters at hand before that happened.

We finished our circuit of the block and decided to head back. The others had been kept waiting long enough. Besides, it was probably only a matter of time before Gan lost her cool with my friends.

As we approached the top floor apartment, I began to

suspect we might have already been too late. Loud voices could be heard coming from inside.

I rolled my eyes. "Oh, for Christ's sake."

"We better get in there before they kill each other," Christy said.

I opened my mouth to reply, just as my key turned in the lock, but it was as if all the air had been sucked out of my lungs.

For fuck's sake. Not now.

One of my legs buckled beneath me and I fell into the door, pushing it open as that strange lethargy overtook my body. Another of those magical pulses had begun.

"For the last time, do not speak to me. I have no interest in you or your paltry wares."

I staggered in the doorway for a moment, long enough to see Dave standing in front of me with Gan a few steps beyond.

"But it's a great opportunity," he replied. "Trust me. You'll make back ten times your investment, guaranteed. It's ... whoa. Hey, watch it!"

Gan snatched up one of the boxes of Dave's hand cream and, perhaps not realizing her powers were back, flung it at him. My former DM somehow managed to dive out of the way. I, currently possessing all the strength of a newborn kitten, wasn't so lucky.

All I could do was watch in morbid horror as the box flew at me like some sort of cardboard missile. It slammed into my chest, sending me stumbling across the hall and causing the contents within to splatter out in a greasy arc.

A wave of white goo covered my face, quickly fading to black once my head collided with the far wall.

A sound, not unlike the buzzing of a thousand mosquitos, filled my head. I really hoped that was just metaphor and not reality. Talk about gross. Also, I'd have to wonder what the fuck Dave had put in that shit of his.

No, it wasn't mosquitos. It was more like a radio with dozens of voices all babbling at once, but the reception was too shitty for me to understand any of them, as if they were too far away for a clear signal.

The buzzing increased for a moment, almost enough to rattle my teeth – not that I could feel them. Then it died down again, like I was losing the signal, leaving me certain I was about to fall back into the blissful silence I'd been resting in. But then much closer voices began to speak.

"Come on, Bill. Wake up."

"Should we call an ambulance?"

"Do not be foolish. My love has survived far worse."

"Easy for you to say. You're the one who..."

"Look! I think he's coming to."

"More like cummed on."

I blinked a few times but when I tried to look around I saw nothing but a fluffy white mass obscuring my vision. *What the fuck?*

"Here, let me clean those off for you."

A pair of hands removed my glasses and suddenly I could see again. Everything was fuzzy, but I could make out the faces of my friends looking down at me ... including one who was semi-transparent.

"Goddamn, dude," Tom's ghost said. "You look like you pissed off the world's angriest jizz mopper."

"You're back." I coughed out a mouthful of moisturizer. *Yuck.* It might smell good, but it tasted like shit.

"I never left."

Christy leaned in. "It was another of those pulses. Short..."

"But not sweet," I croaked. "Ugh. I feel like a bus ran me over."

"You're lucky Dave cheaped out on the packaging," Ed said, cleaning my glasses off.

Christy threw a glare Gan's way. "He's not the only one who's lucky."

"Nonsense," she replied. "My beloved cannot be defeated so easily. Though his power might be gone, his spirit remains as formidable as ever."

"I'm pretty sure my spirit is bruised, too," I said, trying to sit up. *Ouch!* Oh well, at least nothing seemed to be broken.

"Here." Ed handed back my glasses just as I realized that I looked like the Stay Puft Marshmallow Man's personal love doll. I guess that explained why everyone was standing close by, but nobody was actually offering me a hand. "Anyone got a few napkins?"

"A few?" Christy was grinning, but I could see the worry on her face.

"It's okay. I'm fine. Nothing damaged but my ego."

"Good thing those were free samples," Dave muttered from near the door.

"Yeah, I'd hate to inconvenience your inventory."

"Don't bitch at me. I'm not the one who overreacted."

I glowered at him. "No. You're just the one who gave little Ms. Murder here a sales pitch when I told you not to."

"Not a sales pitch, an investment opportunity."

Gan leaned down toward me. "If you wish, my love, I can end his life in a way that will cause minimal suffering."

"Let me get back to you on that minimal suffering part."

"Oh. Then I am happy to..."

"I was kidding, Gan. No killing my friends, please. Even the ones who might deserve it."

"Very well," she replied in an unconcerned tone. "I believe there are more pressing matters to discuss anyway."

More pressing than the fact that she'd almost killed the shit out of me? But, yeah, she probably had a point. "Agreed. We still need to discuss how we're going to save Sally."

"No. I am unconcerned regarding her welfare."

What?! Before I could ask what she meant by that, Ed leaned down and helped me to my feet, or did after a few tries ... I kept slipping out of his grasp.

Tom, of course, had to offer his two cents. "Damn, dude. You look like you just gave Bill the world's sloppiest hand job."

Ed glared at him. "Don't you have a house to haunt or something?"

Tom backed up a step, grinning. "Hey, it's cool. I don't judge."

I pushed past Ed toward the doorway. "Let's get back inside before the downstairs neighbors wonder what the hell is going on." Then, once the door was shut and locked, I turned toward Gan. "What do you mean you're not worried about Sally?"

She shrugged. "I have seldom worried about her, but in this case, I don't believe her life is in immediate danger."

"Because they kidnapped her," Christy surmised.

"Precisely, witch. If they wanted her dead, they could have simply been done with it."

"We still don't know why, though," Ed replied, grabbing a soda from the fridge.

"Exactly." I pulled a towel out of the closet, then grabbed two. One wasn't going to get the job done considering I looked like the guest of honor at a bukakke festival. "Were they purposely targeting her, or are they planning to use her as bait? Because if so..."

"I do not believe she's bait either," Gan said. "They would have approached us with their demands by now."

"Assuming that's true, then what the hell are they after?"

"Intelligence."

Tom grinned. "Why'd they attack Bill first then?"

Gan, thankfully, opted to ignore him. "At this point I believe it's safe to assume that is why they broke into my home. They wanted access to The Source and somehow knew I had that information."

I continued toweling myself off. "Okay, I think I see where this is going. If we can narrow down all the people who knew that, we can maybe figure out..."

She waved me off. "Unnecessary. I have already vetted those in my service. As for the rest, one is present – you, my love. That leaves only..."

"No..."

"Yes. I am afraid at this point we must assume the Shining One is responsible for that betrayal."

"You don't know that! Someone else could have..." I trailed off as I realized Gan's accusation made sense, disturbing as that was. When she'd revealed herself to Sheila and me two years ago, she'd told us about the tunnel leading up to Damascus. *Goddamn it!* I was standing on shaky ground with my denial and knew it. "Never mind. Go on."

"The fact that they took your wh..." Gan met my eyes and saw the daggers I was glaring at her. "...*friend* and did not kill her tells me there is a reason."

I balled up the first towel and tossed it into the bathroom. "But they came for me first."

"Indeed," she replied. "And they failed. However, the fact they did not try a second or third time is telling."

"Of what?" Vincent asked.

"It's merely speculation on my part but, based on the

fact that they have not offered her up for trade or ransom, I must conclude it is some knowledge that you are both in possession of." She locked eyes with me, despite the fact that I looked like the sole XXX VHS tape in a men's prison. "So I must ask, what is this missing factor? What do you both know that they could possibly want?"

"Ooh, I know." Tom raised his hand like this was elementary school. "They both went swimming in Sasquatch shit that one time in Canada."

I glanced at Christy. "Is there any way to turn him off?"

"I believe he will dissipate naturally as he did last time, beloved," Gan said before also turning toward Christy. "I must admit, conjuring a spirit from beyond the veil is potent magic. Impressive after all this time. But I must question the wisdom of wasting such an effort on..."

"Oh, she didn't conjure me," Tom said idly. "I've been here the whole time."

Gan raised an eyebrow. "How is that possible?"

"Dear," Christy warned, "maybe now isn't the time to distract us with..."

"That's easy," Tom replied, Christy's warning flying right over his head. "It's that glowy thingy."

"Glowy thingy?" Gan asked.

"Yeah. What did you call it, babe? Apollo's nutsack or something?"

I saw on Gan's face something I couldn't claim to have seen often: surprise. "You managed to recreate one of Xihe's Tears in so short a time? I would have thought such a task impossible."

"Xihe's..." Dave asked, but Gan was ready for his question.

"Western sorcery refers to them as the prisms of Apollo. I am intrigued to know..."

"Focus, people," I said. "We're not here to tell ghost stories, no offense."

"None taken," Tom replied, already beginning to flicker again.

"Good. Because if we don't figure out what these assholes want, then Sally could very well become a ghost herself and I, for one, don't care to start a collection."

21

GAN-T CHART

Quickly was a relative concept as I excused myself to grab a shower. Toweled off as I was, I still felt like I was entombed in scented sour cream.

Fortunately, for the sake of the fact that he couldn't keep his fucking mouth shut, Tom winked out of existence again shortly thereafter, before Gan could coerce additional information out of him.

At this point I wasn't sure what harm he could cause, but perhaps it was for the best that his loose lips didn't have too many opportunities to sink our ship.

Despite having taken a shower, I still smelled like a reject from the cosmetics aisle when I rejoined the group. Doing my best to not glare at Dave for having sent me that crap to begin with, I suggested we start at the beginning so as to try to figure out what – if any – knowledge Sally and I shared that could be of use to those trying to kick open the door to beyond.

"She and I were both vampires as well as members of Village Coven."

Gan waved her hand dismissively. "Neither presents a

unique factor for anything I can ascertain. Please be more granular, my love."

Grrr! That was rapidly getting old. "Um, fine. We were both in Pandora Coven, too."

"So was Kara," Ed offered. "Oh, by the way, she texted me a little while ago. All's boring on her end, thank goodness."

"Okay, moving on. Here's a good one. We were both present at the Woods of Morning summit."

"As were several of us," Christy replied.

Gan nodded. "Interesting, but perhaps not relevant. The Alma were removed from this world at the time of The Source's collapse."

"Alma?" Dave asked.

"The Feet ... Sasquatch," Ed explained. "Same shit-heads, different name."

"And a stupid one at that."

Gan shrugged. "Regardless, fearsome as they may have believed themselves, I do not think they would be a factor in forcing their way back to this dimension. However, let us continue along this line of thought."

"All right," I said. "We can forget that second summit. I mean, Sally and I *were* the only ones who ended up marrying a Bigfoot, but..."

"Don't forget when Turd adopted me," Ed replied bitterly.

I couldn't help but grin. "Oh, trust me. I could never forget *that*." He flipped me the finger and I continued. "Anyway, hopefully this isn't some sort of reconciliation attempt by our respective spouses because I don't know about you guys, but the Feet were seriously..." I trailed off for a second, a memory resurfacing. Way to go, free association psychobabble.

"What is it?" Christy asked.

"Maybe we're too quick to dismiss the Feet."

"How so?"

"They were originally nature spirits connected to The Source. After Calibra captured us, she showed Sally and me a vision of the past. When she first discovered The Source, it was basically Sasquatch's swimming pool. She kicked their asses then, later on, experimented on them, which resulted in the accident that turned her into a vampire. Human souls merging with nature spirits. It's part of the reason why the Feet hated us."

Gan raised an eyebrow. "She showed you this?"

"Yep, in glorious, technicolor magic vision."

"Fascinating. I've read legends hinting as such, but our written history doesn't go back far enough to actually confirm it."

"Well, myth not busted," I said. "Is that it, maybe? So far as I'm aware, Sally and I were the only ones she showed her old vacation photos to."

"Maybe," Gan offered. "Such knowledge does fill the gaps in our species' history..."

"Awesome."

"But," she continued, "I'm not certain it is relevant to our here and now. Even if they knew, I'm doubtful the Magi who ventured below would care to subject themselves to a similar accident. The mortality rate would certainly exceed any prospect of success. As for the vampires who went with them, they were of the new breed. Why go back? For all intents and purposes, we are a superior species to what came before."

Humility, thy name is Gansetseg.

"There's also Sheila to take into consideration," Ed replied. "Why would she want to recreate vamps again? Does she really miss kicking their asses that much?"

I found myself glad Tom had become undetectable again, because I had little doubt he'd have an asshole comment for that.

Christy shook her head. "She was obsessed by what she'd done to the Magi. But vampires? No. I don't see it."

"I concur with the witch," Gan said. "I believe we may have the correct focus in The Source cavern. But I'm not convinced that the creation of the vampire race would offer our foes any usable insight."

"So what else do we know about that accursed place?" Vincent asked.

"It was a shithole," Dave said, drawing glares from all of us. "What? It was. Even the palace that bitch had was still lakefront property in the middle of Hell. And don't even get me started on her ego. Statues of herself all over the place, and that big cave painting shining down on everyone like some fucked-up Flintstones selfie."

I let out a laugh. "Yeah, that was all kinds of messed... Hold on a second."

"What is it, my love?"

"The cave painting Dave mentioned. Something else was there before that."

Unsurprisingly, all eyes turned to me expectantly.

Too late I realized I should have maybe watched my tongue in present company. Oh well, what was done was done. Besides, Gan was no mage. What use was it to her? "Back when we were in Vegas, we had to rescue Ed from the Jahabich ... for the first time, anyway."

"Kiss my ass."

"Sorry, man, but you were pretty much our group's designated woman in a refrigerator. Take some pride in your work. You were good at it." Ignoring the double-fisted fingers he shot my way, I continued. "Anyway, back then there was a different mural on the wall, a much older one."

"What was it?" Vincent asked.

"It showed the Jahabich being defeated in the distant past, but that wasn't all. There was a spell written on the pictograph, too. I think it was originally left there as instructions for future generations, in case those fuckers escaped again ... which of course they did."

Vincent nodded. "I see. Do you think this spell could be what they want?"

Christy made to open her mouth, but I shook my head and replied, "I don't know. It feels like a stretch. First off, the Jahabich are all dead. Secondly, Sally and me weren't the only ones who knew about it. Christy saw it, too, or at least the photos."

Ed held up a hand. "Let me stop you there. We don't actually know what these assholes want, so maybe we're only assuming it's something only the two of you know."

"The Progenitor has a point," Gan said. "It would make sense for a knowledgeable strike team to target the easiest prey first. A seasoned witch would make for more difficult quarry than..."

"Those of us who are squishy and easy to beat?"

She smiled at me, showing straight white teeth. "Your way with words continues to warm my heart."

"Wonderful to know. Back to the point. The other problem is we're talking five years here. Hell, I barely remember what the damned thing looked like. As for those pics, that was at least two cell phones ago, and no, I didn't save them to Instagram in case any of you are wondering."

Christy shook her head. "That wouldn't matter to a Magi skilled in mind magic. Memories, even old ones, can easily be coaxed back to the surface."

Okay, she had me there. Score one for magical mind-fuckery.

"Be that as it may," she continued, "the spell on the cave wall was ultimately limited."

True. By then, the Jahabich problem had already

spread far and wide. Containment would have been nothing more than a Band Aid.

"It was limited in its original format," Gan replied. "But I believe you further refined it to be of use, did you not?"

The barest grin appeared on Christy's face. "I was wondering if you remembered that."

"I remember a great many things."

Couldn't say that surprised me. Gan's mind was like a psychotic steel trap. She was the type to hunt someone down because their ancestors didn't bow low enough a century earlier. Regardless, she had a point. Christy had worked hard on the cave spell, expanding upon it and making it something we could use to end the threat that Calibra posed.

"Yeah, but we never even got a chance to use it," Ed said. "Christy was knocked out before that could happen." At her glare, he added, "Sorry, but you were."

"Whatever the case," I said, trying to keep us focused, "Sally didn't know the new spell. Neither did I."

Christy nodded. "That's a good point. I'm the only one who knows it in its entirety."

"Perhaps we are thinking about this wrong," Gan said after a few moments. "Tell me, was the Shining One aware of any of this?"

"Sheila?" I replied. "I guess. She definitely knew about the cave spell and that we were planning on using it. I remember that much."

"But what of the refined version, my love?"

Ignoring her continued creep-factor, I thought back. "I ... actually don't know. I mean, it was kind of chaotic back then and she was out of the loop for a lot of it. Then afterward, well, it wasn't really a memory lane either of us wanted to stroll down."

"Then I submit that perhaps we have found the

missing piece of our puzzle. It is why they attacked you, my darling, followed by your...”

“Don’t say it.”

Vincent leaned forward. “Why would they even want this spell? It was designed to close The Source.”

“Yeah. Not to mention ... holy crap, I’m an idiot.”

“No argument here,” Ed replied.

I ignored him and turned toward Christy, working this out in my head. “Could a spell designed to close a door be reengineered to open it again? Hell, it happens all the time in programming. You tighten up a system, but sometimes that same code functions as a backdoor in case you need to get in.”

“Coupled with ancient gods pushing from the other side?” Ed offered.

Christy nodded. “In theory, yes. But it took me some time to modify the original and even then I was only able to complete it with help.”

“Would a Magi probing the whore’s mind know this?”

“Do you have to keep calling her that?”

Gan fixed me with her green eyes. “Forgive me, my love, but I believe the time for pleasantries grows short.” She turned back to Christy. “Would they?”

Christy met her gaze. “Yes. Any Magi who speaks Enochian well enough would be able to figure out what the cave spell did and didn’t do. The problem for them would be the time and expertise required to modify it for their needs.”

“Except they wouldn’t need to if they were to become aware you had already done the work.”

Oh crap. “Sally. She didn’t see the new spell, but she was definitely aware Christy had worked on it.”

“Then I suggest we depart for your home post-haste, witch. There have been more of those pulses since the whore was kidnapped, likely enough for our foes to have learned all of this already."

"Tina," Christy said in a low voice, barely a whisper.

Gan nodded. "If they've figured out you are the sole holder of this incantation, then they will be seeking you, or any they can use as leverage against you, to get what they need."

22

BEATING THE AMBUSHES

A part of me refused to believe Sheila was behind this. But I'd seen the proof. It was hard to dispute and, besides, there was no time. For now, I had to push my doubts to the side.

Even so, I could understand her guilt causing her to do something stupid. Hell, I'd been there and done that. But I had a hard time believing that she'd purposely endanger a child.

Regardless, both Christy and Vincent called ahead, or tried to, sealing our next course of action.

There was no answer from either Christy's landline or Kelly's cell. Sure, it was possible she and the tyke had decided to crash. Probable, even. Nevertheless, that got our asses moving.

Dave *graciously* declined to join us, wishing us well in our quest to stop Apocalypse 2.0. It was probably for the best. Even knowing what he did, he still wasn't a part of this. Besides, neither Gan nor Christy liked him much. If he opened his mouth at the wrong time, I couldn't promise there wouldn't be any not-so-friendly fire.

Gan summoned her limo, offering to give the rest of

us a lift. Despite it being the size of a bus, far from ideal for Brooklyn streets at rush hour, her driver navigated the route to Christy's like a taxi driver on crack. Sure, it resulted in lots of angry horns blown, but fuck those guys. If they knew we were trying to stop hell from returning to earth, I have little doubt they'd have ... probably still honked at us. This was New York, after all.

Interestingly enough, I noted, at no point did the driver ask Christy for an address. He simply took Gan's orders to head to the "witch's place" at face value, leading me to remember she'd been playing the part of voyeur with my life for the better part of five years.

Oh well, we could discuss her creepy proclivities at a later time. For now, it saved us precious minutes.

Not to diminish our panic, but the interior of Gan's limo was pretty goddamned swank. She definitely didn't believe in suffering for the cause. We're talking jade arm rests, a wet bar, and even a big ass TV. Hell, if we hadn't been in a hurry I'd have checked to see if there were any new episodes of *Game of Thrones*, as I was pretty sure she got every channel known to man in this thing.

However, not all the décor was designed purely for hedonistic comfort. Some of the designs throughout the interior – inlaid in silver, of course – looked strangely familiar. "Are those..."

"Enochian sigils," Christy said, eyeing them. "Scrying wards."

"Indeed," Gan replied. "Specially crafted so as to work in a moving conveyance such as this."

"Seems a bit ... paranoid," Ed replied. "I mean, if none of this had happened..."

Gan smiled, her eyes glittering. "Then it would have merely been a wasted expense, minimal for one such as myself."

They were both right. It was paranoid to build a bomb

shelter ... until such time as missiles rained from the sky. Then you instantly went from eccentric to insightful.

Following that exchange, silence descended in the back where we sat. I noticed that Christy kept staring at her hands, held a few inches apart on her lap. I'd seen enough spell casting to know she was calling upon her power, keeping an active watch for any pulse activity.

I should have told her to keep an eye on me. If I keeled over, it was magic time. However, I didn't want her worrying about me at that moment. If it happened and I fell behind, so be it.

Just to be clear on that, though, I pulled Ed aside once we made it to Christy's place.

"If one of those pulses hits again..."

"I'll tell them you fainted or something so nobody loses focus on Tina."

"Thanks. Although you could also go with something more manly. Just saying."

"Yeah, fainting works."

I offered Sheila's sword – having grabbed it on the way out – to Vincent before we headed up. As a former Templar, he was far more adept with such weaponry. He wasn't too keen on taking it, being a holy relic and all, but relented when I pointed out we needed every advantage we could get.

That done, we raced up to Christy's apartment at a pace that made me rue not having vampire stamina anymore. Gravity really was a bitch for us normal folk. On the other hand, my godchild was well worth a potential heart attack.

We got to Christy's floor, her and Vincent in the lead. It seemed all was quiet, just how we hoped to find it.

"Hold," Gan replied just as Christy was about to put her key in the lock.

"What is it?"

"The door."

"The door's fine," Christy snapped. "I set up wards in case anyone tried anything during one of those..."

"*That* door is fine," Gan replied, cool as a cucumber. "This one is not." She walked over to the apartment next door and tapped a finger against the doorknob. It clattered to the floor. Someone or something had snapped it off, then simply hung it back on the broken jamb to make it look intact.

Oh, shit.

Almost as if in response to the ruse being discovered, the door in front of Gan was pulled open and a man dressed in body armor stepped out holding an assault rifle. He was fast, but Gan was faster. She disarmed him with a quick twist of the gun's barrel, flipped him onto his back, and slammed the butt of his own weapon into his face before he could so much as tell us to put our hands up.

Sadly, he wasn't alone. Doors up and down the hallway opened and more armed invaders stepped out, weapons at the ready. Vincent managed to fend off one with the sword before another, a woman, came up and clubbed him in the back of the head, dropping him to his knees.

Ed and I were, unsurprisingly, the least useful members of our party. By the time either of us responded with anything other than shocked stares, it was all over. Guns were pointed at us, at least three locked onto Gan alone.

We'd underestimated our opponents, assuming they'd attack when they were at their strongest. Thing was, we were at our most powerful during those pulses, too ... and by we, I meant everyone else. Turns out they'd learned from their earlier mistake with me, realizing the smarter move was to surround us when we were at our weakest, their guns being more than enough to tip the balance.

"Keep your mouths shut and do as you're told," one of them growled at us in a low voice, making me think perhaps they hadn't overrun the entire building. If we made enough of a commotion, maybe someone on another floor would hear it and call the cops.

Sadly, that seemed like a sucky strategy, as the ruckus needed would likely involve gunfire. Considering who had the weaponry, that probably wouldn't work out for us in the short term.

Either mindful of the wards Christy had put on her door, or just being extra cautious, they shuffled us into the apartment neighboring hers.

The place was a mess, and that was just the furniture. I caught the barest glimpse of slippered feet lying unmoving in the living room and then we were directed toward a gaping hole in the wall. It had been crudely made, and probably quickly, too. If I had to guess, one of those neo-vamps had waited to power up and then plowed straight through it into Christy's place. Effective, not to mention hell on her renters insurance.

"Her name was Greta McDavish," Christy said from somewhere behind me. "She was a nice woman with two grandchildren. I just thought you should know that."

"One sacrifice made for the greater whole," the woman who'd clubbed Vincent replied.

"I thought you were better than this, Liz."

"Better? I was, but then you betrayed our coven, our whole damned race. Spare me the lecture."

I decided to go out on a limb and assume they knew each other. Before I could ask, though, we were shunted into Christy's apartment, me first with Ed on my six.

Despite the weapons pointed my way, seeing Tina unharmed was a massive load off my chest.

She was sitting on the couch with a few of her toys. She wasn't tied up, but there was something around her waist, a wide belt or harness of sorts. Before I could get a better look, however, one of the armed intruders pointed his gun in my face.

Somewhat less well-off was Kelly, Christy's former and, I guess once-again, coven sister. She'd grown her hair out and either switched to contacts or gotten Lasik since last I'd seen her. It was a good look for her, or would have been minus the shiner under her right eye and her hands being trussed up behind her back.

"Are you okay?" I asked just as Vincent entered the room behind me.

He tried to push his way past me to get to his wife, but all that did was get him clubbed again for his troubles.

"Leave him alone," Kelly protested to no avail.

As the rest of our number were brought in, Tina cried out, "Mommy!"

For a moment, I feared Christy would get the same treatment Vincent had, but she managed to keep a cool head about her, although I'm not entirely sure how. "Are you okay, honey?"

"I'm fine, but they were mean to Aunt Kelly." She lowered her voice to a loud whisper. "I tried to stop them, but my fire didn't work."

Hmm. Earlier there'd been a long pulse, followed by a much shorter one – one which ended with me doing an impersonation of a cream pie. I wasn't exactly a tactician, but if they'd somehow timed it right with that second one, I could see how that might've played out in their favor.

Considering the lack of scorch marks around the place, it made sense.

They'd struck fast, breaking into the surrounding apartments and then busting through the wall – unwarded like the door. The pulse, however, had been short enough to end before either Kelly or Tina could blast these assholes back to the Stone Age. After that, it would have been a minor issue to take them captive.

Of course, this assumed they knew when to expect these pulses, something that was starting to seem more and more likely. First my place, then Sally's, and now here. The timing of these strikes was too perfect to be mere coincidence.

They herded everyone into the living room and made us all kneel. We hadn't exactly come well-equipped, but they took what little we had on us – mostly Sheila's sword and Christy's purse – and tossed it all into the corner.

I counted more than half a dozen armed intruders, most of them aiming their weapons at Gan.

"Tie them up," one of them, possibly the head fuck-wad, said. "Secure the witches and other threats. Wire ties on the rest."

Liz, the woman who'd traded barbs with Christy, stepped forward. She had short, brown hair and appeared to be a few years older than Christy, although that might have been deceiving. There was a world-weary appearance about her that might have added to her years. Mind you, her looks were far less important than what she was holding: a pair of old manacles with sigils clearly etched into the iron.

Holy shit.

It had been five years since I'd seen anything like them. They were designed specifically for Magi, the glyphs on them somehow canceling out their magic. I glanced over at Kelly. I couldn't see her wrists from my vantage point, but it seemed a safe bet she was wearing them, too.

But what about...

I craned my neck toward Tina, even as another of our captors pulled my arms behind my back and laced them together with zip ties. Guess I counted as one of the rest.

She was still untied, thank goodness. But, now that I had a free moment, I was able to get a better look at the thing around her waist. It was made of worn leather, with more of those sigils etched into it. Suddenly it made sense. Tina was too small for old-timey manacles. She'd have slipped out of them no problem. This must've been the witch hunter's equivalent of a booster seat. They'd come prepared, which didn't exactly give me warm fuzzies about our predicament.

Glancing at the rest of my fellow prisoners, I saw Gan and Ed had apparently been labeled *threats*. Their arms and legs were shackled with heavy-duty cuffs, the type you'd expect to see used on a guy like Luke Cage. At least Vincent got wire ties, too, making me feel slightly less insulted.

More importantly, this confirmed that whoever was behind this knew who we were and what we were capable of.

What have you done, Sheila?

Once they were finished tying us up, the one in charge removed his helmet, revealing himself to be one of the assholes who'd kicked in my door the prior week – Blond Crewcut. It wasn't exactly a reunion I'd been looking forward to.

"I know you," Gan said, her tone indicating she still considered herself firmly in control. Gotta love the criminally insane. "You were assigned to the Boston prefecture. I must apologize, but while your face is familiar, I never bothered to make note of your name."

Blond Crewcut gritted his teeth and said, "Komak. Ernest Komak, formerly of Boston Strike Team Draco." The pleasantries out of the way, he turned toward Ed and gave him a curt bow. "You may not believe this, considering the circumstances, but it's good to see you again, sire."

The fuck?

23

LAST OF A DEAD SPECIES

"I can't help but notice you're all staring at me like I have any clue what's going on," Ed said after several seconds of stunned silence.

Komak nodded as if he expected this. "That's okay. The esteemed members of the Last Coven all remember you. How could we not? You're the reason we're alive today."

Ed appeared as confused as the rest of us, but then recognition began to dawn on his face, giving way to a look that screamed "oh shit!"

"The battle with Calibra," he said more to himself than anyone else. "But how?"

Komak nodded. "I'm sorry we didn't rise in time to help, I would've liked to have taken a chunk out of her myself."

Gan turned to Ed and narrowed her eyes. "Those vampires you attempted to turn during the battle?"

Despite the fact that she was trussed up like a Thanksgiving turkey, my former roommate still turned a shade paler. "You remember that, eh?"

"I remember..."

"Yeah, yeah, a great many things," he replied. "I get it."

"Care to fill the rest of us in?" Kelly asked, looking even less pleased than when I'd first laid eyes on her.

"It's quite simple," Komak said. "I was part of a strike force that Lord Alexander led to liberate Boston from Vehron the Destroyer. We were captured, taken below, then left to rot in a cage. And why not? I was nobody, fodder for that witch to turn into one of her slaves. But then, just when I thought I'd go mad from hunger, a riot broke out. Those of us not already beyond help escaped and came across Ib's chosen one here." He gestured toward Ed.

Holy crap! These were the same guys we'd talked about when I picked Ed up from the airport, the vamps we'd casually dismissed as being long dead. Guess we weren't exactly batting a thousand with that one.

More and more, my theory that the differences between vampires and these neo-vamps ran deeper than mere resistance to sun tanning seemed to make sense, much to my dismay.

"I'll admit," Komak continued, seemingly caught up in the memory, "having already died once, the prospect terrified me, but being free from that whore's compulsion was worth it."

"But you guys never woke up," Ed replied. "No offense, but I kinda assumed..."

"That we died with the rest?"

"Seems to be a lot of that going around," I muttered

The witch, Liz, threw me a glare. "Keep your mouth shut, *Freewill*. You may have been hot shit back then, but you're nothing now."

"And yet you assholes still trashed my apartment."

Komak put a hand on her shoulder, likely staying her from caving in my teeth with the butt of her rifle. When it came time to kick this guy's ass, I'd have to remember that.

God, what a joke. There I was, falling into the old mindset. She was right. I wasn't the Freewill anymore. I was William Anderson Ryder, a regular guy who stood absolutely zero chance against anyone with "strike force" on their resume.

Once we made sure Sally was safe, that was it. I needed to back away from this shit. This was a big boy game, and I was all out of quarters.

Komak turned back toward Ed, apparently not done monologuing yet. "I'm not entirely sure what happened, but when we finally awoke, it was in darkness. At first, we didn't know what to think. All we knew was that there were a handful of us ... alive among a veritable sea of dead bodies."

I remembered it well. Corpses – Magi, human, and other – had littered the place by the end, and that wasn't even counting the mounds of ash. But we'd rounded up any survivors and brought them with us. Komak and his buddies must have revived after the rest of us escaped.

"Judging by the smell of decomposition," he continued, "we'd been lying there for days, far longer than it should have taken us to turn. But, as we all now realize, the old rules went out the window that day. I suppose we were lucky to have woken up at all."

"Let me guess," Ed replied. "You were all surprised as hell to discover you were human again, right?"

"Hell yeah. Talk about being terrified. Before we got our shit together, at least a few of our number lost it and ran off screaming in the dark. No idea what eventually happened to those poor fools."

"What did you do?" Christy asked, no doubt hoping to keep them talking.

"The only thing we could. We searched every corpse in

the area until we got lucky and found one with a working flashlight. As for finding a way out, I didn't know it at the time, but this little lady here was our savior."

I turned my head toward Gan, wondering if this was confession time, the part where we learned she was the mastermind behind everything. However, she merely raised an eyebrow, about as close as she came to looking confused.

"Your footprints, Prefect Gansetseg," Komak said. "We would have been lost down there, would have surely starved to death. But, while looking for a way out, one of us happened to spot a tiny pair of footprints leading into one of the tunnels. Lo and behold, it wasn't a dead end."

"So as way of celebration, you guys decided to call yourselves the Last Coven?" I asked. "Catchy name, by the way."

Rather than kick me in the teeth, as I probably deserved, Komak laughed. "No, sir. That came a lot later. We were too busy enjoying the sun again. We traded the supplies we'd scavenged and got drunk as fuck in broad daylight."

Despite our predicament, I couldn't help but crack a smile. I remembered those early days, drinking Coronas at the beach like there was no tomorrow, even as the world was still scratching its head as to what happened. And I fucking hate the beach. Can't say I could blame these guys ... for that part anyway.

"But eventually the cash ran out and with it came damning sobriety," Komak continued, starting to get lost in his tale. Pity I wasn't in much shape to do anything about it. "It soon became obvious we were alone, lost in a world that no longer feared us. Everything we knew, *all* of it, was gone. But eventually we began to realize we weren't as alone as we thought." He reached out and took Liz's hand.

Uh huh, so that's how it was.

"When Ernest first confessed to me what he was," Liz replied, giving him goo-goo eyes, "I was taken aback, frightened. How could such a thing be? But, I soon realized this was a sign, that there was still hope for the Magi ... for both our people ... to be whole again."

Son of a bitch. Why couldn't these assholes just fuck their problems away like everyone else instead of trying to screw the world in the process? But I guess what they say is true: crazy attracts crazy.

"It didn't start off that way, of course," Komak said, returning her gaze. I swear, if these two started making out in front of us, I was going to ask to be put out of my misery. "At first it was just talk, trying to understand our place in this world."

"Yes." Liz turned to face Christy. "But whereas *some* tried to convince us to accept the hand fate had dealt us, to live the rest of our lives as less than what we once were..."

"We saved the world," Christy countered.

"You're talking to a brick wall," Kelly said to her. "I already tried that."

Liz wasn't done yet, though. "You killed the White Mother!"

"She wasn't the White Mother," Christy replied through gritted teeth. "At least not the one whose teachings we'd been taught to revere."

'You don't know that."

"She was beyond redemption and there was too much at stake to do otherwise. The war would have consumed us all had it continued."

Liz narrowed her eyes. "So rather than work with your brothers and sisters, you instead sided with our destroyer, condemning us to a half-life. You may as well have cut off our legs when you cut off our magic."

"Don't speak to me of loss."

"You act all smug and righteous," Liz replied, "but who were you to decide what was right for the rest of us?"

"This is all truly fascinating," Ed interrupted. "And I'd love to continue debating the ethics of saving the world versus letting it turn into a cesspool of infinite darkness. But I'm going to venture there's a point to all this exposition."

"The point, sire..." Komak said.

"Could you maybe not call me that?"

Komak shrugged. "The point is that we all thought we'd have to accept this new world, but we were wrong and, ironically enough, hope came in the form we least expected."

"The Icon," Liz said, grinning at Christy. "Believe me, it wasn't easy to accept. Hell, I wanted to spit in her face the first time you brought her to one of our meetings. But it was the best thing that could have happened to us. Unlike you, she genuinely wanted to help."

She was right. Sheila did care, a unique trait among Icons apparently, most of whom history remembered as arrogant jackasses. Sadly, her caring for others had come at the cost of her caring for me.

I shook my head. Enough of that shit. I'd already thrown myself plenty of pity parties. Now was not the time for another, especially not while these two dick biscuits were busy spilling the beans.

"Okay, I think we get it," Ed replied. "She was all 'hey, let's go invite all the ancient evil back into this world.'"

Even Gan rolled her eyes at that one.

"Hardly," Liz said with a huff. "The truth is, all she offered was hope. She listened, talked to us, cried with us over what was lost, and eventually a few of us started to listen. The tenet of an Icon is that faith in oneself can overcome all obstacles. Once we got past feeling sorry for ourselves, it was easy to internalize that."

Komak put an arm around her. "I think she meant for us to use our unique knowledge to move forward with our lives, but instead it kick started discussion between our peoples. Imagine, the mystic knowledge of the Magi combined with the wisdom of the ages."

I perked up, feeling a slight sliver of hope. According to this clown, Sheila had merely been trying to tell these guys to get jobs as history professors or something, but he'd taken it as a cue to get the old band back together. Of course, that still didn't answer why she'd been with them in Damascus.

"We must have gone over it thousands of times," Komak continued. "We filled whole rooms with charts, maps, and theories. It was maddening ... until we eventually stumbled onto something that might work."

"How?" Christy asked, sounding genuinely curious.

"You were the key," Liz said, her grin wider than ever. "Sheila, she told us how you got everyone out once The Source collapsed. How you realized there was still power in..."

At this, Komak put a hand on her shoulder. "I think we've said enough."

Now? He decided now was enough? They'd just talked our ears off, but then, right as shit was getting interesting, they decided to play it coy? Fucking A!

"So what now?" I prodded, hoping to open the floodgates of his lips again ... and really wishing I'd come up with a better analogy.

"For you, nothing," Komak told me. "Your former coven mistress gave us what we needed."

"Is Sally..."

"She's okay, for now. Think what you will of us, Freewill, but the old ways are no more. We are the injured party here, seeking only to right our grievances. Should we succeed, there's no reason to think we won't show mercy."

"How generous of you," Gan said. "Know that if we find our positions reversed, the same shall not be offered."

Gotta love Gan. Always striving to make our situation *better*.

"I would expect no less, Prefect," Komak replied. "But then, you *are* a product of a dead era, I suppose."

Liz nodded. "Agreed. Perhaps it's time for you to join your ancestors in the..."

"Now, now," her boy toy interrupted. "We still have use for the Prefect. She's staked a claim over what is rightfully ours. It would be a shame if something happened to her before we could rectify that."

Gan merely stared back, seemingly nonplussed by the threat.

After a few moments, when nobody said anything, I finally snapped, "Okay, I'll bite since no one else is asking. What does she have that you want?"

Komak let out a chuckle. "Our birthright, of course."

"Not following."

"I'll give you a hint. We are the Last Coven, rightful heirs of the First Coven."

"Okay, so? Is she holding on to your membership rings or something?"

"Far more than that. Gansetseg here has appropriated the near limitless resources that the First once controlled."

It figured. "So is that what all of this is about? You're nothing more than a supernatural Hans Gruber?"

"Hans...?"

"Hardly," Liz said. "This isn't some mere bank robbery..."

She was interrupted by an electronic chirp from Komak's side. He reached down and unclipped a satellite phone from his belt, then held up a hand as if beckoning us all to give him a minute.

"We have her," he said into the receiver, forgoing any basic pleasantries.

Considering the way he was looking at Christy, I had to assume our assumptions were correct. They were aware of the spell and that she was the only one who knew it.

And, hey, look at us. We'd waltzed right in and handed her over on a silver platter. Yep, just like old times.

"Can you tell them to hold off?" he asked. "We're not in a position to... What?! Three at once? No ... we're not ready."

Huh? Three what?

"Isn't there any way to ... no, I understand. We'll do what we can. Komak out." He hung up and frantically clipped the phone back to his side. "Shit! Secure the prisoners. All weapons up and at the ready."

"What the hell are you..."

But there was no opportunity or reason for me to finish my question. I knew what was happening a scant second later as my heart skipped a beat, then another, as I slumped over onto the floor.

24

AND A CHILD SHALL LEAD THEM

I almost certainly would have passed out – that sluggishness was worse than ever – but then I caught a boot to the side which cleared the cobwebs ever so slightly.

"Stop playing games, Freewill. It won't work."

I really wished that were the case. Pity I could barely pull in enough breath to tell the goon who'd shit-stomped me to go fuck himself.

Sadly, I couldn't even make for a decent distraction. My friends, on the other hand...

Gan blinked and her eyes flashed yellow. However, even as there came a groan of metal fatigue from her cuffs, several weapons were leveled at her.

In addition, Liz and another of the goon squad began to glow an angry red. "Don't," she warned.

Powerful as my allies were, they were outmatched with little chance of breaking free before their brain pans could be perforated.

One of our other captors stepped over to me and removed his helmet, revealing himself to be none other than

Hipster McFucknugget, the other asshole who'd kicked my door down. I'd been wondering where he'd gotten off to. And, of course, he was now sporting yellow eyes and fangs. Lucky me. "It's funny. Freewills were unique in their ability to feed upon others of our kind. Now, though, I have to admit to being curious what you taste like."

Oh fuck.

"Don't you dare..."

"Or what?" Liz asked, pointing a glowing hand at Christy. "Give me an excuse, you traitorous bitch."

"You leave my mommy alone!"

"All right, that's enough," Komak barked. "Nobody needs to get hurt, but know that if you try anything, we are more than capable of neutralizing any..."

"Neutralize my cock, asshole!"

Weak as I was, I was still able to smile. Komak and his buddies had captured seven of us, but were apparently unaware that we actually numbered eight. With the power back on, that meant so, too, was Tom. He stepped through the wall shouting obscenities and drawing their attention. Half their number turned their guns on him and one actually opened fire, the bullet striking the wall behind his ghostly form.

Heh. Tom was definitely not part of their plan. But if I thought that was cool, what came next was icing on the cake.

Even as Komak shouted for his men to hold their fire, Tina cried out, "You hurt my daddy!"

She began to glow, a chaotic mix of colors. With that belt around her, I was certain it would be little more than a light show, but Christy had been right. Her little girl was an atom bomb.

The belt disintegrated from around her waist and, a moment later, her power lanced out in all directions, blasting us with a shockwave that blew out windows and knocked everyone, human or not, off their feet.

Fortunately, I was already on the floor. That was good, because someone could have bowled me over with a Nerf gun at that point.

I quickly saw that nobody was spared an up close and personal meeting with the carpet, including – amazingly enough – Tom.

"Holy shit," he cried. "I actually felt that."

It was a safe bet that everyone had. That said, the overall effect wasn't the same. Though most of his forces, Liz included, were slow to recover, Komak and Hipster – both neo-vamps – sat up and shook off the attack.

Too bad they weren't quick enough.

Before either could reestablish control of the situation, there came the groan of metal shearing and then Gan was on the move. With one hand she ripped the cuffs off her ankles, while with the other she sliced through the manacles still holding Christy's arms in place.

"It would be prudent to not tarry, witch," she said before launching herself toward Hipster, the nearest of the two vamps. Holy shit. I remembered Gan being fast beyond her years, but seeing it in action after all this time was still a mind-blower.

But it wasn't anyone's mind I needed to worry about right then.

Komak stood up right next to me. As he raised his weapon and prepared to pepper her with bullets, I managed to kick out at his leg.

The result was next to nothing. Between my weakened state and his far more powerful one, I might as well have been trying to trip a mountain. At best, I barely bought Gan an extra second.

But sometimes an extra second is enough.

That was more than she needed. Even as Komak began to put pressure on the trigger, she tossed Hipster McFucknugget his way, knocking them both to the ground. Then, without missing a beat, she turned on another of his men, a mage who'd been powering up for an attack. Before he could hit her with so much as a single spark, she'd twisted his head around with a sickening snap of bone.

"What have you done?" Liz cried.

"You were warned my mercy would be nonexistent," Gan said dispassionately. "Know that I do not make false promises."

It was as if time stopped to allow us all a moment to take this in. Back then, the casual erasure of life had been commonplace for us all. Outside of Tina, I doubted anyone in this room could claim innocence to the violence of the supernatural world.

But that had been five years ago, giving us all time to readjust to a life without it.

So much for that.

Tina, interesting enough, was the first to react following this, seemingly unconcerned with anything except protecting her loved ones. A bright green orb of flame appeared in each of her hands, both looking far nastier than what she'd conjured in my apartment just a few days earlier. Goddamn, remind me to think twice about ever sending her to bed without supper.

Mind you, her mother wasn't chopped liver either. She screamed out an incantation and bright blue beams of force flew from her hands, striking Liz and another of our foes and sending both to the ground twitching – a stun spell, if I remembered my color coordination correctly.

While this was going on, Gan leapt at Komak, taking two bullets in the gut for her troubles. Too bad for him that was barely a tickle fight for her. With her vamp powers back, an attack like that might hurt, but it wouldn't stop her ... unless of course the power abruptly cut out.

However, judging by Komak's reaction while on the phone, I got the feeling whatever was happening was destined to last a bit longer than usual.

Good for my friends. Less good for me. My eyelids were growing heavy, and I was finding it hard to draw breath. I wasn't sure how much more I could take. Even if this pulse ended, there was still the question of what would happen when the next one hit. I, for one, didn't really care to place bets when the only options on the wheel were heart attack and stroke.

Christy threw a concerned glance my way, but she was smart enough to realize that saving me wouldn't mean much if we lost this fight. She let fly another incantation in that unintelligible language of hers and, this time, a purplish dome of energy rose up around her, Tina, and those of us still tied. Unsurprisingly, Gan didn't rate in this equation, but then she probably didn't need the help.

Next on Christy's list was melting Ed's cuffs, but not before telling Tina, "Protect your Uncle Bill but ... um, don't vaporize him."

Well, that was reassuring as all fuck. At the same time, I had to admire her not giving into the parental cliché of telling her child to run and hide, especially since we needed the help and Cat had firepower in spades.

Ed stood up a moment later, freed. "Thanks. I was just about to do that." He immediately hit the deck again, though, as our remaining enemies finally got their shit together and opened fire. Fortunately, Christy's shield was up to the task, the bullets doing nothing more than causing sparks as the magical force field deflected them.

Holy shit! There was both gunfire and fucking magic being thrown back and forth. Where the fuck were the police in all of this? You can't tell me nobody in this fucking building had heard any of this?

Or maybe you could.

As Ed was freeing Kelly, I spied a shimmer of power behind him. Christy's wasn't the only shield in place. I glanced around from my low vantage point, realizing one of Komak's men had disengaged from the battle and stood with his hands raised, sadly not in surrender.

Smart. They no doubt realized that outside help wasn't likely to advance their cause. It wouldn't be much of a covert mission if the NYPD was all up in their asses.

Speaking of assholes, Hipster was back on his feet. He grabbed his weapon and turned it toward Gan, who was still wrestling with Komak. I opened my mouth to croak out a warning, but Ed was already on the job. He rushed through Christy's shield and began to grapple with Hipster for control of the weapon.

"About ... fucking ... time," I muttered, just barely able to raise my voice above a whisper.

"Better late than never," Ed growled, sparing a glance my way. "Oh shit, man. You don't look good."

I didn't feel particularly good either. It was like my systems were shutting down one at a time.

Or they might have, had Tina not picked that moment to perch herself protectively over where I lay. The energy crackling around her was awesome to behold – less awesome to experience. This close, it was like sticking a penny in an electrical socket. My body began to vibrate from the proximity to so much raw power, and not in a good way.

Painful as it was, though, it definitely woke me up a

bit – like some sort of whole body defibrillator. Glass half full and all that.

"Tina!" Christy cried. "You're too close."

"N-no," I managed to sputter out, my teeth chattering uncontrollably. "It's f-fine."

All right, it was far from fine. But I didn't want her worrying about me in the middle of this shitstorm, especially since our other big gun was turning out to be a peashooter.

Hipster contemptuously pimp-slapped Ed with a backhand, sending my former roommate flying ... right into Vincent, who'd just been freed.

"Who would have guessed our sire would be so weak?" Hipster proclaimed.

What a prick. Mind you, when one is a complete prick, one shouldn't act surprised when they get totally fucked. "Cat! T-that man hurt Uncle Ed. H-hurt him back!"

Tina didn't question me. She didn't need to. All she saw from her perspective were big, mean assholes threatening her loved ones. Unlike most little girls, though, when she kicked you in the shins, you *really* felt it.

She held out her hands and a gout of green flame shot forth toward Hipster. I'd only meant for her to incapacitate him, realizing a second too late I should have perhaps been a little clearer with my instructions.

The spell hit the neo-vamp dead on in the torso, utterly erasing everything it touched. When it was finished, he dropped to the floor in two pieces.

Holy shit!

Tom turned from where he'd been continuing to harass Komak's people. "That's my girl!"

A moment later, the remaining parts of the now very dead vamp flared up like they were made of phosphorous. They burned white hot for several seconds before turning to ash, leaving the carpet a charred and smoldering mess. Huh. Seems these neo-vamps bit it somewhat more dramatically than the old breed. Something to remember, perhaps.

Gan followed up by launching Komak at two of our remaining attackers, scattering them like human bowling pins. One landed in the corner where Christy's purse had been set, knocking it over and sending Max Adventure rolling out – aglow from the seething energy within it.

I closed my eyes for a moment, half expecting it to explode and render the whole battle moot, but fortunately that didn't happen.

"Hey, watch that shit," Tom protested, stepping in front of the lone gunman still firing upon Christy's shield.

The distraction proved to be just what was needed as Kelly, now freed, blasted him with a beam of blue magic that left him a twitching heap on the floor.

Liz was finally getting back to her feet along with the wizard Christy had stunned. Too bad for them Gan was on the move again.

She intercepted him first, took a swing, and ... eww ... basically exploded his head with a single punch, sending bone and brains flying everywhere.

Liz, not an idiot and apparently realizing the battle was lost, screamed for the remaining mage, the one keeping the shield up around the apartment, to retreat. Then, without waiting to see if he did or not, she threw herself atop Komak's prone form, cried out an incantation, and the two of them disappeared in a flash of light.

The shield Magi grabbed the other two survivors and did the same a scant second later, leaving us with a trashed apartment, two dead bodies, and even more questions than we'd started out with.

25

INSURANCE CLAIM

Tina's jolt had brought me back a bit, but I was still in shit shape to do much more than watch as Ed raced to put out the fire caused by Hipster's rather violent dusting.

Mind you, I wasn't so far out of it that I couldn't chuckle when he slipped on some brain matter. Yeah, it really wasn't funny, but it was either that or pass out.

This pulse was definitely turning out to be a long one. So far as I could tell, everyone was still powered up, except for me. Even Vincent was back on his feet doting over Kelly who – despite the shiner on her face – seemed ready for round two.

Christy was all over Tina, hugging her like there was no tomorrow. All the while, Tom stood close by expounding on what a badass his little girl was.

There were bruises and abrasions aplenty, but all in all, we'd gotten lucky.

"It's not funny," Christy finally told Tom, as he continued to brag about how much ass Tina had kicked.

"Sure it is. She fucked him up six ways to Sunday."

"That's exactly my point," she snapped. "Our daughter is five. Her introduction to magic shouldn't be this..."

"Awesome?"

"No. Dark."

"I'm okay, Mommy," Tina replied. "I'm not even tired."

"That's not what I mean, baby girl," Christy said, rubbing her eyes. "Why don't you go play in your room while we clean up out here?"

Tina must have realized her mom wasn't really asking, because she ran to her bedroom without further protest.

"Speaking of cleaning," Tom said, stepping over to where I still lay. "Looks like we missed a spot."

I lifted my hand, feeling as if it weighed a hundred pounds, and flipped him off. It was a lot of effort, but worth it.

Gan saved me from further humiliation – sorta – by dragging me up and laying me on the couch. "Did one of our foes strike while you were unprepared, my love?"

"Nobody hit him," Ed replied, finishing up what he was doing. The fire was out, but the rug was clearly ruined. Mind you, the headless body still bleeding out all over it was likely not helping.

Kelly, in the meantime, finally managed to pull away from her husband. "Wow, dude. You look terrible."

"Nice to see you, too," I croaked. "That bad, eh?"

She hooked a thumb at Tom. "You're almost as pale as him."

Christy stepped over and gave me a long look. "Oh my goddess." Apparently realizing I wasn't merely stunned, she knelt down and started checking my vitals. All things considered, I couldn't blame her for not noticing before. She'd had more than her share to worry about during the battle.

I tried my best to crack a smile. "Sorry."

"About what, this?"

"No ... Tina. I didn't mean for her to do ... what she did."

A mix of sadness and fear flashed across her eyes, but she simply said, "We can talk about that later. For now, I'm worried about you."

"But not too worried, right?" Tom asked, drawing glares all around. "What? He's obviously more alive than me. He can't be that bad off."

Dumbass.

Speaking of my former roommate, while everyone else was busy gawking at me, Gan wandered over and picked Max Adventure up.

"Give me that," Christy said, taking notice.

"Is this..."

"I said give it to me. It's not yours."

Gan appeared to consider the implied threat for a moment. With both of them powered up, things could get nasty real quick although, truth be told, I didn't like Christy's odds in these close quarters. Fortunately, after a tense second or three, Gan relented and placed the action figure in Christy's outstretched palm.

"The original prism," Gan remarked, one eyebrow raised. "The same that closed The Source." Christy didn't reply, so she continued. "Remarkable that it survived. I see your former lover wasn't exaggerating when he said he'd been here all along."

"What do you mean former?" Tom asked with a huff.

An uncomfortable silence descended until Ed, no doubt trying to deflect everyone from the rising tension in the room, addressed me. "It's getting worse, isn't it?"

As much as I wanted to nod, I could barely lift my head to do so.

"Worse?" Christy asked.

"Yeah. You probably should know, since he's in no

position to tell me to shut up, that these pulses have been affecting Bill in pretty much the opposite way of the rest of us. He's been getting weaker every time."

"That shouldn't be possible," Gan said, giving me her full attention now that she realized her *beloved* was in shit shape. "You're fully human, my love. None of this should have any effect on you at all." She raised an eyebrow. "Your whore. Has she experienced...?"

"Sally," I corrected weakly. "No. When last ... we spoke, she hadn't even noticed ... the pulses."

"Neither have I," Vincent said, quickly adding, "Don't forget, my fellow Templar and I were turned, albeit for a short time."

"And you're okay?" Kelly asked him, concern coloring her voice.

"Aside from the embarrassing beating I just took?" he replied with a laugh. "I haven't felt a thing."

"This makes no sense." Christy reached out and checked my pulse again.

"Please tell me it's still there," I said with a brittle chuckle.

She nodded, her face grim. "There, but weak. I think we need to get you to the hospital."

"What? No."

"Listen to me, Bill. What if this is unrelated to the pulses? You could be sick or... Maybe those vampires hurt you worse than you realized the other day."

"No..."

"Don't be stubborn."

"I'm ... not. I'm saying it isn't that. Believe me. I'm not ... acting brave. Do me a favor, and try something."

"The only thing I'm doing is calling 9-1-1."

"Trust me, please."

Christy looked split, but then Ed stepped in. "Let's give him the benefit of the doubt."

"Fine," she replied, seeing I wasn't backing down. "But then I'm calling an ambulance. What do you need?"

"That time stop spell. Do it again."

"But..."

"Just for a few seconds. Please."

"I'll help you," Kelly told her.

"No, you're..."

She pulled away from her husband's doting. "I have a black eye and a few bruises, that's all. I'm more than capable of lending some power if it'll help."

The matter settled, Christy and Kelly sliced open their palms, joined hands, and closed their eyes. A few moments later, two things happened: a shimmer of light encompassed the room, and suddenly I felt a hell of a lot better.

It wasn't a cure-all. Don't get me wrong. I could still feel that weakness within me, threatening to take over again at any moment. But even so, it felt as if a hundred pound weight had been lifted from my chest.

To prove it, I got off the couch and stood up. "See? Would I be able to do that if I was standing at death's door?"

Outside of Ed, the rest of the folks in the room looked surprised at my sudden *resurrection*.

"I don't understand how this is possible," Christy said after several seconds.

"You said time is stopped, correct?" Vincent asked.

"In a sense, hon," Kelly replied. "We're actually a step out of sync with the rest of the world. This is a form of pocket dimension, if you will, existing in the space between seconds."

Tom raised a hand. "Anyone else not understand a fucking word of that?"

"Like we're in the TARDIS," I explained.

"Gotcha!"

I turned to face the rest of them. "Okay. We already know Tom still works here, for lack of a better term. What about the rest of your powers? Do they ... whoa!"

Ed grabbed hold of my shirt collar and lifted me off the ground with one hand.

"The fuck, man?"

"Sorry, always wanted to try that." He lowered me back down. "But I think that answers your question."

"Same here," Kelly said, waving her hands and conjuring a small shower of multi-colored sparks.

"So why are you the only one affected?" Christy asked me. "This isn't healing magic. Someone who was injured out there would still be hurt in here. At best, it might slow down blood flow enough to staunch some bleeding, but that's it."

"Hold on," Ed replied. "Kelly said this was a pocket dimension. Is that true, or were you just dumbing it down for some of us?" He inclined his head at Tom.

"In essence it's true. We're one step removed from the reality we know, but the walls are paper thin. You could step right through and normal time would resume for you."

"What about someone or something on the outside?"

Christy glanced at Kelly for a moment and then shrugged. "Unlikely, unless we allowed it. A skilled enough caster could bend the construct around anyone she didn't want to enter. And on the outside that person would be moving too slow to compensate."

"Skilled enough?" I asked with a smirk. "As in present company included?"

Christy flashed me a smile, the first I'd seen since we'd gotten here. "Guilty as charged."

"Don't butter up my woman, dude."

"Oh, Jesus Christ!" I turned toward the ghost of my best friend. "It's not like I was dry humping her in front of company."

Christy cleared her throat, reminding me I'd said that in front of everyone. Oops.

"Why would you wish to..."

"Just a figure of speech, Gan," I quickly amended, doing my best to cover my tracks and praying to whatever gods could see us in this time bubble that Tom ceased flapping his translucent gums.

"Speaking of spells," Kelly said, "how much longer are we going to keep this one up? Because I'm starting to feel it."

"Me too," Christy said. "Bill, maybe we can..."

"It's okay." I sat down and made myself comfortable on the couch. "There are bigger fish that need frying than me. Let's focus on saving Sally and stopping this. I can ... I don't know ... always drink a few Red Bulls. That might help."

"Good plan," Ed replied with an eye roll. "That oughta work."

I flipped him off as Christy released the spell, my body once again feeling like it had the weight of the world upon it ... perhaps literally this time.

The pulse lasted for at least another hour, a near eternity for me. Several times, I came close to passing out. But thankfully my friends were there to keep an eye on me. Christy conjured that time bubble a few more times whenever she felt my heartbeat was getting too slow. I won't lie, tired as it made her, I appreciated the momentary reprieve.

When they weren't helping me, my friends were hard at work vaporizing any evidence, scrubbing blood stains out of the carpet, and conjuring wards to prevent our enemies from teleporting back in – that sort of stuff.

Even Gan helped, if indirectly. She made a few phone calls and then announced the building was now under surveillance and that any further intrusions would be dealt with.

Christy's poor neighbors, at least the ones Komak hadn't killed already. I could only hope none of them returned home after some grocery shopping only to end up with a sniper bullet in the back of the head.

At long last, the pulse finally ended. The result was instantaneous. Not only did I immediately feel better, but Tina came out of her room to complain that she couldn't make her stuffed animals fly anymore.

The only indication any of it had even happened – aside from the damage, hole in the wall, and aforementioned dead neighbors – was Tom. His *battery* had apparently gotten a good charge as he remained with us even as everyone else reverted to normal.

"Ah, that feels so much better." I stood up and stretched. Not to be overly melodramatic, but it was like rising from the dead.

"I'm glad you're back on your feet," Kelly said. "But damn, did it feel good to..."

"Be your old self?" I offered.

She nodded. "I know we left that life behind, and I accept that. Life's been good to me." She blew a kiss Vincent's way. "But still, stretching those muscles again, it just felt so ... natural."

From the look on her husband's face, I wasn't sure he agreed with that last part. With the end of all things supernatural so, too, had ended the vigil of the Knights Templar. They'd existed to protect the world from things that went bump in the night. That charter, however, included people like Kelly. I could understand his worry. If this kept up, he was probably wondering what that would mean for their relationship.

I shrugged and turned my attention elsewhere. There wasn't much I could do about that. Ultimately, that was their marriage counselor's problem, not mine.

26

TUNNEL OF BLIND LOVE

Even with the pulse over and me back to fighting shape, in a sense of the word, Christy still insisted I stay off my feet.

Regardless, I knew we couldn't stay at her place forever. The entire floor of this building was a crime scene. The best we could do was sanitize it of our presence and then play dumb later, much like I'd done at my apartment.

However, we were neither ready to leave yet, nor had clue one as to where our next stop would even be.

Christy, Gan, and Ed stepped into the kitchen to discuss exactly that ... albeit I had a feeling Ed was mostly there to play referee between them. Despite being a vamp, his knowledge of the supernatural was about on par with mine, which was to say limited. Kelly and Vincent, meanwhile, entertained Tina so as to calm her down from the *excitement* of the last hour or so.

That left me and Tom. With a bit of time to kill and curious to see if the rest of the world was noticing these pulses, I flipped on the TV.

Tom settled his incorporeal ass next to me on the couch. "Change the channel. I think Shark Week is on."

"How about we check the news instead?"

"But they're doing a follow-up to that Megalodon documentary."

"You do realize that was bullshit, right?"

"Maybe they just wanted us to believe it was fake. Ever think of that?"

I stared at him for a long second before turning back toward the TV.

The top stories seemed to be normal shit: politicians fucking over their constituents, celebrities fucking each other, that sort of stuff. Stupid as this might sound, I found it reassuring. It meant the world as a whole wasn't freaking out ... yet.

When they got to local news, though, things took a turn for the weird.

...as seen in this footage, the structure is clearly engulfed in green flame. Let's go to our chief science consultant to hear what might have caused this phenomenon...

Locals are claiming ghost lights suddenly appeared over this remote lake seventy miles north of...

"And then it disappeared in front of me, just like that. I ain't normally a prayin' woman, but..."

Thirteen residents of this small senior community collapsed at the exact same time. Authorities are investigating food poisoning as a culprit, but the staff are claiming that couldn't be the case...

We reached out to a representative of the Church of the Green Unity for a comment. He issued a statement proclaiming the Strange Days had returned...

Oh yeah, we definitely weren't alone in noticing things. The upside, however, was the media didn't appear to be taking it too seriously yet.

That didn't mean they wouldn't eventually. But hopefully we could stop things before it reached the point of devolving into a witch hunt for...

"I already concurred, witch. Do not let it go to your head."

Hmm. Only Gan could agree with something and remain that condescending in the same breath. I turned to find her and Christy marching out of the kitchen.

"What's up?"

"Hold that thought," Christy said, continuing past us. "I have to grab something from my bedroom."

Tom turned to me. "She means alone."

"I didn't move."

"I know how your mind works, dude. To steal a phrase, lack of pussy makes you brave."

Gan, rather than acknowledge Tom's jealous idiocy, sat next to me, right in the spot where he was. A disturbing double image stared at me, but only for a second before Tom leapt to his feet.

"Personal space, lady!"

She gave him the barest of glances before turning back toward me, her green eyes locking onto mine as if they had laser guidance. "Your revenant grows tiresome, my love."

"Oh, I don't know. He kind of grows on you, in a House on Haunted Hill sort of way."

She smiled. "I have missed your sense of humor these last few years. Tell me, how are you feeling now?"

"Um, pretty good, I guess."

"As I knew you would. Yours is a destiny of might, not weakness."

"Well, isn't that ... comforting."

"I offer no comfort, merely fact. It is as I have foreseen."

"Wait, what do you mean *foreseen*?"

"You're speaking metaphorically, right?" Ed asked, joining us in the living room.

"Not at all, Progenitor," she replied.

"You do realize calling me that creeps me out, right?"

She shrugged as if that were his problem to deal with. "It is a title of honor I bestow upon one who has risen from the ashes of the old race to create the new. For without you, I would not be here with my beloved today."

I mouthed, "This is all your fault," at him, catching a dirty look in return. It felt good to lay the blame on someone else for ...

Fuck! There I was, getting distracted again. "What did you mean by you'd foreseen it, Gan? Did you buy a magic eight ball or something?"

I was hoping she'd throw back some bullshit about love conquering all. That was easy enough to dismiss. But what she said next sent chills down my spine.

"You remember the Château de Chillon, of course, do you not, my love?"

"I do," Tom said. "That's the French castle where Alexander the Great cornholed Bill."

I turned and gave him my best withering stare. "First off, it's in Switzerland. Secondly, he only wanted to wrestle ... in the nude."

"I rest my case."

Grrr. How could someone dead be so fucking irritating? I sucked up any response I had and turned back to Gan. "Yes, I remember. It was the headquarters for..."

"For the First, yes," she finished. "But upon their death, the Swiss government reclaimed it for themselves, including the lower levels. I was forced to step in and convince them otherwise."

"Convince them?"

"I understand their economy is doing quite well these days."

"Oh." I suppose bribery was marginally better than the atrocities I immediately envisioned for her.

"As my father's heir and former hopeful to the First, I

felt my claim was solid to all they possessed, so I took steps to secure it."

"Okay, fine. So you own the dungeon in a drafty old castle. Congratulations."

"You know as well as I what lies in those depths."

I glanced at my two former roommates. "You don't mean..."

"The cave of seers," she replied. "Of course, is it not obvious?"

The underground cathedral the seers inhabited was one of the more frightening places I'd ever been, and I'd seen some scary shit in my day. We're talking a smoky cavern inhabited by a bunch of crazy fucks from the dawn of time. And that says a lot when we're discussing vamps. I got the impression that even the First Coven were afraid of them.

Forced to blind themselves on an hourly basis, these vampire psychos sat around huffing fumes until they hallucinated something of significance. Far be it from me to judge anyone high as balls, but the bullshit they spewed forth was then interpreted as prophecy ... of which Sheila and I apparently ended up as the subject of a few.

Ah, good times, I tell ya.

Still, all of that shit was dead and buried, or at least I hoped it was. But with my horoscope seemingly calling for miraculous resurrections, who was I to say?

"The seers were, of course, all dead by then," Gan continued, "their ashes mixed with the soot from the everburning incense of that pit."

"And yet you still wanted this shit hole?" Tom asked.

"Indeed. One need not be either Magi or vampire to be gifted with the burden of sight. One simply requires their mind to be elevated to a state beyond this mortal coil we inhabit."

"That sounds kinda hippyish," I said.

"You see, beloved, it was my theory that even the destruction of The Source could not fully obscure the mists of time." She smiled at me. Ugh, so creepy. "It was a minor matter to recruit volunteers, blind them, then set them to plumbing the mysteries of what the future holds."

"Definitely less hippyish now."

"Unfortunately, it isn't nearly as efficient as it once was. Humans are far more fragile than the old seers. Their viability within the mists is ... limited."

"Meaning?" Ed asked.

"On average, they last less than seven months before I am forced to replace them. However, I have been making strides in extending their use. For example, rather than waste the bodies of their fallen colleagues, they instead utilize them as..."

I held up a hand. "I *really* don't want to know. Your point?"

Gan smiled. "My point, beloved, is that my efforts have begun to yield fruit. For you see, I have learned a glorious truth."

"And that might be?"

"You, Dr. Death. Your involvement in all of this, our glorious future, it is just beginning."

"You're wrong."

"Am I?" she asked. "Who better for fate to choose, my love?"

"How about anyone?"

"I disagree. Think about it. Since the time when man

first fell from the trees, we have walked side by side with creatures from beyond the veil. Millennia existing alongside, and being guided by, those who walk in the shadows ... until now. For the first time in all its long history, mankind is alone, free to dictate its own fate, and it is *all* because of you."

"Um..."

"Who better to lead the charge into this bold new future which awaits us?"

It took some effort to keep from freaking the fuck out. The last thing I wanted was for my name to come up again in some half-assed Chosen One lottery. I'd done my part, paid my dues. As far as I was concerned, I was square with fate.

No, fuck that. Considering how things had played out, fate probably owed me one.

Scooting away from Gan, I took several long breaths, trying to rationalize what she'd just said. I wasn't exactly a neutral party in her eyes. For all I knew, she had these so-called seers tortured until they gave the answers she wanted to hear.

Sucked for them. But that was more a problem for Amnesty International than me. No, my problem was the little psycho herself, sitting there making crazy proclamations like she was Lo-Pan to my Jack Burton.

Fortunately, before she could get to the part about how we were fated to live out this *glorious* destiny together, or some other such bullshit, Christy mercifully walked back into the room.

She was carrying a massive and ancient looking tome — something I sincerely doubted she'd gotten from the local chapter of the New York Public Library. Laying it down on the coffee table in front of us, she called for Kelly and began flipping through the pages.

"I take it we're not looking at yearbook photos," I said.

"Not quite. But I think we may have figured out what's been going on."

"That's great!"

"Not only that," Christy smiled at me and it lit up her whole face, erasing the fear I'd felt only moments earlier, "but we might actually be able to stop it."

27

LEY LINES IN THE SAND

"Liz tipped me off," Christy explained. "She mentioned something I did *after* The Source collapsed as being the key to opening the gateway again."

I shrugged, not following. "But all the magic was destroyed at that point."

"That's exactly what I said," Ed replied.

Gan turned his way. "And hence why you added so little to our discussion, Progenitor."

I may have snickered a bit at that.

"That's what I thought at first, too," Christy said. "It's been five years and I freely admit my memories of that time are a bit fuzzy for ... reasons." Though she didn't elaborate, I saw her glance Tom's way. "But then I forced myself to think about what happened, what really happened, step by step."

She opened the book to what appeared to be a crude map. The continents were all askew and missing were any country markers, making me wonder if whoever drew this had been drunk off their ass. Making things even more chaotic were a series of interconnecting lines scribbled across the whole thing.

But then Christy pointed at a spot on the map where the squiggles all seemed to converge. "Ley lines."

That seemed to ring a bell. "Weren't those the portals we used to get to The Source?"

"That was simply one use for them, my love," Gan explained. "A quick means of ingress and egress that Ib utilized. The lines themselves are much more, though. They are the former conduits through which The Source's power flowed to all corners of this world."

"Exactly," Christy said. "Look at this. It's a reproduction of an ancient map, one of the first and only attempts by the Magi to map the ley lines." She tapped her finger at a spot where the lines converged. "There's been debate for millennia about this focal point, what it meant and where it was. As you can see by the map itself, there isn't a lot of detail to go off."

"The Source?" I offered.

"Yes. We know that now, as well as where it's located. Because of that, we can add context that never existed before." She pointed elsewhere on the map. "For example, this is most likely the line that runs beneath Boston. You remember that, right?

"Bunker Hill? Hard to forget."

"And I think this is the one under Las Vegas."

"Why the big mystery?" Tom asked. "If you can find one line, just follow it back to where it came from."

"It's not that easy," Kelly said. "Legend tells us there're thirteen major ley lines zig-zagging across the globe, crisscrossing each other. Good luck tracking one with even modern technology."

"And yet somehow they managed to do it thousands of years ago," Christy replied, her eyes still on the map.

I exchanged glances with my former roommates, living and otherwise. "Okay, and this means what for us?"

"Remember what happened," Christy asked, "after The Source was gone? We weren't sure how to get out, but then I realized the ley lines themselves still held some power, enough for us to escape."

I nodded. "Yeah. Saved us a lot of walking. But why does that matter now?"

"Think of these lines as rivers of pure magical power, with The Source being the mountaintop they all flowed from to carry that energy across the world – energy that empowered my people and connected this world to all other worlds of the multiverse."

"Getting kind of trippy," Tom remarked.

"So says the guy with the transparent body." I turned to Christy again. "Okay, I sorta remember you explaining this. But, if I recall correctly, you said the magic in them would dry up pretty fast without The Source."

She nodded. "I did and still believe that's the case. But, continuing the water analogy, when a river runs dry, sometimes small ponds or creeks are left behind – not much more than puddles but still there."

Kelly snapped her fingers. "Where the ley lines run deepest."

"Indeed, witch," Gan replied.

"Hold on," Tom said, crossing his arms smugly as if he thought he had something useful to contribute. "I thought we were talking about gods kicking down doors."

Gan waved her hand dismissively. "An early hypothesis, nothing more."

Christy nodded, the look on her face saying she wasn't overly happy to agree with Gan on anything. "What cemented it for me was what Komak said before that last pulse, about three at once."

I nodded. "Yep, that one was a doozy."

"I think what's happening is that Komak's coven are working with the Magi to search the ley lines for these deep wells of remaining energy."

"But why?" Kelly asked. "Even if they managed to tap into some residual energy in the surrounding rocks, it would be finite, like taking the last few nuggets of gold from a spent mine."

"So that's why these pulses have been so short," I surmised. "They've been digging for magical gold, spending the shit out of it, then moving on to the next one."

Tom tried to clap me on the back, doing nothing more than sending a static shock down my arm. "So that means there isn't anything for us to do. We just wait for these fuckers to tap all the wells and then shit goes back to normal."

"A gross oversimplification," Gan said. "And also incorrect."

Christy again nodded. "She's right. I know Liz. I doubt she's in this for one last fling to get it out of her system. No. She and Komak want to turn the lights back on full time. And that's where Sheila comes in."

"How?" I asked, despite not wanting to. "Sheila's power helped close The Source."

"What better way to unlock a door, my love, than with the same key that closed it?"

"I don't understand."

"Neither do we. Not fully," Christy said with a heavy sigh.

Gan looked like she wanted to say something to that, but Christy shot her down. "Nor do you. Admit it." Gan's response was a silent glare, so she continued. "Our working theory, however, is that The Source cave is the central focal point where all of these ley lines used to be fed from. That's why Komak's people commandeered it."

She was definitely starting to lose me. "Yeah, but it's a dead end."

"Maybe not," Kelly said. "If what Christy's saying is right, then The Source chamber would be the first place to check for residual energy since all the lines interconnected there. It would be a big gamble, don't get me wrong, but all things considered, it's probably safe to assume they struck gold."

So what if they did?" Ed asked. "Even if they found some old magic, they were still stuck miles underground. The shit Komak was doing sounded like a coordinated effort. Hard to do with people who are trapped in a mineshaft."

Christy smiled at him. "Not at all. Stuck is a very minor matter for a re-empowered mage to overcome. It would have been nothing for them to strike down any of the White Mother's old wards, allowing sending to and fro."

"But not Sheila," I said. "Don't forget, her power futzes with magic." It was part of what made Icons so dangerous. Their energy burned some supernatural creatures and negated the powers of others. Hell, so far as I was aware, their only weakness was the blood of Baal ... a corrupting black spooge that only a handful of ancient vamps had known the recipe for, present company included. Speaking of which...

"Agreed," Gan replied. "Hence why she was with the group in Damascus."

"But then..."

"She would still be trapped, yes. But what of it? The Magi could easily ferry fresh supplies to the caverns below."

"I still don't understand how any of this shit would work," Tom said.

Sad to say, but I wasn't too far ahead of him on this one. What Christy and Gan were explaining kept flying way over my head. But maybe that didn't matter so long as it made sense to them. Hell, it wasn't like I was studying to get a PhD in wizarding. Besides, in the end, they were the ones who would make a difference in this, not me.

"As I said," Christy replied, "a lot of this is assumption on our part. But it seems to make sense. Hear me out. The energy that flowed through this world came from The Source via these ley lines. But it's dried up now, meaning the current has been cut. I believe they're trying to turn it back on, but in reverse – tapping into this residual energy and sending it back upstream like tributaries. And waiting there at The Source for it all..."

"Is Sheila," I said.

Gan nodded, her eyes glittering despite the shit show in front of us. "That is our guess. The Shining One is acting as a conduit. As the energy flows into The Source chamber, it both empowers her as well as counteracts against her faith energy."

Christy stood up, stretched, and then pointed at the map again. "Those pulses we've experienced, I think those are happening whenever a ley line is tapped and the flow reversed. It's creating a temporary breach between worlds. That's why the last one was so long. Three ley lines were tapped at once. They're accelerating their efforts, coordinating with each other across the globe. Who knows how many Magi they have working together on this? But I think it's safe to say it's more than a few."

"It wouldn't have been hard to find volunteers," Kelly replied. "Especially with the carrot of getting their old lives back."

Christy let out a long sigh and nodded.

I raised my hand. "Okay, so they're finding old magic and shooting it back upstream. But even the longest of these pulses hasn't been *that* long. And that one earlier was barely a few seconds."

"I know," Christy said. "That was likely a line that was nearly spent, but I don't think the pulses are the key here. They're just a side effect. Wasting all of that energy wouldn't do them any good. No. They'd need to keep the flow of power steady, even if it was just a trickle."

"For what?"

Christy and Gan exchanged knowing glances. "We don't have a lot to go on, but my guess is they believe that if they can tap all thirteen ley lines, then they might have a chance of cracking open the door again – *permanently*."

28

THE ASS-CRACK OF DOOM

"That's why they wanted the spell," Christy explained. "Reversing all of the ley lines themselves wouldn't be enough. The Source isn't some swimming pool they can just fill up again. But, if they had the spell to act as a catalyst, along with Sheila's power..."

"They could blow it wide open?" Ed asked.

Gan turned to him. "Not quite, Progenitor. The Shining One's power runs deep, but is not limitless. She is no goddess."

A few years back, I might have argued with her, but that was before my heart was trampled into dozens of pieces and tossed into a wood chipper. Now ... well, I won't lie, the thought of seeing her again did bring some fluttery butterflies to my stomach. But I mostly wanted to hear her out, have her tell us this was all some mistake.

"Okay, so then it wouldn't work?" Tom replied, sounding about as clued in as he was when still alive.

"It's hard to say," Christy said. "I'm doing a raw calculation here, but I very much doubt the residual power left is enough to punch through the veil between worlds, at least fully. Even with the spell and Sheila as a foci, my best guess is it would only open the doorway a crack at most."

"A crack?"

"Yes. I'm not even sure the expertise to do more than that exists anymore. A good deal of the Magi's best and brightest perished during that final battle."

"Present company not included," Tom added, no doubt trying to earn some brownie points.

"Regardless," she continued, throwing him a quick smile that set off my envy circuits, "I'm pretty sure that's the most they could hope to achieve. A permanent breach is possible, but it would be much weaker than the original Source."

"And that would do what, exactly?" I asked.

"It's hard to say, but I think it could, at best, empower a Magi to a mere fraction of their former ability."

"What good does that do them?"

"You'd be surprised," Kelly replied, a wistful look on her face. "Think of it like being blind but having a chance to regain a tiny bit of sight in one eye. It might not be an earth-shattering result, but it could easily be life changing."

Christy nodded. "I hate to say it, but it would certainly offer many Magi a chance to regain their self-esteem, their sense of worth."

"Okay, so you guys could do card tricks again." Ed hooked a thumb at Gan. "What about folks like ... us?"

"Trickier to deduce, Progenitor," Gan said, "but still possible to hypothesize. I surmise that beings such as ourselves would likely be minimally affected from the way we are now by this so-called crack between worlds. I would expect slightly heightened abilities, perhaps a marginal increase in lifespan, but for all intents and purposes, we would remain mortal."

"Would we still have to drink blood?"

"Doubtful."

"Okay. I can live with that."

Tom tried slapping him on the shoulder, but his hand went right through. "You mean my sister can live with that."

"But what about you?" I asked now that Tom had our attention again.

Christy's face fell. "I simply don't know. He'd likely be relegated to a true ghost of the past – able to be seen on occasion, no more. But he'd be stuck forever in this state of limbo. There wouldn't be enough ... of anything to bring him back." She paused for several seconds. When she spoke again, her voice was ringed by sadness. "Our only other option is to release him.

"How?"

"By destroying the prism once and for all."

"Whoa," Tom cried. "Don't I get a vote? If so, I'm dropping my ballot in the ghost slot."

"You would be able to move on," she said.

"I don't want to move on. All my shit is here."

I stood up to make sure Tina wasn't eavesdropping. "Okay, fine. So, whatever needs to be done to bring him back, we do it before they finalize the ass-crack of doom."

"It's not that simple," Kelly said, putting a hand on Christy's shoulder.

"No, it isn't," Christy said in agreement. "The problem is, we don't know how. The doll, the prism, the glamour we constructed for him back then, it was all meant to be temporary. He needs to be re-integrated with a mortal coil."

"And that's a problem?" I asked.

"It's a sin against nature," she snapped before calming herself again. "Even if it wasn't, his body was cremated."

"That's okay," Tom replied. "It'd be pretty fucked up by now anyway."

Christy stood and began to pace. "It would be different if we had time to research our options and find a way to properly pull him back into this world."

"But we do not," Gan stated flatly, showing that her empathy hadn't improved over the years. "Komak's words suggest that time is short. Their plans are accelerating."

"Perhaps," Vincent offered, stepping to the door of Tina's room. "She's napping, by the way. It's been a long morning for her. But if I'm hearing correctly, we're at a stalemate. They can't move forward without the spell you prepared, which they failed to get in their latest assault. Unless...?"

Christy tapped her forehead. "No. It's all up here. It's one of the few incantations I've never committed to paper. I was tempted to over the years, but never got around to it, thank goodness."

Vincent turned toward his wife and raised an eyebrow.

"I only know bits and pieces," Kelly said. "Not enough to recreate it."

"So, then we're..."

"Still fucked," I said, interrupting. "Don't forget. They have Sally."

"It seems an easy enough equation, my darling," Gan replied. "Her life obviously does not compare to the fate of the world. I have little doubt she would agree."

I glared at her. "Obviously you don't know Sally very well. More importantly, *I* don't agree."

"I still can't believe Sheila would be okay with this," Kelly said, echoing my own thoughts.

"It's possible she isn't." I realized I was trying to comfort myself as much as her. "For all we know, she's onboard with opening this little sliver to beyond and nothing more."

"But..."

"We don't know," I repeated.

Kelly nodded and then, after a moment of silence, said, "Okay, so call me crazy, but why don't we simply trade the spell for Sally?"

Christy's mouth dropped open at the suggestion. "What?"

"You said it yourself, this crack would be nothing compared to The Source itself. The Magi would get a tiny portion of their mojo back and these new vampires could maybe try out for the NFL, but that's about it. As for him..." She gestured toward Tom. "Maybe Tina can help. If the tyke gets even a fraction of her natural power, then that might be enough to do something ... if we can eventually figure it out. If not, then we'll move on to Plan B: put his soul to rest."

"I can still hear you," Tom replied.

"Sorry, but you know what I mean."

"No," Christy said.

"Why not? Think about it. If we offered our help, it could heal a lot of old wounds."

"What do you mean?" Ed asked.

"We don't talk about it much, but there's still plenty of bad blood. Even though we did the right thing back then, a lot of our brothers and sisters still consider us traitors for turning against the White Mother. This could fix all of that. We'd have our cake and finally be able to eat it, too."

Christy shook her head again, but I was beginning to see Kelly's logic.

"Far be it from me to argue that we should open doors best left closed, but let's not throw this away so casually," I said, half-surprised to find myself agreeing with this plan despite what it could mean for Sally. "It sounds like this so-called crack isn't exactly Armageddon 2.0. Sure, maybe Ed likes his steaks a bit rarer going forward, but that's a fuck-ton better than turning the neighborhood into his own personal buffet."

"True," Christy said tentatively.

"Also, let's not forget that the main reasons we closed it in the first place are all gone. Alex, Calibra, the Jahabich, the Feet, all of them are either dead or back where they belong. Hell, aside from these Last Coven bozos, there's no more vampires either."

"And I'm not planning on making any new ones," Ed added.

"I was really hoping you'd say that." I turned my attention back to Christy. "The playing field will be level. No monsters in the woods, no desperate peace summits, no Humbaba Accord to break. It's all gone. We did what George Lucas couldn't and brought balance to the Force."

"What about other ... stuff?" Ed asked. From the tone of his voice, I could tell he was considering this plan, too. "Let's not pretend vamps and witches were the only things out there."

"It is conceivable," Gan said, "but I believe passage would likely be limited, at least for lesser beings."

"Meaning we'd be fucked if one of the elder gods decided to force their way through."

"That is always going to be a threat," Gan replied. "But if they are not a factor in the Magi's plans now, then I don't consider it worth worrying about. Once our business is concluded, I can order my people to seal off The Source chamber for good, lessening the risk."

"After warding it against magical intrusion," Kelly added.

"A prudent idea. Agreed."

Vincent didn't appear exactly overjoyed by this, but as a former Templar, I doubted he'd be good with anything that didn't involve smiting evil and dropping half his paycheck in a collection plate. But if he had serious objections, he kept them to himself, and I could sorta imagine why.

Despite the monsters lurking in the shadows, I was still able to live the first twenty-four years of my life blissfully unaware that the paranormal was real. I'd entered this crazy world by sheer dumb luck. It wasn't as if there had been vamps standing on every corner, even back then.

Reopening The Source at a mere fraction of its former strength would likely go unnoticed by the vast majority of the world, even more so than before. The threat to most would be minimal.

This could work. But it also wasn't my call. My days of being the de facto leader of this bunch were over.

Christy was the one who needed to either agree or douse this fire, and I think everyone realized she was the deciding vote.

After a minute or so of quiet contemplation, she turned to face me. "But what will happen to you?"

"His dick will stay sad and dry," Tom said.

I narrowed my eyes. Freaking idiot! Did he not realize how much he was tempting fate with the resident psycho in the room?

Fortunately, before he could say anything further that might cause Gan to become murderously suspicious, Christy herself replied, "What I meant is the way these pulses have been affecting you. We have no way of knowing what opening the door for good, even a sliver, might do."

She had a point, but there was no way I was letting anyone use me to cockblock a possible rescue plan. "If it's the same as how we think it'll affect everyone else, then I should be fine. I mean, heck, if it saves Sally, I can deal with being narcoleptic."

"Bill's used to being a pussy," Tom added. "So being an even bigger pussy won't be much of a change."

"Thanks," I replied dryly.

"Anytime, bro."

I could tell Christy was weighing her options as she stood facing the window.

Yeah, we could do nothing. From the sound of things, the Magi orchestrating this lacked the time to rejigger the cave spell before the flow of power ran dry. Waiting them out, though, ran the risk of another attack, not to mention would almost surely doom Sally in the process ... maybe Sheila, too.

Going on the offensive might sound cool in a comic book, but it was suicidal idiocy at best, especially since we'd nearly gotten our asses kicked by one small strike team.

Much as I didn't like handing the other side a win, Kelly's compromise was probably our best bet ... even knowing it might end up a notch in my personal loss column.

I wasn't worried about what would happen to me — well, okay, I kinda was — but becoming a Magi again, even at a fraction of her old power, would pull Christy back into that world. I knew her. She'd already lost one human lover to the forces of darkness. The possibility of losing another would surely eat at her, even if I had no plans to stick my neck out once this was over with.

Still, I'd sooner relegate myself to a monastery than doom my friends. As far as our options went, I was happy to take one for the team. Okay, maybe not *happy*, but willing.

At last Christy turned back toward us, just as the sound of sirens could be heard from outside. There came a collective beat of silence, then they thankfully sped off into the distance again. Regardless, we needed to bug out of here. We'd already pressed our luck staying as long as we had.

"I ... propose we approach Liz and her people under the ancient rules of parlay. The old ways might not hold much weight anymore, but I'm hoping their sense of tradition is strong enough so they at least hear us out."

"Attacking us would only acknowledge their own failure," Gan replied. "They cannot succeed without your knowledge."

"True, but that won't make me feel any better if they shoot us in the back."

"Sheila won't let that happen," Kelly said, echoing what I hoped to be the case.

Christy raised an eyebrow. "Like she didn't let those monsters hurt you?"

"She wasn't behind that."

"How do you know?"

"Because I know her," Kelly snapped.

Before this could devolve into a full-blown argument, Tom stepped between them. "Sounds like it's settled, then," he said cheerfully. "So ... how do we do this? Anyone got this chick's email address or something?"

Christy took a deep breath, no doubt calming herself down. Then she locked eyes with Kelly again, but this time it was far less acrimonious. "That part at least is simple. We know exactly where they are."

Oh crap.

"It's time for us to return to The Source."

29

MINER SIXTY-NINER

"Oh, is that all?" Ed asked, echoing what I'm sure most of us were thinking. "Because I was *really* hoping to be able to see that shit hole again one day."

"Trust me, I doubt any of us have rosy memories of that place."

"In that you are incorrect, my love," Gan replied. "It is where Alexander was finally laid low. I consider that a most fond memory."

"You would."

"Much as I would like to put my faith in the Blessed One," Vincent said, steering us back on track, "times have changed. Even if she is, as we hope, still our friend, there's no telling what her allies may do. What if we hand over this spell and they turn on us?"

"It would be a violation of parlay," Christy said. Yeah, no shit there. "But you're right. We should go into this assuming a worst case scenario."

"I may be able to assist with that," Gan replied with a nod of her head. "Following the assault upon my facility in Damascus, I set my people to work excavating the collapsed section of tunnel. Upon last report, they are within reach of achieving their goal. I have a sizable force on standby for that eventuality."

Tom turned to face her. "Okay. So why not let them handle this shit instead?"

"Because this is supposed to be a rescue mission, not a bloodbath, genius," I pointed out.

"You speak true, my love. And though I have already calculated the potential losses and deemed them acceptable..."

"Of course you did."

"...I also realize doing so would cause you consternation. Therefore, I propose we follow our set course and utilize my people as a backup solution should we fail."

"A fuck you from beyond the grave," Tom said. "I dig it. So what do we need to do to make this shit happen?"

Turned out the *what* was easy compared to the *who* and *where*.

Our course of action required us to be ready to go at a moment's notice. Problem was, we didn't know when that moment would be. We couldn't afford to wait where we were much longer.

Sadly, our options were pretty much limited to my place, which would put Dave back in close quarters with Gan, joy of joys. Given enough time I had little doubt he'd mouth off again, and I *really* didn't care to get pummeled with another case of moisturizing cream.

However, she offered an alternate suggestion that was quite possibly even nuttier.

"We should return to the whore's domicile and set up there."

"First of all, stop calling her that. Secondly, need I

remind you her place is an active crime scene, much like this one?"

"Yeah," Ed replied. "You were right there with us."

"Ah, Progenitor," Gan said, "I see you share my love's youthful naivety, albeit in a less endearing fashion."

Tom chuckled. "Epic burn from the former half pint."

"Bite me, Slimer." Ed turned to face Gan again. "Why her place? Don't tell me you don't have a penthouse apartment somewhere in the city."

"Several, as a matter of fact," Gan replied. "However, I am aware of the witch's base distrust of me. Neutral ground will likely cause far less consternation during a time that is best spent focused. Besides, I disagree. The whore's abode may have suffered damage from our intruders, but it is not, as my love professes, an active crime scene."

I was about to argue when I realized she might be right. Had the cops been notified in any way, they'd have been swarming the place by the time we got there. But they hadn't been. Coupled with the lack of neighbors and the overall fortified structure of the building...

"I see you are putting two and two together, my darling. It stands to reason that the only ones aware anything there is amiss are us and Komak's people. And I can see no reason for them to revisit her home, having already gotten what they came for."

Damn it all, but she had a point. We bantered back and forth a bit more, but with few options left to us, it was quickly, if reluctantly, agreed upon. In a way, I guess it was fitting that the place Sally had been abducted from would serve as the kick-off point for her rescue.

As we prepared to move out, the conversation turned toward the obvious problem of Tina. Thankfully, not even Gan was insane enough to suggest we bring her along to

Hell's front porch. Walking thermonuclear weapon or not, she was still a small child.

Sadly, we were short on babysitters. Tom's parents were down in New Jersey, too far a drive to risk missing our window of opportunity ... and way too risky in case any vamps came knocking.

What we needed was someone close by and knowledgeable enough to keep an eye out for Komak or Liz ... which meant a member of our already small circle.

Christy and Kelly were must-haves on this expedition. No question there. Gan, too, both for her skills as well as the fact none of us were insane enough to entrust her with a goldfish much less Tina.

Fortunately, Kelly stepped up to the plate with the perfect volunteer – her husband.

Vincent wasn't happy with the idea, mostly the part about letting his wife go into danger without him. But as an ex-Templar, pledged to protect the innocent, he couldn't really claim he wasn't qualified for the job.

He accepted the task stoically, after a bit of browbeating on her part. However, he argued against waiting for us at Sally's place, as it had already been breached once. Vincent instead suggested he and Tina remain mobile so as to decrease their chances of being tracked by Komak and his whack pack.

Remembering the time I'd almost lost her in the Manhattan Mall – damn, kids could be quick when they wanted to be – I suggested perhaps two heads might be better than one for this job.

Christy concurred, but before she could point out the obvious choice, I pulled her aside ... or as much as I could do without Tom hovering. "I know what you're going to say."

"You..."

"Need to be there."

"For Sally?" she asked.

"For all of you. Besides, the moment a pulse hits, I'll be useless to help Tina and you know it."

"What about down there?"

Touché. "True, but you can take care of yourself. If Vincent stops to help me..." I trailed off, allowing her to fill in the blanks.

After a moment, she nodded. "You're right, but then who?"

"Fortunately, I think I know someone who might be right for the job."

"Not fucking happening," Ed said. "I'm going."

"You make the most sense to watch Tina," I told him.

"No. I make the most sense to be down there. Need I remind you, I'm a vampire, whereas you're not?"

"Yeah, but you're a shitty one," Tom said with a smirk. "You totally got owned in that fight."

"He's right," I pointed out. "No offense, but you're the weakest link on the vamp chain. Against an army of mages, you'll last maybe a second longer than me."

"Okay, but that would be an extra second to..."

"However," I interrupted, "if they do manage to somehow track Vincent, it'll likely be with a lot less people than will be down below. If things are normal, he can take point. But if one of those pulses is going on, you'll have a much better shot than any of us at keeping our little Cat safe."

"Cheetara," Tom corrected. "Get it right, dude."

"Bite me."

He hooked a thumb at Ed. "That's his thing now."

Christy stepped in. "I can't believe I'm saying this, but Bill's right. Much as I'd appreciate the extra muscle where we're going, we've got enough." She threw a sidelong glance at Gan. "I'd feel much better if you were looking after my little girl instead." That was probably enough to seal the deal, but she twisted the knife a bit to be sure. "Besides, she'll be with her uncle. In case anything goes wrong, I know you'll take good care of her."

Tom chuckled. "That means get her to her grandparents before any of your bad habits rub off."

Christy turned to him next. "Maybe you should stay here, too."

"What? No fucking way!"

"There's not much you can do down there, and Tina needs her..."

"I disagree, witch," Gan interrupted. "He could prove useful as both spy and distraction."

"Yeah, what she said," Tom replied. "Besides, there's no way I can be less useful than Bill."

"At least I can pick up a pencil."

Christy shook her head. "No. I want you to stay..."

Gan held up a hand. "There is also the Jahabich to take into account."

"What?" Christy and I blurted simultaneously.

"They are, of course, no more. But I've been thinking about the manner in which they were created. Even if The Source is only reopened a mere fraction, it stands to reason we might be able to recreate the process by which..."

Christy's eyes opened wide. "You want me to turn him into one of those mindless monstrosities?"

"Hardly," Gan replied. "With Ib gone, so, too, is the control she exerted over her creations. He would be of his own mind and, with The Source weakened, likely mitigated to whatever form he arose in."

I met Christy's eyes and though I could see she didn't want to admit it, she knew Gan potentially had a point.

The Jahabich were shapeshifters, granite abominations

reborn from the souls of the dead. But I'd seen them being made, and they always awoke in the form of their original bodies. If it still happened the same way, Tom would essentially be himself again, or close to it.

Kelly joined us, an apologetic look on her face. "You have to admit, it's a step up from being stuck as a ghost."

"Not to mention," Tom added, "a fuckload better than being put to rest. What do you say, Bill? You in?"

"I don't know," I replied, not wanting to play devil's advocate. "On paper it sounds good, but let's not forget it's also kinda batshit."

"Really? Is it any crazier than bringing you along, Mr. Collapses the Second Magic is Turned Back On?"

Goddamn it. He had a point there. I turned to Christy. "He's right. If that happens, you need to leave me behind."

"Yeah, Bill's used to being left in the..."

"Enough." Christy turned and walked over to the curio where Max Adventure had sat until recently.

I knew she was warring with the logic of leaving the prism – pretty much a miniature fusion reactor – behind on the surface versus the hope of putting Tom in a better state than he was currently. It wasn't quite Sophie's Choice, but I can't say I envied her the decision.

When at last she turned back toward us, I could see her mind was made up. "I need to think about this some more."

Or maybe not.

"Need I remind you that we don't have the luxury of time."

Christy locked eyes with Gan. "No, just as I don't need to remind you this is *my* decision."

Tom opened his mouth to say something, but Christy held up a hand. "The truth is, you're all correct."

"We are?" I asked, probably with less conviction than I should have.

"We don't have the time to wait, but I still need to think this through." She turned to Tom. "You can come along. As for you..." I assumed she was going to say she'd changed her mind about letting me go, but she surprised me. "There's no way I would ever leave you behind."

"Oh, well, that's good to..."

"Besides, I think I have an idea that will keep you safe, as well as maybe give us all time to think things through."

30

INTO THE BELLY OF THE BEAST

Christy had once used the energy of the prism to power a self-sustaining glamour for Tom. Now, working with Kelly, they raced to jury-rig something similar for me while Gan summoned her limo driver to take us to our next and hopefully not final stop.

The idea was simple enough. They fashioned a charm necklace, utilizing the stored energy that was keeping Tom visible – causing him to fizzle out early. But that was fine. It would probably be easier anyway to step outside without a fucking ghost following us.

Besides, he'd be back once the next ley line was tapped. When that happened, the charm, which was now tethered to the prism, would power up, too. It contained, in essence, a watered-down version of that time dilation spell she'd used earlier – both witches having contributed a drop of blood to seal the deal, so to speak.

The hope was, Christy explained, that it would be depowered enough for barely any discernable change between my time and the rest of the world, maybe a half second delay or so, but I'd be out of sync just enough to keep from being knocked on my ass.

I swear, magic really was like riding a bicycle for her. A little bit of practice and she was ready for the Tour de France.

While that bit of sorcery was afoot, Ed and Vincent packed some snacks and discussed their plans for the day. The only issue was a car, as both mine and Christy's had been left behind in our race to get over here.

Gan, however, in a rare show of comradery, stepped up, offering the limo that would once again ferry us all. Considering her foresight – or paranoia – in having the interior etched with anti-scrying wards, it was perfect.

Now all they had to do was keep one little girl safe and entertained enough to not conjure fireballs in public.

All in all, I wasn't sure which of us had the more daunting task.

"Why can't I come with you?" Tina asked, looking up from where she'd been playing with the limo's satellite radio system. "I can help."

"I know you can, honey," Christy said, struggling to keep the tears from falling, "but I need someone to take care of Mr. Vincent and your uncle Ed. Can you do that?"

"Can I play with the TV, too?"

Christy smiled. "You can play with whatever buttons you want to, honey."

Before Gan could comment, Tina turned serious. "Are those bad people going to come back?"

"They might," her mother said. "That's why I need you to be big and brave."

"But what about you, Mommy?"

Christy leaned down and kissed the top of her head, the tears falling freely now. "Don't worry about me. Besides, your daddy and uncle Bill will both be there."

I was glad she didn't say we were coming along to protect her, since the opposite was likely true. Tina might've been young, but she wasn't stupid.

She cast a doubtful glance at her mom then turned toward me. "You promise to keep her safe?"

I leaned forward in my seat toward her. "Cross my heart. Nothing will get past me."

"But ... what if there are monsters?"

"Monsters? Hah. I'm not afraid of them." Okay, just a bit of a lie.

"No?"

"Nope. Because I used to be a monster, too ... except scarier."

She giggled as I made a face. "You're not scary."

Ed laughed from his spot in the cavernous limo interior. "That's exactly what the other monsters used to say."

"Bite me, dickhead."

Tina stared at me tight-lipped. "Ooh. You said a..."

"Yeah, I know. I'll write you a check when we get back."

Gan's driver once again made ridiculously good time, navigating the city streets back to Sally's place like a pro. But therein lay another problem – sending my friends with a driver whose loyalties didn't lie with them.

But Gan was generous there, too. Once we arrived, she spoke to him for less than a minute. When she turned back with the keys, he was already walking away. Hopefully it wasn't to commit seppuku on her orders, but I figured it was best to not ask.

We took our sweet time saying our goodbyes to Tina and her designated guardians, most of us teary-eyed by the time they pulled away and disappeared around the corner. Then we headed in to get ready.

Sally's apartment had more than enough room for what we needed. After we cased the floor and determined it empty, Christy and Kelly got to work on a sending circle, prepping it so it could shunt us where we needed to go the moment the power came back on again, whenever that might be.

While that was going on, I used the time to rearrange Sally's upended furniture so we could at least be comfortable while we waited.

And wait we did. Several long hours of tedium passed, with not much to do except avoid Gan and sneak some of the shitty health food Sally kept stocked in her refrigerator.

I was just contemplating giving up and grilling myself a tofu burger when I almost jumped out of my skin.

"Could you maybe warn me next time before draining my batteries?" Tom complained, appearing right next to me. Though his bitching was no surprise, his reappearance was, as well as his cadence. It was off, lower pitched than normal as if he was speaking in slow motion.

My heart skipped a beat as a wave of tiredness washed over me, but it wasn't nearly as bad as it could have been. I glanced down as he continued to whine and saw a dim shimmer of light from the charm around my neck. The magic was back, but Christy's spell was working to keep it at bay.

There was no time to waste.

I grabbed Sheila's sword from where I'd left it on the couch, then shouldered the backpack lying next to it, one of Tina's. Yeah, it was a bit embarrassing to be heading into the unknown with *Paw Patrol* emblazoned on me, but I figured it was safer than stuffing Max Adventure into my belt alongside the blade that had blown it up the last time we'd been down there.

Out of the corner of my eye, I saw Christy watching me, concern etched on her face. Not wishing to distract her from our objective, I threw her an overly-enthusiastic thumbs up. "Let's do this."

"Your vigor is no surprise to me, my love," Gan said, stepping up beside me.

Ugh! I swear, if I had even a bit of sense in my fucktard brain, I'd have hopped into that car with Ed and hauled ass out of town. But I had to do this. I wouldn't be able to live with myself sending my friends to rescue Sally with only Gan – someone who wasn't exactly renowned for her restraint – as their backup.

All I really had was my wits and reputation to go on, which meant I had my wits. Maybe it was a good thing Sally was still held captive, because I had a feeling she would have pointed out that left me with jack shit.

Regardless, if this went well, she'd be able to tell me in person.

And if it went extraordinarily badly, well, maybe the afterlife had enough sense of humor to let her tell me anyway.

Knowing my luck, I didn't doubt it.

"Everyone hold hands and step into the circle."

Three guesses who decided to hold mine, and if you didn't say "Gan" for all of them, then count yourself a fucking idiot.

Her hand locked around mine in a vice grip, reminding me there was zero chance of breaking free if she decided to not let go. For a moment, I was tempted to draw the sword and preemptively hack my arm off at the wrist, but decided to save that option for later if need be.

Besides, I had another plan in mind for it beyond self-mutilation. Sheila had once told me the sword made her feel complete. That was a long time ago, but I was hoping it might act as a peace offering, a way to remind her of what she'd once stood for.

If not, then at least it didn't leave me totally defenseless, since we'd opted to not bring any of the weapons we'd scavenged from Komak's strike team. All things considered, a John Woo style entrance might have conveyed the wrong message.

All of that went through my head in the time it took us to step into the circle, Tom included, although technically he couldn't hold anyone's hand.

Christy and Kelly closed their eyes once we were in. A moment later, bright light flashed around us and reality winked out of existence.

It wasn't the first time I'd been teleported, apparated, or whatever the fuck the Magi liked to call it. But it had been years since I'd visited this theme park, more than enough time for me to forget the reasons I didn't like riding this particular roller coaster.

Imagine having every molecule in your body unglued then tossed into a margarita blender. I had no idea what that would actually feel like, but it couldn't be any less pleasant than being nowhere and everywhere at once as Christy zapped us to The Source.

Fortunately, we all had a pretty good remembrance of that hell hole. It was a hard place to forget. There was the inner chamber, a massive underground cavern that housed The Source and had been the main home for Calibra and her legion of Jahabich slaves. That was probably where the big show was going on.

It was also likely where, if we simply popped in unannounced, we'd be gunned down before we could say a word to the contrary.

However, there was also an outer chamber, equally as massive, but separated by several narrow tunnels. It was doubtful that it would be entirely unguarded, but there would almost certainly be fewer people trying to kill us before we could express that we came in peace.

And I had to think they'd be expecting company, especially after Komak's botched abduction attempt. The bigger question was how pissed off they'd be to see us.

And then we were there ... except we weren't.

Oh crap!

The light from the spell faded and before us lay the seemingly infinite darkness of the void.

What the hell had just happened?

"Hold on a second."

A moment later, a sphere of dim light appeared, illuminating the fact that we were actually standing in what appeared to be a narrow cave.

Oh yeah. The Source was deep underground. And, minus any illumination, caves tended to be dark. Silly me. Guess I should've scoured Christy's junk drawer for a flashlight before heading down.

"Well, this is spooky as fuck all," Tom's said, nearly giving me a heart attack. In the dim light he was barely visible, nothing more than a shadow.

"So says the boogeyman," I muttered.

"Heh, you sound like you're huffing helium," he replied.

I guess that made sense since everyone else seemed to be talking slowly and deliberately, a side effect of the time spell. Albeit I didn't exactly feel better knowing I was heading into possible danger sounding like a chipmunk. I turned to Christy. "Are we..."

"Yes. We made it." Her voice was hushed despite the silence around us. "I shunted us to one of the tunnels branching off the outer chamber."

Probably a smart choice. If I remembered correctly, this was one of dozens of narrow tunnels which had once led to portals connected to ley lines at various points around the world, providing a near seamless transition between locations. One step you were where you'd been, and the next you were here ... all without realizing you'd moved thousands of miles.

Of course, that was the past. Now they were just an endless warren of passages that dead-ended on one side and hopefully led to the outer chamber on the other.

"Which way?" Kelly asked.

"Right hand rules, as any seasoned gamer can tell you." I turned in that direction. "Let's go."

"That would be a waste of time, my love," Gan said. "That way ends in a rock wall. Our quarry lay in the other direction."

"How do you..."

"I can smell them."

Oh, yeah. Forgot she could do that. "You could have just said that to begin with, you know."

It was yet another reminder that I was even more out of my depth now than I had been all those years ago.

31

PARLAYING IT ON THICK

"Tell the specter to conceal himself."

"Eh?" I asked.

"The revenant," Gan explained. "He will be more useful if his presence is not painfully apparent."

"She does have a point," Kelly said. "That trick with Komak only worked because he popped up out of nowhere."

I turned to Tom. "So ... can you switch yourself off?"

"How the fuck am I supposed to know?"

"Try."

"Fine." Tom squinted his eyes as if he were concentrating.

"You look like you're trying to take a dump. Just imagine yourself, I don't know, being invisible."

He nodded. "Yeah, like I was back at school trying to sneak into the girl's locker room." Then, upon seeing Christy's expression, he amended, "Or just because I want to be invisible."

Goddamn. Even dead, he was still a whipped moron.

Unfortunately, he was also still there. I turned to Christy, my eyebrows raised.

"Don't look at me," she said. "I've been working all week to make him visible, not the opposite."

Damnit.

"Duck down beneath the ground," Gan said. It was more command than suggestion. "That way you can move unseen"

"Yeah. I should be able to do that." Tom stared at the floor for several seconds, as if trying to figure it out, then he took a step and his foot sank, as if he were descending a hidden stairway. A few moments later and he was completely submerged, at least until he stuck his head out again. "Just for the record, this is really fucking weird."

"Because everything else going on is super normal?" I offered, to which he shrugged and popped back into the floor.

Now to hope the idiot didn't get lost. Fortunately, that wasn't likely. Far as I knew, he couldn't move further than maybe a dozen yards from the prism currently in my backpack.

A few minutes later, Gan paused, her head cocked to the side. "There's machinery ahead – generators, I believe."

Soon enough, the light at the end of the tunnel was upon us. Despite knowing what was likely waiting, I was glad to see it. Protective spell or not, I was starting to get winded.

There was no reason to be stealthy as we approached the mouth of the cave. This was a case where surprise could work against us, but fortunately we had witches to help with that.

As we neared the cave exit, the massive outer chamber partially visible beyond, Christy and Kelly worked their mojo. The latter conjured a purplish dome of energy in front of us, just in case, while Christy cast a spell that amplified her voice.

"WE HAVE COME SEEKING THE PROTEC-

TION OF PARLAY UNDER THE OLD WAYS. WE WISH TO NEGOTIATE WITH YOUR LEADERS."

Not quite how I would have put it, but probably for the best. "Give us Sally, you kidnapping cock-hamsters" likely wouldn't have won us any brownie points, hence why my chosen profession was programming, not hostage negotiations.

Several long seconds passed in which I nervously wondered if we were about to be hit with a concentrated Death Star beam by a dozen angry sorcerers. Go figure – plans like ours sounded awesome right up until you actually had to do them.

Finally, though, there came an answer, one not wrapped in death magic. A booming male voice replied, "PARLAY IS GRANTED. STEP FROM THE TUNNEL WITH YOUR HANDS RAISED. NO HARM WILL COME TO YOU SO LONG AS YOU OFFER NO RESISTANCE."

I glanced at Christy and she nodded, although I could see the uncertainty in her eyes. Something like this used to be law among her people. Now, all we could do was hope the other team was nostalgic enough to not blast us to bloody chunks.

Kelly dropped the force shield and we continued onward. There was no sign of Tom as we walked. Good. Now to hope he didn't pop his head out at the wrong moment and end up making us all ghosts.

I glanced over at Gan and saw her flex her hand. The nails on it momentarily extended into wicked claws before she retracted them again. She was playing nice for now, but no doubt readying herself in case the need to filet some wizards arose.

Maybe I should've worn a rain slicker for our trip down here.

As expected, the outer chamber wasn't empty by any stretch, but it wasn't exactly standing room only.

Half a dozen people met us as we stepped out. Five were aglow with energy, no doubt ready to blast us to atoms if we made the wrong move. One held an assault rifle, either a human who'd been recruited or another of those neo-vamps. Regardless, I didn't recognize any of...

What the fuck?!

I realized, after a moment, there was a seventh among their number. At first I thought it was maybe a shadow or trick of the light, but then I looked closer and saw it blink at me ... from about twenty different spots.

It was a blob of goo, about knee high, and filled with eyeballs of various sizes.

Needless to say, that was a bit unexpected.

But then I remembered what Gan had told us. Not every creature had been shunted back to where they belonged when The Source closed. There had been stragglers from elsewhere. Call me crazy, but that thing definitely looked like it was from out of town.

It must have noticed me staring – how could it not – because an air bubble appeared in its gelatinous body, floating to the surface where it popped, producing sound.

"It's the Freewill," it said, sounding like a drowning man gasping for one last breath. Talk about creepy.

"I can see that," the man with the gun – a tall fellow with five o'clock shadow, thick black hair, and an angular face, said. "We are honored by your presence." He blinked and his eyes turned yellow as he nodded toward Gan. "Prefect Gansetseg."

She, in turn, didn't even acknowledge him. What a surprise.

"You asked for parlay," one of the Magi, a middle-aged

male with thinning salt and pepper hair, said. "What do you wish to discuss?"

I opened my mouth before clamping it shut again. For a moment, it was as if the years melted away and I was the one expected to speak for my motley crew. But those days were dead and buried. This was Christy's expedition.

Now to only hope Gan understood that.

"We have come to speak to your leaders," Christy said, taking a single step forward, her voice formal. "We offer an exchange – that which you seek in return for one held prisoner."

"A prisoner?" the blob slurped. "We don't have any…"

"That'll be quite enough," the vamp interrupted before turning to Christy. "Please be more specific. I'd prefer to know what we're negotiating for before we decide whether or not to execute you right here."

"Parlay has been granted, Jasper," the Magi said. *Jasper?* We were talking to a vampire named Jasper? So much for the mind-numbing fear coursing through my veins. "I would ask you to honor it until such time as it is rescinded."

I personally would have let the two argue it out. Vamps and Magi historically had a kind of mutual don't-fuck-with-each-other policy. They didn't go out of their way to start shit but also weren't shy about murdering each other if it suited their needs.

Christy, however, proving she was the right person to lead this adventuring party, said, "I am the bearer of an incantation known to myself alone, one capable of augmenting the Icon's power and cracking through the veil to what lies beyond."

There came a beat of silence. Our theory about what was going on was exactly that, a theory. If they replied with, "Da fuq?" that would tell us we'd screwed up and had, in essence, given ourselves up to these assholes with absolutely zero leverage to show for it. Wouldn't that be the perfect cherry atop this shit sundae of a week?

"A way home?" the blob thing sputtered, the excited air bubbles of its speech splattering the floor around it. *Eww.*

It definitely didn't have much of a poker face, but that was probably because it didn't really have a face to begin with.

Finally, the Magi in charge spoke again. "You're Christine Fenton, correct?"

She nodded.

"I've heard of you. A lot of us have been wondering where you would stand in regards to our efforts. Very well. If what you say is true, then we will hear you out. But know that if you're planning any duplicity, you can expect no quarter in return. There are many here who do not speak fondly of your name."

The words were chilling, but she took it like a trooper. "I speak true."

Can't say I or my former roommates would have been so neutral on the subject, but that's probably why Ed was on the surface, Tom was stuck in the floor, and I was doing my damnedest to keep my fucking mouth shut.

Unsurprisingly, they relieved me of Sheila's sword before leading us away. However, I took some small bit of amusement in seeing that none of them – mage or vamp – was all too eager to touch it. In the end, the high-muckety mage ordered one of his minions to carry it, much to the poor guy's apparent chagrin.

I took the time to look around. The folks who'd commandeered this cavern had been busy. Heavy duty electrical wire ran everywhere. Some were connected to work lights while others led off into the darkness to points unseen. As we walked, there came a massive flash of light about twenty yards to our left, followed by a tanker truck bearing the ExxonMobil logo appearing out of thin air.

Guess that was one way to keep the generators running. Christy was right. When the magic was flowing again, it was apparently a minor issue for the Magi to keep this place supplied. Judging by the multiple stacks of crates we spied along the way, the people here were ready to go the distance.

I dared a glance back over my shoulder and an involuntary shudder passed through me at the expected sight of dozens upon dozens of tunnels lining the far wall of this chamber. All of them were pitch dark, offering the promise of any of a thousand horrific nightmares, although they probably led to nothing more than dead ends these days.

All except one, that is. One tunnel to the far right was aglow with light. Several people stood guard at its entrance.

"Hey Gan," I whispered under my breath. "Do you think that's the..."

"It is," she replied, no doubt anticipating the rest.

If I was reading her right, that tunnel was the one which led up to Damascus ... a place I actually had no interest in visiting.

"No talking," Jasper the vamp warned. Five years of living as a human was apparently not enough to erase centuries of being an asshole.

Big surprise there.

We were about three quarters through the chamber, massive as it was, when I suddenly realized I had a lot more spring in my step. It was as if I'd been wearing weighted clothes and had stripped them all off ... minus actually whipping my dick out. At the same time, the voices of our captors seemed to rise both in pitch and speed.

The pulse had ended as abruptly as it had begun.

Almost as if in response, half the Magi leading the way drew guns from their sides.

Maybe I'm crazy, stupid, or both but – despite their weapons – the threat of regular people seemed to pale compared to what they could do when the juice was flowing. Yeah, it made no sense for me to be emboldened, but then I never claimed to make much sense.

Fuck it.

"Yo, Jasper," I said, trying to keep the smirk out of my voice. "What's your story? I mean, what were you doing before the shit hit the fan ... you know, human to human?"

For a moment, I wasn't sure if he would answer or simply shoot me in the face and be done with it. But he actually glanced back and replied, "If you must know, I was the second in my coven."

Where at?"

"Cambridge."

"What happened?"

"The Destroyer happened," he replied before turning back.

He didn't need to explain. Vehron the Destroyer had cut a swath of destruction from New York to Boston, decimating covens along the way and *recruiting* them for his master, Calibra.

It was perhaps best to not mention *I* was one-hundred percent responsible for that happening.

That was fine. There was no real need for more words as we reached the far end of the chamber and entered another narrow tunnel. This one I remembered well. Where there were dozens, maybe hundreds, along the outer wall, there were only a small handful on this end.

And they all led to the cavern that would either prove to be our salvation or final resting place: The Source chamber.

32

CRAZY EX-GIRLFRIEND

Stepping from the tunnel into the vast chamber beyond was like falling into a nightmare from the past.

When last I'd been here, I'd been lucky to make it out. Not all of my friends had been so fortunate, including the one who was hopefully still hidden by the rocky floor beneath our feet.

As we emerged, I half expected to see the grinning stalagmite teeth and jack-o-lantern eyes of the Jahabich waiting for me, knowing if that happened I'd have likely screamed like a little bitch and shit myself.

Thankfully, my companions were spared that display of raw manliness.

I blinked and the past retreated into the far corners of my memory where it belonged, allowing me to behold what had become of this place.

Missing, thank goodness, was the perpetual blood-red twilight The Source had once cast upon this cavern, aglow for time immemorial ... at least until I'd come along. What can I say? I used to have a nasty tendency for fucking things up.

The Source had once lay at the far end of this cavern. Now it was merely a massive depression in the ground – an empty lakebed – the earth beneath it cracked and dry.

However, this place wasn't as devoid of power as I'd thought. Above us, scattered throughout the ceiling, twinkling lights could be seen – crystals or bioluminescent lichen maybe. Those lights had been in the process of dying last time I'd been down here, slowly plunging this cavern into perpetual darkness. But now they were once again aglow, a testament to the fact that the assholes fucking around down here had been at least partially successful.

If that natural luminescence was the main source of illumination, I wouldn't have been able to see much, but more of those high-powered work lights were scattered about, illuminating the small tent city that presumably housed the cavern's current residents.

I'd been half expecting to find an army of angry Magi waiting for us, but maybe that was just my imagination running wild. That said, this cavern was definitely busier than the outside one. And, judging from the small sample of beings walking about, more varied, too. Just for the record, though, aside from a pair of oversized bipedal otters, nothing seemed to come close to the blob of eyes still slithering alongside us.

Speaking of ... *it*, more of those air bubbles formed inside its body, bubbling to the surface where they created the equivalent of words, just a lot more gross.

"Is it true what they say about you, Freewill?"

"My love is legendary in his feats," Gan replied from beside me, close enough to remind me of a bad rash.

Ugh! Ignoring her, I glanced down at the creature to find half a dozen eyeballs staring at me. Damn, this thing was freaky as fuck. "Depends what they say."

The thing quivered in place for a moment, then it

slurped out some more words. "They say you slaughtered dozens, maybe hundreds of the Feet singlehandedly." There was a breathy quality to its voice that hadn't been there before, as if it were nervous or excited.

The Magi who'd been leading us turned toward Blobby. "That will be enough, Glen. This is serious business. Please don't drop your guard."

Glen?! The blob's name was Glen? Sure, why the fuck not?

I looked down to find most of its eyes fixed straight ahead. But one or two swiveled in its gelatinous mass to stare up at me. Oh, what the hell?

"We can talk later if we get the chance, but I'd be happy to tell you about the time I dropped the mother of all Turds."

Kelly snickered from up ahead of me. Even Christy dared a glance back my way, one eyebrow raised.

Sue me. Terrifying as some of my memories were, they were also pretty fucking ridiculous, too.

Last time I'd been here, I'd gotten some serious shade from just about everything present. Being the legendary Freewill had come with a few perks, but it mostly seemed to be a giant "kick me" sign stapled to my back. However, as we walked, I found myself split.

A part of me was disturbed to see the angry stares pointed in my girlfr ... err, Christy's direction. But I can't lie. A small slice of my subconscious was kind of relieved to see it directed at someone other than me for a change. Besides, once the juice was flowing again, Christy could handle herself against just about anyone looking to talk smack.

We stepped around what appeared to be a communications array — they really had gone all in with this endeavor — and I caught a clearer view of the empty lakebed that had once been The Source.

Or maybe not so empty. In the middle of it stood a single tent, away from all of the others.

Though I didn't see any movement near it, I could guess who it belonged to and it gave credence that Gan had been right all along, damn the luck.

Goddamn it, Sheila. What the fuck are you thinking?

"Oh my God," Kelly said. "Can you feel it?"

"Feel what?" I asked, pulled from my darkening thoughts.

"The power flowing through this place, through the people here." She twirled her fingers and a small ribbon of flame appeared above her hand, despite the fact that we were between pulses. All at once, our escorts turned toward her, weapons raised.

"Oh, crap!" Kelly quickly doused the flame. "Sorry. It's just..."

"Been so long?" the wizard leading us replied, not unkindly. "Catalysts such as yourself feel it most strongly in this place, attuned as you are to external energy. It's like missing a limb, only to wake one day and find it regrown."

She nodded, obviously following his rambling discourse. That was fine for her, but I was a little less forgiving of the fact that they'd nearly ventilated my friend.

I stepped in front of her. "Y'know, you could have just warned us without stuffing a bunch of guns in her... oof!"

Jasper slammed the butt of his rifle into my gut, dropping me to my knees. On the upside, without one of those pulses going on, it simply hurt instead of outright impaling me. "That's enough talk."

Beside me, Gan tensed up. Much as I might have enjoyed watching her feed this guy his own weapon rectally, it would have put a serious damper on any plans to end this peacefully. I grabbed her hand, more than aware that I was probably going to regret it later. "Don't."

"As you wish, my love," she replied in a cool voice.

"Really?" the head Magi asked, a touch of disapproval in his voice as he addressed Jasper. "Was that necessary?"

"Don't lecture me, Hershel. We're not here to make friends with these people. Don't forget what happened up top. They killed Abner."

"I am well aware," Hershel, presumably, replied. "Do not forget two of my brothers also failed to return. But, unlike you, I'm willing to allow that unfortunate misunderstandings are to be expected."

Unfortunate mis...

Glen the blob slithered over to me, air bubbles popping out from the surface of his slime. "Are you okay, Freewill?"

Gross as he was, his concern was almost cute. "No worries," I replied with more bravado than was warranted. "It takes more than that to take out the mighty Freewill."

"Oh, for fuck's sake," came a barely audible murmur from somewhere below my feet.

"What was that?" Hershel asked, one eyebrow raised.

Hoping to cover for my ghost-tard of a friend, I replied, "Sorry, clearing my throat."

Thankfully, nobody's super hearing was working at the moment.

"Let's keep moving," he said after a moment when nobody else offered up any objections. "The sooner we can conclude this business, the better it will be for us all."

I wasn't sure if it was because of Glen's attitude toward me or something else — especially since I was pretty sure the two-legged members of this party could do it faster — but Hershel looked down at him. "Go and fetch the Icon. She'll want to hear this."

And just like that, eyeball blobs and angry vamps aside, I had a feeling my day was about to get even more stressful.

Glen veered away from us, moving at a speed that one might expect from the equivalent of a three foot slug. I figured we'd be lucky if he returned with Sheila before we all died of old age.

However, as we were steered into a tent much larger than the rest, I began to suspect that was purposeful.

Inside, I saw a tack board full of charts and graphs. There was also a whiteboard covered in what appeared to be times and geological coordinates. I wasn't exactly a tactical genius, but even I could tell this was a working command center.

A row of folding tables sat at one end. Several people were already seated behind them including – surprise of surprises – our old buddies Komak and Liz. To say they didn't look happy to see us was an understatement. I couldn't exactly blame him. Vamps didn't like to lose, especially those who'd once worked for the First Coven. Failure simply wasn't an option for that bunch. As for Liz, well, maybe she just didn't like us.

A couple of others – either vamps or Magi, I couldn't tell – sat with them. There was also at least one non-human among their number, a winged, four-armed imp. I'd seen his species before, although obviously it had been a while.

We were led to a spot in front of the table. There, Hershel and Jasper left our side to take seats with the others. The rest spread out behind us, no doubt to kill our asses if things went south.

It served as a harsh reminder that I was far more vulnerable than during my last visit here. It would probably be best to keep my tongue in check.

What the fuck had we been thinking? We'd marched right in and surrendered, and for what ... a fucking pipe dream that these guys would play nice once we gave them what they wanted?

Holy fucking shit. Why is it that bad ideas were never painfully obvious until it was too late? "Um, I don't suppose you guys have a bathroom down here?"

"Latrine's out back," Komak said without much humor. "But I think that can wait."

Fine, be that way. I at least comforted myself in knowing that if I shit my pants out of fear, it would be epic.

Liz glared at Christy. "Are you finally ready to admit that you want your life back?"

"No. But I am ready to admit that I'm outmatched. Know that I do this only to protect my daughter."

"Don't be so sanctimonious..."

"Wait," Hershel said. "Her daughter? What does she have to do with..."

Komak held up a hand. "Later. Let's stay on point for now." He locked eyes on Christy. "Is it safe to assume you figured things out on your own?"

She nodded. "The ley lines."

"Lizzy knew you would. She seems to hold you in high regard."

"Could've fooled me," I said.

The imp stood and stared at me, his eyes black coals in his oblong head. "Why are *you* here, Freewill? Is it to give us the..."

"The spell on the wall?" Christy replied. "You know as well as we do that it's useless to your cause."

"Useless? What do you mean?"

Liz put a hand on his shoulder, causing him to ruffle his wings ever so slightly. "Sorry, Ux, but things have been ... busy. We've since learned that the spell we sought was only a precursor to what was actually needed. It required further ... refinement."

"Refinement that you don't have time for," Christy added, "and which I've already done."

"I see," the imp, Ux, replied, taking his seat again.

"What she said," I added lamely. "I'm just here for moral support."

There came a beat of silence as everyone stared at me. So much for keeping my mouth shut.

Finally, Gan broke the impasse by, of course, changing subjects to something I was pretty sure nobody cared about.

"So is this your so-called Last Coven?" She glanced at Komak, then Jasper. "I sense only two of you. Or have you invited these Magi to sit..."

"The others are in the field," Jasper replied, his eyes narrowed. "Unlike the First Coven, we don't sit on our accolades and let others do our dirty work."

"A new day dawns," Komak said. "It's a chance to rebuild our world from the ground up, but the right way this time, with cooperation. Pity you don't seem to understand that. You could have been a part of it all, but now, thanks to you, there's only twelve of our number left."

Gan raised an eyebrow. "Oh?"

"If you're hoping for an invitation, I'm sorry, but I think our sire will make a better candidate."

"The Progenitor?" Gan asked, barely concealed amusement on her face. Oh yeah. She might have filled out, but she hadn't mellowed at all. At her core, she'd always be an arrogant little psychopath. At least now, assuming everything worked out as planned, I could sleep better knowing that she'd do the world a favor one day and die of old age.

"Yes, where is he?"

"Ed?" I shrugged. "He had some errands to run. Groceries to buy, a little girl to keep safe from you fuckers, that sort of thing."

"No matter. We'll find him once this is..."

"Hold on," Hershel interrupted. "That's the second time they said that. Did you endanger a child?"

Komak turned to the mage, but Liz spoke first. "You knew she stood against the White Mother, Hershel."

"As well as I understand the returned White Mother had become ... erratic in her teachings."

Erratic? That was one way of saying it. Talk about putting lipstick on a five-thousand year old pig.

Liz nodded. "Perhaps, but this witch was almost directly responsible for plunging our world into the darkness we have lived in ever since."

"I am well aware..."

"You have to understand, we needed to ensure her cooperation. Failure was *not* an option."

"But a child?" Hershel asked, visibly disturbed. He wasn't alone. Both Ux and one of the other mages in their number also didn't appear to like what they were hearing.

The group began to squabble among themselves. Guess all wasn't wine and roses in the new order. It began to paint a picture. All of these yahoos were aiming for the same goal. Problem was, some of their go-getters were a bit more extreme in their methods.

But I also saw they'd kept the others in the dark about it, no doubt hoping that the ends justified the means.

It gave me cause to hope that at least a few of these guys might not be in favor of going trigger happy on us once we gave them what they wanted. If so...

There came the rustle of a tent flap behind us. I glanced back to check it out and immediately felt my train of thought go flying off the rails.

Sheila stood there glaring at us all, an unreadable expression on her face.

She put her hands on her hips. "What have you done?"

33

TEST OF FAITH

"We've been waiting for you," Komak said, indicating an empty seat at his end of the table.

The surreal aspect of the entire situation was only augmented by a vampire offering the Icon a seat instead of ordering her killed.

We truly did live in strange days.

"I asked a question." Sheila stood there unmoving. Her blonde hair was up in a ponytail and she wore functional work fatigues, looking more like an archeologist than a warrior of faith. Though her expression remained neutral, I could see in her eyes ours was a reunion she hadn't been looking forward to.

I couldn't imagine why. I mean, she'd only dumped my ass, then set about kicking down a door that we'd all shed blood, sweat, and tears locking in the first place. Surely that wasn't reason for this to be awkward.

Oh well. Sue me for being petty but – unlike some folks in this room – I was only human.

Nobody said anything for several long seconds – a Mexican standoff at the Earth's core.

My former infatuation with Sheila was over and done with, mostly. Don't get me wrong, she looked pretty good doing a Lara Croft impersonation. It was more what had happened that had me all in a kerfuffle. Ending up single again had sucked, but I couldn't say it wasn't a road I hadn't walked before. And hey, I'd rebounded pretty darn well, even if those waters were currently looking a bit muddied. Being back down here again, though, was a bit harder to swallow, made more bitter by the fact that she'd had a hand in it.

The impasse was finally broken as Glen came oozing in to, err, quiver at her side like the world's freakiest Jell-O mold. The multitude of eyes in his body all blinked excitedly. "I don't know if it's too much to ask, but is there any chance you two could reenact your epic battle? I would so love to get a picture for my album."

Something was telling me that I'd somehow attracted a seriously weird fanboy.

Sheila looked down at him. "Not now, Glen."

"Oh. Sorry."

Christy apparently had enough of this. She pushed past me and headed toward Sheila.

The guards in the back raised their weapons, until Sheila turned to them. "What are you doing? Put those down."

"Belay that order," Komak said. "They're under protection of parlay, but make no mistake, they're not here as friends."

"And I wonder why that is," I replied. "Oh, yeah. It's because you threatened a small child, beat the hell out of my friend here, and murdered a bunch of innocent people. And let's not forget kidnapping..."

"Enough!" He locked eyes with me. "As the least important member of these negotiations, I will remind you that you no longer have anything we need. I call you

Freewill as a reminder of your past, but don't think you hold any sway because of it. Your presence here is superfluous at best."

I half expected Gan to make him eat his own tongue, but she held her ground. Oddly enough, she was keeping her cool, small miracle that it was.

"I agree," Sheila said, her gaze locking on Komak. "That *is* enough. Is he talking about Tina? She's five years old, for God's sake."

"You didn't know?" Kelly asked.

"Of course not," she replied. "They were supposed to approach Bill for the spell we needed. Barring that, the plan was to..."

"Attack Sally?" I offered.

Her eyes opened wide. "No! Ask her."

"Didn't really work out that way."

"What the hell is going on?" She stepped in further and faced Christy. "You have to believe me. I'm trying to help these people, but I would never condone..."

Christy slapped her across the face before she could say more. Can't entirely say she was in the wrong. "The road to hell is paved with good intentions." She lowered her voice. "You picked the wrong friends, and they put my little girl in danger."

"Yeah, you tell her, babe!" Tom said, popping his head up from the floor.

Oh, fuck me sideways with a blender.

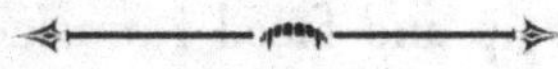

Two of the guards opened fire at Tom's dumbass reappearance. The bullets passed through him and hit the ground, thankfully not ricocheting into someone else ... like me.

"Cease fire!" Komak ordered. "I should have known this was rigged."

If Christy's slap was a surprise to Sheila, Tom's appearance was a sledgehammer to the face. Her jaw practically dropped to the floor, a grab bag of emotions passing through her face in the space of seconds. "How? It's not..."

Tom, seemingly pleased with himself, replied, "Oh yeah! I am Powermaster Optimus Prime, bitches. Just when you think the Decepticons have won, I return and kick everyone's ass."

I glanced down at him, nonplussed. "I would have gone with bad penny myself."

"That's because you're a small-dicked loser."

"B-but, how?" Sheila asked, horror dawning on her face as the modicum of authority she'd exuded upon her arrival slipped away. It was a far cry from her old confidence as the Icon, "How are you ... you ... Tina ..."

Despite being at the mercy of a group not entirely friendly to our cause, I immediately felt better at seeing her surprise. Whatever she'd come in here expecting, this wasn't it. I knew Sheila. She wasn't this good of an actress. I wasn't dumb enough to think her hands were entirely clean here, but seeing she hadn't been the one to give Komak his marching orders was a sizable weight off my chest.

"None of *this* was supposed to happen," Sheila continued, more to herself than anyone. "All I was trying to do was fix the lives I destroyed."

Hershel stood up and faced Komak. "As am I. There had better be a very good explanation for all of this."

"Yes, Ernest," Sheila added. "There had better be. All we needed was the spell. There was no reason to hurt anyone."

"The spell is useless," Liz snapped. "It's the wrong one. You, the all-powerful Icon, were wrong about it."

"But…"

"And we don't have the time to refine it ourselves. So we did what needed to be done. End of story."

"But how could you even know that?"

Ignoring Komak's assertion that I was the tits on this bull, I added my two cents. "Because they kidnapped Sally and ripped the information from her mind."

When nobody said anything to the contrary, Sheila pointed a finger at him. "Is this true?"

"I judged her unlikely to cooperate," he said. "So we took what we wanted. Sadly, it wasn't what we needed."

I turned to him. "Is she…"

"Let her go, *now*," Sheila interrupted, obviously feeling more optimistic than I was.

"No," Komak stated flatly.

"What do you mean, no?" Ux cried. "The council did not agree to this."

"Yes you did. You all did. The moment you signed on to this endeavor. You want to go home, see your people again. Same with Glen. And you, Hershel, you've been in and out of rehab these last five years, desperate to get your old life back."

"He's right," Liz said, standing up. "Unspoken or not, we all knew what we were getting into."

"But this is…"

"Exactly what you bargained for," Jasper replied, sounding way too smug for my personal tastes. "And I offer the mosque above us as proof. None of you had a problem with that."

He kind of had a point there. What they'd done in order to reach this place was kind of hard to write off as an oops.

Liz nodded. "So don't any of you get on your high horses now. We all knew we'd need to get our hands dirty, probably more than once. Even if you didn't pull the trigger, none of you did anything to stop it from happening."

"This is intolerable!" Ux banged one wispy, um, pincer on the table. "You can't do things like this without consulting the rest of us first. And I won't be a part of it."

It was like standing in the middle of a bunch of YouTube commenters. Much as I liked to see infighting amongst the other team, it wasn't doing much to get us what we needed.

I held up my hands, more as a peace gesture than surrendering. "Okay, I think we get it. None of us are the good guys, not even us."

"Speak for yourself," Tom said.

"No comments from the ectoplasm gallery. I'm trying to make a point here. We just want our friend back. No tricks. No deception."

Komak raised an eyebrow.

"Okay, except for him, but he's a ghost. What's he really going to do?"

"Bill's right," Kelly said. "What's done is done. We can't change that, but we can still move forward and make this a win-win for everyone. We have the spell you need. Give us our friend and it's yours. We won't stop you. Heck, I'm not going to lie and say I'd mind getting some of my mojo back."

The people on either side of us were silent as they continued to glare back and forth. I could tell there was unfinished business here, but that was their problem. I just wanted to rescue my friend and get the hell out of here.

"How do we know this isn't a trick?" Komak finally asked. He might've been stone cold with his poker face, but I could see hope glimmering in his girlfriend's eyes. I had a feeling we were almost there.

Jasper turned to him. "Surely they would know…"

"That if we fucked you over, we'd end up filled with

lead?" I interrupted. "Yeah, been there, done that. Don't forget, I dealt with the First Coven, too. I know how this shit works." Then, realizing my tone might have been a tad more aggressive than intended, I pointed toward the wizard still holding Sheila's sword. "Besides, if we were planning on screwing you guys over, we wouldn't have brought the Icon a peace offering as a show of, dare I say it, good faith."

Sheila turned toward the weapon, her eyes wide. "You kept it?"

"How could I not?"

"Yeah," Tom added. "Fucking thing's worth a mint. You don't just throw shit like that away."

Goddamn it all. Was it too much to hope his batteries ran out anytime soon?

34

GREEN-EYED MONSTER

Things were still tense as we headed back toward the outer chamber, but it wasn't nearly as bad as it could have been. We had definitely moved the doomsday clock back a few minutes as evidenced by the fact that we weren't all bullet-ridden corpses.

That didn't mean they trusted us by any means, but whatever the fuck.

Liz and Jasper had stayed behind to start prepping the mages for the final pulse, the last ley line, the one that would make or break this deal, or at least they claimed. Personally, I hadn't been counting.

The rest of their leadership, friend and foe alike, accompanied us to make good on the first part of the deal: freeing Sally.

Komak had tried to convince Sheila to go prepare, too, but she wasn't having any of it. However, she did send Glen ahead with her sword, instructing him – after plunging the weapon, scabbard and all, into his goopy form – to place it in her tent. Hopefully she had plenty of wet wipes in there to clean it off with afterward.

We mostly marched in silence. Even Tom seemed to

have little to say. Talk about awkward. As far as reunions went, I'd have sooner attended my high school one and I mostly hated that place.

After several minutes of uncomfortable quiet, Kelly decided to cut the tension by sidling up to Sheila. "How are you doing?"

"I've been better."

"I know the feeling."

Sheila turned and looked at her, sorrow etched on her face. "I don't think sorry begins to cover this."

Kelly, however, smiled. "It's a start. So ... how are things down here?"

Sheila nodded, no doubt grateful for the change in subject. "Boring mostly. The shower facilities suck, and don't even get me started on chemical toilets."

"That's fucking gross," Tom replied, keeping pace with us now that the secret of his presence was thoroughly blown. "Although I have to admit I do miss the joy of a good shit."

I let out a sigh. "Thanks for sharing."

"Anytime, bro."

"I know this is going to sound ... wrong." Sheila turned to him, a wide-eyed stare still on her face. I guess I couldn't blame her. Last time she'd seen him, she'd been busy plunging a sword through his chest. "But how are you here? I thought ... we all thought..."

Christy stepped forward. For a moment, I thought she might lay into Sheila again, but she appeared to have calmed down. "We all did. But then he appeared. Turns out he's been here all along. We just didn't know. And..." She took a deep breath. "We never would have if you hadn't started this." After a moment, she added, "Sorry about earlier. You have to understand..."

"Don't," Sheila replied. "I deserved it. There's no

excuse for what happened, and I have to take responsibility for it. I could have..."

"Asked me yourself instead of sending the goon squad girl scouts to my door?" I offered.

The look on her face suggested she knew her apologies were not even remotely done for the day. "You would have said no."

"You don't know that... Okay, fine. I would have. But you could have at least tried."

She shook her head. "No. I couldn't. I didn't want to see you." No doubt realizing what she'd implied, she quickly added, "Not like that. But I knew you'd talk me out of it. And I didn't want you to. I was trying to hold on to that same sense of purpose I had when I was the Icon. But it's not that easy now. That unearthly confidence, it turns on and off with the flow of the ley lines. One moment I'm certain this is the right path. The next..."

"This *is* the right path," Komak said with a surety she didn't have.

"Perhaps, although we may have to disagree on the methods involved," Ux said, a note of disgust in his voice, even if his weird imp face was unreadable.

"When we're finished, the world will be a better place. Just wait and see."

I chuckled. "For some of us."

"Why not for everyone?" he asked, actually sounding serious. "The old ways are dead and so are those who enforced them. They're the ones who made the world the way it was, divided – one half in the light yet ignorant, the other confined to the shadows. We have a chance to change those rules, enlighten the denizens of this world as to its true nature."

"I disagree," Hershel said. "The Magi will not be strong enough if the humans turn against us again."

"This isn't the Dark Ages anymore."

"I'm going to assume you don't use Twitter often," I replied.

Sheila watched us as we talked. "I just want the sadness, the suicides, to end. I want to wake up and not feel all of those lives I destroyed."

I looked hard at her. We'd discussed what cracking open The Source a smidgeon could do for vamps and mages but hadn't considered what it might do to her. If I had to guess, it wouldn't affect her much physically, but perhaps subconsciously she longed for enough of that old self confidence to stop second-guessing herself ... maybe even allow herself the happiness I began to suspect she didn't think she deserved.

I noted the sleeves on her shirt were rolled up, the scars crisscrossing her left arm plainly visible – scars I'd given her during our final battle all those years ago. She'd suffered permanent nerve damage as a result, but I realized she probably could've healed herself during those pulses, yet hadn't. But maybe that was the point. Those scars were more than skin deep.

And what about me? I'd been so happy to be in a relationship with her that I hadn't noticed any of it. Maybe a part of this was my fault. If I'd been a better listener and less of a self-absorbed douche, perhaps this could have been...

Tom stepped past me to walk beside her despite there not being enough room . One of the benefits of being a ghost was apparently not giving a shit about personal space. "Y'know, I've had a bit of time to think the last couple of years while everyone was busy ignoring me."

"We weren't ignoring you," I said.

"Whatever." He turned back toward her. "Anyway, the truth is, I'm cool with it. You should be, too. Most of the people who were down here when we blew the fuck out of this place were dicks. Fuck them."

Needless to say, our *gracious hosts* all glared at him, the looks on their faces ranging from outrage to anger.

I raised a hand to the bridge of my nose. Why the hell did we think bringing him along was a good idea?

"It was the right thing to do," he continued, oblivious. "Even ganking me, which you actually didn't. But if I had to do it all over again ... well, I'd try to figure out a way that didn't involve having to watch Bill getting all cozy with my woman while I was invisible, but if I couldn't find one, then I'd do it the same way."

Oh fuck!

Both Gan and Sheila glanced toward me, eyebrows raised. So much for dead men telling no tales.

"What?" I asked, doing my best to play dumb. "I'm her godfather. Of course I'm going to spend time with Tina. She needs positive..." *and not fucking dumbass* "...male role models in her life."

"That's not what I..."

Thankfully, Christy was there for the save. "Where are you taking us?"

"To retrieve your friend, of course," Komak replied. "We had to keep her ... segregated from the rest."

Hershel and Ux didn't seem overly appreciative of that, but arguing was likely pointless, especially since we – and probably they – had no idea who was on Komak's side. It was possible that most of the folks down here were in the hippy camp, assuming this was all lollypops and sugarplum fairies. I mean, Glen the blob had sure as hell seemed surprised, so why not others?

At the same time, Komak didn't strike me as stupid. I had a feeling that the majority of those *escorting* us to hopefully wherever Sally was were firmly in his employ.

I wondered how many in my group realized that. Gan almost certainly. She was usually about ten moves ahead of me in the chess game of life. Christy probably, too.

Tom, no. But at least he was immune to bullets.

We were led into the far more sparsely manned outer chamber. If they decided to try anything out here...

No. That was paranoid. I needed to remember that these fuck-weasels wanted their precious spell. Without it, they'd get dick all.

Of course, only Christy knew how to cast it. The rest of us weren't worth jack shit to them.

Oh yeah, gotta love positive thinking.

"Let's hurry," Komak said. "The time is near. The final ley line is almost ready to be harvested. You should go and get ready, Sheila."

"I'll get ready once I see that my friend is okay."

"As you wish, *Shining One*. Although I must warn you, we still have a ways to go."

Komak steered us in the direction of the countless side tunnels. Smart. One could have held a hundred prisoners in them and nobody would have been the wiser.

Surprisingly, though, it was the one lit tunnel out of all of them – the one leading back to the surface – that he guided us toward.

Bundles of heavily shielded cables ran into it – power for lights and probably communications too. Pity that wiring wasn't the only thing inhabiting it. There were armed guards inside, too. Lots of them. There was a pair stationed maybe every ten yards.

And Komak had been right – this was no short jaunt. We kept walking and walking, passing more and more guards. I had little doubt they were mostly Magi, but none were taking any chances in the defense department. That meant there was a *lot* of firepower in this cave, perhaps enough to overrun the rest of the place if anyone balked at their leader's methods.

I did a quick calculation in my head as we walked. Far as I could tell, I'd seen a lot more people down here than in that video Gan had shown us. Either they'd been merely the advance force or others had been recruited along the way – a prospect that, judging by even Kelly's response to this, might not have been all that difficult.

We walked for maybe twenty more minutes. The tunnel was broken up every so often by larger chambers inside, big enough for supply caches, but for the most part it was a slog as the path gradually sloped uphill. Thank goodness that final pulse hadn't hit yet, because otherwise – even with Christy's magic charm – there was little chance of me making it.

However, just as I was beginning to rue that normal me was starting to get winded, I spied something up ahead that perked me back up.

There were lights, a small platoon of guards, and what looked like mounted weaponry bolted to the floor the cave.

But it was what lay beyond that really caught my eye. A solid wall of rock, a dead end, but driven into that rock were two pairs of manacles.

And attached to them, pinned to the wall, was Sally!

35

SEGUEING TO THE FINALE

The guards tensed as we approached, but thankfully Komak called out for them to stand down. That was good, because the rest of us had already started racing toward our imprisoned friend. Being gunned down in sight of her would have been the height of embarrassment.

Sally's head hung low, but as we approached, calling her name, she raised it up to look our way.

She was alive, but she looked like shit.

Whatever cuts or abrasions she'd suffered during her abduction had been cleaned and bandaged, but I could still see evidence that she'd been worked over. Both her eyes were blackened and a section of hair on the side of her head had been burnt away, the scarred skin beneath it raw and ugly.

Worst, perhaps, was the glazed look in her eyes. It was almost the same as if she'd been compelled, although that was something these new vamps weren't capable of. So that meant magic.

"Unchain her," Sheila ordered, her voice cracking, a

shell of the former authority she once commanded as the Icon.

The rest of us gathered around Sally. She blinked a few times, then finally appeared to notice us. "About ... fucking time."

"I said release her!"

Komak nodded and two of the guards left their station to do as they were told. As Sally was freed, I stepped in to support her, looping her arm over my shoulder.

Christy stepped in front of us and stared into Sally's eyes, her gaze unreadable. Finally, she said, "We need to get her out of here."

"Hold on..."

She rounded on Komak. "No, *you* hold on. I said we need to get her out of here and I meant it. No negotiations while we're still in this tunnel. And if you don't like it, you can..."

"Come on." Sheila positioned herself on Sally's other side to help me support her. "We can talk more once we're back in the main chamber."

Sally glanced at her groggily and then turned toward Tom, her eyes widening as much as they were capable. "I see ... the gang's all here."

Yep. We were one big family again. Problem was, I had a feeling *happy* didn't exactly fit into the equation.

"They dug pretty deep, didn't they?" Kelly asked, examining Sally closer once we were back in the outer chamber.

I'd given Sally the Cliff's Notes version of Tom's resurrection along the way to help pass the time – leaving out a few key details due to the presence of unfriendly ears.

Now that we were out, I wasn't sure our position was

any better. We were still trapped deep underground. The only difference was we had more room to maneuver if need be. But hey, if Komak decided to plug us now, at least his people might need to aim a bit.

Christy nodded. "Yeah. They definitely forced their way in and went deeper than they should have. But I think she'll be okay."

"It was necessary," Komak replied, his tone betraying no emotion. "You should be proud of your friend. She put up a hell of a fight. It took three Magi to finally pull the spell out."

"Proud?" Christy hissed. "You raped her mind."

"We did what we had to. We didn't know that the spell she had was useless." He grinned, looking predatory despite the lack of fangs. "But you're here now. So in the end, it all worked out."

"Not yet."

Uh oh. I was afraid she might do this.

"I will remind you," Komak said, his tone turning dangerous, "we have a deal struck under parlay."

"You yourself said the old ways are dead."

"And you are heavily outnumbered. I could easily have those chains filled again, with you this time."

Sheila made to speak, but Christy held up a hand. "And what would that get you?"

"You think your will is stronger than hers?"

"Like ... hell," Sally sputtered, apparently too far out of it to understand things like basic diplomacy.

"Ask anyone here who knows me." Christy glanced at a few of the Magi present. "Mind magic is one of my specialties."

"So?"

"So," Gan replied, speaking up, a smile on her face. "Did you think the witch would come down here without having put precautions into place?"

I turned to her. "Precautions?"

Christy didn't seem pleased at Gan's revelation, but she nodded. "A kill switch. You try taking what isn't yours and you'll end up with nothing."

From the look on Kelly's face, she didn't seem surprised by this either. I so hated being left in the dark. "Um, kill switch as in wiping the spell from memory?" I asked.

"No," Gan explained. "A protective ward – a construct, if you will – placed inside her waking mind, designed to destroy it all."

I was kind of afraid that's what she meant.

"Whoa. Hardcore," Tom muttered.

That was an understatement. I turned to her. "Are you insane?"

Christy smiled sadly at me. "Not at all. I simply stacked the deck. And I'm not convinced I want to run the risk of any of this happening again. We sacrificed too much to go back to the way things were." She glanced toward Tom. "No matter how much I might want to."

"You sound like you've already made up your mind."

When she spoke again, however, the steel in her voice had melted away. "I thought I had."

"Not following," Tom said. That made two of us.

Christy ignored him, though, turning toward Ux and Hershel. "You just want to go home. And all you're asking for is a second chance at life." Finally, she glared at Komak. "If they'd all been like you, I would have made sure you ended up with nothing. I have no desire to see monsters such as yourself in power ever again. But I believe now that the majority of those down here have good intentions." She turned to Sheila and put a hand on her shoulder.

Hershel nodded. "We do."

"Home," Ux said quietly, his eyes moist ... although that might've just been his natural state.

Komak, for his part, kept his cool. "So you'll hold up your end?"

"Yes, but there are conditions."

"Absolutely not."

"Fine. Then kill us all. You'll get nothing."

I shared a glance with Tom, who shrugged. Asshole. He knew bullets wouldn't do dick against him. Mind you, if we bought it, he'd be stuck here for all of eternity with nothing but dirt to keep him company.

"Be reasonable," Hershel said.

Christy's conditions had been both simple and direct. Komak and his people needed to step down. She wanted him and his followers disarmed, including the jackboots guarding the passage out of here. Once that was done, she would conduct the ritual with a circle of three other Magi: Kelly, Hershel, and Liz. I had a feeling that last one was a bit of extra insurance. If something went south, Christy could ensure Liz went down with the rest of us.

Following the completion of the spell, whether it succeeded or not, Komak and his people would be the first to leave. Where to? Christy didn't care. She wanted them gone. After that, well, I guess we'd see.

"I don't trust her," Komak complained.

"Nor should you," Gan replied. "But I will remind you, the honor of first treachery fell to you and your minions."

Oh yeah, I'm sure that would go a long way toward helping our cause.

Fortunately, Sheila stepped in. "You may not trust her, but I do. For the sake of your people, those who are broken waiting to be made whole, I'm asking you to have a little faith. If not in her, than in me."

Talk about Irony 101. The Icon, the enemy of both vampires and the Magi, was now negotiating on their behalf, trying to save them much as she'd saved humanity five years ago.

I still wasn't happy at how things had ended between us, but I understood. She was trying to balance the scales she'd tipped all those years ago. While I couldn't exactly forget what had happened, I could forgive ... assuming we didn't all die horribly first.

As we stood there, tension running high among us, there came the faint sound of gravel crunching, followed by a low hum.

What the?

I turned and saw Jasper – Komak's vampire toady – approaching us ... on a Segway, of all things. These guys really had thought of everything.

He waved at us, looking both agitated and excited. "The last one! We just got word. They're about ready to open it!"

Christy blinked a few times at the sight, then turned to Komak. "It would appear the clock is ticking. The ritual will take some time to set up and perform, so I would highly suggest you make your choice now. Your fate is in no other hands but your own."

36

SPLIT THE PARTY

Komak looked like he would have enjoyed nothing less than ordering his men to open fire on us. Human-ish he might be now, but in his mind he was still a centuries-old vampire – arrogant and not fond of taking orders.

Being told to suck it up wasn't unheard of in the old vamp hierarchy, but it always came from those higher on the food chain. To be told that by someone not in a position of power was a hard pill to swallow for those used to being masters of the night.

Finally, a look of disgust upon his face, he unclipped the walkie talkie by his side and spoke into it. "Master Team, this is Dracula..."

Dracula? Oh yeah, that settled it. Five years of mortality or not, this guy definitely thought his shit didn't stink.

"...You are to lay down your arms and surrender them."

If he'd been in possession of his supernatural strength, I had little doubt he'd have crushed the radio to powder, so hard was he gripping it. But instead he kept talking, ordering his men out of the tunnel and letting them know Hershel was now in charge.

Mind you, I didn't know Hershel from a hole in the wall, but he at least seemed the lesser of evils. If worst came to worst I could always tell him I saw a crackpipe in someone's tent.

Komak drew his pistol, spun it in his hand and, in what I can only assume was a show of good faith, handed it to Christy.

For a moment, I was half convinced she'd simply plug him and be done with it. Mother or not, Christy could be scary as all hell when she wanted to be. And with the past beginning to catch up to us, I began to see signs of her old self peeking through her exterior.

However, she simply accepted the weapon and stuffed it into the waistband of her pants.

"If you need someone to keep that warm for you, just let me know," Sally offered.

Oh boy.

Tom leaned in toward me and whispered, "Chicks with guns are so hot."

"Is there anything you don't find hot?" I whispered back.

"Dude, my dick's been in limbo for five years. I almost find you hot."

I leaned away, giving him some serious side eye.

"I said *almost.*"

Jasper didn't seem too happy about any of this – no surprise there – but he did as told, especially once Christy reiterated that time was of the essence. With the final ley line tapped, there would be a finite window of opportunity to perform the spell. I wasn't sure how long that would be, but the more Komak's lackeys dicked around, the smaller that window would become.

Ux recruited a few folks, busy stacking supplies, to wait with him at the tunnel entrance and relieve the guards there of their weapons. Hershel took Komak's walkie and began relaying orders into it as the rest of us prepared to head back toward the inner chamber.

"I need to go ahead and get ready," Sheila said.

There were no objections, so she commandeered Jasper's Segway, looking kinda embarrassed while she climbed on board, and started back ahead of us.

Before she got out of earshot, I called to her, "Good luck!"

The smile she threw back suggested she appreciated the words of encouragement.

I'd meant them but, truth be told, good as things appeared to be going, I also had a feeling we'd all need it.

For as long as they'd apparently been planning this, chaos still reigned in the inner chamber. Excitement filled the air and the denizens of this place – mages and more – ran to and fro, some of them seemingly with no idea what they were doing.

"It looks like ... Christmas Eve at Macy's," Sally said with a pained wheeze. We probably should've asked for another Segway. She was in rough shape, and it would also have been kind of funny, too. Nevertheless, if she was feeling strong enough to quip, then that was a good sign, even if I suspected a long hospital stay lay in her future.

"Yeah," I replied. "Except these merry little elves shoot death rays instead of candy canes."

She chuckled then coughed. "Ugh. I need ... to rest. Sit me down over there and go on ahead."

"No way."

"I'll be fine."

"I can carry you."

"*You* carry me?" She rolled her eyes.

"Come on. You don't weigh a lot, old and brittle as you are."

She glared but, with me supporting her, it didn't leave her in a good spot to elbow me. Timing is everything. "I'm serious, Bill."

"Fine." I raised my voice. "The rest of you go on without us. We'll catch up." Christy opened her mouth, probably to protest, but I shook my head. "You need to do this. We'll be okay."

She locked eyes with me, no doubt happy for any excuse to tell Komak to take a flying fuck off the nearest stalagmite.

Much as I wouldn't have minded that, I still wanted to make it home alive. Extenuating circumstances aside, I was no hero. I had no intention of dying for the cause. "We made a deal. You're the only one who can see it through. Trust me, we'll be fine."

After what seemed a near eternity, she pulled the gun out of her pants and handed it to me. "Be safe."

She leaned toward me, but I held up a hand, remembering that a certain someone was way too close for comfort, and I didn't mean Tom. "Save it for after."

Christy wasn't stupid. She understood. "Okay," she whispered. "It's a date."

Well, that was certainly promising.

She turned and started walking away with the others. I half expected Gan to plant herself by my side, because nothing would make this situation more wondrous than her trying to crawl up my ass. However, she instead kept pace with the group headed toward The Source.

Who knows? Maybe the little nutball was finally taking the hint. Go me!

I eased Sally down onto a nearby crate just as Tom stepped up to us.

"Just for the record," he said, poking a spectral finger into my chest. "It is *not* a date." He, too, turned and began to walk away. After a few yards, though, he stopped in his tracks ... almost as if he'd hit an invisible wall. Spinning on his heel, he marched back. "Come on, man! I want to see this shit."

"So then go."

"I can't. I'm tethered to you like your personal gimp."

"Thanks. I really needed that image in my head."

Sally let out a sigh. "This is like the Amityville Horror, only stupider. And what does he mean you're tethered to each other?" After a moment, she shook her head. "You know what? Scratch that. I really don't want to know."

"Oh please," he replied. "Like you didn't cry at my funeral."

"It was a high pollen count day."

"You were bawling like a baby," Tom said with a grin. "And you know it."

She turned to me. "You should ask if any of these magical morons moonlight as exorcists."

"Play nice, you two."

"Oh, speaking of which, where's the other chuckle-head?" she asked. "I kind of figured, with shit going down like it is, you three would be tied at the hip again."

"Ed?" I offered my apologies on his behalf, explaining where he was and the precious cargo he was in charge of.

"Smart." Sally took a deep breath, sounding a bit stronger. "Glad to hear you guys didn't bring the tyke along. She doesn't need to be a part of this. But I'm still surprised *you* agreed to it."

"It was the only way to save you."

Sally smiled, but then lowered her voice, not that

anyone else was close enough to eavesdrop. "Christy's got a plan to stop this from happening, right?"

I shrugged.

"She does, doesn't she?"

"Um, not really."

"Are you fucking kidding me?" She started coughing from the exertion. I stepped in to help her, but she waved me off. "I'm fine. Don't worry about me."

"You're not..."

"Seriously, what the fuck are you all thinking? Do you really want to deal with vampires, Sasquatches, and God knows what else again?"

"We won't be." I explained to her our hypothesis that, outside of divine intervention, the spell only had enough juice to open things a crack. It would allow the Magi a modicum of power at best and the vamps barely any at all.

"And you're sure this asinine theory is sound?"

"Christy thinks it is."

"And him?" She gestured at Tom.

"If my woman says it's going to work," he said, "I trust her."

"Not that, genius." She turned to me. "What happens to him?"

"Um, I don't think any of us really know."

"Glad you thought this through before coming down here. You really are lost without me."

I shrugged. "You have no idea."

"Oh, shit!" Tom cried. "Me!"

"Huh? Me what?"

"Dude, we need to get moving. Remember, she's going to toss me into that orange jizz and see if I go all rock monster or not."

I quickly turned to Sally. "That's not exactly what we're hoping will happen."

She raised an eyebrow. "What's the difference? His

head is already full of rocks." Then, after a beat, she said, "Go."

"I can't..."

Sally made a face that suggested what she was about to say was hard for her to digest. "Will it help him?"

"Um, I guess. It should hopefully at least make him better than he is now."

"Then go."

'But..."

"He's your friend. And..."

"I'm your friend, too," Tom added.

"Don't press your luck. I'd like plausible deniability in case we live through this." Then she turned back to me. "Go on. This needs to be done."

"But you..."

"Can't help much until I get my second wind. Sorry, but I need to sit this one out."

"I won't leave you alone here."

She reached toward my pants, causing my eyes to open wide for a moment, then grabbed the gun out of my belt. "Don't get your hopes up, Romeo. There, see? Now I'm not alone. I have the best friend a girl could ever hope for." She ejected the magazine, checked it, and then slammed it back home. "And at least this way you won't accidentally shoot your own dick off."

"Are you sure?"

The snark dropped off Sally's face and she suddenly looked very tired. "Tina needs her father. Bring him back to her."

That settled it although, in truth, the matter was already settled the moment she told me to go.

I stepped in and gave her a big hug. "Stay safe."

"Ow. Not so hard. I'm not as young as I used to be." Then she hardened her voice, sounding for a moment like the old Sally. "Don't worry about me. Worry about anyone who tries to fuck with me."

I pulled away and faced Tom. "Ready to reenter the world of the living, buddy?"

"Fuck yeah, man! And hopefully I'll even get *rock-hard* abs out of the deal."

I didn't know if that would be the case or not, but we certainly had rocks in our heads to be trying this.

37

THE ROOM OF DOOM

No doubt in part because everyone down here was familiar with magic — and was busy running around like chickens with their heads cut off — nobody seemed to give a second glance at the full-bodied apparition by my side.

Well, okay, we did catch some shade when Tom turned to a nearby group of witches and announced, "I'm Casper, the friendly-dicked ghost."

The more things change, the more they stay cataclysmically stupid.

I hoped Sally would be all right, but seeing how the vast majority of the denizens here appeared preoccupied with heading toward the former site of The Source, I had a feeling she was low on their priority list.

"Dude, check it out. Castle Bitchenstein is still here!"

I turned toward where Tom was pointing. He was right. It was hard to see, as there were no work lights stationed there, but enough illumination shone down from above for me to make out Calibra's old lair, still standing off in the corner of this chamber.

It shouldn't have been a surprise. After all, it had been

carved, via magical fuckery, from the same rock that made up the walls. Unlike what the movies would have us believe, it hadn't fully collapsed when she died, although some parts had definitely gotten an impromptu remodeling during the big battle five years ago. Now it stood there in the gloom like some kind of haunted manor, minus the entrance fee.

"We should go take a look."

"Really?" I asked. "You want to do that now?"

"Why not?"

"I thought you were in a rush."

"Nah. I was just bored. I mean, it's not like Christy's going to throw her hands up, go poof, and shit will happen."

Idiot! Although, maybe he wasn't totally off. She did say it would take some time to prepare everything. There was also the fact that the final pulse hadn't hit yet. Still, dawdling didn't sound...

What the?

As I stood there debating with myself, I realized Calibra's former lair wasn't as empty as I'd assumed. Maybe it was a trick of the light, but I could've sworn I saw movement around it. Huh. That was odd, considering everyone seemed laser focused on the grand reopening.

"You see it too?" Tom asked, echoing my thoughts. "What the fuck are they doing over there?"

"Who knows? Maybe some of the Magi decided to slip away for a quickie before the festivities got started."

"We should definitely go check it out, then."

I turned to stare at him.

"Seriously. They might be up to something."

I raised an eyebrow. "You just want to watch people fuck, don't you?"

"Who doesn't?"

Okay, maybe he had a point there.

"C'mon, man, don't you think it's odd?"

"That people might be boning in that horror house?"

"No, that Pornhub doesn't have a witch sex channel yet?"

"Why the fuck would I care if ... wait. How would you even know that?"

"Christy occasionally checks it out when she thinks nobody is watching."

"Really?"

"Yeah. It's hot as fuck."

I ... actually couldn't disagree.

Even so, now was really not the time for that. Tom was right, however, to question what people might be doing over there. Maybe something was going on while everyone else was busy. But if so, what?

It was stupid to even think about investigating, especially now, but would any of my old D&D characters have been happy with not knowing?

That settled it. When in doubt, let the gamer win out.

"All right, let's go."

There wasn't a lot of cover between us and the Hall of Doom, so we tried our best to hug the cave wall as we made our way over, letting darkness be our camouflage. Fortunately for us, unlike the prism itself – which was stuffed safely in my backpack – Tom didn't seem to glow with his own light, becoming little more than a sentient shadow.

As we drew near, I didn't see any more movement. Either it had been a trick of the light or whoever was there had gone inside. Hopefully it was the latter, because otherwise we were wasting time that could have been better spent ... um, waiting, I guess.

"Walk faster, slowpoke," he complained.

"Fuck you."

"Not if I grew tits and had a hankering for sausage."

"Thanks for the visual. Now shut the fuck ... ugh!"

I dropped to one knee, my breath caught in my throat. All at once, it was like my entire body decided to seize up. My heart skipped a beat, then another, and for one terrible moment I became certain this was it. I was going to die down here, with only the dead as my witness.

But then, just as quickly as it hit me, I felt better – not entirely, but mostly.

"Are you okay, Bill?" Tom asked, speaking somewhat more slowly than the situation warranted.

I looked up, noting that he seemed slightly more visible than he had a few seconds ago, almost as if he'd been running off battery power and been plugged back in to charge. When at last I stood up, it felt like I'd instantly gained about fifty pounds, but at least I was able to stand. Christy's spell was working again.

"The final pulse. It's here."

"Shit," he drawled, his voice pitched lower than normal. "We don't have much time."

"Yeah. We should..."

"All right. A quick peek, just to see if anyone is boning, and then we're outta here."

He started forward without me, forcing me to catch up. The funny thing was, he had no autonomy of his own, yet – like an idiot – I decided to play the good friend and indulge him.

Calibra's fortress loomed large in front of us. This close up, it was both massive and terrifying. My resolve was definitely beginning to falter, and it had nothing to do with the fact that the only thing keeping me on my feet was the magical proton pack I was wearing.

"Come on. Don't puss out now."

I so hoped he was able to get a physical body back, because I really wanted to smack him upside the head. But I forced myself onward. If the incorporeal fucktard could do this, so could I ... the guy who bullets could actually hurt.

Goddamn. What the fuck was I thinking?

We rounded a corner, hugging the wall of the palace of pain, and spied the entrance. There was no door, just an opening in the rock wall. Calibra had once been the baddest mofo down here, so there wasn't much need for a security sys...

"Oh crap!"

Tom spun around. "Dude, keep it down. What the fuck are you ... oh shit. Gnarly."

He had no idea. Slumped against the wall, hidden in shadow until I'd almost stepped on it, was a skeleton. No. More like a mummy. Down here in the deep, the process of decay had been retarded. The corpse's skin had dried and shriveled up, but the mouth was agape as if letting out one final scream – probably from the bullet hole that could still be seen in her forehead.

It was Firebird, a ginger-haired vamp formerly of Village Coven, at least until she'd fucked us over royally. In the end, Sally had gotten the last laugh, plugging her at close range. This was where we'd left her to rot, forgotten.

Talk about a bad way to go. That said, she'd kinda deserved it. I would shed no tears for...

"What the fuck are you doing?"

Tom crouched down over the body and was thrusting his hips into its face. "Check it out. I am the ghost of skull fucks past."

I vaguely wondered if Sally would be horrified at the

sight – her murderous proclivities having subsided some time ago – or laugh. Maybe I didn't want to know. "Knock it off, let's…"

"That's far enough."

Tom and I turned toward the sound of the voice. I had just enough time to make out two forms silhouetted against the darkness before I was enveloped by a pale blue glow. *Oh crap.*

What felt like thousands of volts of magical energy lanced through my body, dropping me to the ground like a bad habit.

But that wasn't the worst of it. I heard a snap, crackle, and pop from around my neck. Though my muscles weren't currently on speaking terms with my nerve endings, I managed to glance down enough to see sparks flying from Christy's charm.

That couldn't be good.

"Biiiillll," Tom shouted, drawing out the syllables way too long.

Another spell hit him, blue energy lancing through his body as if in slow motion, but it didn't appear to faze him as…

Wait. Slow motion?

Fuck! The time dilation spell!

The charm sparked again and everything resumed its normal pace. Whew, that was a close one. Oh, wait, no it wasn't, as I was still twitching on the ground like a bug on a zap racket.

"Eat fist, asstard!" Tom threw a punch right through one of the Magi who'd waylaid us. So nice to see he was as useful as ever in a fight. His one-liner game was rusty, too, but that was the least of my worries.

The Magi who Tom tried to hit raised his hands for another spell, but the second put a hand on his shoulder.

"Hold on, Bob. I think maybe he's the one we were told about."

"Yeah, fuckers," Tom replied. "They told you to hide your women and protect your dicks because I'm here to kick them both ... err, your dicks, anyway."

Oh God, this was embarrassing.

"Where's the...?"

"It has to be on him somewhere," the second mage said, pointing at me. "Drag him inside and we'll search for iiiiiitttttt."

That last word played out way too long, telling me the charm was still on the fritz. I watched helpless as the two black-robed mages took what seemed to be about an hour to grab hold of me. I kept hoping the stun spell would wear off, allowing me to recover and smack the shit out of these assholes at Flash-like speeds, but all it did was go on and on.

Sadly, I had no real clue how spells worked or affected each other, and with my brain synapses being fried, it wasn't like I could put much thought into it. I could only guess that since they'd hit me with their stun hex before Christy's time charm futzed out, that it could conceivably last as long as they held it in real time. If so, I'd have all the time in the world to kiss my crispy ass goodbye.

A small eternity passed as I was dragged inch by inch toward the entrance of Calibra's lair. Had my nerves not been on fire, I could have easily taken a nap in the time. My only solace was that the charm kept sparking. Each time it did, the spell would change from normal to bullet time and back – the few seconds of normalcy in between at least allowing my captors to make progress.

Progress toward what, I didn't know. But I'd have

sooner they put me out of my misery than experience being tazed for what felt like hours on end.

Tom, bless his non-existent heart, kept trying to attack them, but by the time we reached the doorway, the two Magi – both dressed as if they shopped at the same evil cult emporium – had grown used to his incorporeal state and were ignoring him.

At last they pulled me inside and, as time resumed its normal pace again, I was relieved to find the stun spell finally wearing off. Sadly, it had taken its toll, meaning I still couldn't do much more than twitch. On the upside, if the charm fritzed out again, the effects could potentially wear off in bullet time, meaning I could get back up and ... um, scream for help, I guess.

I needed to remember, I was me, nothing more. Hell, it was doubtful I could have taken one of these guys in a fair fight, much less two.

No! That was quitter talk. Save that shit for the guy currently drooling all over himself.

Oh, wait. That was still me.

My two captors eventually dumped me in a large chamber, deep enough in the fortress that I wouldn't easily be found. Guess Tom had been right to want to investigate, although things appeared far more sinister than the mere quickie he'd been hoping to find.

Bob pulled out a flashlight – surprisingly mundane for a guy who'd just blasted me with magic – allowing me to see that this place wasn't nearly as empty as it should have been. Multiple summoning circles were inlaid in the floor, while crates of supplies were stacked against the walls. A communications array, far more advanced than the one I'd seen outside, stood off in one corner.

Whatever this was, there was some serious shit going on in here, and it had been planned in advance. Fucking Komak! I had no idea what his game was, but it had to be some contingency designed to fuck over anyone not on his team.

Bullshit stories about his self-respect aside, I began to see what a dickhead he was. And why not? He was a vampire. It was practically ingrained in his unholy DNA.

"Search him!" the second mage ordered.

"Not full body cavity," Tom pleaded. "Nobody needs to see that."

I tried to flip them all the finger, but found my muscles unwilling to comply. Damnit! Fate couldn't even give me that one small bit of defiance.

"Wait!" Tom cried as they yanked the backpack off me. "The only thing Bill keeps in there are his tampons."

Moron.

The first mage, Bob, looked at the bag for a moment, then glanced down at me. "Paw Patrol? Seriously?"

Fucking A!

"Open it!"

"All right already. Relax." Asshole Bob unzipped the pack and white light began to spill out of the opening. "This has gotta be it!"

"Don't touch it with your bare hands."

"Yeah," Tom agreed. "Don't touch it at all. That's part of my collection. Nobody sells that shit except me and my little girl."

The two wizards continued to ignore him, which I couldn't really blame them for. "Are you sure about this?" Bob asked.

"Not really, but it's the only chance we have. You want it back, right?"

"You know I do."

"All of it?"

"Of course."

"All of what?" Tom asked, sounding frustrated. "My dick? Because if so, open wide, fuckers."

"Then this is what we need to make it happen," the second mage replied, ignoring my friend. "Let's go."

Go?

"What about him?"

"Leave him," number two said. "We need to get this back to the boss."

"And who's that," Tom asked, continuing to harass them, "Prick Fury, Agent of C.O.C.K.?"

Okay, that was a slight bit better than his earlier efforts but still not good enough.

Tom stepped in front of the door and put his hands out, blocking the exit ... at least until the two mages stepped right through him.

They continued onward, heedless of his protests.

"Don't worry, Bill," Tom said, turning toward me. "I won't leave you. Fuck these Asssshoooolesss."

Despite his protests to the contrary, I watched as Tom was dragged away against his will. It was as if he were being pulled away by invisible chains, but painfully slowly.

I forced my eyeballs to comply and saw the charm sparking again. Time was slowing down. Yes! Now if it would only stay that way long enough for the effects of the stun spell to...

Another spark and Tom was dragged from sight as the Magi reached the end of his tether and kept on going.

No!

I needed to ... needed to...

All at once I felt woozy. It was as if the weight of a truck fell onto my chest from nowhere. I tried to take a breath and couldn't. *What the ... oh no!* Christy's charm. Yes, it messed with time, designed to keep me safe from those pulses, but it was also powered by the prism. Tom had a short leash, but apparently the power cord for the time spell was equally as limited.

It became hard to think, and my lungs refused to fill with air.

Tom's protests faded in the distance, leaving me in silence. The only sound I could hear was the beating of my heart, and it was growing slower with every second that passed.

Not now. Not like this.

I thought of my friends as I tried to fight through the sludge slowly descending upon my mind. Tom and Ed. Christy and Cat. Sally. Even Sheila.

My heart beat again, sounding both dreadfully slow and weak.

I began to slip away as the darkness at the edges of my vision closed in around me.

There came a bit of light, dim, as the amulet sparked once more, but by then it was too late. The darkness consumed me, and there was nothing I could do about it except wait and see what awful place it led me to.

38

FREE WIL-LY

*T*hud thud
    I sat up with a start, finding myself in familiar surroundings. Apparently that awful darkness had led me ... back to my own apartment?

It had all been nothing but a dream – a seriously fucked-up, not even remotely wet, dream, but somehow that made sense.

As if I'd ever agree to go to that godforsaken cavern again.

Thud thud

I turned toward Tom's room, preparing to yell for him to turn his fucking radio off. There was a hideous bass beat, but beneath it was annoying static – voices barely audible – as if the antenna were broken. The idiot had probably knocked it off the...

But then I remembered that had been part of the dream, too. Tom wasn't back. That had been nothing more than wish fulfillment by my subconscious. Strange that I'd be dreaming about him now, after so long. But then who the fuck was playing shitty music in his room?

Dave!

Suddenly it all came back to me. No wonder I'd been dreaming about the past. Dave was in town, hawking his shitty moisturizer, and Ed had flown in, too, for a sort of mini reunion. So maybe it wasn't such a strange thing to dream about after all.

If the past was gonna come back to haunt me, then wouldn't it make sense to do so when the old gang was back in town?

As for waking up on the couch, I'd probably indulged in a few too many toasts to the not-so-good old days and passed out where I'd lain.

Fuck it, I was due. It had been a while since I'd let myself have some fun. I...

Thud thud

For a moment, the whispering static became louder, sounding like a thousand voices all trying to speak at once. The shit that passed for music these days.

Oh, for Christ's sake! I picked up the TV remote and chucked it at the door of the bedroom. "Turn it down, asshole! Don't make me kick your ass."

Not that I expected him to listen. Dave was probably too busy counting all the Social Security money he was siphoning off old ladies with that crap he was selling. I mean, yeah, it actually wasn't bad stuff, but that's only because he'd sent me a free case.

No. Free was too strong a word. The fucker expected me to be his personal Avon lady.

Yeah. With Dave, nothing was free...

Thud thud.

"Will you..." I paused. *Heh. Free ... Will.* Not really a pun I wanted to wake up to.

There came a knock at the front door in the same moment that static became louder than ever, almost understandable in its babbling.

I ignored it and turned toward the door, confused. Who would be visiting at this hour?

Actually, I had no idea what hour it was. Likewise, I couldn't recall buzzing anyone in. Of course, I owned the building these days, so it was entirely possible it was simply one of the tenants here to bitch about something I wasn't qualified to fix.

Thud...

I glanced toward the bedroom again. Maybe they were here to complain about the shitty music my ex dungeon master refused to turn down.

"Hold on, I'm coming!"

I got up, put a hand on the door knob, and then froze. From out of nowhere, a sense of dread filled me, as if every instinct in my body was screaming for me to back away. Staring at the door, I got the strangest feeling that opening it meant never truly closing it ever again.

That feeling persisted for a moment more and then I let out a laugh. Knowing this shithole, that wasn't entirely out of the question. Even so, it's not like I couldn't fix it with a screwdriver and some WD-40.

Thu...

The bass beat ended. Simultaneously, that whispering static fell quiet and silence descended.

I called out, "It's about fucking time!"

Then, before I could creep myself out with more stupid thoughts, I unlocked the door and opened it.

"I dare say, it is indeed about time," my visitor replied.

Yeah, I should have heeded those warning bells in my head.

Standing just outside the door, carrying a suitcase of all things, was ... me.

If you think that's crazy, you're not the only one. But then I realized it wasn't actually me. No. If the soulless black eyes staring back from behind my – *his* – glasses were any indication, it was far worse.

The other me smiled, revealing long, sharp canines.

I should have slammed the door shut, locked it, and then dragged the fucking refrigerator in front of it.

But all I could do was back up in horror at the sight before me, a distant memory yet one terrifyingly familiar.

"Dr. Death?"

Before evil alternate me could answer – likely with something pithy and assholish – the world went black, as if I'd forgotten to pay the electric bill.

For a moment, there was nothing but numbness around me, like my body had been encased in a satanic cocoon of nightmare cotton candy.

Long seconds passed and sensation began to return. I felt something pressed up against my backside. Panic flared as I wondered what my evil twin was up to, but then realization hit. I wasn't standing in my apartment after all. I was lying on the floor.

And the reason I couldn't see anything was because my eyes were closed. Duh!

I tried to command them open, but they refused to obey.

Oh crap.

An unpleasant memory flashed through my mind. I'd been here before or someplace like it.

No! That can't be happening. It's impossible.

Back then the floor beneath me had been soft, a shag carpet I'd landed on after having my throat torn out. Now, whatever was beneath me was hard, rocky. That ... and I couldn't recall anything bad happening to my throat.

That was odd.

Last time, the memory of my death had clearly gelled in my mind: the party at the loft, Sally and Night Razor, dying, that sort of shit. Now, though, all I could remember was ... being zapped by a couple of assholes. They'd stunned me, nothing more.

I should be waking up and running after them to ... probably get zapped again, but hopefully not before telling them what a pair of treacherous ball-suckers they were.

Instead, my tongue flopped around in my mouth, seemingly of its own will – *Freewill* – for a moment before it decided to listen to the neurons telling it to get its act together. Finally, I was able to run it across my top teeth and...

Ow!

I had fangs. Fuck me!

Well, it was either that or I'd been sucking on a piece of glass when I'd passed out. But somehow I didn't think so.

Sensation continued to return. I could feel my arms and legs. I opened and closed my mouth ... *fuck* ... puncturing my lower lip in the process.

How the hell was this possible? The vampire race was dead, extinct.

Yeah, there were a handful of those neo-vamps running around, but the only guy who could make new ones was Ed and – so far as I was aware – he was thousands of miles away protecting my goddaughter.

Problem was, that was all elementary at the moment. How and why kind of took a back seat to the reality of my situation. I mean, sure, there was the possibility that someone had stuffed plastic fangs in my mouth and I'd wake up surrounded by laughing friends to find a dick drawn on my face. Oh, how nice that would be ... sorta.

Speaking of which, my eyelids fluttered, telling me I was just about in full control of my faculties again. I opened my eyes to find, sadly, no party happening around me this time. I was alone. The ceiling above was the only thing staring down at me, and I seriously doubted it had been drawing dicks on anyone.

Mind you, that didn't mean I hadn't been dicked over royally.

The thing was, if I was right, I now had the means to do a little dicking myself ... figuratively speaking, anyway. I pushed myself up, noting that I could see the room around me better than before despite the mages taking the only light source with them. Everything was in almost painfully sharp relief. I'd almost forgotten what a sensory trip being a vamp could be.

My body was still a bit shaky, coming out of the deathlike state I'd been in, so I sat there for a moment, acclimating. Just for shits and giggles, I removed my glasses. The sharp lines of everything around me instantly blurred into unrecognizable blobs.

Fuck me! I thought I was past that. Or I had been once, right before we'd shut things down for good ... albeit not as good as we'd all thought.

My stomach rumbled, but I tried to ignore it for the moment ... knowing that was a near impossibility in the long run.

Replacing my glasses, I pushed myself up. That shakiness I felt quickly passed and I was left feeling much lighter on my feet than I could remember feeling in a long time.

That wasn't such a bad thing, but the tradeoffs ... *no*. I couldn't concentrate on that for now. I'd cross that bridge when this was over and done with. For now, I needed to stop those wizards from...

Those thoughts ground to a screeching halt as more memories came back to me. The process of turning took hours. You didn't just get bitten, then pop up with a whole new outlook on your death. There was a whole metamorphosis involved, one which, I'd learned from Calibra, involved an outside spirit – something from beyond the veil – invading your body and merging with it into a whole new being.

Dr. Death.

Gah, I really needed to focus. That shit could wait. First things first: I had to expose Komak for the asshole he was. Unfortunately, he was likely already long finished doing whatever he'd been scheming to do.

Though it felt like minutes to me, long hours had passed, hours in which I was unable to stop...

A small spark from my chest area caught my eye and I looked down to see the faintest fizzle of power on that charm Christy had given me.

The time spell!

Right before I'd gone under for the third time, the charm had sparked again, meaning maybe the spell had activated one last time before Tom was fully out of range.

It had been designed to protect me from whatever had been happening – which, I now had to assume, was some weird drawn-out death on my part. But maybe this time I'd been too far gone or maybe, with the spell fizzling out, I'd been only partially protected as time slowed to a crawl.

Either way, it was possible that hours had passed for me, but here in the real world...

It seemed a long shot, but it was the only shot I had.

That said, there was little need for the charm now. Whatever it had been protecting me from had won in the end.

I ripped it off then hesitated, my nose catching wind of the dried blood contained within. It was all I could do to keep from popping it in my mouth and chewing it up like a wad of bubble gum.

Gah! Not how I wanted to start things off.

Resisting the urge, I crushed it instead, enjoying the feel of my newly regained vampire strength ... before remembering the charm had been pretty flimsy to begin with. Okay, so maybe I shouldn't use that as a benchmark of my undead power.

Regardless, I needed to get out of this place and see if my theory held. If so, then there might still be time to stop whatever the fuck needed stopping.

I turned toward the door and smiled.

"Get ready, motherfuckers, because once again, I am the terror that flaps in the night."

39

FROM HERO TO ETERNITY

I paused after taking two steps, repeating in my mind what I'd just said.

Ugh, I was already starting off my second death sounding like a dork.

My stomach grumbled again, this time a lot more insistently, but I ignored it. Blood could wait. My friends couldn't.

Or at least I hoped so.

Stepping to the exit, I took a moment to survey the cavern before me. The Source chamber was still barely aglow from above. That hadn't changed. However, the darkness no longer meant dick to me.

Looking around, I spied figures in the distance scurrying about. Most were headed toward The Source itself. There were too many tents and other obstacles in the way to see clearly, but if folks were still gathering, then maybe there was time to...

"You dickless losers are going to get my spectral foot up your asses."

The voice was distant, faint, but unmistakable ... Tom! Thank goodness for vampire hearing! Even better, if I could hear him, that meant...

Turning my head to follow the sound of his voice, I spied two figures in the distance. They were heading parallel to The Source, not toward it. I couldn't see Tom, but that wasn't a surprise. He didn't emit his own light. At this distance he'd be nothing but a shadow at best. But if they were still walking away from me, that meant ... *yes!*

Mere minutes had passed in the real world while I was busy being dead behind the protection of Christy's spell. Yeah, maybe *protection* was a somewhat contentious word there, but whatever. The important thing was I hadn't missed anything important.

I made it a point to give Christy a big kiss when next I saw her, assuming she wasn't completely repulsed by me now, but that was a worry for later. Her thinking of me as little more than a monster would suck, but ultimately it would be a small price to pay for us all living through this.

Besides, for all I knew, that sliver she planned to open would have the same effect on me as we'd theorized it would have on Gan and Ed ... minimizing my vampness and effectively allowing me to live a normal life.

Or so I hoped.

For now, though, I turned to the wall nearest me and took a swing at it.

Ow!

Fuck, it was solid! However, even as I bruised the shit out of my knuckles, a chunk of it broke off and shattered.

Super strength. That meant the magical pulse was still in effect, which likewise meant I could catch those two assholes with relative ease.

I crouched into a runner's stance, or what I assumed to be one since jogging wasn't really my thing. Then I took off, feeling my body accelerate far past its normal limits.

"WOO!" It was pretty goddamned heady.

It was also unsubtle as fuck, or at least my whoop of

joy was. I'd closed enough of the distance between me and the two Hogwarts rejects that one of them turned his head to see what the commotion was all about.

I put on more speed, but it was too late. In my stupidity, I'd tipped my hand before I was in attack range.

The mage who'd looked back, Bob, screamed to his companion, "Run!"

As I continued to close on them, Bob began to glow red. Being that it wasn't Christmas yet, it was probably safe to assume he wasn't planning on wishing me holiday cheer.

The second wizard – the one holding my backpack, of course – turned, saw me racing toward them, and took the fuck off without needing to be told twice.

I had a second in which I finally spied Tom, superimposed over the second mage – probably in an attempt to be annoying, since there wasn't much else he could do. Then a beam of red-hot death came racing my way.

There was a moment, no more, for me to consider what a stupid fucking idea this was, then I leapt with everything I had.

Fortunately, Bob was apparently as rusty at this as I was. It was a sloppy leap for me, but an equally shitty shot on his part. I felt the bottom sole of one of my sneakers melt, and then I cleared the blast.

A hot foot wasn't such a high price to pay for survival, even if it wasn't exactly a wonderful sensation.

That was the big problem with being undead – well, aside from needing blood to survive and being deathly allergic to sunlight – our nerve endings worked just fine.

I'd always thought that was weird, but I guess technically my body wasn't dead. It was just in a sort of weird limbo as a result of the fact that an outside spirit was now sharing it like some sort of fucked-up duplex.

I quickly pushed that thought away, realizing this was

a piss poor time to wax philosophical on the nature of life ... or death.

My momentum carried me the rest of the way toward the mage. As I descended upon him, I flexed my hand, preparing to slice and dice this motherfucker with my claws – a small part of me horrified at how quickly I'd accepted that course of action.

It was too late to change tactics, though. I landed before Bob could charge up another spell, swinging my hand with enough force to ... bitch slap the shit out of him?

He went down, his nose spraying a fountain of blood from the force of the blow, but I hadn't bisected his face as had been my original plan. No wonder, too. I glanced at my hand to see ... goddamn it ... nothing more than my regular fingernails.

Guess I needed to start practicing this shit all over again. Talk about unfair. Christy got her powers back and, within five minutes, she was casting advanced time magic while I couldn't even get my fucking fingernails to grow.

Nevertheless, this was a win. Bob was down for the count. That was the important thing. Best of all, it meant I'd managed to overcome my initial murderous impulses, sorta.

Now to catch his buddy and see if I could...

I could...

I glanced downward again at the mage, focusing on the blood still pouring out of his broken nose.

The scent of it enticed me like a two for one sale at a gaming convention. My stomach grumbled in response, sounding like a hungry jungle cat.

I remembered that a lot of newly turned vamps woke up feral, the hunger all-consuming for them. Others were lucky in that there was something present to distract them from becoming bloodthirsty beasts. The last time this had happened to me – heh, how many others could make that claim – I'd been dragged to my feet and faced with the choice of fighting my way out or getting staked.

Something like that tended to make lunch a secondary priority. Now, though, I was standing triumphant over the equivalent of a hot lunch. There were still bad things afoot that I needed to stop from happening. Problem was, physically anyway, it wasn't quite as strong of a motivator as having the shit beat out of me had been.

I could feel my fangs descend, not of my own accord. A sliver of drool collected on the side of my mouth as I made the mistake of breathing in the heavenly scent again.

That pushed me over the edge. Even as a part of my consciousness screamed out that I needed to save Tom, the rest ignored it. And why not? It wasn't like he could get any deader.

As for Bob here...

I fell upon him, intent on feeding.

My only solace in doing so was that I somehow managed to have the good graces to at least not suck on his nostrils.

Feeding isn't a pretty thing, especially when the vamp in question is hungry. There's no time for table settings or figuring out which one is the salad fork. It's like being in a contest to see who can scarf down the most hot dogs and the judge has just rung the bell.

It's all about eating your fill and getting to the juicy center. Not making a mess is a tertiary concern.

I'm happy to say I didn't go quite as nuts as Ed did with that homeless guy the other day. That had been some fucked up shit. However, it wasn't like Bob ended up any less dead. And I was pretty sure he'd stay that way. Aside from special circumstances – like trying to punch a hole in the universe – Magi couldn't be turned into vamps.

That was probably a good thing. In Calibra I'd seen what a lethal combo that could be. It was likely for the best that she was a one-off freak show, no repeat performances.

My head cleared and I stood up. Looking down at myself, it wasn't as bad as it could've been, but a case of wet wipes would certainly not have gone unappreciated at that moment.

At that moment...

Shit!

There was no telling how long I'd been sucking on Bob's neck. It couldn't have been too long, though. Feeding on a victim wasn't like some Italian family get-together where dinner lasted seven hours and fourteen courses. However, it had apparently been long enough. Taking a moment to wipe the gore off my glasses, I looked around. There was no sign of the second mage.

Either serious about whatever course of action Komak had set him on, or just a big old pussy, the other wizard hadn't stopped to help his friend. The fucker had taken off and kept on running while I was busy sucking Bob dry like the last rib on the rack.

I shook that thought from my mind and scanned the direction I'd last seen him heading in – damn, this cave was big – but he was gone. Nor did I hear Tom cursing up a storm anymore. Either they were out of range, the mage had found a way to mask them, or my friend had run out of insults.

No, I didn't consider that last one likely either.

"Damn it!" I kicked Bob to let off some steam, then turned around to consider my next course of action – stopping dead in my tracks at what I saw.

Glen, the multi-eyed blob of goo, sat before me. He

must have slithered up at some point while I was busy making the mage into my personal Happy Meal. Who knew how long he'd been ... err, pooling there?

All I knew was that every single eyeball in his gelatinous body was currently staring unblinkingly at me.

Oh crap.

40

TONGUE TIED

The freaky ass little blob began to quiver all over. Considering the dead body just a few feet away – the one I'd just finished kicking – I had to assume the worst. I no doubt looked ever so slightly to be the *aggressor* here.

That meant Glen was either getting ready to scream or fight. Neither was a good option, but that latter kind of freaked me out. In the back of my head I envisioned a vile acid attack melting me into sludge where I stood. Or maybe he planned to shoot his eyeballs at me, like hypersonic golf balls.

Regardless, I hadn't faced too many blobs in my day. Hell, even in my D&D game the closest I'd come was the occasional gibbering mouther and those tended to...

Uh oh. Several air bubbles began to form in Glen's blobby form. That was it! He was going to unleash a sonic attack meant to confuse and incapacitate me.

I needed to stop him, but how? It wasn't like he had a jaw to punch and there were too many eyes for me to try poking before he could...

"That was so cool!"

The fuck? I continued to stare at him, dumbfounded. "Um..."

"Oh, man! I so wish I had a camera on me," he continued. "Or hands to use a camera. Who would have thought when I woke up in my bucket this morning that I'd have a chance to watch the legendary Freewill in action?"

"Hold on," I said. "You're not freaked out?"

"Freaked out?" he bubbled. "I'm totally psyched. I swear, if you're planning to reenact your big fight with the Icon, too, I might just die of happiness."

"You do realize I killed this guy, right?"

Glen bubbled excitedly. "Yep, that's pretty clear. I only wish I'd been close enough to hear what he'd said to impugn your honor. It was something reprehensibly vile, wasn't it?"

"Impugn my honor?"

"Sure. Why else would the Freewill vent his vicious wrath upon such an undeserving foe?"

"Um ... yeah. He was an asshole, all right."

"Would you mind if I kept a piece as a souvenir?"

"*What?*"

Glen quivered again, more hesitantly this time. "This is kind of embarrassing for me to admit, but I'm a big fan."

"Oh," I replied, still taking this in. "Then, I guess ... help yourself."

"Ooh! Thank you."

Glen slithered atop the mage's body. I wasn't sure what he planned to do ... maybe that acid thing was still on the table. But then he undulated right off again, leaving the mage intact — if still dead. The only difference was ... *whoa.* He was entirely clean now. All traces of blood and gore were gone from the body. It was as if Glen had hoovered everything up. With the exception of the wounds visible on Bob's corpse, you could have easily thought he was simply taking a nap, right there in the middle of the floor.

I was tempted to ask if Glen could do the same to me, but then stopped when I realized how weird that might be. We were already pushing the boundaries of strange with this one. I had to wonder if any other *celebrities* – outside of maybe Keith Richards – could claim a groupie quite this ... unique.

"This is definitely going in my scrapbook," Glen said excitedly before once again turning a dozen eyeballs my way. "So what's next, mighty Freewill?"

Next? Oh yeah, I'd almost forgotten I still needed to rescue Tom, stop Komak, and do it all on a very short timetable.

It was just like old times except Sally was currently sidelined, leaving me with a goopy pile of snot as backup. "You didn't happen to see another mage dragging a ghost with him, did you?"

Glen blinked several dozen times. "Excuse me?"

"Never mind. Was a long shot anyway. So why exactly are you here?

"I came looking for you because I didn't want you to miss the ... um ... thing that those people are doing."

"The grand reopening?"

"Yeah, that works."

Without any other leads, it was probably the only place to start the search. Besides, whatever evil Komak and his witchy girlfriend had planned was bound to be tied to what Christy was doing. It was either that or run around randomly and hope I got lucky.

"Let's not keep them waiting. Lead the way."

Thankfully Glen was faster than he looked, able to tumble along the ground like a water balloon rolling downhill when the need called for it.

Truth of the matter was, we couldn't have missed our target had we been blind. It was where nearly all of the mages, vamps, and other thingamabobs in this place had converged. The problem was more finding the specific asshole I wanted – a needle in this haystack of magical beings.

They gathered in small crowds all along the perimeter of the dried up lakebed that once housed the portal for all of this world's magic. Bursts of power lit up the cavern in front of us as we approached, causing me to jump a few times. However, I quickly realized they weren't aimed at me. A few of the Magi were apparently tossing random spells into the air like firecrackers as their friends cheered.

I can't say for certain that alcohol was involved, but I wouldn't have doubted it.

All in all there was a sense of excitement in the air but, based on what I could hear in quick snippets, it was colored with a mix of both hope as well as the fear that it wouldn't work.

I had to admit, much as I'd been ready to dismiss the masses down here as nothing more than assholes, the sight of so many standing hand in hand, along with the whispers of quiet desperation that caught my newly enhanced ears, brought a lump to my throat.

I'd previously regarded our course of action to be a minor win for the bad guys, a necessary evil to save Sally. But I began to see that Komak's group was merely a militant fringe amongst the masses united in the hope of getting their lives back.

A part of me could understand why Sheila had decided to help them.

Don't get me wrong. We did the right thing five years ago. I'd go to my deathbed swearing on that. But I'd never stopped to consider the consequences of those actions. So many of those aligned against us had been utter dick biscuits that giving them all a giant "fuck you" had been my main focus.

It was one of the oft-forgotten aspects of war – the people caught in the middle, the ones whose lives were left in ruins no matter the outcome.

I slowed down as we entered the fringes of the crowd, keeping my eyes peeled. Komak was up to no good. Of that I was convinced. He'd already proven himself capable of committing needless atrocities in the name of getting what he wanted. There was a vast difference between stealing a loaf of bread to feed your hungry child versus killing everyone in the store. His excuses to the contrary wore thin indeed.

But perhaps letting Christy finish her ritual was ultimately the right thing to do. Most here could then get on with their lives again. As for the serpents in this Garden of Eden, well, hopefully we could stomp them out now before they could spread.

I wasn't sure what that meant for me, but I guess I'd soon find out. With any luck, Dr. Death would be minimized to nothing more than the occasional bad dream. There was also the fact that Christy, Tom, and I had a lot to discuss ...

Shit! Tom!

I'd gotten lost in my thoughts, paying more attention to the shit going on around me than on finding him. Goddamn, I really needed to consider ADD meds at some point.

Problem was, outside of spotting a transparent guy

cursing out his kidnapper, I had no idea how to find him. He didn't have a scent to track, and so long as the prism remained closed in that backpack, it wasn't obvious from a distance.

"Are they almost finished?"

"Shh, don't bother them."

"Have you ever heard anything like this incantation?"

The sound of conversation different than what I'd mostly been hearing up until now caught my ear and I followed it to a large group milling about near the shoreline. Glen and I skirted around their periphery to get a better look.

For a moment I was afraid I'd have to start tossing people to the side, but finally the crowd parted enough for me to catch sight of Christy.

Sure enough, she was seated in the center of a circle that had been carved into the ground at the very edge of where the orange goop of The Source used to flow. Holding hands and encircling her on three sides were Kelly, Hershel, and – of course – Liz.

Their eyes were all shut and they were chanting something unintelligible, probably in that Enochian language they liked to use. Or, hell, it could have been French for all I knew. My grasp of most languages outside of English was shitty at best.

Regardless, based on the paraphernalia around them – burning incense and other shit straight out of *The Craft* – it was a fair bet they were well along in the process of casting the spell.

Tempting as it was to interrupt them with news of Tom, I wasn't sure what that would do ... aside from probably get my ass kicked by the rest of the crowd.

But if they were in the middle of performing the spell, then where was...

"Look!" Glen bubbled, "The Icon!"

I turned toward The Source itself. The flap of the lone tent sitting in the middle of it was pushed open from the inside. Sheila stepped out and, despite everything, my breath caught in my throat.

Gone was her cave explorer chic. In its place she'd donned her old Templar armor – gleaming chainmail topped with a crimson cape. Far as I was aware, she hadn't worn it in five years, not even that time I begged her to put it on for a Ren faire we were attending.

It was quite the sight and – based on the crowd's reaction – I had a feeling that was purposeful. A collective gasp rose up at her appearance, quickly turning into a cheer as she drew the sword from her side. Almost immediately, like some kind of She-Ra fetish cosplay, her whole body erupted in white flame.

Despite the display, a small sliver of fear began to worm its way into my gut. It was the memory of what had happened here all those years ago – she and I locked in mortal combat, the prophecy between us fulfilled at last.

She'd won that battle. I happily admitted that. However, once again – beyond all logic – I was the Freewill of vampire legend. I couldn't help but feel that us both being here again couldn't be a coincidence, as if destiny were demanding a rematch.

Heh. At the very least that would make Glen happy.

No! That was silly. I pushed that thought aside as nothing but paranoia, my mind playing tricks on me. Komak, asshole that he was, had been right. The past was dead...

But not as dead as I hoped, as a hand fell upon my shoulder and I turned to find golden eyes staring at me with such intensity that I was certain I'd burst into flames.

Pity that I didn't.

Gan's nostrils twitched ever so slightly as she took in my undead scent. "How is this possible?" I tried to think of an answer, but she stepped in and whispered, "Fate is indeed kind, my love."

Then, before I could so much as blink in protest, she grabbed hold of me and pressed her lips to mine.

I was wrong. History wasn't repeating itself.

No. What was happening now was so much worse.

41

GRAND REOPENING

*G**ah!** It was like being Frenched by a hungry cobra. She wasn't kissing me as much as mapping the inside of my mouth with her tongue.

Either way, I was stuck fast. My power was nothing compared to hers. Hell, I doubted I could have pried her off with a crowbar. Goddamn, I'd forgotten how much strength she possessed.

Or how disturbingly into me she was.

On the upside, she wasn't twelve anymore. That had to count a little toward keeping me off the sexual predator watch lists. Sadly, she was still Gan, which meant she was a sociopathic nutcase with enough blood on her hands to fill a swimming pool.

"It's good to be the king," Glen bubbled from somewhere beside me. Little asshole. He had no idea how *not good* this was.

At last, I managed to pull back enough to excise her creepy little tongue from my mouth and clamp my lips shut.

She finally got the hint and let go. *Eww.* Good thing I

325

was a vampire again, because hopefully my constitution was now strong enough to keep me from contracting her crazy.

I stepped back, only for Glen to sidle up next to me. "High five, buddy!"

"Oh, shut up." Then, before Gan could resume her game of full-contact tongue hockey, I said, "Please don't do that again."

"It is quite all right, my love," she replied. "I don't mind if everyone watches."

Gross! Oh God! She was a murderous psycho and an exhibitionist, too. I could only imagine what other shit she was busy planning in her twisted little mind. "Yeah, well, I kinda do."

Jesus Christ, I sounded like a prude. Then again, where she was concerned, I'd have happily joined a monastery and taken as many vows of celibacy as necessary to keep this particular demon at bay.

"I told you my seers foresaw a glorious future for you, but even I could not dream this would be possible."

"Trust me, it wasn't exactly on my horoscope either."

"But how? The old race is dead, gone. Did the Progenitor perhaps feed upon you incorrectly?"

"No. Ed and I don't have a Netflix and chill kind of friendship. We keep our mouths to ourselves, thank you."

"Then how can this be?"

Gan seemed genuinely flummoxed, something rare for her. It made me wonder if maybe she was right about fate choosing me for a second go at this life. After all, I hadn't been bitten. Strange as magic could be, my turning made zero fucking sense.

Once again, though, this wasn't the time or place. I shook those thoughts from my head. We could speculate on how this happened later ... preferably with a lot of people between us. For now, I had more important matters at hand. "Tom's been kidnapped."

"Tom?"

"The ghost."

"Oh, yes. The specter of that annoying human. What of it?"

"He's been taken."

"He?"

"The prism. Komak's people have it. They're up to something."

"Tell me what you suspect, beloved."

"I ... don't know. But we need to do something. Liz is over there with Christy. She's Komak's main fuck buddy, so I don't doubt for a second she's a part of whatever is going on."

"Your fiery words cause my insides to quiver with excitement."

"Stow the hormones, Gan. I'm serious."

"As am I," she replied with a devilish grin. "But so be it. I believe I saw Komak and his lieutenant over in this direction. Come with me and we shall confront him."

"But Christy..."

"She must finish her incantation. They are too far along, I'm afraid. Interrupting them could have dire consequences."

"Really?"

"Are you not versed in the ways of magic?"

"Um, no."

"Fortunately, I am. But fear not. If Komak and his so-called Last Coven are indeed planning something nefarious, I have little doubt the two of us can easily best him."

"Three," Glen said, but then quickly added, "Um, can I at least come and watch?"

I was tempted to tell the little blob to go find a nice

latrine to splash around in, but he'd probably follow us anyway. "It's cool. He's with me."

"As you wish, my love."

Glen began to bubble uncontrollably. "This is so exciting!"

"Shift it into neutral, blobby," I said, letting Gan take the lead.

I wasn't sure if we could stop whatever Komak had planned, but I sure as hell aimed to try.

We maneuvered to the fringe of the gathered crowd so as to move more freely. Gan took a right and I followed with Glen in tow.

"Tell me, beloved, how does it feel to once more have immortality running through your veins?"

The truth was, it was terrifying – like waking up from a nightmare, only to turn over and fall back into it. But that was only half the story and I knew it. There was definitely a part of me excited to feel this powerful again, to know that I could heal from nearly any injury.

And then there was the blood. It was both blessing and curse. To have to live off of something else's life essence was horrific. But the truth was, holy shit, it was good. I mean, it was like every taste bud on a vampire's tongue was wired to think blood was the best fucking thing ever. Much as I hated to admit it, draining that mage had been like the best Thanksgiving dinner, and that's not even counting the lack of family there.

Mind you, there was also a bit of jealousy mixed in, too. Gan and Ed were upgraded models, yet somehow I'd gotten stuck with the old sun and faith allergic downgrade. I mean, I didn't know that for certain, but Gan's nose seemed to confirm it and inside I felt the same as before. Talk about unfair.

However, the last thing I wanted to do was encourage her. So, rather than give voice to any of that, I simply said, "It sucks."

I figure that about covered it.

Rather than be put out, Gan replied, "If I may say so, it suits you, my darling. Do not misunderstand. I would love you no matter how fragile your body. But now, it is as if you are truly whole again."

Well, if that didn't ruin my day, I didn't know what would. Fortunately, I didn't have too much time to dwell on it as we rounded the shore of this once infernal lake.

"Over there, my love." Gan pointed. "I believe we have found him."

Komak was a couple dozen yards ahead of us. He was standing at the edge of The Source away from the main crowd, with Jasper and a few of his other asshole buddies who'd recently been deposed. He was staring intently, a little too intently, toward where Sheila waited in the center of everything.

"He's planning something."

"Then we should dispatch him before it is too late."

"Yeah!" Glen cried. "Just let me find a good spot where I can watch."

"Um, okay."

He slithered away from us, no doubt to find better seats.

We were almost upon them – close enough for them to have easily spotted us if their attention wasn't focused elsewhere – when there came a flash of light from above.

I looked up and stopped dead in my tracks.

The twinkling lights in the ceiling, which had been providing modest illumination up until now, began to glow brighter, pulsing as they did and somehow also rearranging themselves.

Soon I began to see a pattern: lines of light converging on a point on the ceiling that seemed to be directly above where Sheila stood. I took a quick count, knowing what I'd find – thirteen in all, each coming from a different direction on the compass.

Sheila raised her sword with both hands, white fire engulfing her entire form. Up above, where the ley lines converged, the energy began to slowly swirl, multiple colors shimmering in the growing tempest.

This was it. We needed to stop Komak now, because whatever he had planned, it was no doubt about to happen.

42

VICTORY DANCE

As Gan and I approached, Komak and his minions continued to pay rapt attention to what was going on up above. I overheard him say, "At last."

"At last what, asshole?" I cried, unable to control myself. Stupid. We were still too far away to do anything … scratch that. *I* was still too far away.

Gan bolted before the words had finished leaving my mouth, stopping right in front of Komak in the time it took me to blink.

It was impressive as all hell, but risky, too. With the power still on, he and his mage buddies could... Oh who was I kidding? This was Gan we were talking about. She could have gutted half the people in this place before the rest noticed.

"What the hell do you want?" Komak asked, backing up a step. Beside him, Jasper and a few of the Magi tensed up.

Movement from the direction of The Source caught my eye. Sheila had spotted us. She lowered her sword, concern etched onto her face, but before she could do

331

much else a booming chant cried out in the cavern, seeming to come from everywhere and nowhere at once.

"*OME LAVERUS GOHED MAELPEREJI!*"

What the fuck?

The unearthly voices repeated their strange words, almost making me piss myself, but then I glanced across and saw Christy's circle aglow with power. It was them. The spell was working.

Much as I didn't want to take my attention off Komak, it was hard not to. The energy above Sheila began to coalesce into a pinpoint of brilliant light, a miniature sun almost too bright to look at. Risking my retinas burning to a crisp, I watched as a beam of energy slowly began to descend.

"This is it," Komak cried.

The hell with that noise. Impressive as the light show was, I was here to make sure he didn't fuck with the festivities. I stepped in front of him, blocking his view. "Where's Tom?"

"What are you talking about?" Even with my freshly vampirized ears, it was hard to hear him above the chanting, rising and falling in both pitch and cadence as Christy and her makeshift circle continued to wedge open the doorway between our world and what lay beyond.

"You took him. Don't try to hide it. I..."

"What was that?"

"I *said* you took him. I saw what was in Calibra's lair. You can't deny it."

"Calibra?"

"The White Mother, fucktard!"

The chanting was now loud enough to make my teeth rattle. The mages standing nearby, rather than fry me for my aggressive stance, were all mesmerized by what was taking place behind me. Oh fuck it. I dared a glance over my shoulder. Sheila had once again raised her sword high.

The brilliant beam of light struck it, its power mixing with hers.

At the convergence point, high above her head, that ball of energy began to grow, white at first but then turning a sickly orange, the same unholy shade The Source had once been.

It's only a crack, I told myself, forcing my attention back toward the matter at hand.

My timing was perfect, as a dome of purplish energy about seven feet in height appeared about ten yards beyond where Komak stood.

The magic within it swirled for a moment, then began to dissipate, revealing ... fuck me! It was no wonder I hadn't been able to find Bob's friend, the one who'd stolen the prism. He'd been hiding behind his magic, concealing Tom with him.

Backpack in hand, he came running our way.

"I have it!" he cried. "I have ... URK!"

Gan, once more proving her power put mine to shame, intercepted the wizard before he could take more than a couple of steps. With one quick move she popped him in the jaw, grabbing the backpack even as he collapsed unconscious onto the ground.

It was a surprisingly restrained move on her part. Maybe she was learning after all, but we could take stock of her personal growth once we were finished here. The deed done, easy-peasy, she turned toward us backpack in hand.

"Yeah, you got yours, fucker!" Tom cried, just barely audible over the continued chanting. He tried to kick the mage's prone form, but his foot flew right through it. Idiot.

Seeing that was pointless, he hurried to catch up to Gan as she strolled our way.

Komak seemed split between what was going on out

in The Source and us, but apparently he gauged – correctly, if you ask me – that we were the more pressing matter. "What are you doing?"

Finally, the chanting began to decrease in volume, thank goodness. So I was fairly certain he heard me when I said, "Fucking up your plans, asshole."

"You tell him, Bill," Tom said, stepping to join us.

"Are you okay, man?"

He flashed me a thumbs up. "Yeah, but for a minute there I was worried. Thought that asshole might try to cornhole me in private."

I shook my head. "You do realize you don't have a hole to corn, right?"

He shrugged as if he hadn't considered that, but before he could stupid things up further, Gan stepped through him and held the backpack out to me. "I believe this is yours, my love. Use it as I know only you will."

"Thanks," I replied, just as the light began to change.

It was subtle, not nearly as overpowering as it had been when last I was down here, but the illumination in the cavern began to take on a slightly reddish hue.

The chanting continued to diminish as if they were nearing the end, so I dared another glance back. Sheila was standing roughly ankle-deep in what appeared to be a puddle of orange goo maybe ten or fifteen feet across.

The light from above began to dissipate and along with it, too, so did the glow of faith around her.

Thud thud.

I nearly jumped out of my skin as there came a pounding in my chest, weak at first, but slowly gaining strength and rhythm.

Was that ... my heart?

Thud thud.

Holy crap, it was!

I turned to Gan. "Quick. Flash me your fangs."

She raised her brows over eyes their normal green color and then smiled, revealing teeth that were disturbingly straight but not even remotely sharp.

One of the nearby mages held out his hands and chanted something. My instincts screamed that I should react, but nothing more than a small spark of energy appeared between his fingers. It was barely enough to light a cigar, but from the look on his face you'd have thought it was the best damned cigar lighter in the world.

"It worked," Komak said.

"No thanks to you, dickhead." I pointed a finger at him from outside his reach. He might've been mostly human again, but he still had a shitload more combat training than me.

He glared back. "If you're through making a fool of yourself, I don't know what you're talking about."

I was about to call him out on that, but Gan put a hand on my shoulder and pointed out toward where Sheila still stood. "This can wait. Go, my love. The energies from the ritual have not fully stabilized. If you are to help your friend, it must be now."

Her words caught me by surprise. It was rare to hear her say something so ... human. For the barest of moments, I was touched, forgetting she absolutely terrified me.

But Gan was right. Everything else could wait. We'd achieved a partial victory for almost everyone here, but there was still work to do. We needed to see if we could help Tom ... and then figure out how to get the fuck out of here before anyone changed their mind about our truce.

I gave her a quick "we're friends, nothing more" grin, then stepped off the shoreline and waved for Tom to follow – not that he had much choice. "Come on, bro. Let's see about getting you a body."

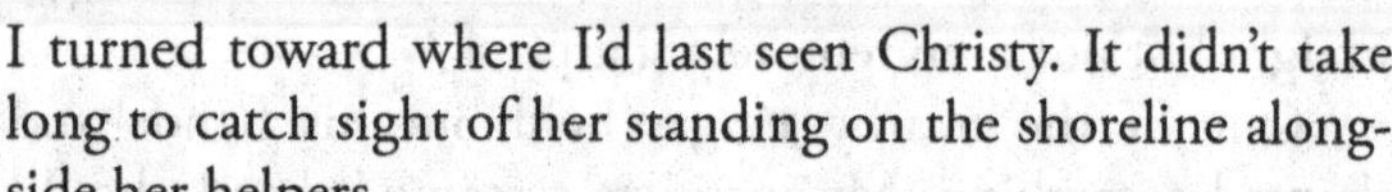

I turned toward where I'd last seen Christy. It didn't take long to catch sight of her standing on the shoreline alongside her helpers.

All four of them looked exhausted, but each was wearing a look of satisfaction upon their face. They knew what they'd accomplished, although Lizabitch would probably be a bit less smug when she learned we'd fucked up whatever scheme her boytoy had planned.

"Christy!" I shouted. "Over here!"

"No. Over here!" Tom cried from right behind me.

"Same difference, asshole."

"Yeah, but I want her running to me, not you."

Either way, she noticed. A big grin lit up her face and she headed our way.

Much to Tom's chagrin, I'm sure, she reached me first, throwing her arms around me.

"You did it," I said.

"We all did," she whispered back.

"Hey!" Tom protested. "Save one of those for me."

She disengaged and turned to him. "I've been saving one for five years. Let's see what we can do about it." Gone apparently was her former pessimism, and why not? She'd just done the impossible. Now it was time to see if the universe had one more miracle left for us.

We turned as a trio toward where Sheila still waited. She, too, looked winded. She stood bent over, with her hands on her thighs, having sheathed her sword.

As we approached, she locked eyes with me and frowned. "Choose the form of the destructor."

I stopped dead in my tracks. "What?!"

"Psyche! Made you look."

I couldn't help but laugh. Guess some of me had rubbed off on her after all.

There was still a lot to answer for between us, but it was hard to not be happy right at that moment. I doubted we'd ever go back to the way we'd been, but hopefully we could at least salvage our friendship after this.

Crazy, huh? A few years ago there wouldn't have been any doubt about my course of action. I'd have thrown myself at her feet and screamed, "All is forgiven, take me back!"

Guess this was part of that maturity thing I'd heard so much about. Even if my current relationship was still uncertain, it was time I took fate's hint that Icons and Freewills were at opposite ends of the compatibility scale. And, truth be told, even if we only maintained the barest fraction of our abilities going forward, that's what we were. There was no denying it anymore.

Still, this wasn't the time to depress the shit out of myself. We'd won. Holy shit! We'd actually won.

Now to see if fate was generous enough to give us one more victory.

43

LITTLE PIGS, LITTLE PIGS

I unzipped the backpack and gingerly pulled the broken Max Adventure doll out. It was glowing, still charged up with energy from that last pulse, but there wasn't any question that it was finite. Once it ran out, the Prism would be about as potent as a nightlight and Tom would be left as a mere ghost.

"Is that...?" Sheila asked, her eyes growing misty. No doubt she was remembering back to when she'd been forced to ram her sword through it – Tom's body – unleashing the vast energy within.

"Yep," he replied with a grin. "I told you fuckers last time that I'd be all right, but none of you listened."

"At least we don't need to stab your ass again." I turned to Christy. "What do you think? Is it bath time?"

She took a deep breath. This wasn't exactly our ideal scenario, and we both knew it. "I think ... it's our best shot."

Sheila raised an eyebrow. "What is?" Then stark realization filled her features. "Oh! You're going to make him into one of those..."

338

"We're making him whole," Christy corrected. "Or as whole as we can."

"Do you think that's wise ... err, I mean, will it work?"

Christy glanced among our quartet. The indecision drained from her face and a look of determination took over. She'd obviously been giving this some heavy thought. "I think so. The teachings of magic tell us that a soul remains tethered to its body for a time after death. Under normal circumstances, that tether quickly fades and the spirit moves on. But I think this place somehow acted as a conduit, breaking the existing tether and reconnecting it to another receptacle – in the case of the Jahabich, the very stones that make up this cavern. It's much weaker now, but it might still work. And the Prism should be stable enough to not..."

"Blow us the fuck up?" Tom offered.

"React badly," she countered with a sigh.

"Too bad we don't have another body to act as the receptacle," Sheila said.

I blinked at her. "Would that even work?"

Christy shrugged. "In theory, but it would need to be undamaged to be viable. A body that died from heavy trauma would simply die again."

"But who gives a shit since we don't have one?" Tom rightfully pointed out.

Christy nodded. "True."

I briefly considered Bob's corpse, but quickly pushed that thought away. Trauma free was the key phrase here, and that didn't really apply to him. Pity. If I'd known sooner I'd have ... probably still drained him like a stuck pig. There was no fighting the bloodlust once it took hold.

And since I doubted anyone here was willing to volunteer for a non-traumatic death, that left us back at square one – turning Tom into a hopefully non-grotesque and far less murderous rock monster.

Speaking of volunteers, though, I took a quick look around. There was still a lot of activity back at the shore, but many of the groups were beginning to disperse. Guess they realized it was time to wrap things up here.

Glancing over my shoulder, I saw Gan was still standing with Komak and Jasper. They appeared to be arguing, but my super hearing was currently turned off and I was otherwise too occupied to try making out what they were saying. Besides, Gan could handle herself.

"Okay, then," Tom said, drawing my attention back. "Let's do this shit."

That broke the impasse. You could always count on him to not waste time with silly things like sentiment or consequences. I held the doll out to Christy, but Sheila stepped forward.

"Can I? I was the one who caused all of this. It's only right I be the one to make it better."

"You weren't..."

She cut me off. "You're wrong, I was. *All* of it. Five years ago and now. Bringing him back won't erase any of what I did, but maybe it'll be a start."

Christy took a moment to consider this, then she nodded at me.

I handed Sheila the doll and she stared hard at it for several long seconds.

Tom, in the meantime, walked to her side, his feet disappearing into the ooze of The Source puddle as if it weren't there. "Just like old times."

Sheila looked up at him and laughed. "Hopefully not."

Christy and I both backed up a few steps, our hands subconsciously intertwining with each other.

Sheila noticed it and, for a moment, stared at me quizzically. But rather than say anything, she apparently decided it could wait. We could always discuss weird-ass love triangles – like the ones in those trashy harem books – another day.

As Tom looked on, Sheila bent at the knees, preparing to submerge Max into what would hopefully be his next big adventure.

The doll's feet were about an inch away from the surface of the magical pool when a deafening roar filled the air, as if someone had driven a riding mower into a pride of lions.

"RAAAAWWWWRRRRRR!"

What the fuck?!

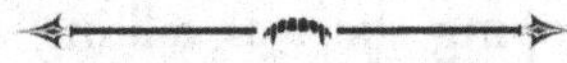

The entire cavern shook from the force of it. Hell, I was lucky to not be knocked on my ass. Christy and I held onto each other as much for balance as support.

In the very center, Sheila fought to keep her footing as the strange interdimensional waters of The Source began to churn, forming mini breakers of orange goop around her feet.

"Is this supposed to happen?" I cried out.

"No!" Christy shouted, although I wasn't sure if she was answering me or just screaming in general.

She turned her head skyward, eyes wide, and I followed her gaze.

You've gotta be fucking kidding me!

The swirling disc of energy from the ley lines, which had been in the process of dissipating, suddenly flared up to at least five times the size it had been. It spread along the ceiling as what appeared to be a funnel cloud of raw power began to form in its center. It was like the beam of energy that had touched down on Sheila earlier, except increased by a magnitude of power.

That can't be good.

Crackles of oddly-colored electricity lanced out from it and I had to blink a few times to make sure I wasn't losing my mind. The energy appeared to take on physical form for a second or two – massive clawed hands grasping for purchase in the air – before dissipating and reappearing elsewhere.

Yeah, this was definitely not normal.

"My God, she was right!" Christy cried from next to me.

"Who?"

"Gan!"

Oh boy. "About what?"

I was really hoping she was talking about something benign, maybe a harmless comment about someone's hair, made when I wasn't paying attention. Sadly, it wasn't to be, as Christy turned to me, her face pale with fear.

"Something is trying to force its way through."

"Goddamn it," I replied, the sound coming out as more a growl than anything.

In response, Christy's eyes opened wide and she backed up a step, letting go of my hand.

I was about to ask what was wrong – outside of every-thing that actually *was* wrong – when my tongue ran over my teeth, answering that for me.

My fangs were back.

Just for shits and giggles, I reached a hand up to my neck. I was no EMT, but I was pretty sure that was nada on a pulse.

"It can't be," she said.

I had no answer for her. She was right, but that didn't change my reality.

Christy shook her head, the shock disappearing from her face. "We can talk later. Stopping this takes priority."

I nodded, grateful. She was a true pro when the chips were down. and I had a feeling that's what we needed more than anything.

That was confirmed in spades a moment later when the monstrous growl gave way to an equally terrifying voice. "***GIVE WHAT WAS PROMISED!***"

It was different than what I'd heard from Christy and her circle. More importantly, I was hearing it in my mind as well as with my ears. Whatever was communicating with us was beaming its commentary track straight into our heads, with the volume set to twelve.

I looked back at the shore. Unsurprisingly, panic seemed to be the soup of the day for most. However, most was not all.

I spied a witch, wearing the same black robes as Bob and his buddy, standing at the shoreline waving her arms about. Either she was practicing some sick new dance moves or casting a spell.

And she wasn't alone. There was another a ways down. Then still more further along. It took me a moment, but I quickly realized they'd encircled The Source, each of them undulating in tune to the rest as if dancing to a beat only they could hear.

I didn't have time to count, but wouldn't have been remotely surprised to discover there were thirteen in total.

Too bad for them I'd never been a fan of raves.

"Come on!" I shouted to my friends, turning back toward where I'd last seen Komak.

It didn't take more than a second to spot him. He stood where he'd been on the rocky shoreline, his eyes turned upward, probably creaming his pants in anticipation.

I took maybe two steps when another voice caught my ears.

"What the hell are you doing?!"

It was Kelly. She was standing with Liz at a different spot along the shore. However, where I expected the latter to be partaking of this fuckery, I was wrong. *What the?* Both she and Kelly were being restrained by a pair of black-robed mages as a third undulated upon the shore, performing the same unholy dance moves as the rest.

His hood flopped off his head, giving me enough of a glance to see Hershel's face. *Fuck!*

The asshole had been one of Komak's men after all, stringing us along so he could play double agent. Well, if that didn't chap my ass, I didn't know what did.

I pointed him out to Christy. "Go help them. I'll take care of Komak."

She didn't look pleased at the prospect of splitting up, but she was far better suited for a wizard duel than me, and I was certain she knew it. Rather than argue, she gathered energy around her and turned to help Kelly.

"Keep your eyes open," I called after her, certain Liz was only biding her time before turning on us. "Something isn't right here."

Talk about a talent for understatement.

I turned back to find Sheila standing where she'd been. Tom was alongside her, mostly because he couldn't move very far from the doll in her hands. What worried me more, though, was the look of disbelief on her face, about as far from her Icon self-assurance as you could get.

"This wasn't supposed to happen," she said.

"I believe you. But we really can't dwell on that right now."

"I..."

"The world, these people, need the Icon. Do you think you can do that?"

That seemed to get through to her. She locked eyes with me for a moment and then nodded, drawing her sword with her free hand. Before either of us could make a move, however, she cried out, "Look!"

I spun, expecting to see Komak doing something ... diabolical, I guess. But he continued to stand there staring, a look of pure confusion on his face.

After a moment more, he met my gaze and cried out, "What is this?!"

I wasn't sure how to respond. I'd expected arrogance and triumph from him, not this.

The cavern floor shuddered beneath us, shaking me from my indecision. I opened my mouth, knowing he'd hear me over the rumbling. "You can't fool me, you lying..."

My accusation was interrupted by a hand erupting from his chest cavity, showering him in gore. Komak looked down at it, a mix of horror and surprise on his face, then he turned his head, trying to face the lithe figure behind him who'd done this.

Uh oh.

In the next instant, his body exploded in white-hot flame from the inside out, immolating him where he stood.

When the spots finally cleared from my eyes, he was gone and in his place stood Gan.

More chilling than her presence, however, was the smile plastered upon her face, as if she'd known all along that this would happen.

44

THE GODS MUST BE CRAZY

Any delusion that Gan was simply taking Komak out of the equation, before he could do something nefarious, dissipated in an instant as Jasper stepped next to her, likewise grinning.

She gave her arm a shake, the charred and burnt flesh already beginning to mend, and cried out, "Is it not glorious, my love?"

"What have you done?" I asked, knowing full well she'd hear me just fine despite the distance between us.

"What those leading this endeavor were not bold enough to do."

Whatever spell those mages had been preparing went off. Shimmering bolts of energy shot upward from their bodies to a point maybe halfway between them and the ceiling ... spaced so that they were directly beneath the ley lines still glowing above us.

There, the power from each collected, expanding until they formed a series of brilliantly shining disks, each roughly twenty feet high.

What the?

Remembering my video games, I half expected to hear that the cake was a lie as people started leaping out of them with portal guns.

I realized the truth wasn't too far off from that as images began to form in each of the ... portals, I guess, taking on shape and substance until it was as if there were thirteen windows to elsewhere above us.

In each could be seen groups of people. No, not people, at least not all of them. I spied yellow eyes among the masses – vamps and mages, if I had to guess. Some appeared surprised at what they were seeing. Others were far less so, wearing knowing grins upon their faces. And maybe it was just me, but it seemed the vamps were all among the former.

What the fuck was going on?

A group of black-robed mages approached Gan from her flank as she stood there smiling. One let loose with a bolt of yellow-tinged magic, giving me hope that maybe one of them was a double-double agent. Gan made no attempt to dodge it, however, despite her senses likely being heightened enough to hear a spider take a shit from a block away.

The spell engulfed her, lighting her up with its power, but still she stood facing me as if everything was right as rain.

"HEAR ME," she said, her voice echoing in my mind as well as my ears. All around, I could see the various beings in the cavern stop as if to listen.

It was some sort of communication spell, possibly meant to compensate for the fact that she was no longer capable of compulsion – handy for getting everyone's attention in the middle of the apocalyptic chaos going on above us.

"THIRTEEN HAVE BEEN PROMISED," she

continued. *"FULFILL THE PACT, SO THAT WHICH WAS STOLEN FROM YOU MAY BE RETURNED IN ALL ITS GLORY."*

Call me pessimistic, but I had a feeling she wasn't talking about some wallet she'd found on the sidewalk.

I couldn't hear what was being said on the other side of those portals, the spell apparently being a one-way thing, but there appeared to be some dissent going on. The vamps in particular, visible in all but two of the windows I could see, appeared confused by what had been said.

A moment later, however, that confusion turned to horror as the Magi turned on them. Flashes of lethal magic – green and red – flared up all around, engulfing neo-vamps wherever I could see them. It made me glad the sound was turned off, because there appeared to be a lot of screaming going on at the other ends ... for a few seconds anyway.

Then it was all over as the Last Coven lived up to their name, being disintegrated to the man, present company excluded.

I heard Christy cry out, "Have you gone mad?!"

Sparing a glance back that way, I saw her lash out with a spell of her own toward Hershel, still aglow from conjuring the portal hanging high over his head. Sadly, it fell short as the mages restraining Kelly and Liz let go long enough to erect a purple force dome around him.

"That's eleven! We need two more."

Jasper, still at Gan's side, was pointing my way. "Finish the covenant!"

That was finally enough to break Sheila's impasse. She stepped to my side, albeit fortunately not close enough for her shield of faith to vaporize me. "No more! Whatever you're doing, it ends now."

"Yeah," Tom echoed, joining us. "Kick their asses, sexy lady, oppa Icon-style."

Ugh! Five years in limbo definitely hadn't made his puns any better.

"I think not, Shining One," Gan replied in a voice probably too low for her to hear. "Thirteen were promised and thirteen *shall* be delivered."

The red glow from the nascent Source began to turn a sickly green as the energy continued to collect above us. More of those spectral claws reached out, raking furrows across the ceiling, and another hungry growl rose up, causing the ground to shake.

Oh, this was definitely not good, and we'd walked right into it. All that shit about primal gods clawing their way into this world, that had been Gan's idea all along – hidden in plain sight right in front of our noses. As for the rest, I had no idea how she was able to convert so many mages here to her whim, but I doubted any answers were forthcoming.

More importantly, I had a bad feeling about the final two sacrifices. Following their break-in at Christy's, only twelve of the Last Coven had been left, Komak had confirmed as much himself. Ed was safe, and I sincerely doubted Gan planned to off herself. But the way her asshole partner in crime was staring our way told me all I needed to know.

However, before they could make their move, a group of Magi apparently not cool with any of this crap launched an attack, firing beams of magic at any black-robed assholes in sight. The cavalry had arrived.

Too bad Gan and her new lackey weren't alone, as more of her black-robed minions raced to protect her. Nevertheless, it gave us an opening, however small.

I turned to Sheila. "Think we can take them?"

"The Freewill and Icon together again?" she replied. "I

like those odds." But then her confident tone wavered. "But what then? Will stopping them stop this?"

"I ... have no idea."

"Fuck that noise," Tom said. "If that's the case, we can end this ourselves."

"What do you mean?"

He pointed toward the doll still in Sheila's hands.

"You can't be serious," I said.

"Yep. Repeat performance, bitches." He smiled at Sheila. "What do you say? We closed this fucker once. Care to do it again?"

What?!

"No!" I cried. "We don't know what that will do to..."

"To me?" he asked, his expression turning serious. "Don't sweat it, man. I know that my little girl is in good hands and ... I guess so is Christy. Besides, she was probably right about me moving on." He grinned again. "But if I gotta go, go with a bang."

"Y-you can't. We've come so far. The Magi..."

"Fuck 'em," Tom said. "They can get jobs like everyone else. Beats the world being ass-raped by Gozer."

Amazingly enough, as he'd done before, Tom – normally the one to shoot his mouth off when it was best to keep his trap shut – had somehow become the voice of reason.

That said, I didn't give a shit about most of the Magi here. We, I, *his daughter*, had just gotten him back.

I opened my mouth to protest, but he held up a hand. "No offense, dude, but can we skip the next part? We don't have time for you two to fight again. Let's just assume you got your ass kicked so you can cover ours while we do this."

"But..."

Tom stepped up to me and put a spectral hand on, or

through, my shoulder. "It's time to do what you do best, buddy – fuck up their plans."

He'd been right five years ago. Now, with something unknown trying to force its way into our world, I couldn't help but think history was repeating itself. This needed to be stopped, but we didn't even have a backup plan in our pocket like last time. Gan had spoon-fed us what she wanted us to hear, leading us by the nose the entire time. The only option we had left was to do the unthinkable.

Goddamn it all!

I could see the indecision on Sheila's face, her faith aura faltering. This whole thing had been her attempt to make things right for the Magi. But now it was being perverted far beyond what even Komak had done.

She looked at Tom, then back at me, tears in her eyes. "I don't know if I can do this. Not again."

Tom was offering to make the ultimate sacrifice – once more. I realized the least I could do was be strong for both of them. "I do. I have faith in you."

There came a cry from the shore and I glanced back to see Gan dispatching one of the witches who'd attacked her.

Time was nearly up, but we weren't ready. Not yet. "Christy. She needs to..."

Tom shook his head. "I suck at long goodbyes anyway. Tell her for me. She'll understand."

"I..."

"Come on," He turned and held out a hand to Sheila, as if she could take it. "Once more, for old time's sake?" After a moment, she gave her head a single nod. "Awesome! I always wanted to slam the door in a god's face."

I turned away, sick to my stomach. We'd come so close only to have it snatched away at the last second. Nevertheless, if they were willing to do this, then I had to be prepared to do whatever was needed to buy them the time.

There was no time to falter. I had to be strong, even if I didn't want to be

"Bill?"

I looked back to find Sheila aglow with the power of faith, tears streaming freely down her face.

"I know you don't have any reason to believe me, but I will make this right."

"I know you will," I whispered to myself as I once again faced the shore.

There was so much to say, far more than I could have conveyed in an hour, much less a few moments. And mine wasn't the only voice that deserved a chance to say goodbye.

But alas, time – and apparently fate – were not on our side. The cavern rumbled beneath me once more as if in agreement.

Gan and Jasper had just finished ganking a pair of mages, tossing their bodies to the side like they were nothing more than garbage. A group of black-robes formed a defensive perimeter around them, no doubt to free them from further distraction.

Jasper saw me approaching and smiled. "Do you honestly believe you can stop us?"

"I'm the Freewill, Assper. What do you think?"

"The Freewill?" he scoffed. "The old ways are dead. All I see before me are the last few sacrifices needed to usher in a new era."

"As do I." Gan stepped to his side, her eyes glittering with a combination of greed and madness – in short, her usual look. Then, almost faster than my eyes could follow, she lashed out with her claws and erased Jasper's throat in a spray of blood. "But my beloved is not one of them."

Vampires can heal from a lot, but she'd nearly decapitated him with a single blow. Another quick swing from her and the nearly part of that equation was erased, along with Jasper as his body flared up in white-hot flames, giving to this place another life that had been denied it all those years back.

A part of me wasn't entirely surprised. She was Gan, after all. Every time I'd gotten comfortable thinking I knew the answers to her crazy-ass mind, she'd changed the questions. Why should now be any different?

"How long have you been planning this?" I asked, making sure I stood between her and Sheila. Gan was fast, far faster than me. But if I kept my eyes on her, I might be able to intercept her if she tried anything.

"Since the day destiny chose to spare me."

Okay, that was a bit longer than I would've guessed. "And Sheila, all of this?"

"A mere catalyst spurring me to action, albeit earlier than I originally planned. Nevertheless, I knew her involvement would draw yours, which in turn would provide the missing pieces I required."

"But how?"

"The Shining One is not the only creature upon this world to possess the conviction of faith." She took a step forward. "I did tell you, beloved, did I not, that fate continues to smile upon you?"

I readied myself, praying that Sheila was in place and hadn't changed her mind. "You want her to be the thirteenth, don't you?"

"I told her I would return for you one day. Did you think me a liar?"

"You do realize we broke up, right?"

She shrugged. "Then her fate should be all the more easy for you to accept."

Goddamn, that was cold. The light in the cavern

shifted again, growing darker, more ominous. I dared a glance up. The energy gathered at the ceiling was starting to swirl, forming a diabolical funnel cloud of sorts. I had a feeling that when it touched down, the effect would be ... not good.

"So you tricked us?" I asked, trying to stall her. Gan was scary smart, but she had a bit of a blind spot where I was concerned. I was hoping I could get her to monologue long enough for us to stuff her plans down her throat with an extra helping of boot. "Tricked us into coming down here so you could get Christy's spell?"

To my surprise, Gan actually laughed. "Of course not, beloved. I have known the intricacies of the witch's ritual for some time."

"You're shitting me."

"Hardly. As I told you, I've kept close tabs on you and your life, including the pieces of it you may have discarded along the way."

My eyes opened wide as realization hit. "Hold on. You didn't go dumpster diving for my old phone, did you?"

"Not personally," she replied, "but in essence. The data contained within was most enlightening. I especially enjoyed the video you surreptitiously captured of your whore being wed to the Alma leader." *Oh, yeah. Almost forgot about that.* "More importantly, my servants have long had access to the photos you took of this place, including the ritual once inscribed upon the walls."

Oh boy. I could only imagine what blackmail dirt she had on me from the last laptop I tossed out.

"Where Komak and his pet witch lacked the time to properly distill it," she continued, "the mages in my employ have had years to do so and more."

And more? That didn't sound good. "Then why lure us all down here?"

"The others are inconsequential, the fodder of fate. But you wouldn't have come if they hadn't."

I narrowed my eyes and pointed to my fangs. "So you wanted this to happen to me?"

Gan broke eye contact for a moment, seemingly embarrassed. "Alas, that was … not anticipated. All I knew was that I wanted you by my side as we embraced a new beginning."

I was tempted to call her out. If this wasn't her doing, then whose was it? But before I could do so, Sheila cried out from somewhere behind me.

"Bill! It's almost here."

I let a fanged smile play out across my lips as I continued to face Gan. "Yeah? Well embrace this. DO IT!"

I expected to see any of a dozen different emotions cross Gan's face: shock, anger, batshit crazy, or some combination. But the fact that she merely smiled chilled me to the bone.

"Yes," she replied in a bare whisper, "do it."

What?

Her words from mere moments ago played out in my head. *The mages in my employ have had years to do so and more.*

Was it possible she'd prepared for this, too?

And just like that, it made sense why she hadn't killed that mage earlier, the one who had Tom. It wasn't mercy. It was because the fucker was working for her, too, setting up the opportunity to hand Tom over to me so we could carry out the … plan Gan had suggested in the first place. She wanted him out there in The Source.

"No, wait!" I spun, quick as my vampire reflexes would allow, but it wasn't nearly fast enough to make a difference.

I could only watch as Sheila – Tom's shade by her side

– tossed the doll into the air and then sliced it neatly in half with her sword.

The two ends fell into the magic goop pooled at her feet just as that sickly green funnel of power descended upon her.

For a moment, I lost sight of her amidst the swirling torrent of energy, and then it all exploded in an eruption of light, sound, and fury.

45

BODY OF EVIDENCE

The shockwave from the explosion hit me like a truck, sending me tumbling end over end like a ragdoll all the way back to the shoreline.

I'd forgotten what being cock-punched by magic was like. Needless to say, I hadn't missed it much.

Dazed and bruised to all hell, I skidded to a halt, *enjoying* the sensation of my skin shearing off against the rocky ground. Thankfully I landed in a position conducive to see what was going on. Back in the center of The Source, a rising dome of swirling energy was forming – myriad colors fighting for dominance: orange, white, and green, like the Irish flag trying to teabag itself.

Bracing myself best as I could, I waited for the primal scream of souls being dragged back to whatever hell they'd been unleashed from – the cry that would tell me we'd once again closed the door, hopefully for good this time.

Sadly, where I'd been caught unprepared by the blowback, I saw that others were not. The mages who'd created those thirteen portals somehow continued to stand their ground against the cascade of power. Worse, they weren't finished yet.

The fuck?!

As they gesticulated, sickly green energy flared forth from each of the portals – their color matching whatever was trying to break through to our world – and struck the swirling center.

A scream rose up, but it wasn't that of spirits being dragged away. It came from inside that vortex of energy. There was no fury or defiance to it. It was a cry of terror, of pain, and it was coming from Sheila.

"No!"

"*HAHAHAHAHAHA!*"

Sadly, my voice was lost as booming laughter echoed from above, once more shaking the very foundation of this cavern.

There was only one chance. I focused on the maelstrom of power, the cry of pain that continued to issue forth. I needed to stop this. I needed to save her but couldn't as myself. I could only do that by letting the beast inside of me out to play. "Come on, Dr. Death! Get your ass out here and fuck these guys up."

Reaching deep down inside, I tried to remember the rage, the anger, the pain, all the things that used to summon my own personal demon forth from deep inside my head.

If I gave him control, I could do this. I could get in there, break through whatever was happening.

I could still win this.

Any minute now.

Yep, any time...

But nothing happened. No red haze of rage. No transformation. Hell, there wasn't even a hiccup of mocking laughter from inside my head.

Fine! Be that way, asshole. If I have to take both of us out to save her, I will.

Shaking my head to clear it, I pushed myself to my

feet. But before I could take more than a step or two, the maelstrom flared up and a tidal wave of orange goo poured forth from the center, racing out in all directions as if someone had turned on a giant spigot connected to Hell itself.

The Source had been opened wide again.

The wave of primal power raced toward the shore at tsunami speed. I was certain I was about to be bowled over by a King Kong-sized money shot, but then it simply stopped – freezing in place mere feet from its former edge.

For a moment, I wondered whether Christy had cast her time spell again. If so, maybe we could...

The orange goo – in reality, a gateway to worlds beyond our own – held its place for a moment longer and then it began to recede, even faster than it had come pouring out.

Okay, that's new.

It was pulled back into that swirling dome of energy as if someone had activated a Mega Maid-sized vacuum cleaner.

Yes!

She was doing it. Sheila was fighting back. More importantly, she was winning.

The screams that had been coming from that awesome display of power fell quiet against the thunderous crackle of raw energy, and a moment later, the center of it all flared out in thirteen different directions, blasting toward those still-opened portals.

Whatever the mages had been trying to do, Sheila had somehow found a way to turn it around and ram it down their throats.

Yeah! Fry, you fuckers!

The energy struck each of the portals simultaneously, filling them with explosive orange radiance. There came a crackle of thunder from each and then they winked out, leaving nothing but acrid smoke behind.

The crackling dome of power at the center of The Source was next, sizzling for a moment and then likewise reversing itself. The funnel of otherworldly energy blasted back up toward the ceiling, leaving a dense cloud of dust and debris behind.

The energy fed back into whatever had been coalescing along the ceiling, causing it to collapse in on itself until it was little more than a few crackles of magical power still arcing along the roof of the cavern.

Thank Goodness.

I dared a glance at the nearest of those black-robed assholes, expecting to see confusion etched onto their stupid faces. But instead I saw the opposite. Where fear seemed to reign supreme for nearly everyone else in sight, expressions of rapturous joy beamed from Gan's mages.

The fuck? Had these guys suddenly turned stupid or something?

They'd lost. The Source had been destroyed again. Everything, even that small puddle that had formed in the center, had dried up. Gone was that reddish glow that had suffused the cave.

It was over.

Wasn't it?

I turned toward the center to see if I could catch sight of Sheila, but it was still too obscured by dust and smoke. Whatever had just happened was weird as fuck, but I had faith that she'd...

"What have you done, you monster?!"

I spun automatically at the sound of Christy's voice. She was clambering to her feet about fifteen yards away.

Kelly and Liz were both on the ground nearby, dazed but alive – not exactly a win in that latter case.

For one terrible moment, I thought she was yelling at me, but then I realized she was directing her fury at a group of black-robed wizards, Hershel among them.

He and the wizards who'd been protecting him stood on shaky legs, looking winded. But the expression on his face was still one of gleeful defiance. "I've done what a heretic like you was too weak to do."

He raised his arms and began to chant. *Idiot.* The Source was gone. Magic was once again as dead as...

Christy held out her hands and a beam of angry red energy shot out, blowing a hole right through Hershel's chest.

Jesus fucking Christ!

Yeah, she'd just murdered the shit out of him. But how the hell was that even possible?

"Do you find it as marvelous as I, my love?"

I did a one-eighty and found Gan standing upon a small rise maybe thirty feet away from me. Four black-robed and hooded witches stood around her, facing outward as if to ward off a potential attack.

That itself wasn't promising. However, what caused my balls to truly shrivel was the sight of her eyes – golden orbs of yellow malevolence staring back at me.

No way.

Not really wanting to know the answer, I raised a hand to the side of my neck again. Sure enough, there was nary a peep from my pulse. "How?"

She grinned, displaying her fangs. "Is it not obvious?"

Had there been a desk nearby, I'd have gladly beaten my head against it. "No, not really."

"One portal to beyond, one Source," she explained. "Powerful yet vulnerable."

"And now gone forever."

"Yes, beloved." She continued to smile. "*Sacrificed* so that thirteen others, dotting this world, could be birthed. Combined, they shall open the veil in ways not seen since the dawn of man. It shall be glorious to behold."

Glorious was really not the word that came to mind. It was trumped ever so slightly by pterodactyl-shit crazy. "How the fuck is that possible?"

"It is not," she replied as the black-robed figures standing around her raised their hands into the air. "At least not without ... assistance."

Behind me, I could hear more blasts of energy being unleashed, could feel the hair on the back of my neck standing up from the discharge of magic. Christy, and hopefully others, were engaging the true traitors among their number, helpfully identified by their poor choice in fashion.

I should've turned and helped her, but somehow I couldn't. Before me was Patient Zero of this cancerous outgrowth. Everyone else was merely a pawn.

Gan held out a hand toward me. "Join me."

It was straight out of supervillain 101. "Join you? You're all kinds of..."

"*HAHAHAHAHAHAHA!*"

Sadly, my litany of colorful words describing what a psychotic shit-burrito she was were drowned out as that creepy-ass psychic laughter started up again, louder than ever.

"*THE OFFERING IS ACCEPTED. RECEIVE MY BLESSING SO THE WORLD MAY TREMBLE ONCE MORE.*"

Call me crazy, but that didn't sound particularly promising.

Gan's smile widened as she continued to hold out her hand toward me. The four mages around her looked up as thunder sounded from above. I followed their gaze to find that crackle of green energy, still playing across the roof of the cave, beginning to once again grow in intensity.

Oh for Christ's sake, what now?

"Tremble at this, asshole!"

At the sound of the familiar voice, Gan's smile faltered and her face took on that rarest of expressions for her — surprise.

I spun, praying that my ears weren't deceiving me.

The smoke had finally cleared from the center of The Source, giving way to the white glow of faith.

Sheila was alive, and she looked pissed.

46

TIT FOR TAT

"Impossible," Gan said, her voice betraying both surprise and fear, although far more of the former.

Yet it was true. Guess it was a good day for the impossible.

Sheila began heading our way just as that sliver of power above us flared up. That was all the incentive I needed. It was time to kick some ass or die trying – even if that second one was more likely.

I didn't see any sign of Tom but that, along with my grief, would need to wait until we'd finished what the crazy bitch with a SpongeBob fetish had started.

Gan, however, was apparently through playing games as well. "Kill the Shining One," she ordered. "Her kind are obsolete in this glorious new age."

Too bad for her the classics didn't die that easily.

Sadly, intent wasn't the same as reality. I quickly realized that neither of us were going to make it there in time. With another rumble that left me staggering off balance, the power above us coalesced into a crackle of green lightning which arced across the ceiling until it was right above where Gan stood triumphant.

Or where she *had* been standing triumphant?

One of the hooded mages guarding her raced up and tackled her from behind, sending the teenaged hellion stumbling forward.

Her attacker tossed her robe to the side, revealing ... Sally's smiling face.

Holy shit!

Guess she'd finally caught that second wind. "Way to go!"

She took a moment to toss me a wink before raising the gun I'd left with her and taking aim.

The other three mages turned toward her, already gathering power. They were too late, though, Sally was already in a shooter's stance.

"I've been waiting for this a long time, bitch."

As the words left her mouth, three things happened in near synchronicity, and it was as if time slowed down just long enough to mark the occasion.

Sally pulled the trigger just as the mages unleashed beams of red death at her.

The spells struck their mark in the same moment the green lightning lanced down and engulfed her in an embrace of fire.

Oh, God, no!

There came a hum of power as if an electrical transformer had just blown, followed by a blinding flash and the awful smell of burnt flesh and hair.

Sally didn't even have time to scream as the power consumed her whole.

I saw red, albeit my body still refused to transform. But it would have to be enough. Later I would cry. For now, I focused all of my rage, grief, and outrage into savage action, baring my fangs and charging forward.

No more!

The combination of death magic with that green lightning caused a feedback of power that arced out from where Sally had stood — weak enough to not affect me much but more than enough to stagger the witches who'd killed her.

Good enough for me.

Gan lay unmoving at their feet. But the fact that she wasn't dust spoke volumes. She would have to wait, though. My window of opportunity wouldn't last long, and the first rule of any dungeon encounter was take out the ranged fighters first.

I reached the witch closest to me just as she was regaining her footing. She looked up, delicious terror on her face as she saw me close the gap.

"Masenko!" I cried, clocking her hard enough to ensure they'd need a spatula to rebuild her nose.

To my right, Sheila tackled another of the witches from the side, dropping her, too. It wasn't the most graceful move I'd ever seen her perform, but considering everything she'd just gone through, I wasn't about to critique her performance.

She popped the witch in the jaw with a sloppy right, putting her out of the fight, then turned toward me. "Masenko? Seriously?"

"It's a move from *Dragonball...*"

"I know what it is, dumbass," she replied. "Next time yell Final Flash or something cool. Don't embarrass me with that pussy shit."

Huh?

Before I could say anything to that, movement registered in the corner of my eye. There was one witch still standing and we were both caught flat-footed as she let loose with a blast of explosive green energy.

"Oh shit!" Sheila cried as the bolt of death flew toward her.

Her aura flared up just as the spell hit home, dissipating it harmlessly around her. I was already on the move but realized I had, at best, a fifty-fifty shot of reaching our attacker before she got off another shot.

Time seemed to slow as I closed in. The witch raised her hands and ... stumbled?

The blast she'd meant for me flew wide and I realized why a moment later. A quivering ball of eyeballs had pooled around her leg, pulling her off balance.

That was all I needed. I let loose with a backhand, hard enough to ensure she'd be enjoying a good long stay in traction before trying any shit again.

Satisfied she was out of the fight, I turned to the little snot ball. "Thanks, Glen. I owe you one."

"My pleasure," he bubbled excitedly. "But watching you and the Icon in action is all the payment I require."

The Icon? *Oh, shit!* I spun back to make sure Sheila was all right.

She was alive but looking down at herself wide-eyed, as if surprised she'd survived the attack. "Um, Bill?"

"Yeah?" I replied, worried that maybe she wasn't as okay as she looked.

"When did I grow these?"

47

ESCAPE FROM THE
CENTER OF THE EARTH

"**E**xcuse me?"

Sheila opened her mouth to reply, but was cut short by a groan from nearby.

"Oh fuck! She's still alive." Sheila drew her sword and held it out tentatively in front of her, the blade shaking in her grasp.

This was definitely not normal Icon behavior, especially coupled with her newfound knowledge of *Dragonball Z* moves. I mean, heck, she'd watched it with me a few times while we'd lived together, but I'd gotten the impression it had been in that way couples had of humoring their significant others by doing things they didn't give a shit about.

That would all have to wait, though. Gan was rising. There was a bullet hole above her right eye but even as I watched, the skin around it bubbled and then the slug itself was pushed out as the bone beneath it began to knit back together. Sally's shot had been dead on, but alas, the bullet hadn't been high enough caliber to get the job done.

Not good. We stood no chance against her, not with Sheila acting all squirrely.

There was only one thing to do if we wanted to win this, something I would have traded my left nut to avoid.

The thing was, Sally had bought us this chance with her life. Could I dishonor her sacrifice for something so petty as personal disgust?

That was all the answer I needed.

Before Gan could fully recover, I grabbed hold of her and sunk my teeth into her neck.

I'd forgotten what it was like. Blood, human blood anyway, was the greatest feast one could ever hope for. Vampires were attuned to it in a way that made human food pale in comparison. Your favorite chocolate chip cookies? That burrito place down the road that was to die for? A home cooked meal by someone who knew what the fuck they were doing? They were crap compared to the drug-like euphoria of a mouthful of blood.

But that was human blood. Freewills like me had an extra trick up our sleeves. We could also drink the blood of other vampires, something they couldn't do in return. Better yet, doing so temporarily added their power to my own. Gan was, as far as I knew, one of only two other vampires left on the planet besides me. And she was by far the most powerful.

With that first bite, Gan's blood tingled in my mouth. Then I swallowed and it hit my gut like liquid fire, her power becoming mine. I grasped hold of her arms, now with strength rivaling her own, and held tight so she couldn't escape.

Of course, that assumed she actually wanted to get away.

"Oh, my love."

Fuck me! There I was, tearing into her throat, and she couldn't even do me the favor of screaming in terror. She really took the joy out of kicking her ass.

I pulled back before she could really get into it. Blood oozed out of a ragged wound on her neck, but she was looking at me as if we'd gone back to my place at the end of a date. Ugh, I was going to need a lot of alcohol to purge that imagery from my mind.

Holding onto my anger, I balled my fists.

However, Gan merely stood there smiling at me, the wound on her neck stitching itself back together before my eyes. She glanced back at where Sheila stood, then shifted her position so that neither of us could make a move without her seeing it.

Smart, but possibly also pointless, seeing that Sheila still looked too freaked out to do much more than gawk. Guess whatever had happened to her and Tom inside that pillar of energy had been seriously messed up...

Tom!

Knowing it was risky, I dared a quick glance back to where it had all happened. The smoke had finally cleared, revealing ... nothing. There was no sign of Max Adventure, Tom's ghost, anything. It had all been consumed in the maelstrom. Nothing but cracked earth remained.

In an instant, it all became clear. Gan had meant for Sheila to be her thirteenth sacrifice, but he'd taken her place instead – completing the unholy covenant but ensuring the Icon remained alive to fight whatever evil Gan had consorted with.

I should have focused on the task at hand, but all at once I couldn't. Thoughts of my best friend filled my head and I couldn't shake them loose. I'd mourned him five years ago, thought I'd moved on, but to be given him back only to have him taken away again reopened those wounds, making them feel as fresh as they once had. What a sick joke by cruel fate.

Worst of all, Christy didn't know yet. What would this do to her, losing him twice?

I turned back to find neither of the two women had moved from their spots. Sheila still looked like a deer in the headlights, her faith aura nowhere to be seen. I thought perhaps Gan was waiting for me, her twisted sense of honor insisting I make the first move. But she was actually staring past me, at the spot where...

Oh God!

The pause in the action brought with it a cessation of the brain chemicals keeping me from facing the awful truth.

Tom wasn't the only casualty this day.

I forced myself to turn and look. Sally's body, blackened and charred, stood fused to the spot where it had been consumed by magical energies – much like the doomed citizens of Pompeii had been entombed by volcanic ash.

Even the expression on her face was still visible – surprise, with maybe a tinge of annoyance. In some ways it was a fitting, if awful, memorial to the person she'd been.

"How bothersome," Gan said with a sigh.

"Bothersome?" I snarled, turning back toward her. Fuck it. I didn't need Sheila's help for this. "She was more than you could ever hope to be and you killed her!"

"Doubtful, although I must admit," Gan replied nonchalantly, "the whore has always been something of a wild card. I regrettably failed to plan for her interference."

"Regrettably? Plan for this!" I launched myself at her, willing my claws to extend, and swung hard enough to knock her head right off her fucking shoulders.

Sadly, fast as I was, it wasn't enough.

At the last second, she raised a hand and blocked me, knocking me off balance. I expected a counterattack, but none came. She continued to stand there, staring at Sally's remains, as if too preoccupied to pay me any heed.

Fine by me. I went after her again, looking to rip her spine out and enjoy the feel of her combusting around my arm – even if it would probably give her one last thrill.

As if I needed that thought in my head.

"Go, Freewill!" Glen bubbled.

Sadly, his shout of encouragement tipped her off because she side-stepped me neatly, sending me stumbling past to land at Sally's feet. I looked up at her remains, tears in my eyes, and realized she smelled like burnt barbecue. Fucking vampire senses.

Forcing myself to focus I spun, quick as the wind, and prepared to try again. If I could tackle Gan, get her down, then she'd be at my mercy, advanced combat skills or not. Even she wasn't powerful enough to...

There came a low rumbling from off in the distance, causing the cave floor to vibrate beneath my feet.

I glanced up, afraid that whatever had tried to enter this world had returned to kick down the door for good, but the energy that had been arcing across the ceiling was gone. Nothing but the twinkling lights of this place remained.

Yet the floor continued to shake.

"Bill, look out!" Sheila cried, finally snapping out of her funk.

Movement from behind caught my attention, and I turned to find Sally about to tip over. *No!*

Using Gan's stolen speed, I stepped in and caught her before she could hit the floor. Sally was beyond help, but the least I could do was ensure her body wasn't further defiled by this accursed place.

Gently laying her on the ground, I once again prepared to take the fight to Gan.

However, she merely sighed as if annoyed. "Go."

"What?"

"It would be prudent for you to leave this place, beloved," she said. "Take your friends and depart."

"What are you..."

"That sound you heard was my people breaking through the Damascus tunnel. A sizeable force will arrive here within minutes to secure this location and all remaining within." At my questioning gaze, she continued. "I assumed, quite correctly, there would be resistance to the dawn of this new age. So their orders are to quell any such ... disputes."

She gestured for me to take a look, forcing me to realize I'd been so focused on her that I hadn't paid any heed to the small war being waged all around us as mage battled mage.

Casualties littered the ground as myriad spells continued to flare throughout the cavern, lighting this place up like a lethal Fourth of July.

Guess more people had taken offense to what Gan had done than I'd first guessed.

I caught sight of Christy. She and Liz – of all people – were lobbing spells at a group of black robes while Kelly held a protective shield around them.

The problem was, even without Gan's reinforcements, I could tell it was a losing fight. There were flashes of light as mages all over the battlefield cut their losses and ran. And why wouldn't they? Come tomorrow, I was willing to bet most would probably change their tune and hail Gan as the savior of their race.

Almost as if reading my mind in that creepy way she had, Gan proclaimed, "The day is won, beloved. Once more the veil lies open to us, its mysteries even now permeating the stale husk this world has become. I know you may disagree with me now, but I have faith that soon you will come to understand. Until then, I shall count the days."

"Wait. What do you..."

She turned and walked up to Sheila, who continued to stand around like some newb at a ren faire. Gan looked her in the eye, as if daring her to attack.

Come on, do something!

"Um, hi?" Sheila said.

Fuck it. If she wasn't going to be useful, I'd at least say my piece. "You haven't won shit. You failed. My friend sacrificed himself, but you missed your true target. And, believe me, that's something you're going to regret." *Hopefully.*

Gan glanced back toward me, an enigmatic smile on her face. "In that, my love, you are incorrect."

She stepped past Sheila then spun, quick as a rattlesnake, pulling something from her pocket in the same instant. Her blood must have already started wearing off because my eyes were barely able to follow her, much less do anything to stop it, as Gan took advantage of the moment and stabbed Sheila in the back.

No! Please, not another!

Sheila's faith aura flared to life in response, but only for a moment. Before I could step in to do something, *anything*, it began to falter, growing dimmer, until finally her eyes rolled into the back of her head.

"What a twat," she slurred before collapsing in a heap onto the ground.

"My gift to you," Gan replied with a brief nod of her head, before turning and walking away, heedless of the fighting going on around her.

Gift to me?

I debated for a moment between trying to take her

down and helping Sheila, but there really wasn't any question which was of greater importance. Revenge would have to wait.

I bent down and checked for a pulse, finding Sheila's strong and steady. She was merely unconscious. Rolling her over, I saw a syringe protruding from her shoulder blade. I pulled it out and took a closer look, already knowing what I'd see – tar black residue.

It was the blood of Baal, an unholy corrupted substance, the only thing that could harm an Icon.

I didn't understand. In the past, vamps had coated their weapons with it. Injected, though, it merely robbed an Icon of their powers, leaving them vulnerable for a time. Gan could've easily twisted her head off but had instead chosen to walk away. Why?

"I'm gonna go out on a limb and assume you won't be fighting the Icon today."

"Not now, Glen," I snapped, but then a thought hit me. There was one advantage to an Icon's power being taken away. "Actually, you could do me a favor."

"Anything, Freewill."

I looked around, then pointed toward where Christy continued to battle Gan's forces. "Go over there and convince my friends to come back with you."

"Oh? Are you going to fight the witches instead?"

"No. We're gonna get the fuck out of here."

A part of me desperately wanted to go and help Christy pound the crap out of every asshole I could get my hands on, but I couldn't leave Sheila unguarded. I was also well aware that once I started punching mages, I might not want to stop.

None of that would bring my friends back, though. We'd already lost. Continuing to fight was pointless.

Mind you, that wouldn't have stopped me from gutting anyone who dared try to start shit with me at that moment. But none did. The black-robed mages, if anything, appeared to be fighting defensively. And why not? They were the victors. There was no reason to press their advantage.

Still, it was probably best to not push our luck.

Fortunately, Glen quickly slithered over to where my friends continued their attack.

I couldn't hear what he said to them with all the other ruckus going on, but it didn't seem as if Christy – or Liz, for that matter – were too enthused to call things off. Not that I gave a shit what Liz did. She could get blasted to her component atoms for all I cared.

Kelly, however, seemed willing to listen. She stopped what she was doing and started talking, eventually getting the other two to drop their assault. Thankfully, the black-robed assholes didn't seem interested in pushing the matter. Once my friends disengaged, they did the same. Hell, it was probably fucking Miller time, as far as they were concerned.

No matter. There would be a reckoning later.

After some more cajoling, Christy finally turned back toward where I stood guard over Sheila. Less fortunate was that there seemed to be a two-for-one sale on witches going on as Liz followed in her footsteps. Good thing for her I was beyond caring. Otherwise...

Christy's eyes met mine and it was as if the fight drained out of her. She doubled her pace back toward where I waited and stopped in front of me. For several long seconds we just stared at each other, communicating with nothing but our eyes. Then she stepped in and buried her head in my shoulder.

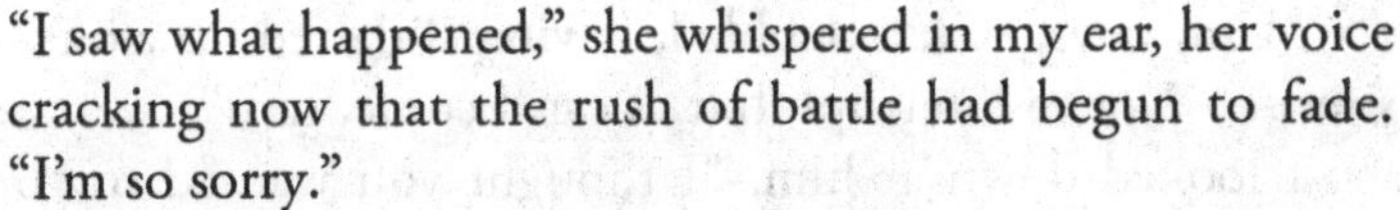

"I saw what happened," she whispered in my ear, her voice cracking now that the rush of battle had begun to fade. "I'm so sorry."

There was nothing I could do except repeat her own words back to her. She'd lost as much as me down here, maybe more.

Kelly caught up to us and knelt down over Sheila. "Is she..."

"She's ... okay," I croaked. "Just out cold."

She stood up, a look of relief on her face, then glanced past us to where Sally lay. "Oh my God!"

I wanted to laugh. I'm sure her husband would have agreed that no loving God had anything to do with what happened down here.

Kelly stepped past where we stood, but I didn't try to stop her. I was too busy taking what small comfort I could and offering what little I was able to.

Christy, for her part, let out a quiet sob but didn't ask about Tom. I had a feeling she didn't need to.

"What are we waiting for?"

I looked up to find Liz staring at us. My fangs descended and I clenched my fists.

However, before I could put them to use, Christy tightened her grip on me and simply said, "Don't."

"They betrayed me, too," Liz said, the attitude all but extinguished from her voice. "That ... bitch killed Ernest."

I was tempted to tell her I was glad the asshole was dead, but the fire inside of me was dying down as well. Enough harm had been done here. We'd all lost today. And though we might not exactly be allies, we were united in our misery.

"Let's get out of here," I said, pulling away from Christy.

Tears were streaming freely down her face, but she managed to nod.

"Um, guys," Glen bubbled, having slithered up alongside us. "Not to interrupt, but ... can I come, too?"

I looked down at him. "I thought you wanted to go home."

"Oh, I do, Freewill. There's just one small problem..." He trailed off, sounding almost embarrassed. "I have no idea how."

Christy wiped her eyes and smiled at him. "Then I guess we'll have to help you find the way."

He blinked, err, gratefully I guess, at her. "Thank you!"

"Bill's right. It's time to go. There's nothing left for us here."

Christy carved a shallow circle in the dirt around us with Liz's help. When they were finished, they linked hands while I called Kelly over. "All aboard for the last train back home."

She stood from where she'd been crouched over Sally's body. "Hold up, guys. We can't leave her."

I'd already given that some thought, though. "It's okay. This place has a lot of history. There's plenty of old..." I'd meant to say ghosts, but the word got caught on my tongue. "...memories here. It could use some good ones. I think she'd be okay with this being her mausoleum. It's almost large enough to suit her personality."

Christy let out a sad chuckle and nodded.

"That's not what I meant," Kelly said. "I'm serious. We can't leave her."

"Listen, I knew her, maybe better than anyone. She..."

"No. You *know* her." At seeing my confused glance, she continued. "That's what I'm trying to tell you. I think she's still alive."

48

HOME IS WHERE THE HORROR IS

With no safe houses or coven lairs left, and the fact that Christy's building was likely swarming with cops, we rematerialized in the only place that made sense: my apartment. More precisely, my living room, eliciting a shriek of panic as we appeared.

The light from the spell cleared and I found Dave standing there staring wide-eyed at us. "Fuck me!" he cried. "You almost gave me a heart attack."

"Not now, Dave..."

"Pleasure to meet you," Glen bubbled.

"What in the fuck is that?!"

"His name is..."

Dave turned to where Sally had materialized on the floor. "And is that a dead body?"

"It's ... Sally."

"Oh. She's ... seen better days."

It was all I could do to keep from decking him. Instead I chose the high road, picking Sheila up and laying her on the couch as Kelly continued to examine Sally.

Liz stepped over, but Christy moved in front of her. "You need to go."

"I'm just trying to help."

"You've helped enough," Kelly snapped, standing up and poking her with a finger. "Consider our temporary truce at an end."

"You need to get out of my face, catalyst witch."

"Or what?"

"What's a catalyst witch?" Dave asked, looking about as confused as I felt.

"None of your business." Christy grabbed Liz by the arm and steered her to the door. "Like I said, you need to go. And you need to stay gone. Don't let me see you again."

She opened the front door and Liz stepped through. Before she walked away, though, she said, "Just so you know, you're not the only one who lost someone today. For what it's worth, I'm sorry."

I thought Christy's response might be in the form of explosive death magic, but she merely shut the door before sinking down against it and burying her face in her hands.

"So what was that all about?" Dave asked, stepping over Glen. "You know what? It doesn't matter. Not after the day I've had."

"The day *you've* had?" I asked, half tempted to send him following in Liz's footsteps.

"Yeah, you wouldn't believe it. Everything was going great, then all of a sudden the emails started coming in."

"I really don't..."

"Fuckers cancelling their orders left and right and using the stupidest fucking excuses. 'My grandma just died.' 'My aunt is in the hospital. She's not expected to make it.' Yeah, right."

"Here's a thought. Shut up before I shut you up." I nodded toward Glen. "If he says anything else, melt his face off."

"How?" he asked, blinking several eyeballs in unison.

"I don't know. Figure it out." I turned away, preparing to pepper Kelly with questions. There'd been no time to talk following her bombshell. We'd simply dragged Sally into the circle and gotten out of Dodge. Now, though...

But before I could start, Glen started quivering excitedly. "Freewill! The Icon is waking up. Oh, how exciting."

"How the fuck does this thing even talk?"

Kelly stood up, wisely ignoring Dave, and hurried over to the couch.

"Hey, what about..."

"It's fine," she told me. "Sally's not going anywhere, at least not yet."

"What do you mean..."

But Kelly was already busy hovering over Sheila. "Come on, Sheils, you can do it. Come back to us."

I should have been glad for this one small victory, but it was hard to be. What a fucking nightmare. It was as if everything we'd fought for five years ago had been for nothing. I dared a quick look back at where Sally lay but couldn't hold my gaze, not seeing her like that. I really hoped Kelly wasn't just blowing smoke up my ass, but there didn't seem to be much I could do about it right at the moment. All I could do was hold onto a thin sliver of hope.

I glanced over at Christy, but she hadn't moved. At least I had hope. For her, there wasn't any. I was tempted to go and offer what comfort I could, but I had a feeling she needed some time to be alone with her thoughts.

"Uhhhh."

"Come on, girl," Kelly said as Sheila finally opened her eyes. "There you are."

"What ... the ... fuck?" she asked weakly.

"Gan stabbed you with the blood of Baal," I explained.

"I got stabbed with the what of what?" Sheila focused

her eyes on me and shook her head. "Holy shit. I had the weirdest dream, Bill."

"It wasn't a dream."

"I dreamt I had..." She looked down at herself. "Goddamn, I do!"

"Do what?"

"I have tits!" She ran a hand over her chest. "And I can feel them!"

What the?

She grabbed her crotch next, something I hadn't known her to do in front of company. "Where the hell did my dick go?"

Christy looked up from where she sat. "What's ... going on?"

Sheila pushed herself to a sitting position and smiled at her. "Oh, hey, babe."

Babe?! Oh, shit. No. It couldn't be.

"Um, Sheila, are you okay?" She didn't answer, prompting Kelly to lean in and put a hand on her shoulder. "Hey, I'm talking to you."

"What? Do I look deaf or something?"

"So are you?"

"Am I what?"

"She asked if you were okay," I said.

"No. She asked Sheila if she was okay, dumbass. By the way, where is she?"

Uh oh. "You're her."

She fixed me with a gaze that said her opinion of my intelligence was dropping rapidly. "Dude, has celibacy made you stupid or what?"

Glen slithered over. "What's going on, Freewill?"

"I have no fucking idea."

Christy, however, was able to give voice to what I was unwilling to acknowledge. "Tom?"

Sheila smiled. "Yeah. Who else would I be? Oh, hey!

Check it out. I can touch shit again."

"Well, if this isn't all sorts of fucked up," Dave said, "I don't know what is."

I turned to the others. "Does anyone have a mirror?" It was a stupid question. We'd just come back from the center of the Earth, not exactly a place where anyone needed to retouch their makeup.

"Hold on," Dave replied. "Use my phone."

He handed it to me. I turned on the front facing camera and held it up to Sheila.

Her eyes became as big as saucers as she saw the face staring back at her. "No fucking way." She reached up, touched her cheek, then stuck out her tongue, as if expecting her reflection to do something different. "Well, damn. This is kinda messed up."

"No shit," Dave replied.

"But, I have to say, I do wear it well."

"Um, guys," Kelly said. "How is ... this even possible?"

"The Source," Christy replied, her voice shaking.

"Gan won after all," I muttered, just barely able to process this. "She killed her."

"What?" Kelly cried.

"But how..."

"Sheila," I said. "It has to be." I turned to Christy. "Before it all blew up, she told me she'd make it, all of this, right again."

Sheila, Tom, or whoever they were, nodded. "Weird as that sounds, man, I think you might be on to something there. I remember her stabbing me, or my action figure anyway. Then there was nothing but blinding light. Suddenly I was having one of those weird ass, out-of-body experiences they talk about."

"You do realize the last five years has been an out of body experience for you, right?"

"Whatever the fuck." The voice was Sheila's, but the

mannerisms and inflection were one-hundred percent Tom. "Anyway, I felt myself floating away, when all of a sudden it was like a hand closed around mine and yanked me back down. The next thing I knew, witches were trying to kill me and then I woke up here."

"Do you think she knew?" Kelly asked, her eyes glassy.

I shook my head. "I don't think anyone could have. Gan played us all from the start – both sides, here and below. I get the impression everything that happened was meticulously planned out." Before Kelly could reply, though, I continued. "Except for this part. Gan counted on Sheila's despair, her guilt. But in the end, she remembered what she'd once stood for and that gave her the strength to make one last choice nobody, not even Gan, could have foreseen."

"She gave her life for his."

I nodded. "It was her way of atoning and, in doing so, making sure the world still had an Icon." I watched as Tom felt himself up. "Or some semblance of one, anyway."

A swirl of emotions clouded my thoughts as Tom stood up and took a few steps, looking uncertain in his new skin.

I walked over to Christy, her expression blank as if she'd reached her limit and was incapable of processing anything else. That was something I could understand. "Are you okay?"

"Okay?" she asked incredulously. "I don't even know what that is anymore."

"I get it, babe," Tom replied. "This is pretty fucked up for me, too. But the important thing is I'm still me on the inside." I was about to comment with something affirmative, but he wasn't finished yet. "As for the rest ... we could always try scissoring."

I sighed. "You really are a fucktard, you know that?"

"Takes one to know one, bro." He smiled, his expression upon the face of the woman I'd once loved. To say it was strange wasn't even close to the truth.

"Listen ... um, Tom," Kelly said. "You might want to take this more seriously. You're ... the Icon now and that means..."

"Hold that thought. This whole name thing is going to get confusing quick, but I think I have a solution."

"A solution?"

"Yeah. I'm me in Sheila's body."

"And...?"

"Tom, Sheila ... you can call me..." He paused dramatically as if expecting a drum roll. "Teela!" Stunned silence descended upon the room for several seconds. "C'mon, guys, think of how awesome that is. Me with Cheetara by my side. We will fucking own Comic Con."

I looked him in the eye. "There is no fucking way that I am ever calling you Teela."

"I actually think it's kind of cool."

"Shut up, Dave."

Tom excused himself to borrow some of my clothes, despite me doubting anything I had would fit him anymore. He claimed Sheila's armor chafed in all the wrong places. Thankfully, he didn't elaborate.

That left the rest of us pretty much stunned into inaction. I couldn't begin to make sense of how I felt, not yet. Kelly, in particular, seemed to be hit hard by this.

But I gave her credit – rather than break down at the

loss of her friend, she instead refocused on examining Sally. After a few minutes, Christy joined her.

They worked in silence for several minutes, casting a variety of spells that I guessed were meant to poke and prod the charred statue on my living room floor.

I watched as they worked. "How ... um ... is she?"

"I don't know. I ..." Christy's voice cracked. "I should probably focus on what I'm doing."

I put a hand on her shoulder. "We did it, you know."

"Did what?"

"The impossible. We brought him back. That has to count for something."

Christy looked up at me and smiled. "It does. I'm just not sure what it means for..."

She was interrupted by the sound of my phone ringing, causing both of us to jump.

"It's probably that Vincent guy again," Dave said dismissively, stepping to the fridge.

"Hold on," Kelly replied. "What do you mean *again*?"

"He's been calling on and off for the last hour. Left a bunch of messages for you guys to call him back."

I stepped up and got in his face. "And you didn't tell us this *why?*"

"One, I'm not your fucking answering service. And two..." He gestured toward Sally and Glen. "I've been a bit distracted."

Christy and Kelly both bolted for the phone, not that I could blame them. In all the craziness we'd forgotten that the most precious of our new fellowship was still out there somewhere.

They reached for it simultaneously, but then Kelly pulled back. "You answer it."

Christy looked like she wanted nothing better than to do that, but she replied, "No, he's your husband. He's probably just checking in."

"Are you sure?"

Christy nodded and Kelly picked it up.

"Hey, honey! You have no idea how glad I am to hear your voice. Yeah, we just got back. I know, things are a bit ... whoa, slow down. I'm not getting all of that."

Christy's eyes opened wide, but Kelly held up a hand, no doubt to keep her from jumping to conclusions. "Is Tina... Okay. Thank goodness." She gave Christy a thumbs up.

"Tell her mommy misses her."

"Daddy, too," Tom shouted from my bedroom.

"Yeah. I know," Kelly continued. "I'll explain later. For now... What's that? He did? But how? Do you know where? Okay, okay. Just head over. We're all at Bill's place. We'll figure it out. No, they're not going to be a problem anymore. Trust me on that. Okay. Love you, too." She hung up the phone, her face a shade paler than when she'd answered it.

"What is it?" Christy asked.

"Tina's fine," Kelly replied. "Vince, too. He's just a bit frazzled." She ran a hand through her hair. "They're only a couple of blocks from the subway. They should be here in an hour or two, depending on the connections."

"Why don't they just drive?" I asked.

"It's Ed."

"What? Did he double park and get that land yacht towed already?"

"It's not that," she replied, turning to face us all. "He's gone."

"Wait, what do you mean gone?"

"Tina had to use the bathroom," She explained. "They stopped at a gas station on the west side. Vincent took her in then they went to buy some snacks. But when they came out, Ed and the limo were both gone."

"Did he try..."

"Of course he tried calling," she said. "That's the first thing he did. But then he heard a phone ringing. It was Ed's cell. Someone had tossed it in the trash."

"Well that's fucking stupid," Tom called out to us. "Dude needs to be more careful with his..."

"He didn't drop it," I snapped, putting two and two together. "Gan took him. It's the only answer that makes sense."

"You don't know..."

"I'm pretty sure he didn't spontaneously decide to throw his phone away so he could take a joy ride."

"Damnit!" Christy said, a crackle of red energy flashing in her eyes. "Why didn't we see this sooner? The car. It was hers."

I nodded, starting to feel quite stupid at how easily we'd been played. "What did she care if she handed the keys over? She probably had GPS installed to track it."

"And those sigils," Christy added, "so we couldn't."

Kelly shook her head. "But why him? And ... don't get mad at me for saying this ... not..."

"Tina?" I offered. "Gan doesn't have any interest in her. Never did. That was Komak's thing. Gan already knew everything she needed to. But Ed..."

"She need a new fuck boy or something?" Tom asked, stepping out of my room. He was wearing a t-shirt and an old pair of my jeans, the latter cinched up tight with a belt.

"Vampires," I corrected with a sigh. "Aside from her, Ed and I are the only two left."

Tom reached down and picked the seat of his, her, pants. "Christ, I have no idea how anyone can wear a thong. This thing keeps shooting up my ass."

"TMI, dipshit."

He shrugged. "So why Ed and not you?"

"I think I know the reason," Christy replied. "She and him. They're both that new breed."

"Neo-vamps," I offered.

"Yeah, but he's the only one capable of siring more."

"But I thought they can't be compelled," Kelly said. "Isn't that kinda the whole point?"

I waved that off. "Doesn't matter. Gan's the type who instills absolute loyalty into her servants. Hell, even before she changed she told me she used compulsion sparingly. But now the slate has been wiped completely clean. Out with the old, in with the new. She can force Ed to create a whole new race of vampires, one that she can mold into her own twisted image."

Tom stepped over and clapped me on the back. "I know we've been here before, Bill, but it bears repeating. Your wannabe girlfriend is a fucking nutcase."

I automatically moved to smack him upside the head, but then paused when I saw Sheila's face staring back at me.

He smirked at my hesitation. "Pussy says what?"

Yeah, this was going to require some getting used to.

49

THE HELL IN A HAND
BASKET EPILOGUE

The sky began to lighten in the east, meaning I'd need to head inside soon. Back when I'd first become human again, I used to come up here to the roof and enjoy both the sunrise as well as not being immolated by it.

The novelty soon wore off, though, and I eventually stopped. Hell, even when Sheila and I were together, I don't think we came up here more than once or twice.

Now it would never happen again for either of us. But she wasn't the only one on my mind as I...

There came a knock from behind me. "Penny for your thoughts?"

I turned to find Christy climbing out of the trapdoor.

"Just thinking about ... stuff."

"Sally or Sheila?"

"A bit of both. It's weird. A part of me insists I should be crying my eyes out over Sheila, but I can't because she's down there looking as alive as ever."

Christy stepped up beside me and rested her head on my shoulder. "Believe me. I understand."

"I don't know. Maybe she did me a favor walking out

when she did. Let me get my mourning out of the way ahead of time. Either way, it all feels a lot weirder than it does sad."

Christy let out a long breath. "There's gotta be something karmic in all of this. My ex-fiancé's soul in your ex's body."

"Fate can be a fucked up thing," I said. "Speaking of which, what's he up to?"

She gave a small chuckle. "He's ... trying to figure out how to use the bathroom again. I figured it might be best to slip out before he asked me to come in and give him some pointers."

"Just wait until it's that time of the month."

"Wonderful. And here I was thinking I wouldn't have to worry about tampon advice until Tina was older."

Speaking of which, both Tina and Vincent had arrived some hours earlier, neither worse for the wear. After doting on her little girl – who seemed far less freaked out than the rest of us – Christy had tucked her into my bed. It hadn't taken long for her to fall asleep. Despite the excitement, Cat was thoroughly exhausted from the past day.

Her daughter safe and sound, Christy had gotten back to work examining Sally, prompting me to head up here once it became painfully obvious I was annoying them with my constant questions as to her condition. "So..."

"You can ask. We've done all we can do for now."

"How ... is she?"

"Alive."

"Are you..."

She looked up and met my gaze. "Yes, I'm sure. It's weird, though. Like she's in some sort of chrysalis. I can sense her in there, but something is happening."

"You're certain?"

Christy raised an eyebrow. "Even if my magic wasn't back I'd still make that guess."

"I don't know. I was standing right there. You should have seen all of that..."

"Power?" she finished. "That's exactly how I know. Do you think for one second Gan would've let that much energy rain down upon her if she thought there was a chance she'd die?"

I considered that. "With her ego? I doubt it."

"It's not just her ego." Christy gritted her teeth as if she found her next words to be bitter. "She doesn't do anything unless she has the advantage. The old gods, they can be treacherous, but they don't break a bargain lightly. There's power in a promise, and that's not just a saying. This wasn't merely some crossroads deal with the devil, trading her soul for money."

I shook my head. "Not her style. She probably had a thousand mystics pore over the contract before she even considered signing on the dotted line."

"Lawyers, too. Whatever she bargained for, I guarantee it was in her favor."

"Except it missed her and hit Sally."

Christy nodded, then turned to face the sunrise. "Exactly. The only question now is what that bargain was for."

"So that means we wait?"

"Yes, but not here."

"Huh?"

"I want to take Sally back to my place where I can keep a proper eye on her. Make sure nothing goes wrong."

"Your place? But the police..."

She held up a hand, sending a spark of yellowish energy crackling through it. "Trust me, nobody will ever know anything amiss ever happened there."

I paused for a moment. "Are you happy to have it back?"

"My apartment?"

"You know what I mean."

She blew out a long breath. "Do you want the truth?"

"Always."

"I'm terrified and excited at the same time, and it's not just for me. Take a sniff of the air. Can you sense it?"

"Garbage and car exhaust?"

She chuckled. "No, energy ... the power of the veil mixing with this world. It's all back again, stronger than ever. Everything has changed."

"It has, hasn't it? But how much?"

"Who can say?" She took my hand in hers. "Besides, whatever happens, we'll get through it."

"We?"

She smiled coyly. "In some form or another."

"After we figure a few things out first?" I offered.

"I have to admit, it might take some time to..."

"Sorry to interrupt, Freewill ... err, madam witch."

Saved by the blob. We turned back toward the maintenance trapdoor to find Glen and his multiple eyeballs had made it onto the rooftop.

"How the hell did you get up the ladder?" I asked.

"Wasn't easy." He bubbled a few times. "The others requested your presence."

"Is it Sally?"

"No. There's something on the TV they said you might want to see."

"Oh. Okay. We'll be there in a second." I turned back toward Christy after Glen had dripped back down again. "We should probably get going anyway. Looks like the sun will be up any second now."

"Probably a good idea. So, just out of curiosity, what are you going to do about ... him?"

"Glen? I don't know. I figured I'd give him Ed's room for now, or at least his waste basket."

She grinned up at me. "That's awfully generous of you."

"He's a blob. How much space could he possibly need? Oh, and I think maybe I should let Tom have his old room back, at least until such time as..."

"We figure this out?" She nodded. "That's probably for the best. And it's not like Tina and I are far away."

"Exactly." I took a step toward the ladder, but then stopped and let out a bark of laughter.

"What's so funny?"

"I was just thinking. Back when I first got turned, Tom and Ed had a ball testing my powers, usually ending with me on fire. Anyway, I used to think that my roommate situation couldn't get any weirder. Guess I was wrong."

We returned to my apartment to find Kelly, Vincent, and Tom all seated on the couch watching TV. Dave, meanwhile, was in the kitchen nook helping himself to my Keurig machine.

Coffee was sounding pretty good right about then. Christy said as much and went to grab us a couple cups.

I plopped down next to my once again roommate to see what everyone was paying such rapt attention to.

Tom turned to me as I sat. "Bill..."

"Relax. We were just talking."

"Good, then I won't have to kick your ass."

"Nice to know."

"Anyway, that's not what I wanted to tell you." He lowered his voice. "Taking a piss with this equipment..."

"I *really* don't want to know."

"It's like a whole new adventure."

"Come on, guys," Kelly admonished. "Pay attention."

"Oh, right," Tom said, shaking some of Sheila's hair out of his face. God this was weird. "You gotta see this shit."

Kelly clicked the remote. "Hold on, I'll turn it up."

I forced my attention away from the strange mashup of my best friend and former lover sitting next to me. There was a news report playing on the TV. A reporter was standing in front of a brick building. Behind her could be seen cops, police tape and, far back and out of focus, there appeared to be a pair of broken doors.

"...I'm here at the Paradise Valley retirement complex, the scene of what residents are calling a miracle turned massacre. Witnesses are claiming the impossible – that several of the elderly residents died overnight only to rise again in the early hours of the morning and turn upon their friends and neighbors, ripping them to pieces..."

"Hold on," Dave said from the kitchen. "Did they say Paradise...?"

"Not now," I hissed.

"One of the survivors managed to capture the following on his phone. I must warn you, what you are about to see could be disturbing to some viewers."

A video began to play, presumably taken from inside the facility. Lights were blinking on and off and screams could be heard in the distance. A muffled voice, probably whoever took the video, said, "Oh *bleep*. There's one of them."

It felt like a cheesy promo vid for a Halloween haunted house, at least until I saw what he was talking about. An old woman leapt into view, dropping down from the ceiling. She turned toward the camera, her head raised as if sniffing the air. The video cut out mere moments later, but not before catching a clear view of soulless black eyes staring out over a set of fangs.

No fucking way.

"In the past few hours, similar incidents have been reported throughout the city, all of them claiming the same thing. Already, some on social media are laying blame on the bizarre occurrences of the past week, claiming that the Strange Days are here again."

"You've gotta be fucking kidding me!" Dave cried.

"What is it?" I asked, turning toward him.

He looked up from his phone. "Paradise Valley."

"What about it?"

"I knew that name sounded familiar. It's one of our big accounts. They placed a bulk order just the other week. I swear, those assholes had better not be trying to weasel their way out of paying. Not my fault that they..."

"Bulk order?"

"Yeah, the old geezers love Immortalis. Anything to make them feel less decrepit."

The rest of Dave's rant was lost to me as I considered this. "Wait a second. Weren't you complaining earlier about cancellations?"

"Yeah," he groused. "What a fucking pain in the ass."

"Because people were dying?"

"If you believe that bullshit."

"Like in that piece we just watched?" An unpleasant thought began to form in my head.

"Yeah, I guess."

Christy joined us, carrying two steaming mugs of coffee, but I barely noticed her. "Did I hear that right?" she asked.

"Vampires." I stood up, the allure of caffeine all but forgotten. "The original kind, like me."

"But how?"

I barely heard her, though, a recent memory playing in my mind as if I'd DVR'd it. *What sets Immortalis apart from other so-called age defying creams are special patent-pending proteins.*

I strolled over to where my former dungeon master stood, looking more put out over the hit to his wallet than the human misery we'd just witnessed on the TV. "Dave, can I ask you a question?"

"Sure, what do you need?"

"What is that hand cream of yours made of?"

"Nothing special. Coconut oil, beeswax, generic shit like that. We buy it in bulk from some sweatshop in Central America. Those fuckers make it for pennies on the..."

"Not that stuff. I meant those proteins you talked about."

"Oh, that? We inject a couple milligrams per batch so we can differentiate ourselves from the other crap on the market..."

"Fascinating I'm sure." I held up a hand. "How exactly did you develop those proteins?"

"Develop?"

"Yeah. That's what you said on your infomercial."

"That's just for marketing purposes. We have to establish me as a subject matter expert..."

I slammed my hand on the counter, cutting him off and drawing everyone's attention. "Where did you get them from, Dave?"

He held up his hands. "Fine, you got me. I had some of my old samples in frozen storage from back in the day."

"*Your samples?*"

"Well, technically yours. But you have to understand, everyone in the product department thought it would make a killer selling point."

"Are you telling me that stuff contains my blood?"

"No."

"Oh, thank goodness."

"All of your blood samples were contaminated. These

were from your venom. My lab managed to synthesize it ... after a little trial and error."

Son of a bitch.

Vampire venom, the very thing that once created new vamps – acting as a lure to hungry spirits from outside our world. Hungry spirits like the one I called Dr. Death.

"So, let me get this straight." I grabbed hold of Dave's shirt and lifted him off the ground. "You made this crap – the same shit I practically took a bath in yesterday – out of vampire venom? Is that what you're telling me?!"

"Y-yeah, but it was all inert."

"*Until* these pulses started," I snapped.

Stunned silence met the room for several seconds.

"If you need to kick his ass," Tom said, "I'm pretty sure we can all turn a blind eye."

Vincent opened his mouth, no doubt to protest, but I dropped Dave before that advice began to sound a little too tempting.

Christy stepped to my side, glaring at my former DM. I got the impression she was firmly in the blind eye camp. "Am I hearing this right? Are you saying that everyone who bought that stuff..."

"Has either turned or is in the process of turning into a vampire," I finished.

"Not only that," Kelly said, "but they're waking up hungry."

I nodded. "And with no covens left to rein them in."

"That's ridiculous," Dave said. "If that's the case, then how come nobody else here is ... vamping out?"

"Sally didn't open hers. No offense, man, but she really doesn't like you."

"I threw mine away," Christy replied. Can't say that was a surprise either.

"Same here," Kelly added.

Jesus Christ! Was I the only one? No. That still left

Dave and he at least seemed human, physically if not emotionally.

I said as much, but he smiled sheepishly in return. "First rule of being a doctor: never become your own customer."

"That's drug dealers."

"Same shit really," he replied. "Besides, I have naturally moist skin."

Son of a... It was all I could do to not put him through a wall. What Calibra had once done through playing with forces beyond her control, this stupid fuck had managed to recreate with nothing more than the dumb luck of having a working freezer.

"Everyone calm down," Vincent said. "The sun's up now. That should help."

"It might," Christy replied. "But it won't matter for those who've been bitten since then."

"I understand that. What I meant is we need to stop it from spreading."

I was tempted to laugh at him. Just like a former Templar. Bet he couldn't wait to dust off his old cape. Pity he was talking about a job that was easier said than done.

"It's too late," I replied. "If it were just one Patient Zero, maybe, but..." I turned to Dave. "How much of that crap did you sell?"

He backed up into the kitchen. "Um, it was a surprisingly effective marketing campaign, and that's not even counting our mall kiosks."

"We are so fucked."

"Maybe not," Christy said after a pause. "Maybe it's not as hopeless as you think."

"How so?"

She flashed me a smile. "Think about it. We have someone on our side with the experience and skills to deal with this."

Kelly hooked a thumb at Tom. "Her?"

Christy shrugged. "If it comes to that, maybe. But these people are victims, and we have the means to contain them." She turned toward me again. "If these vampires are like you, then that means compulsion will work on them. And will you look at that, we are in the presence of someone who knows all about that – the legendary Freewill."

"Yeah, right. Legendary," I scoffed.

"Don't sell yourself short," she replied. "You're the only one who can do this."

"The only one left, you mean."

Kelly stood up. "She's got a point..."

"But..."

"And we're all here to help you. Isn't that right?"

It was tentative at first, but then slowly, all of those in the room began to nod. Even Tom added a quick, "Fuck yeah!"

I let Christy's words and their support sink in.

In the space of a few short days, my entire world had turned upside down. Magic was back with a vengeance – vampires, too. Sally was stuck in a cocoon, changing into *something*. Sheila was gone, but my best friend now stood in her place. And that was just the tip of the iceberg.

Ed and Gan were still out there somewhere. He needed to be saved. She needed to be stopped.

But above all else, I considered, stepping to the window and glimpsing the dawn breaking outside, once again I seemed destined to play a part in it all.

Hell, the little nutcase had even said as much.

Who better for fate to choose, my love?

Hah! Mere minutes earlier I'd have said anyone but me.

Now, though...

I stepped back and saw my own face reflected in the pane of glass and, behind me, those of my friends.

Perhaps we all had our parts to play in this bizarre new world we were waking up to. But if so, we'd have each other's backs. I don't think any of us had any idea what to expect in the near future, but hearing their support now made it all sound a little less terrifying.

The Strange Days had returned, and this time they might be stranger than ever. Whatever happened next, however, I wouldn't be facing it alone.

THE END

Bill Ryder will return in
EVERYDAY HORRORS (The Tome of Bill – 10)
Read on for a sneak preview.

BONUS CHAPTER
EVERYDAY HORRORS

The Tome of Bill - Part 10

"You're the only one who can do this," I muttered to myself as I stepped into my apartment. What a crock of shit. I really needed to stop listening when people went off on an inspirational bullshit monologue. That almost never ended well for me.

I flipped on the light switch, noting the silence and enjoying it. A long shower was just what the doctor ordered, followed by sweeping up the trail of vampire dust I was no doubt tracking in the door.

If this were baseball, two for five would've been a good record. Pity that vamp hunting wasn't nearly as forgiving, not to mention the pay sucked infinitely worse. Speaking of which, I could afford maybe a quick nap when this was all said and done, but that was all. After that, it was back to work. I'd taken a contract to migrate a client's databases to a new platform. Boring as fuck stuff, but I'd ignored it for the better part of a week so it was time to get my ass in gear before the product manager started bitching.

I stopped in the living room to consider how easy it

was to sink back into my old mindset. Here I was thinking about programming when I'd dusted three people tonight ... just barely at that. Mind you, they'd been assholes, so it's not like I probably should feel too bad about it.

Still, Christy's words kept repeating in my head that these people were all victims, so they at least deserved a chance before I shanked them.

She was right, of course, but at the same time not everyone handled becoming undead as well as others. The vast majority became drunk on their new power, giving in to their feral side. It was turning out to be much rarer to find those willing to listen to reason.

And what did I do when I did find them? Recruited them into a coven. What a joke. Much as I'd rued the old days with its frat-boy like vamp covens, it turns out there'd been a good reason for it. Only vamps could keep other vamps in check. Without such a system in place, it would only be a matter of time before we either ended up in some 28 Days Later nightmare scenario, or some yahoo called in the National Guard and decided it was open season on anyone, living or not, stupid enough to be out after dark.

I'd worked so hard to bring down the old regime, only to realize I had no other choice but to rebuild it from scratch. Hah. Night Razor was probably looking up from whatever Hell he was frying in and laughing his ass off.

My only hope was to maybe get lucky and get it all running again in a less assholish way. I had no real interest in establishing a system in which younger vamps became little more than playthings to the older, more powerful...

A sound from down below caught my supercharged ears, and I glanced back toward the door. Footsteps were heading up the stairs, quickly at that.

Most of the building's residents would just barely be getting up for work at this time, much less coming home

– barring any walks of shame of course. Ugh, not a pleasant thought. The tenants who lived here were mostly good, hard-working folks, but not a lot of lookers in the bunch.

The footsteps continued up the stairs, their pace increasing. It seemed a fair guess that it wasn't one of the tenants, at least not from the other apartments.

Despite both me and Christy insisting that he wasn't even remotely ready for field work, Tom had insisted on going out on patrol. As the new Icon, he sort of had a point. Problem was, he treated the whole thing like the plot to a comic book – the only upside being that he kinda sucked at it so far. To date, his record had been a lot of early AM catcalls with zero vamps actually found. Even so, until he figured out how to control his newfound powers, it was still risky for him to be wandering around the city streets alone late at night.

Of course, Glen had been more than happy to volunteer to keep him company. The little slime-ball was ecstatic to accompany the Icon on patrol, despite being about as adept at it as Tom was. In short, they pretty much wandered the streets together – Glen sticking to the alleyways and gutters since he was the equivalent of a living Jell-O mold – not accomplishing much but also not getting into too much trouble.

So then why the frantic footsteps now?

That question was answered a few moments later as Tom burst through the door, causing my breath to momentarily catch in my throat as I still wasn't quite used to the fact that he was now inhabiting Sheila's body. Whenever he came home, I was reminded of an earlier time when she and I...

"Outta the way," he cried in her voice. "I gotta take a massive piss."

And then he'd speak and the spell would be broken.

"Um, where's Glen?" I asked, as he darted past.

"Bringing up the rear. Should be here in a few. Can't talk, about to blow!"

He raced into the bathroom, slamming the door shut behind him.

Sadly, awesome as vampire senses could be, there were some horrific downsides, too ... such as clearly hearing him pee, followed by a sigh of relief and, "Oh, that is so fucking good."

I left the door open for Glen, not that he couldn't ooze beneath it if he wanted to, and headed for the fridge – hoping none of the downstairs neighbors decided to pick that moment to pop their heads out. It was only a matter of time before that happened and when it did ... fucked if I knew.

Despite being moderately well-suited to rounding up vamps, I wasn't nearly strong enough to compel humans. The only way that was happening was if I was amped up on vamp blood, which sadly was easier said than done these days as there were only two other vampires in existence older than me and they were both currently MIA.

The sound of the toilet flushing caught my ears as I pulled a plastic container from the refrigerator. Pig's blood. Not my favorite, but workable, even if the folks down at the Asian market charged me extra to buy it by the bucketful no questions asked.

I popped it open and took a sip as Tom stepped out, adjusting the crotch of his pants. "That is so much better," he said with a sigh, looking at me. "Oh, for Christ's sake. Put that shit in a cup or something."

"Nobody told you to look. And you do know that there's these things called restrooms, right? This isn't the only toilet in Brooklyn."

"Dude, I already explained it to you. I don't know which one to use."

"I believe the socially acceptable norm these days is to use the restroom of the gender you associate with."

"Fuck that shit," he replied, his voice and mannerisms coming from my former girlfriend's body – still weird after several weeks. "Guys freak out whenever I do that, and it's not like I can even use a fucking urinal anymore."

"Well, you could if you got creative."

"Bite me, asshole."

"Alright, then use the ladies' room."

"I can't."

"Why not?" I asked, stepping out of our kitchen nook. "You go in, do your business, and leave."

"It's not that simple." He fixed me with a stare, the eyes Sheila's but the semi-crazed expression firmly Tom's. "First of all, there's always a line, which sucks balls as it is. But also, chicks *know*."

"What do you mean, they know?"

"They do. It's like women's intuition or some shit. I thought at first it would be rad as hell stepping freely into the forbidden zone, but it's not that easy, man. They don't say anything, but they don't have to. I can see it in their eyes. It's like they know I'm an imposter."

"I'm willing to bet they don't."

"Yes, they do. It's like deep down they have boner sense."

"Pretty sure that's not a problem for you anymore."

He nodded sadly. "Don't remind me."

Amusing as it was to give him shit about his lack of junk, something that seemed to annoy him to no end, I changed the subject, despite knowing what I'd hear. "Any luck tonight?"

"With vamps? Not a peep. It's like they know to fear me."

"Yeah, uh huh."

"But we did score big elsewhere."

"What do you mean by..."

"*Bark*."

I spun back toward the sound coming from the door ... and almost shit a brick. "What the fuck?!"

"Isn't it awesome?" Tom asked.

Awesome wasn't quite the word that came to mind. Before me stood a large, rather raggedy looking dog. It looked like maybe some kind of Irish Setter mix, but mixed with what? Its coat was a dirty mess, but that was nothing compared to the big bulging eyes staring out of its head, as if they were getting ready to pop right out of its skull.

"Bark", it repeated, the word sounding disturbingly like it was being spoken.

I glanced back at Tom. "What the hell is that?"

Almost as if in response, the dog-thing opened its mouth, far wider than a normal dog should be able. It then vomited forth a viscous goo – the sludge continuing to pour out, spreading across our entranceway.

Then an even stranger thing happened. Those bulging eyes in its head pulled back in, leaving gaping holes where they'd been, as eyeball after eyeball fell out of its mouth into the rapidly growing pile of slime on the floor.

When it was finally finished, the *dog* collapsed into a heap, like a deflated balloon, while the eyeballs in the sludge pile all turned my way and blinked.

"Glen?"

"Isn't it great?" he replied, sounding way too excited for my own personal sanity.

"Yeah," Tom said, stepping to my side. "We got to discussing about how much it sucked that he has to be all secretive and shit."

I glanced between him and the dog ... err ... body lying on the floor. "Not really seeing how this fixes any of that?"

"Well, we were talking about finding him a disguise. And I swear, it was like fate was listening, because not even five minutes later we found this dead dog lying in an alleyway."

I held up a hand. "You do realize that one, that's gross as fuck, and two, that's not even remotely inconspicuous. Oh, and did I mention how gross it is?"

"Twice," Glen replied, his responses bubbling to the surface of his pliable body. "But it's fine, trust me. It was a minor issue to remove the major organs, and I think after a little bit of practice I'll..."

"What? Horrify everyone who sees you into a coma? That's the worst fucking dog disguise since Invader Zim, not to mention it's disgusting as..."

The phone rang, interrupting what was almost certain to be an extra long rant on my part. All I could do was stare blankly at it for a few moments. It was way too early for the telemarketers to start and I was far too freaked out to process anything else.

It wasn't until the third ring that I finally snapped out of it.

"You," I said to Tom. "Close the door before someone sees ... *any* of this. And you, um, move that thing somewhere else for now, preferably the garbage can." I picked up the receiver, feeling my left eye beginning to twitch. "Yeah?"

"Oh, thank goodness," Christy said from the other end. "You weren't picking up your cell."

"Sorry," I replied numbly. "One of the vamps I was chasing after bit it. Need a new screen." Off to the side, Tom and Glen were conversing over the dog's body like it was the most normal thing in the world. "Listen, Christy. Can I call you back later, it's a bit weird here..."

"That's why I'm calling. You need to get over here. If

you leave now, you should be able to make it before the sun rises."

As much as I was typically in favor of a booty call, the situation in my living room was the poster child for killing the mood. Not to mention, the fact that I'd already said her name aloud meant there was no way I was escaping without Tom in tow.

"Maybe we can catch up later," I replied. "I need to hop in the shower and there's a bit of a ... situation here that I need to..."

"It's not as big as the situation here," she replied, cutting me off. "Trust me."

Glancing back at the dead mutt currently serving as the apartment's doormat, I sincerely doubted that. However, I also wasn't in favor of ticking her off, and not just because she could blow a hole through me big enough to step through. "Okay, fine. What's up?"

"It's Sally," she replied.

"What about her? Is she okay?"

"It remains to be seen. That cocoon she's in, it's starting to crack. I think she's about to wake up."

⇐————— ⟡ —————⇒

To be continued in...

Everyday Horrors (The Tome of Bill – 10)
Available in ebook, print, and audiobook

AUTHOR'S NOTE

Writing is kind of like being a kid playing with Legos. You build something fabulous, only to knock it all down when you're done, like Godzilla stomping through Tokyo.

But then, the time comes when you start building all over again.

Truth be told, I've been waiting a long time to write this book. I've known that I'd be coming back to Bill's world, but felt both he and I deserved a break after *The Last Coven*. For him it's been five years, for me about half that, but I wanted to make sure all the sacrifices made in the previous chapter of *The Tome of Bill* had weight, that they hadn't been for nothing.

But now it finally feels right. I've heard from readers all across the globe, some who loved the ending of the last book and others who perhaps loved it a bit less. Either way, folks have hopefully had time to come to grips with what came to pass.

Which means it's time to shake things up again!

I'll also admit, the fact that the timelines between the books and reality match up again, makes me happy. The first eight books of *The Tome of Bill* cover a span of maybe two years, followed by a five year gap until the events of this book. However, the series itself took about five years to write, followed by a two year break since *The Last Coven* was released ... bringing Bill's world and the real world back in sync, which admittedly is something that probably nobody but me cares about. Oh, well. At least my OCD is happy.

Before you ask, I'm not sure how many books this new story will entail, yet anyway, other than to say it will be finite like the previous storyline was. I'd sooner change things up and start anew again every so often than risk running across any sharks that need jumping. That said, we're at a new beginning, so it's a bit premature to start worrying about the end. It'll get here in due time.

For now, let's have some fun.

I hope you'll continue to join me for this new ride through the world of the strange, supernatural, and snarky. I've said it before, but I have a lot of fun writing these books. I sincerely hope you enjoy reading them as much.

Rick G.

ABOUT THE AUTHOR

Rick Gualtieri lives alone in central New Jersey with only his wife, three kids, and countless pets to both keep him company and constantly plot against him. When he's not busy monkey-clicking words, he can typically be found jealously guarding his collection of vintage Transformers from all who would seek to defile them.

Defilers beware!

Also by Rick Gualtieri
THE TOME OF BILL
Bill the Vampire
Scary Dead Things
The Mourning Woods
Holier Than Thou
Sunset Strip
Goddamned Freaky Monsters
Half A Prayer
The Wicked Dead
Shining Fury
The Last Coven
BILL OF THE DEAD SAGA
Strange Days
Everyday Horrors
Carnage À Trois
The Liching Hour

FALSE ICONS
Second String Savior
Wannabe Wizard
Halfhearted Hunter
Deviant Dark Dryads

HIGH MOON
The Girl Who Punches Werewolves
The Girl Who Fights Witches
The Girl Who Hunts Fairies
The Girl Who Defies Fate